SHIELDING KINLEY

Delta Team Two, Book 2

SUSAN STOKER

Edited by Kelli Collins

Cover Design by AURA Design Group

Manufactured in the United States

For Shawn
You never know how strong you are, until being strong is the only choice you have.

CHAPTER ONE

"You seen her yet?" Trigger asked Lefty as they leaned against the wall and watched the politicians entering the large room being used that morning as a meeting place.

"No," Lefty said without elaborating. He knew who his friend was talking about. Kinley Taylor. She was the assistant to Walter Brown, the Assistant Secretary for Insular and International Affairs.

As part of their job, the Delta Force team was sometimes sent overseas to protect important political and military figures. They'd even been sent to the last Olympic Games to help make sure the American athletes were safe. Babysitting political figures wasn't their favorite assignment, but Lefty was more than happy to be in Paris, France, today.

There was a large gathering of officials from around the world. Lefty wasn't exactly sure what they were discussing, and honestly, he didn't really care. He wasn't a political man, which some people might think was odd, considering the President of the United States could ultimately decide his fate, but he simply didn't care. Whatever job he was assigned, he did the best he could. Period.

But this mission felt different. He was antsy and fidgety and for the second morning in a row, he was hyper alert—and it wasn't because of any danger the man they were tasked to protect, Johnathan Winkler, the Deputy Secretary of Agriculture, might be in.

"Maybe she didn't come with Brown this time."

"She came," Lefty replied. He knew Brown wouldn't go anywhere without Kinley. Even though Lefty had only been around her for a few days all those months ago when they'd met in Africa, he knew she was vitally important to the politician. She was smart and organized. She did what Brown asked her to without complaint and without hesitation. Even if that meant putting herself in danger...as it had back in Africa.

Brown had insisted he didn't like the coffee at the government building where he was attending meetings, and had sent Kinley back to the café at their hotel to get him another. At the time, however, there'd been a protest forming, and Kinley had found herself right in the middle of it. Luckily, Lefty had seen her slip out of the building. He'd followed her and prevented her from being harassed and abused at the hands of the revved-up natives.

Lefty knew from talking to Kinley that she frequently went above and beyond for her boss. She never questioned Brown when he asked her to do things that might be outside the realm of her job duties. Because of that, Lefty was fairly sure Brown would take Kinley with him everywhere he went.

Also...at the moment, the hair on the back of his neck was standing straight up, a reaction he'd had around her back in Africa too. It was as if his body knew she was close and acted accordingly.

"You took guard duty last night," Trigger said. "I've already talked to Grover and Doc...they're ready to take over for us while the meetings are in session so you can concentrate on finding and talking to her rather than worrying about protecting Winkler."

Lefty looked over at his friend in surprise. He'd thought he'd done a pretty good job in hiding how much he wanted to talk to Kinley. How much he wanted—no, *needed*—to find out why she hadn't kept in contact with him after Africa. He'd thought they'd connected, and when she hadn't answered any of his emails or texts, he'd been disappointed.

He had the best friends anyone could ask for. He'd known some Deltas who didn't really get along with their teammates. Luckily, Lefty knew he could count on Trigger, Brain, Oz, Lucky, Doc, and Grover for anything, no matter what time of day, no matter what it was. They'd worked together so long they could almost read each other's minds as well. Which was both a blessing and a pain in the ass.

"Come on," Trigger said with a chuckle. "You think it's not obvious that you're chomping at the bit to pull her aside and talk to her?"

Lefty's lips quirked upward. He should've known his friends would see through his bullshit. "I am, you're right. But I won't put the mission in jeopardy to do so."

Trigger shook his head. "You know that none of us would, either. We might not like bodyguard duty but that doesn't mean we're not going to give it one hundred percent."

Lefty nodded. He did know that. "I'd appreciate it. I think she's avoiding me, honestly."

"She knows how protection duty works. Brown has his own team on him, right?" Trigger asked.

"Yeah. Merlin's team is on him."

Trigger nodded. Merlin and his four teammates were stationed out of Washington, DC, so they were frequently used for these kinds of missions. "They know about what happened in Africa?" he asked.

3

"Yeah. And they weren't happy," Lefty said. Assistants weren't officially included in protection details, but most of the teams sent on these jobs did their best to protect everyone traveling with the person they were sent to guard. In Africa, the Delta teams had been spread pretty thin because of the unrest outside the building where the meetings were taking place, and Kinley had been able to sneak out almost undetected.

Not for the first time, Lefty was very glad he'd seen her at the last second and had followed.

"Right. Anyway, I'm just letting you know that when you do catch up with her, we're willing to give you some time and space to talk," Trigger said.

Lefty knew his friend truly meant that, and there would be no hard feelings about it picking up his slack. Now that Trigger was living blissfully with Gillian, a woman he'd met while on a mission, Trigger wanted everyone to be as happy as he was.

"Thanks," Lefty told him. He was pretty sure he and Kinley weren't meant to be, not with the way she'd ghosted him, but he *did* want to find out why. Find out what he'd done to turn her off so completely.

Ten minutes later, the woman he'd been thinking about nonstop ever since he'd heard Walter Brown would be at the conference walked around a corner in the hall. She came to a halt when she saw Lefty and Trigger standing against the wall.

She quickly regained her composure and continued walking toward them. She had a handful of folders in her arms and looked delightfully disheveled.

Her shoulder-length black hair was a bit mussed, as if she'd been running her hand through it in vexation. She never wore much makeup, and this morning was no exception. Lefty thought she had on lip gloss and a bit of mascara, but that was it. She was petite, only standing at around five and a half feet tall. He felt as if he towered over her, and he'd never been so glad for her slight stature as he'd been that day in Africa. He'd easily been able to wrench her away from the asshole who was trying to stick his hand down her pants and carry her out of the worst of the protests to safety.

Today, she had on a pair of small heels that gave her a bit of height. She also wore black slacks and a short-sleeve heather-red blouse. A pair of gold hoops adorned her ears, the only other jewelry a watch on her left wrist. Lefty silently approved; it was never a good idea to wear a lot of flashy jewelry when overseas, even in Paris...a city that had a higher-than-average percentage of expensive stores for its citizens to shop in.

Kinley refused to meet his gaze, which frustrated Lefty. He had a million questions for her, but here in the hall, when she was obviously in a rush, wasn't the place or time. He really didn't like that she couldn't even bring herself to say hello to him. He wracked his brain trying to figure out what it was he'd done or said that had made her want nothing to do with him, but couldn't come up with one damn thing.

She slipped inside the meeting room without even once looking up at him.

Sighing, Lefty's jaw tightened. Ignoring him wouldn't make him go away. She was going to have to talk to him sooner or later.

"Wow," Trigger said under his breath. "That was the coldest cold shoulder I've seen in a very long time."

"I'm going to take you up on your earlier offer," Lefty told his friend. "I swear to God, I didn't say or do anything to warrant her acting so skittish around me."

"I know you didn't," Trigger said, putting his hand on Lefty's shoulder in a gesture of support and understanding. "Out of all of us, you're the most congenial."

Lefty nodded, his determination rising. If Kinley thought

she could ignore him and pretend they hadn't shared a connection in Africa, she was sorely mistaken.

He hadn't been able to forget her. She was pretty, soft-spoken, hadn't treated him deferentially just because he was a Delta Force operative. He'd had more than his fair share of women throw themselves at him after they'd learned what he did in the Army. He liked that she treated him as a "normal person," that she wasn't impressed by his job. He felt protective of her because of her size, and because she literally didn't hesitate to do whatever was asked of her.

Her vulnerability also struck a chord in him. Made him want to hold her in his arms and protect her from the big bad world.

* * *

Kinley Taylor breathed a sigh of relief when she'd managed to slip inside the meeting room without having to talk to Gage Haskins.

Lefty.

She knew he'd received the nickname in basic training when one of the drill sergeants found out he was left-handed. It seemed rather discriminatory to her, but he'd reassured her that he'd been relieved to get such an innocuous nickname.

But she couldn't imagine calling him Lefty. As far as she was concerned, it didn't fit. He'd always be Gage to her.

She remembered everything about him, from the second she'd first seen the man. They'd been in Africa, and he was standing against a wall, his eyes constantly roaming the room, looking for danger. He hadn't noticed her, as he was too focused on any possible threats, but Kinley had sure seen *him*.

He hadn't shaved in a while, and the stubble on his face was a bit too long to be considered appropriate for a regular soldier, but from everything she'd read and seen on TV, she assumed special forces guys were allowed a little more leeway in their grooming standards. His dark brown hair was kept short on the sides and a little longer on top in a typical military haircut. He had thick eyebrows, and the intense look of concentration he usually wore made her shiver...with excitement. He'd looked completely badass in his black cargo pants and shirt, and for some reason, Kinley had felt safer just because he was in the room.

The second time she'd seen him had been just after she'd been grabbed on the street by one of the men who'd shown up to protest the summit her boss had been participating in. Walter Brown had been pissed—which wasn't exactly a rare thing—when she'd brought him coffee that wasn't up to his exacting standards. He'd sent her back to their hotel to bring him a cup of coffee from the little café inside, as he'd fallen in love with it after their first morning.

Their hotel was about four blocks away. She'd gone out a side door, but the protesters seemed to be everywhere. She'd done her best to ignore them, to try to stay on the peripheral of the crowd, but that hadn't worked very well. The moment a small group of men saw her, they'd followed, verbally harassing her and scaring her to death.

Then they'd escalated from cat-calling. One of them suddenly grabbed her, attempting to drag her into an alley. She'd fought the man and his friends as hard as she could, but she was no match for their size, strength, and numbers.

But then Gage had shown up out of nowhere. He'd taken out the two men who were doing their best to undo the button on her pants, and when the two others backed off, he put an arm around her waist and physically carried her out of danger.

They'd spent the next four days talking whenever their

schedules allowed—and the crush she'd felt the first time she'd seen him had only grown.

But when she got back to Washington, DC, she began to doubt herself. Why would Gage be interested in *her*? She wasn't the kind of person anyone really wanted to get close to. She'd had lesson after lesson in that fact, starting with her birth mom, who'd abandoned her when she was two. Not one of the foster parents she'd had over the years had expressed any interest in adopting her. She'd had a best friend in junior high, but even that girl had moved on after a while, deciding Kinley was too peculiar to hang around with.

Kinley was used to being alone. She'd worked her ass off in high school and got good grades and went to college on scholarships. She hadn't made any close friendships in college, either; she'd been too preoccupied with studying and working. She'd interned in DC, and simply stayed after accepting her first job there.

Somehow, she'd gotten to the ripe old age of twenty-nine without falling in love and without having even one person she could call a true friend.

Most of the time, neither bothered her, but when she'd gotten back to her lonely apartment after returning from Africa, she'd let her insecurities get the better of her.

There was no way Gage wanted to be her friend. Why would he want to befriend her when it was obvious he had a close-knit group of teammates already? Besides, they lived halfway across the country from each other.

She'd talked herself into believing that he was just being polite when he'd said he wanted to keep in touch.

But even when she didn't return his initial texts or calls, he kept on reaching out to her. She wanted to believe his interest was genuine, but she was too wary to take a chance. She'd had other people who'd shown an interest in getting to know her, and she'd jumped at the chance, only to be disappointed when they'd eventually drifted away.

But it was hard to keep telling herself that he wasn't really interested in getting to know her when he kept texting.

Kinley had finally convinced herself to pull her head out of her ass and reply—and he'd stopped writing. She'd missed her chance.

She knew she could reach out to *him*, tell him her phone had been broken or that she'd been busy, or make up some other excuse as to why she hadn't responded, but then she felt stupid.

Her problem was that she overthought everything. If she could be more spontaneous and go with the flow, she'd probably have more friends, be less lonely.

After Gage had stopped contacting her, even though it had broken her heart, Kinley had tried to tell herself that it would've happened eventually, even if she'd written him back. How would things work out between them? They didn't even live in the same state.

Kinley was...odd. She knew it, and usually she didn't care. She was an introvert who liked being by herself. Liked spending most of her time in her apartment, reading. She'd lived in DC for years, and had also been to all the museums. She loved history, and she'd spent hour upon hour soaking up the remnants of the past the varied museums had to offer. She'd done some of the popular attractions too, taking some of the history tours and visiting all the monuments.

She also enjoyed visiting Arlington National Cemetery. She cried every time she walked around the graves, cried for all the men and women who'd died serving their country. It hurt her heart, but she did it anyway, just because she wanted them to know they hadn't been forgotten.

DC was full of things to do, and Kinley had done her best to experience her share...but she'd always done them alone.

For the most part, she'd been all right with that, but lately, she'd begun to feel the weight of her loneliness. She wanted close friends she could call up to go out to dinner. She wanted someone she could talk to about the latest movies and books. She wanted to feel not so alone in the world.

She knew she'd blown it with Gage. That she should've seen where things between them could go. They'd really clicked in Africa. He was funny and attentive and smart. But she'd let her insecurities get the better of her when she'd gotten home. Hadn't thought she was pretty enough, worldly enough, or even exciting enough to be able to keep the interest of a man like Gage.

So she'd done the cowardly thing and ignored him. And she hated herself for that.

In the back of her mind, Kinley had known there would be a chance she'd see him again. She knew Delta Force teams from across the country were occasionally tasked with protecting political figures when they went overseas. Hell, he might even be assigned to protect her boss again... but she'd put the thought to the back of her mind and decided she'd deal with seeing Gage again if and when it happened.

And now it was happening. He was here. And Kinley had absolutely no idea what she was supposed to say to him.

When she'd come around the corner of the hall and seen Gage and one of his friends stationed outside the room, she'd had an extreme case of déjà vu. He was once again wearing all black, and while he had less stubble than the first time she'd seen him, he was no less beautiful.

And yes, he *was* beautiful. She'd been physically attracted to him from the first time she'd seen him, and that attraction hadn't lessened any with the passing of time.

She felt his gaze on her as she headed for the doorway into the large assembly room. Walter had forgotten some folders he'd needed for a meeting this morning and had asked her to go back and get them.

Feeling awkward, and praying she didn't fall on her face in front of Gage, Kinley slipped into the room without acknowledging him in any way. The second she was behind the closed door, she realized she probably should've at least nodded at him. Or said hello or something.

God, she was the worst. No wonder she didn't have any friends. She was completely socially inept.

Feeling depressed, and knowing the rest of the conference would be awkward if she kept running into Gage, Kinley wordlessly placed the files Walter had forgotten next to him on the table. He didn't acknowledge her presence, which was fine with her.

Kinley walked to the back of the room and took a seat and got out a pad of paper and a pen. It was her job to take notes and type them up for Walter later. She knew he wasn't interested in most of the speeches and discussions going on around him, but he needed to at least know the basics later in case he was asked about them.

Walter Brown was difficult to work for. He was bossy and not very astute when it came to things like knowing when he was overworking his assistant, but she stayed because, while tough, he was fair—mostly. He might make her work overtime, but then allow her to leave early another day to make up for it. He'd make her be his gopher when they were on trips like this one, but then he'd bring in doughnuts or treat her to lunch when they got home.

Besides, Kinley *liked* her job. Seeing how the government worked firsthand could be frustrating and irritating, but it was also extremely interesting to see all the ins and outs of how deals were made and how relationships with people and interest groups really made all the difference.

In her opinion, Walter Brown wasn't a great representative, but he had friends in high places who could do some pretty amazing things to help those less fortunate in the country. She'd been doing her best to subtly steer Walter toward doing more good, but many times her opinion was discounted. She was simply an assistant, after all.

To be honest, her thoughts about staying where she was and continuing to work for Brown frequently vacillated between wanting to quit immediately, and being determined to stay and try to make a difference.

For a second, Kinley thought about Gage. How he also worked for his country, but in such a different way. He was fighting for what was good and right, and putting his life on the line. He was honorable, brave, and didn't hesitate to wade into a dangerous situation to save a nobody like her.

Kinley wasn't sure Walter would lift his little finger to help someone else if it meant he might get so much as a splinter in the process.

Though, she supposed she wasn't being fair. Politicians weren't trained for the things special forces soldiers were. But still.

Kinley half listened to a representative from Spain talk about global warming as she analyzed her own bravery. If she'd been walking near that mob in Africa and seen someone being assaulted, would she have stopped and tried to help?

She wanted to say yes, of course she would...but she honestly didn't know.

Kinley didn't think of herself as very brave at all. She wasn't adventurous, and much preferred to hang out in the safety of her apartment or the familiarity of DC than go exploring the world. But she'd like to think if push came to shove, she'd act and put someone else's safety above her own.

Shaking her head and forcing herself to pay attention, Kinley couldn't help but wonder what Gage was thinking after their encounter in the hall. Was he glad to see her?

Pissed that she hadn't answered his texts and emails? Was he thanking his lucky stars she hadn't written him back? She hated not knowing—and wasn't looking forward to the awkward moment when they'd come face-to-face and she'd have to speak to him.

CHAPTER TWO

The following evening, Lefty was feeling anxious because he still hadn't been able to get a moment alone with Kinley to talk to her. Time was running out—the conference was only scheduled to run for another day and a half, and if he didn't get a chance to clear the air between them, he had a feeling whatever tenuous friendship he might've sparked with Kinley would truly be lost forever.

And something within him knew that if he lost her, he'd regret it for the rest of his life.

So Lefty was bringing in reinforcements...the Delta team who was assigned to Kinley's boss. It was late at night, and Walter Brown had retired to his hotel room hours ago. Doc had volunteered to watch his room to make sure he didn't decide to go on a late-night stroll while Lefty spoke with the other team.

They were all sitting in the hotel room Lefty was sharing with Grover and Oz, who were currently watching over Winkler while he met up with other representatives for drinks. The rest of his team were either exploring Paris on their down time or sleeping.

"Okay, we're here," Merlin said. "What's up?"

Looking around at the five men, Lefty wasn't sure where to start. He felt kinda silly telling them he wanted to spend some time with a girl and needed their help, but that's essentially what was going on.

Trying to figure out what he wanted to say, Lefty studied the other men. Jangles, the only blond in the group, with his blue eyes and boy-next-door looks, had no problem with the opposite sex—he was constantly being hit on by women all over the globe. Lefty had heard him bitch about living in DC...and being "pestered" by politicians' wives. He also knew the man disliked when women made the first move. He much preferred pursuing, rather than being pursued.

Woof had brown hair and an uncanny way with dogs, which was how he got his nickname. It didn't matter if the team was on a dangerous mission or on guard duty, like they were now, dogs always seemed drawn to him. He never went anywhere without a few dog bones in his pocket.

Zip was the youngest of the other team, at thirty. He had a gnarly scar on his thigh from a childhood accident that literally looked like a zipper. The man was constantly smiling, and was by far the most positive person Lefty had ever met. And that should've been annoying, but somehow wasn't.

Merlin was the old man in the group, and the unofficial team leader, even though at thirty-five, he was hardly old. But everyone gave him shit because his hair was already graying around the edges. He didn't talk a lot, but when he did, people listened.

Rounding out the team was Duff. He was a big son of a bitch, and surly to boot. Most people gave him a wide berth and did their best not to get on his bad side.

Merlin and his men might spend a lot of their time on protection duty, but that didn't mean they were any less lethal when hunting down terrorists. Lefty had seen the five men in action and couldn't deny they were good. Damn good. There weren't a lot of teams he'd want at his back if the shit hit the fan, but these men were definitely counted in that number.

"I need your help," Lefty said into the prolonged silence after Jangles had asked his question. "It's nothing life-or-death, but since you're guarding Walter Brown, I figured you'd be the best people to ask."

Lefty could tell that piqued their interest.

"Is Brown in danger?" Woof asked.

"Not that I know of," Lefty said honestly.

"He's an ass," Duff said with a scowl. "I wouldn't be surprised in the least if he's pissed someone off who wants to see him dead."

Lefty didn't bother to hide his opinion. "I happen to agree with you," he told the other man. "He's got a lot of people snowed, they think he's a good guy, but we've watched him long enough to know that while he might have his moments, generally, he treats anyone he thinks is beneath him like shit, and it's gonna come back to bite him in the ass sooner or later."

"Can't come soon enough for us," Merlin muttered.

"Asshole made Kinley cry yesterday," Jangles said with a shake of his head. "For no reason other than he could."

Lefty tensed at hearing that. "What'd he do?" he bit out.

Jangles either didn't notice Lefty's pissed-off tone, or he simply ignored it. "She'd spent most of the night typing up the notes from the meetings the day before and the printer in the business center at the hotel wasn't working. She gave him a jump drive with the notes and apologized for not being able to print them for him, and he went off. Yelling at her, telling her there were dozens of people lined up wanting to work for him."

Lefty took a deep breath to try to control his anger, but it didn't do much good. "I need to talk to her," he blurted.

"Without her looking over her shoulder to see where Brown is and wondering if he's gonna ask her to do something stupid, like get him another fucking pastry from down the street."

Five men pinned Lefty with their intense gazes.

"You looking for a piece of ass on the job?" Duff asked.

"No...and fuck you for thinking Kinley's that kind of woman."

"Interesting that he defended Kinley's honor but not his own," Zip said with a smirk.

"Look, I met Kinley in Africa. Brown wasn't very nice even back then, and she ended up in the middle of a fucking protest because he'd sent her out to get him a cup of coffee. We talked a bit and everything seemed good. I liked her, wanted to get to know her more. We exchanged numbers and emails, and I thought she was as interested as I was to keep in touch. But she didn't return even one of my messages. And now, she won't even look at me. I must've fucked up some-how, and I just want to make things right. Besides...the woman needs a break. She's been working nonstop since she got here."

"So what do you want from us?" Jangles asked.

"I want to steal Kinley away for a few hours in the morn-ing. The representatives have some sort of brunch thing tomorrow morning, it's nothing important, just a lot of hobnobbing. But Brown will probably insist Kinley stand against the wall throughout the whole thing, just because he likes having her at his beck and call. I want to take her for a walk. Get some fresh air, see the sights of Paris for a few hours. But I'm not sure how to do that without him being even more of an ass or threatening her job."

"Could she tell him she's sick?" Zip asked.

"Possibly," Lefty mused. "But I'm not sure Brown is the

kind of man to let Kinley take the morning off even if she's feeling under the weather."

"She could claim to have a slight fever and a cough," Duff said without cracking a smile. "If he thinks she's got that Coronavirus, and she could give it to him, he might be willing to leave her alone."

"Ouch, man. Harsh," Zip said, but he was nodding as he said it.

"But it wouldn't keep him from calling her," Lefty said.

"I could slip him a laxative," Jangles said with an evil grin. "He wouldn't even want to leave his room, and it's likely he wouldn't advertise to anyone, even his assistant, that he's having...digestive issues."

"I'm not sure drugging our charge is the best idea," Merlin said dryly.

"If you go with the sick excuse, maybe don't say she has a fever. That could get her quarantined," Woof said. "Maybe just say she has a migraine and is throwing up. Or... Oh! I know. Say she's got really bad cramps. Most men don't like discussing *anything* that has to do with a woman's period. That way she's not contagious and won't have to worry about being quarantined or anything, and she can 'recover' in time for the afternoon meetings. I can even volunteer to be his assistant for the morning. He might not go for it, but from what I've seen on this trip, he's mostly making Kinley fetch and carry shit for him. I can take notes if he needs me too, as well."

Lefty thought about the plan for a moment. It wasn't ideal. Brown could still decide to fire Kinley for being sick at an inopportune time. Or he could refuse to allow Woof to be his assistant. But he couldn't think of anything else that would work. He wanted Kinley to have a stress-free few hours with him, but he didn't want to jeopardize her job in the process.

Then he remembered the story she'd told him about her boss insisting she take an entire week off when she caught the flu a year or so back. She'd mentioned it in Africa. In a rare display of kindness, Brown had even ordered chicken soup to be delivered to her apartment. It had surprised Lefty that her boss had been so compassionate. Kinley had simply shrugged and said he had his moments.

"Okay, menstrual cramps it is," he told the other guys. "Thanks, Woof, for volunteering to be Brown's bitch boy for the morning. I'll owe you."

"Yeah, you will," Woof said with a chuckle.

"I'll put Jangles on duty at her door to make sure no one tries to bother her," Merlin said. "Just in case Brown decides to visit or something. I doubt he will. Woof's right; he's not going to want to discuss her womanly issues. It won't keep him from calling her, but we can at least run interference if he does show up."

"Thank you," Lefty said with a relieved sigh.

"Don't fuck with her," Zip said in an uncharacteristically serious tone. "She's one of the most genuine people I've met in DC. She always has a smile for us and is constantly asking if there's anything we need."

"Yeah. And as you know, a lot of the people we're assigned to protect act like we aren't even here," Woof added.

Lefty wasn't surprised. In the short amount of time he'd spent with Kinley in Africa, he'd come to the same conclusion. She was quiet and introverted, but she never hesitated to try to help someone else if they needed it. After he'd gotten her away from that African mob, she'd actually insisted they stop at a woman's small produce stand, where she'd proceeded to buy every single one of the items.

Then, because she had no use for a cart full of fruits and vegetables, she'd asked that they be given to a nearby woman with a baby strapped to her chest and a toddler in one arm.

Both women had been overcome with gratitude for Kinley's generosity.

But instead of being smug about it, Kinley had waved off their thanks—then asked if she could thank Lefty for saving her by buying him lunch.

Yeah, Kinley Taylor was genuine down to her core, and he hoped like hell working in DC and for assholes like Brown would never change that.

"I'm not going to fuck with her," Lefty assured Zip and the others. "As I said, we...clicked, for lack of a better word. But I'm worried because she didn't return any of my messages. I just want to talk to her, find out what's going on."

"Maybe she was just being polite, and she really thought you were an asshole," Duff suggested.

Lefty didn't take offense. "Maybe so...but again, that's why I want to talk to her. And not just in a hallway for two seconds."

"Full disclosure here," Merlin said. "I'm gonna be on your tail."

"I expected one of you would," Lefty said, not concerned in the least.

"Brown's our mission, but we take the safety of everyone associated with our charge seriously," Jangles said.

Lefty nodded. This was just one more reason he liked these men. They acted the same way his own team did. Assistants, spouses, children...they protected anyone who traveled with the person they were assigned to watch over.

"She'll never know I'm there," Merlin promised confidently.

"Good," Lefty said. Then he encompassed all the men in a glance. "I appreciate it. I know dealing with Brown isn't exactly fun and games."

Jangles waved off his thanks. "We're used to dealing with men like him. He'll never know Kinley's been out running around Paris...as long as you get her back before those meetings start at one."

"I will," Lefty said. He stood and shook each of the other men's hands.

As they left, Jangles turned at the door. Lefty braced himself for one more warning.

"For the record...Kinley's too good for DC. On the surface, she seems almost fragile, but she has to have a core of steel to have lived and worked in DC for as long as she has. Don't underestimate her, Lefty, but at the same time...look beyond the surface to find the real Kinley. I have a feeling she's never had a chance to blossom, to be who she's meant to be."

And with that surprising pearl of wisdom, Jangles shut the door behind him as he left.

Lefty didn't have much time to ponder the man's words when the door reopened and Grover and Oz entered. Winkler must've ended his night earlier than usual.

"Everything all right?" Grover asked. "We saw Merlin and his team leaving."

Lefty nodded. "Yeah, I'm going to be taking the morning off tomorrow. I already cleared it with Trigger."

"Kinley?" Oz asked with an insight borne of the men being so close.

"Yeah."

"'Bout time," Oz said with a smile, then he sobered. "You gonna be all right if she tells you she's just not into you?"

Lefty nodded. "Yeah. If I think she's being honest. But the thing is...we connected, Oz. And I'm not just saying that. She's interesting, and although she's not super chatty, when she does speak, it means something. I don't know what's goin' on in her head, but I want to make sure she's all right. That she didn't ignore my messages because she's in trouble or because of some other bullshit reason. If she honestly doesn't like me, I'll be okay with that. But I don't think that's the case."

"She watches you when you aren't looking," Grover said as he got settled on the sofa bed where he'd been sleeping.

Lefty's head whipped around. "What?"

"When you aren't looking, she follows you with her eyes," Grover repeated.

Lefty should've been thrilled at hearing that, but instead, it only confused him. "Why the hell has she been avoiding me then?"

"Don't ask me," Grover said with a shrug. "Ask her."

"I plan on it," Lefty said with determination.

"I don't understand girls," Oz said with a sigh. "Never have. Not since I was ten and was chased around the playground by one. She caught me, kissed me, then told everyone she hated me."

Grover cracked up, and Lefty couldn't stop the smile that spread over his face.

"She likes you," Grover said after he'd gotten himself under control. "But she either doesn't think she should, or maybe she thinks *you* shouldn't like *her*. I don't know her, but if you say you clicked, I believe you. Especially with the way she watches you so closely."

"And how do *you* know so much about women?" Oz asked.

Grover shrugged. "I've got three sisters."

"Three?" Oz said incredulously. "I mean, I've heard you talk about your sisters a time or two, but didn't realize you had *three*."

"Yup. One younger and two older. I also have a younger brother. I'm right in the middle. I grew up listening to my sisters gossiping about boys in their classes, agonizing about dating, and analyzing every little thing their boyfriends did. Believe me when I say that I'm pretty much an expert when it comes to what girls are thinking," Grover said with a smirk.

"Then why are you still single?" Lefty snarked.

"Because I know how crazy they are," Grover said without hesitation.

All three men laughed.

"Seriously, how did we not know you had three sisters?" Oz asked, obviously not able to get past Grover's revelation.

The other man shrugged. "I don't know. I just don't talk about them much."

"Are they single?" Oz asked.

Grover gave him a look. "Don't go getting any ideas."

Oz held up his hands as if surrendering. "I wasn't. It was just a question!"

Grover shook his head. "Sorry. I'm protective of them. Especially Devyn, my younger sister. She's had a hard life. She's twenty-nine, but she has an old soul. She had leukemia when she was little and missed out on a lot of her childhood as a result."

"That sucks," Oz commiserated.

"Yeah. But she doesn't let it define her in the least. She's more than made up for missing all the fun stuff growing up. I swear to God she's gonna be the reason I go gray prematurely. She's a wild child. If she's not parachuting or bungee jumping, she's riding a camel across Africa. If it's an adventure, she's up for it."

"She sounds fun," Oz said.

"She is. But all the fun is masking some pretty big hurts inside, I'm sure of it. I've tried to talk to her but she blows me off, telling me I'm just being a protective older brother. Which I am, but if she'd just slow down for two seconds, I think she'd actually enjoy life more."

Everyone was silent for a moment. Then Grover said, "Anyway, take my word for it, Lefty. Kinley *is* into you. But for some reason she's keeping you at arm's length. You're going to have to get her to trust you before she tells you the real reason she ghosted you."

"And how do you propose I do that?" Lefty asked, genuinely grateful for any help.

"I'd say rescue her from a crazed mob who wants to hurt her, but you've already done that and it didn't work," Grover said, tongue-in-cheek.

"Thanks for nothing," Lefty grumbled.

"Be patient," Grover told his friend. "Don't jump on her case. Go slow, show her that you aren't going to fly off the handle. Maybe open up to her, tell her something you've never told anyone else before. And definitely make her feel special, so she's sure you aren't just blowing smoke up her ass. For all she knows, you chat up women all over the globe."

"I don't," Lefty insisted. "You know that."

"*I* do, but she doesn't."

That made Lefty pause. He and Kinley *were* essentially still strangers. Yes, they'd talked a lot in Africa, but they hadn't had a chance to really get to know each other on a deep level. He'd told her he was single, of course, but she had no way of knowing for sure. Long-distance relationships weren't his favorite; they were hard, and they were even harder when you didn't truly know someone. He nodded at Grover. "Good point. I'll make it very clear tomorrow that I'm not dating anyone, that I've spent more time on the battlefield than in the bedroom, and that I'm talking to her because she intrigues me."

"Good. Although it'll probably take time for her to really believe you. My best advice is...don't give up. If she ghosts you again, keep messaging her. Even if it's about stupid shit, like what you're eating for dinner. Women usually want to know that you're thinking about them even when you aren't together."

Lefty nodded. He'd be the first to admit that he wasn't

exactly an expert on women. He'd dated, but most of his relationships had left him feeling...blah. He enjoyed spending time with women, but he wasn't constantly thinking about them when they were apart.

He couldn't say the same about Kinley. She wasn't a total constant in his thoughts, but he couldn't deny that he'd see something—a woman sitting in a coffee shop, or a news story about Walter Brown—and he'd immediately be transported back to Africa and how much he enjoyed talking with her.

Lefty got ready for bed, and after he lay down, he stared up at the ceiling for a long time, trying to figure out how he was going to get Kinley to trust him, to open up to him, to truly believe that he wanted to get to know her better. He'd start with being her friend and maybe things would progress from there.

He admitted to himself he wasn't sure how things could work out on a more intimate level, with him being in Texas and her living in DC, but he'd never felt so determined to get a woman to talk to him before. That had to be a sign that maybe, just maybe, they were meant to be more than passing acquaintances.

Determination rising within him, Lefty promised himself he'd do whatever it took to make sure Kinley understood how serious he was about being her friend, about getting to know her better. That he truly liked her.

Somehow he had a feeling it would be easier said than done.

CHAPTER THREE

Kinley opened her hotel door at 7:03 the next morning. Her head was down and she was lost in thought about how much she was dreading the day. She hated the social get-togethers at conferences like this. They were boring, and people rarely talked to her, so she didn't usually have anything to do other than stand on the sidelines.

But it was all part of the job, she told herself. She'd be on her way back to Washington tomorrow, and she'd have the entire flight to read. Hopefully she wouldn't be sitting next to anyone who wanted to talk. She hated that. Headphones helped to make it clear she wasn't interested in chatting, but sometimes even that wasn't enough to deter an overly extroverted seat-mate.

She was so lost in thought about what book she wanted to read on the plane ride home that she didn't even notice someone standing outside her room. Before she knew what was happening, the man had taken hold of one of her arms and was walking her down the hall.

Ready to scream and pull her arm out of the man's firm hold, she looked up just in time to swallow her protest.

It was Gage who had ahold of her arm. He had a determined look on his face and didn't appear to be in any mood to argue.

Kinley looked back toward her room and saw Jangles, one of the Delta Force operatives assigned to protect her boss, standing outside her room.

He smiled at her and tipped an imaginary hat in her direction. "Have fun!" he called out.

Frowning, Kinley turned back around just in time to see Gage open the door to the stairs that led down to the lobby. He'd ushered her through the door before she could say a word. But instead of continuing down the stairwell, he put her back to the wall and let go of her arm. He actually took a step back, giving her some space before he spoke.

"Sorry if I scared you," he said gently. "But I wanted to get you out of the hall before Brown had a chance to come out and see you."

"He doesn't usually get up until around eight," Kinley told Gage. "He stays up late. I think Drake Stryker, the US Ambassador to France, was in his room visiting last night. They hang out a lot when they're at the same conferences, and he told me not to bother him under any circumstances."

"Ah, okay. Anyway, I have a proposal for you."

Kinley could only stare up at the man she'd been thinking about for months. He looked different this morning, more approachable. He had on a pair of jeans and a short-sleeve white polo shirt. She could see a smattering of hair on his chest where his shirt was open, and on his left arm, she saw the intricate black tattoo she'd caught glimpses of in Africa. She longed to push up the sleeve so she could see all of it, but managed to keep her hands to herself...barely.

His hair was sort of sticking up, as if he'd towel-dried it after showering then didn't bother to comb it. He'd also shaved recently; there was no sign of the five o'clock shadow she'd gotten so used to seeing. Kinley wasn't sure if she liked his clean-shaven look or not. She liked when he looked rugged and a little unapproachable. It made her feel as if no one would dare approach them when he looked a little on the rough side.

"Kinley?" he asked with a slight grin on his face.

"Oh...yeah?"

"I have a proposal for you," he repeated. "I'd like to spend the morning with you. There's nothing going on at the conference except for the social brunch."

"Oh, but...Walter expects me to be there," she said, the disappointment easy to hear in her tone.

"I've taken care of that for you. Bought you a few hours," Gage admitted.

"How?"

"I talked to Merlin and his team. He's going to tell Brown that you're not feeling well this morning. That you've got menstrual issues."

"Seriously?"

"Yup. I'm betting he's not the kind of man who will get in your face about your period. Am I wrong? If so, let me know now and we can think of something else. Maybe I can get Merlin to slip him some laxatives after all."

Kinley couldn't help but laugh. "They would really do that?"

"For you? Yeah, they would. They like you, Kins, and they want you to have some time to explore Paris this morning. To have some fun."

Kinley was shocked, but their concern felt good. "I'm pretty certain that Walter won't question it. I mean, I had to call him once to tell him I had food poisoning, and I was throwing up and had diarrhea, and he couldn't give me the time off fast enough. I know you don't like him, but he's not always so horrible. I think traveling brings out the worst in him."

She could tell Gage didn't believe her, but he looked relieved that the excuse he'd made up to get her out of work for a few hours would suffice. She probably should be irritated that he'd planned this without talking to her ahead of time, but she was too flattered he wanted to spend time with her.

"Jangles will stay by your door just in case Brown decides to come down and see you, but I'm guessing that probably won't happen after what you just told me. I'll make sure you're back by one for the last of the meetings today though."

"Thanks," Kinley told him.

"No need to thank me. I'd like to talk to you without having to worry about Brown deciding he needs you, and without you running off to solve the world's problems. I've missed you, Kins...and I'd love to spend time with you in Paris. What do you say?"

Kinley didn't think she could say anything. She'd been longing to talk to Gage since she'd first seen him earlier that week, but the longer she'd avoided him, the more awkward she'd felt.

"Just talk, Kins, Nothing scary. Have you ever been to Paris?"

She shook her head.

"We'll play tourist and talk while we do it. I'll find you some amazing macarons and we can stuff our face while we see the Louvre, what's left of Notre Dame, and of course the Eiffel Tower. What do you say?"

Knowing she *should* say no and go to brunch instead, Kinley still found herself nodding. How could she resist this man? He'd gone out of his way to give her a morning of freedom. Wasn't she just lamenting to herself last night that she was in

Paris and hadn't seen a single thing? Her hotel room overlooked a damn alley instead of the Eiffel Tower, as she'd hoped. It was supposed to be a romantic city for lovers, and she'd been sitting in her hotel room, too intimidated to go out on her own.

The smile that spread across Gage's face was absolutely beautiful. "Good. I promise you're gonna have a good time."

Kinley wasn't so sure about that—she was worried about this talk he wanted to have—but she'd take spending time with Gage over standing against the wall in a room full of politicians any day.

Then, as if he'd done it every day of his life, he reached out and took the strap of her briefcase from her. He opened the stairwell doorway and placed it on the floor inside the hall they'd just exited. Then he turned and took her hand and draped it over his forearm.

Being this close to him made Kinley feel even more awkward than usual, and that was saying something. She felt short most of the time, but next to Gage, instead of being self-conscious about her size, she felt surrounded by him. He was over half a foot taller than her, and she liked having him at her side.

"Jangles will grab your bag and make sure it's at the meetings this afternoon," Gage told her as he steered her down the stairs.

"Okay." There wasn't anything valuable in her briefcase... well, except for her government-owned laptop. She had her wallet in her purse, which was slung around her chest.

"What do you want to see first?" Gage asked as they walked through the lobby toward the exit. "How about breakfast? We can stop at one of those sidewalk cafes and get some coffee and some of the pastry the French are famous for."

Kinley nodded. She didn't care *what* they did. She was spending time with Gage, so she already knew she'd remember this day for the rest of her life.

Her head seemed as if it was on a swivel as they walked. Even though it was early, there were lots of people out and about. The sound of residents speaking French was all around them, making this adventure seem all the more surreal.

Gage found a small café and got her seated, then managed to order them breakfast even though he didn't speak the language. It took lots of pointing and pantomiming, but before too long, they had small cups of espresso sitting in front of them and a huge plate of sweet, decadent pastries.

"This isn't my normal breakfast, but since it's a special occasion, I think I'm okay," Gage said.

Kinley knew she needed to do more than just stare at the man, so she forced herself to ask, "Special occasion?"

He beamed. "Yeah. Our first date."

Kinley was stunned. Her brows came down and she frowned at Gage.

"Aw, don't look at me like that," he said, reaching for her hand. "I wasn't going to get into this so soon, but I think it's better to just get this conversation out of the way so we can enjoy the rest of the day. I thought we decided in Africa that we were going to keep in touch."

It wasn't a question, but it still was. Kinley's stomach rolled. She had no idea how to explain to him that she wasn't worth his time. That she'd had doubts from the second she'd left Africa. She licked her lips and tried to think of the right words. But he spoke again before she could.

"It was brought to my attention that maybe you think I do this all the time...befriend women and give them my number and email. I don't. You're the first, and I'm not lying about that. We didn't get a ton of time to spend together in Africa but I really thought we'd clicked. I was looking forward to getting to know you better, even if it was only over the internet. I was disappointed when you didn't return any of my messages."

Kinley studied the man in front of her. He seemed sincere. She didn't have a lot of experience with men though. Hell, she had *no* experience with men...except for politicians. And every word out of *their* mouths was a lie. Pretty words to sway others into supporting them with their vote or with their wallet.

Gage didn't seem like that. At all. She wanted to believe him...but he had to understand she wasn't like most women.

"I'm a virgin," she blurted.

The three words hung in the air between them during a long pause, and Kinley wanted to die. It was what she'd been thinking, but she hadn't meant to just blurt it out.

"I mean...I'm not like the women you've known in the past. I'm a nerd. I go out and do stuff, but it's generally by myself and not with friends. But I *like* being by myself. I don't get depressed if I sit in my apartment all weekend and don't do anything or go anywhere. I'm perfectly happy with my own company. Most people think I'm weird. And I *am* weird. I'm not good with relationships. I never had anyone to watch growing up to show me how they're supposed to be done. I say the wrong thing all the time—like just now—and I'm embarrassing.

"I just...I didn't write you back because I knew after a while, you'd realize exactly how strange I am. Then you'd have to figure out a way to distance yourself from me. I figured I'd wake up one day and realize that I hadn't heard from you in a while, and when I asked you about it, you'd tell me you'd just been busy and that would be that."

Kinley realized she was out of breath by the time she'd finished speaking, in her rush to get the words out, but she wanted to be as honest as possible with Gage. "If you're spending time with me because you want to sleep with me, it's not going to happen."

"Breathe, Kinley," Gage said calmly, reaching over and

taking her hand in his. "First of all, I'm intrigued by you *because* you're not like any woman I've known before. I think it's great that you're happy with your own company. You don't need anyone else to validate your likes and dislikes. You are who you are, and that's really refreshing. I don't give a fuck if you're strange. In fact, I *like* your kind of strange.

"I'm not going to wake up one day and try to figure out a way to get out of our friendship. Honestly, I figure that you'll be the one who'll get tired of *me*. Kins, it's more than obvious that you're smarter than me. You're nicer, more patient, and most definitely a better person. Why you'd want to even entertain the prospect of being my friend is beyond me, and yet I want that more than I can explain.

"Also...do you think it's a turn off that you're a virgin?" he asked, his tone dropping. "It's not. But for the record, right now, I just want to be your friend. Am I attracted to you? Yes. But my days of one-night stands are over. I want to get to know a woman before I share my body with her. I want to know what makes her happy, what movies she enjoys. I want to meet her friends and family and feel a bone-deep connection before we hop into bed. Maybe that makes me sound like a pussy, but I don't care."

"I don't *have* any friends or family," Kinley admitted softly. She couldn't read the expression on his face, but she didn't want his pity, so she continued on. "I already told you I was an odd duck. I wasn't lying. I was raised in a series of foster homes and none of the adults ever wanted to adopt me. Probably because I spent most of my time hanging out in my room reading rather than interacting with anyone in the house. I was able to get some scholarships to college—being a foster kid helped with that—and when I left my last foster home, I took all my stuff and never went back...not that I was invited.

"I spent all my time studying in college, and when I graduated, got a job in DC, thanks to one of my internships. I tried to make some friends, but everyone's too interested in moving up the political ladder, and I learned, after a few painful mistakes, that in order to have friends, I have to be someone I'm not." She shrugged. "It was easier to hang out in my apartment by myself."

"Listen to me, and listen good," Gage said, putting a hand on the side of her neck and leaning into her.

Kinley stilled. His hand on her skin felt good. Really good. Her nipples puckered under her white cotton utilitarian bra, and she was genuinely shocked by her body's reaction.

"Are you listening?" he asked, and Kinley could feel his warm breath against her cheek.

She nodded.

"I want you to be exactly who you are with me. I like *you*, Kinley. So you aren't like other people, who cares? That makes you unique. I'll share *my* friends with you. And my family. I don't have any brothers or sisters, but my parents would love you. I'd say that they'd be happy to adopt you, but the last thing I want is for you to be my sister...even if it's only on paper."

Kinley barely dared to breathe. All she could do was stare into Gage's brown eyes and wonder how the hell she'd been lucky enough to catch his interest.

"Just give me a chance," Gage said. "We're all strange in our own ways. You know what it is I do, there'll be times I'll be out of pocket and can't communicate with you. It might be a week, or it could be two months. But don't give up on me, okay?"

Kinley nodded. "Okay."

"I thought I'd done or said something that pissed you off," Gage continued. "I wracked my brain to try to figure out what it was that I'd done to cause you to ghost me. I hated the feeling...because I like you, Kins. I like your innocence, and I'm not talking about sex—although again, it is *not* a turn off to know no one has ever touched you before—I'm talking about the way you see the world. It's as if you see straight to the heart of people. You can see through the bullshit. I think that's what intrigued me about you from the start. You looked at me and didn't see a tall, scary soldier, you saw Gage. And no one ever sees *me* the first time they look at me."

"You didn't say or do anything wrong, it was me," Kinley said softly.

"Okay," Gage said. They stared at each other for a heartbeat before he asked, "You feel it too, don't you?"

She'd never heard him sound so unsure before. But she didn't have to ask him what he meant. She knew. Kinley nodded.

His thumb brushed against the underside of her jaw once, before he dropped his hand and sat back in his chair. He nudged her arm and said, "Eat up, Kins. We've got a lot of walking to do this morning, especially if we're gonna see everything before I have to get you back to the conference."

Kinley picked up the croissant sitting on the plate in front of her, but before she took a bite, she said, "If you want to take another chance and email or message me…I'll answer."

She liked the smile that crossed his face. "I'd like that," he said simply.

But for some reason, Kinley couldn't leave it at that. "Sometimes I forget to check my messages, because it's not like I have anyone who emails me other than Walter, so if I don't get back to you right away, don't think I'm ghosting you again. Okay?"

"Okay, Kins. I don't expect you to get back to me within ten seconds or anything. Just don't shut me out again."

"I won't. I swear."

They gazed at each other for another long moment.

Kinley felt as vulnerable as she'd ever been. She tried to let Gage see her sincerity. Finally, he nodded then gestured to her food. "Eat, Kinley."

"Bossy," she muttered.

He grinned. "Yup."

Grinning, she ate.

* * *

A few hours later, after visiting the Champs-Élysées and the Arc de Triomphe, taking a few pictures outside the Louvre, and eating macarons until their stomachs hurt, they'd made their way to the Eiffel Tower.

"Want to go up?" Lefty asked Kinley.

She had her head tilted back, and she was staring up at the iconic French landmark with wide eyes. "No."

"No?" Lefty asked in surprise.

"No," she confirmed. "I researched it before I left DC... not that I thought I'd have the chance to see it up close like this, but...just because. Anyway, the third floor isn't super big. There's not much room. I don't think you'd like it up there and you wouldn't fit very well at all. And...I don't like being that close to people. I just...it's beautiful from down here, I wouldn't want to ruin that by going to the top and seeing the graffiti that I'm sure is up there."

"Okay, Kins. We can stay down here," Lefty said. He wanted to help her get over her obvious fear of the tower, but in truth, they didn't have a lot of time to wait in the long line for tickets. He didn't know if she was scared of heights or if it truly was just being so close to others, but he wanted to help her get over *any* fears.

Baby steps, he reminded himself. Today was about Kinley having fun, not banishing all her fears in one day.

She hadn't looked away from the tower, and Lefty

grinned. He took her elbow and carefully led her to a bench nearby. She sat, still looking up, and Lefty didn't interrupt her thoughts.

She was right, she didn't talk much, but when she did, he always seemed to learn something. She hadn't wanted to go into the Louvre because she'd said it was the biggest museum in the world and, in order to do it justice, she'd need hours and hours to take it all in. She'd also informed him that a mummy named Belphegor was said to haunt the museum.

He'd hated hearing that she didn't have any friends or family, but he didn't think she'd told him that to gain sympathy. She'd said it in the same matter-of-fact way she'd told him what her favorite restaurant was, that she liked vanilla macarons best, and what she did at her job. For her, it was just a fact of her life, and that made Lefty want to show her what true friendship was all the more. He wanted to introduce her to Gillian, to let her hang out with the other guys on his team, show her that she was likeable and worthy.

He'd tried *hard* to block out her admission that she was a virgin, but of course he couldn't stop thinking about it. He knew she was twenty-nine, and it blew his mind that she hadn't made love to anyone. The men around her must be complete idiots, which wasn't exactly a surprise, considering she worked in political circles, but still.

She'd let a few more things slip as they'd talked over the last few hours, and from what he understood, she'd only had a handful of boyfriends in her life, but as soon as they started pressuring her for more than she wanted to give—whether that was physically, or even socially—she broke things off. She'd admitted it was easier to take care of her own physical needs than have to deal with the men's egos.

Lefty knew he'd be lying if he didn't admit he wouldn't mind showing Kinley what all the fuss was about regarding sex. But a few hours wasn't enough to do more than try to cement the connection he felt between them.

Long-distance relationships sucked, and if he could at least be her friend, Lefty would be okay with that.

He kept his eyes on Kinley as she stared up at the tower. He had no idea what was going through her mind, and he found that intriguing as hell. He could just ask her what she was thinking, but he was enjoying simply watching her take in the world around her too much to interrupt.

After another five minutes or so, she blinked then turned her head toward him. "Are you bored?" she asked.

"Nope," Lefty told her honestly.

She frowned. "Most people would be by now."

Lefty shrugged. "I'm not most people." He looked at his watch, then back at her. "We've got another two hours before we need to head back to the conference. If you want to spend that time here, staring up at the Eiffel Tower, that's what we'll do."

"What do *you* want to do?" she asked.

"Whatever you want," Lefty told her without hesitation.

She wrinkled her brow, and Lefty thought it was adorable as fuck. "You don't care if I just sit here and don't talk to you?"

"Nope."

"If I ignore you totally?"

"Nope," he said again.

She made a little sound in the back of her throat, then looked back up at the huge tower in front of them and didn't say anything else. She scooted her butt down on the seat until her head rested on the bench behind them. Lefty got comfortable next to her.

Neither said a word, but when Lefty reached over and took her hand in his, she didn't pull away. If this was Kinley being "weird," then Lefty decided right then and there that he liked weird. A hell of a lot.

* * *

After another ten minutes of gazing up at the Eiffel Tower, she'd decided she was done. He'd gotten her to stand still long enough so he could take a picture of her in front of it before she'd asked if Notre Dame was too far away. He'd reassured her that it wasn't, and off they went. They didn't talk as they walked. Kinley simply took in the sights and sounds around her.

Lefty wasn't surprised when, upon arriving at Notre Dame, Kinley stopped in the middle of the sidewalk and simply stared up at the beautiful ancient building. He stood guard, making sure no one bumped into her as she took in the church.

"I cried when I watched the news clips of it burning," she said after a moment. "I'm glad the stained glass made it."

"Me too," he said. Then, making a split-second decision, Lefty pulled out his phone. He knew his mom was an early riser. A *very* early riser. She went to bed around eight at night and got up around four every morning. When he'd told her she was crazy one day, she'd just shrugged and told him she liked mornings because everything was quiet and still.

Knowing she'd probably be up, even as early as it was in California, he clicked on his mom's number and put it on speaker. As it rang, he felt Kinley staring at him. He met her gaze as his mom answered.

"Hey, son. Everything all right?"

"Yeah, I'm good. I'm in Paris," he said without preamble.

"Paris?" his mom breathed. "Please tell me you're getting to do a bit of sightseeing."

Lefty chuckled. "As a matter of fact, I am, which is why I'm calling. I'm going to FaceTime you, that all right?"

"Of course. It's not like I'm standing here naked and decided I might as well answer the phone when my only child calls."

Lefty chuckled, and he loved the giggle that escaped Kinley's mouth. He clicked on the button that would let his mom see him.

"Hey, baby," his mom said softly when she saw his face.

"Hey, Mom," Lefty said. "You look great."

She rolled her eyes and shook her head. "Always the flatterer," she accused.

"You know I never lie," he said. "Before I get to why I called, I have someone for you to meet."

"Gage, no," Kinley whispered, but he ignored her.

"Mom, I'd like you to meet Kinley Taylor. Kinley, this is my mom, Molly."

"Hello, Kinley," his mom said as Lefty pulled Kinley into his side so her face would be on the screen with his. "I love your hair! The black color looks positively radiant in the sun."

"Um...thanks. I washed it this morning," Kinley said, and Lefty felt her stiffen as if she was embarrassed over what she'd just blurted out.

But his mom didn't miss a beat. "Good for you. I swear I'm addicted to that dry shampoo stuff. Kaden, my husband, has to force me to get in the shower some days."

Lefty felt Kinley relax next to him. "I haven't tried it. Does it really work?"

"Oh, honey," his mom said. "Yes. It's amazing! I'll have Gage give me your email, and I'll send you names of the ones that I've found work best. They aren't all made equally, you know."

"Thanks," Kinley said.

"Anyway, Mom, I wanted to call because we're standing in front of Notre Dame right now," Lefty said.

"You aren't!" his mom exclaimed.

Lefty chuckled. "Would I call you from Paris and lie about something like that?"

"Not if you wanted to live to see tomorrow," his mom retorted. "Lemme see! I get to see your ugly mug all the time. I've never seen Notre Dame in person."

"Just for that, I don't think I should show you," he teased. He turned to Kinley. "My mom loves Notre Dame. As long as I can remember, she's been in love with this building. There were times I thought she loved it more than *me* when I was growing up. For her birthday one year, I managed to get a buddy who was coming here on assignment to pick up a street artist's drawing of the cathedral. I thought my mom was gonna die when she opened it."

"Shut up," his mom complained.

Lefty kept teasing, drawing out the moment for his mom. "She'd planned to come to Paris with Dad one year, but she had to have an emergency appendectomy and they missed it."

"Gage," his mom threatened. "Turn the damn phone around or I swear I'll tell Kinley about the time you peed your pants while you were waiting in line at Disney to see Mickey Mouse."

"I was four," he told Kinley with a wink. "And Mickey was my hero. Of course I peed my pants."

"Gage!" Molly Haskins whined.

Before he could put his mom out of her misery, Kinley took the phone and turned the camera around, pointing it at the iconic building. "From this angle, you can hardly tell there was a fire," Kinley told his mom. "Look, the stained glass is almost perfect still."

Then, as if she gave tours of Notre Dame all her life,

Kinley proceeded to give his mother the thrill of a lifetime by walking around and showing her every little thing.

Lefty didn't mind in the least. He loved that his mom and Kinley were bonding over the building. He'd always thought his mother's obsession with Notre Dame was a little odd, but seeing her love for it being nurtured by Kinley was a gift.

"And look, you don't see this in any of the pictures of the chapel," Kinley said, pointing the phone toward their feet. They were standing in the square in front of the church, looking down at a compass engraved into the stone. "*Point zéro des routes de France*," Kinley said, then translated, "point zero of French roads. This exact spot indicates where all distances to and from Paris are measured."

He heard his mom sigh in contentment. "Thank you for the tour," she told Kinley after she'd brought the phone back up to look into the camera. "You have no idea what this has meant to me. I'm gonna get there someday, but seeing it today, and hearing you tell me all about it, was special."

Lefty saw Kinley had no idea how to respond, so he wrapped his arm around her shoulders and pulled her into his side, reaching out and taking the phone from her. "Anything you want to know about anything, Kinley can probably tell you," he told his mom. "She's super smart."

"What I want to know is when my boy is going to find the time to come visit his parents," Molly quipped.

Lefty chuckled. "Hopefully soon, Mom."

She looked at Kinley. "That's what he always says. I bet you don't tell *your* parents that."

"I don't have any," Kinley said bluntly.

"Oh. Well, crud, I put my foot in it, didn't I?" his mom said with a little head shake. "In that case, maybe you should come visit me and Kaden. Since our son is neglecting us, we can show you around San Francisco. We'd love to have you. Any friend of Gage's is a friend of ours. Have you ever been here? We can get tickets to Alcatraz. It's fascinating. And the sea lions down at the pier are a not-to-be-missed sight—"

"Mom," he interrupted.

"What?"

"Slow your roll," he told her.

He was surprised when he heard a soft giggle from Kinley. He looked at her with one brow raised.

"Slow your roll? Did you really just tell your mother that?" she asked.

"He did," his mom complained. "See how abusive he is?" But she was laughing when she'd said it. "I like you, Kinley. And I was serious about you coming out to visit. I can't imagine how it feels to have lost your parents, and I'm more than willing to be a surrogate mom for you."

"You are *not* allowed to adopt Kinley, Mom," Lefty said sternly. Kinley looked up at him, and continued, "You can befriend her, share beauty tips, and corrupt her into not showering for weeks at a time, but under no circumstances are you and Dad allowed to adopt her."

"Why not?" Molly asked.

Lefty merely raised his eyebrows.

"Oooooh!" his mom said. "Right. Okay, no adoptions, because it would be awkward if you started dating your sister, wouldn't it?"

"Mom!" Lefty shook his head. "You're impossible."

"I learned it from my kid," she said with a smile, then turned her attention back to Kinley. "I'm serious, hon. If you need a break from all the assholes in DC, you're more than welcome to visit us. And before you ask, Gage already told us a little about you, how he met you in Africa and how you work in DC. We've got more than enough room in our house for you to stay for however long you want. My husband will bore you to death by showing you his sports memorabilia room—don't believe him when he tells you it's Gage's inheritance...it's all junk—and I'll take you out one night to the Castro District and we'll party at the gay bars down there. It's super fun, and those boys are so entertaining."

"Okay, that's it. I'm hanging up now," Lefty said.

Kinley put her hand on his forearm, and he knew he'd stand there and listen to his mom talking about getting drunk in a gay nightclub all day if Kinley wanted him to.

"Thanks," she said. "I've never been to San Francisco. If you...if you and your husband ever come out to DC, I'm happy to be your tour guide. I haven't seen everything myself, as I tend to stay inside a lot, but I can see if I can find the good gay bars and take you out."

Molly Haskins threw her head back and laughed hysterically. "I'd love that, thank you, Kinley. Son, take me off video chat and speaker."

Lefty did so and brought his cell up to his ear. "Hey, Mom."

"I like her," she said immediately. "She's different than any woman you've dated before. She's smart and funny and too good for the likes of you."

Lefty almost choked. "Thanks, Mom," he drawled.

"Tread lightly with her," she suggested. "She's shy, and I'm guessing she's not used to someone like you."

"Someone like me?" Lefty asked.

"Yeah. Someone good. Who will treat her like a princess and who doesn't want to hurt her."

It felt great to know his mom saw him that way. "I will."

"Good. And make sure she knows I was serious about the invite to come out here. And if she wasn't serious about Kaden and I going to DC, let me know. Because I'm *so* planning that trip."

"Okay."

"And, Gage?"

"Yeah?"

"Thanks for sharing Notre Dame with me. Meant the world."

Lefty closed his eyes and sighed. "Love you, Mama."

"Love you too, son. Now...off with you. Go save the world or something."

"Will do. I'll call when I'm back in the States."

"See that you do," she said. "Bye."

"Bye."

Lefty clicked off the phone and found Kinley staring at him, curiosity shining in her eyes. "She likes you, wanted to make sure I knew that. And she told me that you're too good for me."

"No, she didn't," Kinley protested.

Lefty took her hand in his once more and started walking slowly back toward the area where her hotel and the conference was located. "She did," he said. "And she also wanted me to find out if you were serious about playing tour guide for them if they come to Washington, DC."

Kinley shrugged. "Yeah, although I'd suck at it since I haven't seen much myself, beyond the museums. But I can do some research if I know what they're most interested in. I can find out which museums they'd like and get tickets. I might even be able to finagle a tour of the White House if they'd like that."

Lefty stopped and brought his free hand up to her neck, as he'd done earlier during breakfast—and felt electricity shoot through his body in an arc. "If they come out to visit, all they'll be interested in is getting to know you, Kinley. You can take them to a museum if you want, or some of the monuments, but all they'll care about is spending time with you."

"But...I don't even know them," she protested.

"You just spent thirty minutes giving my mother the thrill of her life," Lefty told her. "You have no idea how deep her obsession with Notre Dame goes. When you said you cried watching the footage of the church burning, I knew you and her would get along perfectly. And I was right. Thank you for not thinking my mom's crazy for loving that heap of stone as much as she does."

"She's not crazy," Kinley protested. "I liked her."

"Good. Because she liked you too. And I was serious, don't you dare sign any paperwork letting them adopt you. It *would* be embarrassing for me to be dating my stepsister."

Amazingly, Kinley giggled, but she quickly sobered. "They won't want to adopt me. No one wants me."

"Wrong," Lefty said with heat. "I want you as my friend. Gillian, Trigger's fiancée, will want you as her friend as soon as she meets you. The rest of the guys on my team want you as *their* friend. Hell, even Jangles and his team like you. You aren't alone anymore, Kinley, understand?"

She stared at him for so long, Lefty was afraid he'd pushed too hard. That she'd agree just to get him to shut up. But instead, she closed her eyes, took a deep breath, and nodded.

"Look at me, Kins." She opened her eyes immediately. "You need me, I'm there, no questions asked," Lefty told her. "Even if you just need someone to complain to about your day. Okay?"

"Okay," she whispered. "But you should know something."

"What?"

"Donald Duck is more interesting and has more personality than Mickey Mouse."

Lefty snorted. "As if," he said, dropping his hand from her neck and pulling her into his side. He had to let go of her hand to do it, but she felt good plastered against him.

"It's true. He's funnier and has a much stronger presence on screen than Mickey," Kinley said with a small grin.

As they walked back to the conference, Lefty realized that he'd had more fun in the last five or so hours than he'd had in a very long time. He'd liked Kinley when he'd met her in the middle of a crisis, but hanging out with her in a relaxed atmosphere, even he was almost surprised at how attracted he was to her.

They bantered back and forth throughout a short lunch at another café, and he'd learned more about who Kinley was as a person when she ordered a takeout lunch and gave it to a homeless man she'd seen sitting on a bench across from the café.

Knowing he'd have little to no time with her once she went back to work, he stopped her just outside the building where the conference was taking place.

"You're going to talk to me when you get home, right?" he asked, the sting of being ignored still fresh in his mind.

"I promise," Kinley said, grabbing his hand and squeezing. It was the first time *she'd* touched *him*. "As I said earlier, I'll try to get better at checking my email and texts, but it might take me a while to get into a routine with that. I'm just not used to talking to other people."

"Okay, I can be patient. And if I get sent on a mission, I'll be sure to tell you how long I *think* I'll be gone. It'll always be a guess though," he warned her.

"I understand," she said, and Lefty had the feeling she really did.

"I don't know when our paths will cross again, but I'm looking forward to it," he told her.

"Me too," she said shyly. "I can't promise I'll be the best friend, simply because I don't know how, but I'm going to try."

"You just be you," Lefty told her. "That's all I want."

"Okay," she said shyly.

"Okay," Lefty repeated. He wanted to kiss her, but it didn't feel right. He brought their joined hands up to his mouth instead and kissed her fingers. "Be careful out there,

Kins. Watch your back, and if you need me, all you have to do is reach out."

"Thanks," she said.

They stood on the sidewalk for a long moment, staring at each other, before Lefty forced himself to let go of her hand. He took a step back. She gave him a small wave and backed up, as well. She bumped into the door and wrinkled her nose at her clumsiness. Then she turned and disappeared into the building.

Taking a deep breath, Lefty turned and headed for the hotel. For the first time that morning, he saw Merlin leaning against a building nearby. He'd said he was going to follow them, and it was apparent he had. The other man nodded and joined him as Lefty passed him.

"You guys seemed to have a good time today," he noted.

"We did," Lefty agreed.

"I've never really seen her smile," Merlin observed. "You're good for her."

Lefty appreciated the man's insight. He wasn't so sure Merlin was correct, but it was too late now. He'd gotten his wish to know Kinley better, and now he couldn't picture his life without her in it in some way...even if that was only as a friend.

They walked in silence the rest of the way to the hotel. Lefty needed to relieve his teammate and find out what Johnathan Winkler's schedule was for the rest of the day. He hoped to have a chance to see Kinley again, but even if he didn't, he felt much better about where they stood with each other. He just prayed that she'd keep her word and talk to him when she got home.

CHAPTER FOUR

That night, Kinley stood by the window in her small hotel room and stared blankly out at the alley. The afternoon had been difficult. Partly because she wished she was still roaming around Paris with Gage.

Walter hadn't asked too many questions about her morning, other than to inquire if she was feeling better. The excuse that she'd had menstrual cramps seemed to be really effective, and her boss wasn't suspicious at all. He had no idea she'd been out enjoying Paris all morning.

Kinley supposed she should feel guilty about that, but she didn't. Walter was tough to work for, and every now and then he'd do something that would make her decision to stay or go all the harder. Like when he'd sent her chicken soup when she'd been sick the year before.

Apparently, Woof had done a good job at being his temporary assistant, even making reservations for him and Drake Stryker, the US Ambassador to France, for dinner. They were spending their last evening in Paris together, and had wanted to go to some fancy restaurant. Making dinner reservations wasn't in her job description, but Kinley always helped out where she could when they were away from DC. Obviously, Walter was so used to her doing those kinds of tasks for him, he hadn't hesitated to ask a Delta Force soldier to do the same thing.

The closing ceremony for the conference was the next morning, and she and her boss were leaving right afterward. Kinley had hoped to get the opportunity to spend more time with Gage, but she hadn't seen him since she'd left him outside the conference center.

For the first time in her life, Kinley hadn't wanted to sit alone in her hotel room. She'd wanted to have dinner with Gage. Talk to him more. Live vicariously through him.

Sighing, she glanced at her watch. It was one in the morning, and she should be sleeping, but thoughts of Gage kept whirling through her head. She'd been mortified when he'd called his mom, but after learning how much the other woman loved Notre Dame, she'd been happy to give her a tour and tell her as much as she could about the building.

She'd regretted inviting her to DC as soon as the words were out of her mouth, but now that she'd had time to think about it, she figured there was no way Molly and her husband would ever take her up on the offer. The woman was just being polite.

Kinley was so lost in her own thoughts, she almost missed the activity in the alley below.

She'd turned off the lights in her room a while ago, so she could have a better view of the stars, and hadn't bothered to turn them back on. There was literally nothing else to look at from her hotel room—it wasn't as if she had any kind of view of the city. When movement caught her eye, Kinley shifted her focus downward.

A black sedan had pulled into the alley, and she recognized the diplomatic license plate on the back. It took a second for her brain to put two and two together, but when she saw a man heading for the door, it clicked that it was Drake Stryker, the man her boss had spent the evening with.

But he wasn't alone.

He had his hand around the woman's bicep. It looked like she was completely drunk; she couldn't walk straight, and she would've fallen flat on her face if Drake wasn't there holding her up. The pair had exited a side door, which Kinley assumed led out of the hotel, but she wasn't one hundred percent sure.

The woman was wearing a red tank top and a short skirt. She had messy long brown hair hanging wild around her shoulders. She couldn't see the woman's face, as she was looking down at the ground, but Kinley imagined she was most likely beautiful.

But it was her shoes that really caught Kinley's attention.

She'd never been able to wear heels, something that didn't bother her, except when she saw other women wearing shoes she really loved. And Kinley really, *really* liked the shoes the woman with Drake was wearing. They were wedges with silver sparkles in the heels. Even though there wasn't a lot of light in the alley, those shoes still glistened with every step the woman took.

Drake looked up the alley, then down, then put his arm around the woman. He practically lifted her off her feet to help her into his car. Within seconds, they were inside and the car was slowly driving down the alley. It took a right at the end and was out of sight within seconds.

Drake Stryker was married, as was her boss, but having affairs wasn't out of the ordinary in political circles. They were as common as coffee shops. It was a pity that society had changed enough over the years that no one cared if the men and women in charge slept with someone they weren't married to. Hiring escorts and sleeping with prostitutes was a little more taboo, but most people simply looked the other way when it happened. It used to bother Kinley a lot, but after so much time working in DC, she'd become immune.

Kinley sighed once more. She used to want to be just like that woman. Carefree, in charge of her sexuality, and not afraid to have one-night stands if the whim struck her. But the older she got, the more Kinley just wanted to find someone to be able to hang out at home with. Someone who would be happy ordering in and spending an evening watching TV and reading.

The more time Kinley spent by herself, the more she realized finding someone, anyone, to spend her life with was next to impossible. It wasn't as if she met any eligible men she was attracted to at her day job, and because she didn't like bars or online dating sites, and didn't have any friends to introduce her to men they knew, Kinley suspected she was destined to be a stereotypical spinster of days gone by.

Turning from the window, she forced herself to walk to her bed and lie down once again. She had to get some sleep. Walter was bound to be cranky tomorrow, especially if he and his friend had just spent the evening with the woman from the alley. Kinley didn't condone cheating, but what they did was their own business. As long as she got paid, she could turn her head and pretend she didn't see some of her boss's indiscretions.

That blasé attitude toward cheating was another reason Kinley didn't want anything to do with a man who was involved in politics. She never wanted to be with anyone who would cheat on her. While she could admit she wasn't the best catch in the world, she would never cheat when she was involved with someone.

Closing her eyes, Kinley willed her body to shut down. Between the closing ceremony, getting Walter to the airport and checked in, and flying back to the States, tomorrow was going to be a very long, tiring day.

* * *

Kinley rested her head on the seat back behind her and closed her eyes. She was in a middle seat—of course she was —and the people on either side of her had fallen asleep almost as soon as the plane had taken off. Walter was sitting up in first class, so she had the entire flight to relax and not worry about her boss.

He'd been especially difficult all day. From the moment he'd answered his door after she'd knocked to wake him up, he'd been a jerk. He'd yelled at her, saying he wasn't ready, and that she should go get him coffee and a pastry for breakfast and he'd meet her at the conference. Once there, he'd bitched in front of the other representatives because his coffee wasn't prepared correctly. He'd also been surly and disagreeable to the poor driver on the way to the airport, and Kinley had wanted to die of embarrassment when he'd pitched a fit at the airline counter when he wasn't in the original seat she'd booked for him in first class.

All in all, she'd been glad when he'd disappeared into the lounge for first class passengers. It had given her a break from his nastiness and let her sit and regroup.

Kinley hadn't seen Gage again, which had been disappointing, but maybe it was for the best. It was odd how much she missed him. And of course, it was hard not to compare his behavior to Walter's. Where her boss was rude and condescending, Gage tolerated her quirks and went out of his way to be polite, not only to her, but to everyone he came into contact with. She hadn't missed how he'd left large tips for the servers at the cafes, and how, even when she'd stopped in the middle of the sidewalk, he never said a word—and in fact, kept others from bumping into her.

She even had a small box of vanilla macarons in her carry-on bag that he'd picked up for her simply because they were her favorite, and he thought she might like to have the treats to take home.

For the first time in her life, Kinley wished she wasn't who she was. Wished she was the kind of woman who could jump into bed with a man without having her heart involved. That she was more outgoing. More normal. She wished she had someone to talk to about Gage and how he made her feel. If there was ever a time when she needed another woman to help her comb through the feelings coursing through her mind *and* body, it was now.

Other women at least had their sisters or moms to talk to. She had no one. Literally not one person she was comfortable opening up to. It was depressing and discouraging.

Shaking her head, Kinley straightened her shoulders and opened her eyes. No, she wouldn't get sucked into feeling sorry for herself. She was who she was, and her life was what it was. All the mental boohooing wouldn't change that.

She'd worked damn hard to get where she was today and, all things considered, she'd done an amazing job. Kinley had known a lot of girls who'd been in her same situation growing up who weren't doing nearly as well. She had a degree, a good job, a roof over her head. She didn't need friends or a man to make her life good. It was *already* good.

Clicking on her tablet, Kinley opened the book she'd begun reading when waiting for the plane. She might be a loner, and way too practical, but she loved reading romances. Everything always worked out in the end, and they gave her the emotionally satisfying happily ever after her psyche needed. She'd stick to living vicariously through the lives of the heroes and heroines on the pages of the books she loved. Real life wasn't like that, and wishing for it was setting herself up for heartbreak.

She was glad she and Gage had worked things out between them, but he lived halfway across the country. He was also a military man, and from what she'd seen, they were second only to politicians when it came to cheating, abusing their partners, and divorce.

Feeling guilty she was lumping Gage into the same category of some of the military personnel she'd met, Kinley determinedly started reading. She had several more hours of time to herself before they landed and she had to deal with Walter again.

Determined to enjoy every minute, she lost herself in the words in front of her.

* * *

Sighing in relief when she finally walked into her apartment, Kinley dropped her bags in the middle of the room and staggered to her couch. She lived in a studio apartment near downtown, and she had never been so glad to be home in all her life.

Instead of being relaxed after spending the flight in first class, being pampered by the flight attendants, and being able to lie flat to sleep, Walter seemed to be even more on edge than he'd been when they'd left Paris.

When their driver hadn't met them at baggage claim—she'd gotten a text saying he was running late—Walter had bitched under his breath about not being able to find good help these days. He'd left greeting the chauffeur to her and hadn't bothered so much as small talk with the man as he towed Walter's suitcase toward the limo.

It wasn't much fun being trapped inside the limo with her boss while he complained about being tired and jetlagged. She'd also been surprised when, instead of going straight home, he'd told their driver to take them by the office so they could do some work, despite it being late afternoon.

Kinley wanted to object, wanted to remind him that she

hadn't had a reclining seat on the plane and she hadn't gotten much sleep, but when she saw how stressed and grumpy he looked, she kept her thoughts to herself.

At the office, when she wasn't able to immediately recall some of the names of the representatives they'd met at the conference, he'd gotten even surlier.

She'd never been more relieved than when he'd finally had enough and called it a day.

When Walter was dropped off first, he'd climbed out— then completely surprised Kinley by leaning back into the limo and thanking her for accompanying him to Paris. He'd apologized for being so disagreeable and told her to get a good night's sleep.

Even with his politeness at the end of the trip, Kinley thought both she and the driver breathed a sigh of relief once he was gone.

It was late when she let herself into her apartment and, out of habit, she picked up the remote and clicked on the TV. She didn't like watching the news, but because of who she worked for and where she worked, she had to keep on top of political happenings.

Only half paying attention to the newscaster, Kinley was surprised when something caught her eye on the screen. She quickly fumbled for the remote and turned up the volume.

...the fourteen-year-old was found in the Champs-Elysees district in Paris. Cause of death has been determined to be strangulation and, just like the five other young women who've been found in the last six months, her blood-alcohol level was four times the legal limit and she tested positive for ketamine. The citizens of Paris are uneasy as The Alleyway Strangler—or L'Étrangleur des Allées—as the French press has dubbed the killer, continues to claim victims. There have been few clues as to the identity of the killer.

. . .

Kinley couldn't tear her eyes away from the screen. While the reporter was talking, a clip was playing of the actual crime scene. A body was covered with a gray tarp, only her feet showing.

The second the newscaster changed to a new topic, the picture changed.

Kinley leaped up from the couch and grabbed her carry-on bag, frantically pulling out her work laptop. The wait for it to power up was excruciating, and she couldn't get the feet of the murdered girl out of her mind.

The second her computer connected to her wi-fi, Kinley pulled up her search engine and typed in The Alleyway Strangler. All the images that popped up were horrifying and unsettling to see—but it was the most recent victim Kinley was interested in.

She clicked on the picture of the young woman covered in the tarp in the alley and zoomed in on her shoes.

For a full minute, Kinley stared at the image, then sank into the chair at her small kitchen table in disbelief. She'd recognize those shoes anywhere.

She'd just admired them the night before in Paris.

The woman she'd seen getting into Drake Stryker's car had been wearing the exact shoes that were on the feet of the murdered victim in the picture on her computer screen.

It couldn't be a coincidence. She knew the woman from the alley and the victim had to be one and the same.

A fourteen-year-old girl...

If she hadn't admired the girl's shoes so much, she wouldn't have thought twice about the news story. Unfortunately, people were killed every day. But she'd not only seen this poor girl right before she'd been murdered...she had a pretty good idea who'd done it.

Kinley wanted to scream. Wanted to cry. But she did neither. She merely sat at her kitchen table in shock.

It was possible Stryker had dropped the girl off at home, or wherever he'd picked her up, and someone else had taken advantage of her. But something deep inside Kinley knew that wasn't true. Picking up prostitutes was one thing, and something way too many politicians did, but this was something altogether different.

She needed to tell someone.

But who? Who would believe her?

She could go to the cops, but all she had to go on was a pair of shoes; the tarp had hidden the rest of the girl's body, and any clothing she might have worn. As far as evidence went, it was lame at best. Who knew how many pairs of those shoes had been sold and were being worn by Parisian women?

And Stryker was the US Ambassador to France. He'd been appointed by the president himself.

Feeling herself starting to panic, Kinley stood up and paced her small apartment. She *had* to tell someone.

Then something else occurred to her. Walter had spent the evening with Drake.

Had the girl been with them? Had he known how old she was? If she was, Kinley *had* to think Walter hadn't known her age. He wasn't the nicest man in the world, but she didn't think he was a pedophile. He was married, with two teenaged kids of his own. He was a tough boss, yes, but she'd also seen his compassionate side. He didn't thank her all the time, but he didn't need to thank her for doing her job.

He was grumpy when they traveled, but who wouldn't be?

Spending time with his friend during his last night in Paris didn't mean he'd participated in some nefarious rendezvous with an underaged girl.

But Kinley didn't know Drake well at all. He could've been the one to invite the girl. Maybe both men had thought she was older than she was, and after learning her true age, Drake had immediately escorted her home?

That *had* to be it. He'd dropped her off somewhere, and she'd unfortunately run across someone who'd killed her afterward.

But surely her boss would still want to know about a girl they'd been with being found dead. A victim of an infamous serial killer. He'd need to tell Drake, and they'd both need to go to the authorities. Giving him a head's up about the situation seemed the decent thing to do. She'd want someone to call *her* if she were in her boss's shoes.

Decision made, Kinley grabbed her phone and clicked on Walter's number. He wouldn't be happy being interrupted at home; he'd told her if she really needed to get ahold of him after hours, she should text or email, but this was an emergency.

The phone rang four times before he picked up.

"Hello?"

"Mr. Brown, this is Kinley."

"I've asked you not to call me when I'm at home, Kinley. We work hard enough when we're at the office. Anything you need to tell me can wait until work hours."

"I'm sorry," Kinley said quickly. "But I got home and saw the news. Did you hear about The Alleyway Strangler?" she blurted.

"The what?" Walter asked.

"Not what, *who*. The Alleyway Strangler. He's a serial killer in Paris. He killed someone else last night."

"What the hell does that have to do with me?" Walter asked in a confused tone.

"I think I saw the victim last night," Kinley told him in a hushed tone. "I was awake, and my hotel room was facing the alley. I saw your friend, Mr. Stryker, come out of the hotel with a woman. At least I *thought* it was a woman. I admired her shoes, and when I saw the pictures of the latest victim, she was wearing those same shoes. She was fourteen, sir. Was...was she with you and Mr. Stryker last night?"

There was a thick silence on the other end of the line for a long moment before Walter finally spoke. "Are you telling me you think that the ambassador to France is a serial killer, and that I hung out with him and his latest victim last night?"

When he put it that way, it sounded ridiculous, but Kinley stood her ground. "Well, not necessarily. But I recognized the shoes she had on—"

"You've got to be kidding me," Walter interrupted. "I swear to God, that's the flimsiest evidence I've ever heard in my life. No cop is gonna hear that and take you seriously. I'm offended on Drake's behalf. That man is no more a killer than I am! For your information, we were alone last night. We talked politics and about the conference. We had a few drinks, then he left. If he picked up a woman in the bar downstairs after he left my room, that's *his* business. Did you see the woman's face?"

"No," Kinley admitted. "It was too dark, and she had her head down."

"So all you're basing your accusation on is literally the shoes the woman had on her feet," Walter said.

Kinley bit her lip and didn't respond. She could've pointed out she'd also seen the girl's clothing and hair, but it would take a call to the Paris police to confirm if they matched the victim. And considering how upset her boss sounded, she decided to keep her mouth shut. She wouldn't share that information and risk upsetting him further.

"Have you told anyone else this preposterous story?" he asked.

"No," Kinley said honestly. "I wanted to talk to you first because you're friends with him, and you were with him last night. I just thought you needed to know."

"Right. I *was* with him last night, and there was no woman—or girl—with us. I'm certain whatever you saw last night was completely innocent. It's probably pure coincidence that the woman he was helping home last night happened to have the same shoes as the girl who ended up dead in some alley. Understand me?"

"Yes, sir," Kinley said automatically.

"You're tired after traveling all day. It's understandable that you're too exhausted to think straight."

"I'm sure that's it, sir," she replied grimly.

"I'd suggest not mentioning this to anyone else. If you do, you'll be laughed right out of DC." He snorted. "It would be your word against that of a respected and hardworking man... who just happens to be friends with the president. Get some sleep, Ms. Taylor. You'll feel better in the morning. Because you worked tonight, I'm giving you the morning off. I'll see you after lunch."

"Yes, sir," Kinley said. She was glad she didn't have to go in bright and early in the morning, but she still felt unsure about this whole situation.

"Thank you for calling and talking to me," Walter said, his voice dropping and sounding sincere. "I appreciate that you didn't let this fester in your head, and that you didn't do something crazy like call the cops. Accusing an innocent man is serious business and wouldn't have looked good for you—*or* me. I'll see you tomorrow. Good night."

He didn't give her time to say goodbye, and Kinley continued to hold the phone in her hand for a moment before putting it down.

Everything he'd said made sense...but for some reason, she couldn't shake the belief that what she'd seen last night was that poor girl's last moments alive on this Earth. She hadn't been steady on her feet, and now that she thought about it, it seemed as if Stryker had practically forced her into his car.

But Walter's words were enough to make her second-guess herself. And he was right—who the hell was going to believe her? She had no proof the girl had been with Drake and Walter, and who's to say the ambassador didn't pick her up in the bar at the hotel and innocently escort her somewhere?

Feeling defeated and uneasy, Kinley forced herself to stand and go get her suitcase. She unpacked and started a load of laundry in her small closet washer and dryer set even as she continued debating with herself.

By the time she'd changed and gotten into bed, Kinley had convinced herself that she was overreacting. That thousands of people had those same shoes, and she'd simply misinterpreted what she'd seen. It was just the news clip. It had put ideas in her head that weren't true. The power of suggestion was strong, she knew that from years of working in politics.

Despite that, she fell into a troubled sleep, visions of little girls crying for help filling her dreams.

* * *

"We have a problem," Walter told his friend as soon as the other man picked up the phone.

"What?" Drake asked.

"My assistant saw you putting that bitch into your car last night."

There was silence on the other end of the phone for a second before Drake swore viciously. "Seriously?"

"Yeah."

"What was she doing up at that hour?"

"No clue. She's weird. Probably loves spying on people in her spare time. But she called me all worried because the news over here in the States ran a story about the girl's body being found, and she recognized her shoes."

"*Fuck*," Drake hissed. "What did you say?"

"I told her she was crazy. That there was no way you were a homicidal killer. She called me because she knows we're friends—and she *also* knows we spent the evening together. I *cannot* get sucked into this," Walter told Drake.

"Well, it's too fucking late. You're involved as much as I am. It's not like having sex with teenagers is anything out of the ordinary for you," Drake said.

"Maybe not, but having sex with an underage girl is a lot different than killing one," Walter seethed.

"You were the one who came up with the plan to find an underage prostitute to fulfill your ménage fantasy," Drake insisted. "Sharing child porn was no longer enough for you, you said. *You* were the one who set this whole thing up. The fact that I was the one who had to cover our tracks shouldn't be a fucking surprise."

"I didn't know you were going to kill her!" Walter insisted.

"What did you think I was gonna do? Pat her on the head and send her on her way?" Drake asked sarcastically. "Once she found out our names, her fate was sealed. We both assumed we could have our fun and get away with it, but that wasn't the case. Being all paranoid now isn't helping, so quit your whining and figure out what to do to shut up your little narc assistant. If I go down, you are too."

Walter took a deep breath. He didn't like the situation he was in now...but he couldn't deny last night had been exciting.

When he'd first realized he was attracted to underage girls, he'd been shocked, appalled even. But it had been so easy to find pictures and videos online... The internet was flooded with them. What harm could there be in looking?

But before long, that wasn't enough. He'd seduced and paid the few girls he'd slept with stateside.

The tryst in Paris was supposed to be risk-free. He'd broached the subject with Drake because they'd shared child porn videos in a few online chat rooms.

It seemed like a great idea at the time, discussing the idea of a ménage with an underaged prostitute with Drake. And the actual encounter had been one of the most exciting nights of his life; he'd never gotten so hard as he had, taking the girl with his friend and colleague.

Drake had reassured him that he'd get the girl back to where he'd picked her up without anyone being the wiser. No one would know they'd spent the night with a girl young enough to be their daughter. Or granddaughter.

Walter was relieved they'd both used condoms, so there would be no DNA inside the girl's body, but he had no idea if there was any other DNA evidence, like hair or fingerprints, that the forensic techs might find.

And neither of them had expected anyone to see Drake leaving the hotel with the girl.

He had to do damage control, otherwise he and the ambassador were potentially fucked. He might not have murdered anyone, but that wouldn't matter. If his sexual preferences were discovered, both his career and marriage were as good as dead.

"Kinley has no friends or family," Walter told his colleague. "I know someone who owes me a favor. I can have him threaten her to make sure she keeps her mouth shut."

"You can't just threaten her," Drake warned. "She's different from us. She's gonna blab about what she saw to *someone*. She needs to be taken out before that happens."

"I don't know anyone who's into that," he balked.

"Fuck!" Drake swore. "Fine. I'll take care of it. The last thing I need is the president thinking I had anything to do with a murder. I've worked my ass off to get where I am, and no fucking secretary is gonna ruin it. I've got more power now than I've ever had in my life. She's not taking that away from me."

"But don't make it obvious," Walter warned. "It needs to look like an accident. Or like she killed herself or something."

"I know that. I'm not an idiot," Stryker said.

An idea formed in Walter's head. "I can plant something on her computer and make it look like she's committed treason. I'll have no choice but to fire her. No one will dare re-hire her after that. And no one will have a hard time believing the girl with no family, who dared betray her country, stepped in front of a moving bus or train out of guilt."

"Don't get too complicated," Drake warned. "Keep it simple. But I think firing her can help us. At the very least, it'll put some distance between the two of you."

They talked a little longer about the best way to make sure Kinley Taylor didn't tell anyone else what she'd seen. Stryker assured him once more that he'd hire someone to take care of her, which was a relief to Walter.

"Your job is to get her out of your office. Don't call me again until it's done," Drake ordered. He hung up without another word.

Walter sat back in his chair and steepled trembling hands under his chin. He didn't have a lot of time to set things in motion. It would be better if her alleged treachery was found as soon as possible. As if she hadn't covered her tracks before they'd left for Paris.

Nodding to himself, Walter felt confident about his plan. What would be discovered in his assistant's email would give him ample reason to fire her.

He felt a small pang of remorse. Kinley was a hard worker, and he'd never had a more competent assistant. But she'd had the bad luck to be looking in the wrong place at the wrong time. If she hadn't seen Drake putting the girl in his limo, they wouldn't be in the predicament they were in now.

The thought of killing her made him extremely uneasy. But Walter knew he didn't have a choice. He didn't want to go to prison, he was all too aware of what happened to pedophiles when they got locked up. It was his life or hers—and he wanted to live.

Walter actually hated that he was attracted to girls... wished he wasn't...but he couldn't help it. He was the way he was. But he never should've gotten Drake involved in his fantasies.

He had no idea if the girl was Drake's first kill or not, and he didn't want to know. As it was, he knew too much. But if his friend was *actually* The Alleyway Strangler...?

Swallowing hard, Walter closed his eyes. Everything had spiraled out of control, and it was in danger of spiraling further.

"Walter," his wife called from down the hall, "it's late. Come to bed!"

Sighing, Walter forced himself to respond. "Coming, dear."

He knew he should feel more guilty for doing what he and his friend were planning to do to Kinley, should maybe even put a stop to it, but their political careers were more important than some nobody.

She'd thought she was doing the right thing in calling him about what she'd seen, but in reality, it had been the worst mistake of her life.

CHAPTER FIVE

Kinley stood on the sidewalk looking up at the building she'd worked in for the last eight years in stunned bewilderment. When she'd arrived at work that morning, she'd been thinking about nothing other than Walter's next speaking engagement and the research she needed to finish in order to write his speech.

Now, two hours later, she was standing outside after being fired.

It was two days since they'd returned from Paris, and how she'd gone so quickly from having a secure, albeit sometimes annoying job to being unemployed made her head spin.

She'd been called down to the HR director's office and interrogated about an email she'd allegedly sent to a few of the other assistants—*and a newspaper reporter*—before she and Walter had flown to France. It was her boss's itinerary, including times and locations of every meeting at the conference.

Even the lowliest intern knew not to breathe one word of where the politicians would be, and when. She absolutely wouldn't have sent it to a reporter. Making that information public was like inviting an assassination attempt from a terrorist or crazy constituent.

In political circles, it was akin to committing treason.

Kinley had tried to tell the HR director that she hadn't sent any such email, but he hadn't listened. He had the proof right in front of him. A time-stamped email sent from her government email account.

She'd been fired on the spot, and a security officer accompanied her back to her office and watched with a frown and his arms crossed as she'd packed all her personal belongings. She hadn't even been allowed to say goodbye to Walter or any of the other assistants or interns...not that she was that close to them, but still.

She knew she should be upset, should be crying, but she was having a hard time processing everything that had just happened. One minute she was sitting at her desk doing research, and thirty minutes later she was outside with her things in a cardboard box like a pathetic eighties-movie heroine.

Her mind spinning, Kinley turned and started walking down the sidewalk. She wasn't sure what to do next. It was highly unlikely she'd be able to get an assistant job in political circles again, especially if everyone thought she'd committed treason. But what else could she do?

Kinley had no idea.

She trudged toward the Metro station, deep in thought. Her studio apartment was paid up through the month, but rent wasn't exactly cheap...even for just one room. Surely she'd be able to find something else that paid relatively close to what she'd been getting working for the assistant secretary.

Kinley was so lost in thought that she didn't pay much attention to the people around her. That wasn't unusual, because she'd found that if you made eye contact with someone, typically they felt the need to talk to you, which she preferred to avoid.

As she stood on the platform waiting for the next train, it slowly began to sink in that she was well and truly unemployed. It was unfair, as Kinley knew she hadn't done a damn thing wrong. How Walter's itinerary ended up in her email outbox, she had no idea. She certainly hadn't sent it to anyone. But she hadn't even been given a chance to explain.

Hating that she'd simply stood in the HR director's office and stared at him in shock when he was outlining what she'd supposedly done, Kinley made a split-second decision. She was going to go back and demand to speak with the director again. She wanted someone from IT to explain how the hell they'd found that email, when she knew she hadn't sent anyone anything.

The train was barreling into the station, but Kinley didn't care that she was going to miss it. She was focused on how unfairly she'd been treated and wanting to make it right.

Before she'd even turned to leave the platform, someone shoved her hard from behind.

Kinley felt herself falling, but because she had the box of belongings in her hands, she couldn't stop her forward momentum. The box went flying, straight into the path of the oncoming train.

Kinley fell hard onto the polished concrete, and just barely caught herself from sliding right off the platform onto the rails below.

Two seconds later, the train rushed by, crushing her favorite pens, a picture of her and the president that had been taken four years ago, and the other odds and ends she'd accumulated over the years at her job.

Her chin throbbed from where her head had bounced off the ground, but Kinley could only stare in horror at the gleaming metal cars rushing by just inches from her head.

"Holy shit!" a man said from next to her. "Are you all right? Good God, you almost fell right onto the tracks!"

"You're bleeding," a woman added. "It looks like you hit your chin. Does it hurt?"

Kinley couldn't think about anything other than how she'd almost been flattened by the train. In all her years commuting in the city, she'd never, not once, been scared about the possibility of falling onto the tracks.

But as she lay on the cold floor, she realized exactly how close she'd come to dying.

"Sorry about your stuff," the man said as he tried to help her sit up.

Blinking, Kinley allowed herself to be helped into a sitting position. "It's okay," she said, more out of the automatic need to be polite than actually knowing what she was saying.

Someone handed her a handkerchief, and she didn't have time to ask if it was clean before the woman was holding it to her chin. Kinley brushed the helping hand away and held the cloth to her bleeding chin herself. "Thank you," she told the bystanders. "I'm okay now. Go on, you'll miss your train."

"Oh, I can't possibly leave you like this," the woman fretted.

"Look, the bleeding's almost stopped," Kinley said, having no idea if that was the case or not. She hated being fussed over, especially by strangers. She'd never had anyone dote on her or nurse her through her hurts growing up, and it just felt awkward now.

After another thirty seconds, both her helpers finally nodded at her and entered the train. Kinley got to her feet and swayed for just a second.

She could still feel the hand on her back. She knew there was nothing there now, but it felt as if her skin burned.

Someone had *pushed* her! They'd wanted her to fall right onto the tracks in front of the oncoming Metro.

Kinley wasn't an idiot. She'd always been pretty decent at math. She could put two and two together.

She'd witnessed a possible serial killer with his latest victim hours before the girl had been found brutally murdered. She'd expressed her concerns to her boss, who was friends with the alleged killer. Then two days later, she's fired and almost pushed in front of a train.

Surprisingly, the main emotion she felt at the moment was anger, not fear. Oh, the fear was there, but luckily tamped down for now.

Kinley mourned the loss of her phone; she'd thrown it into her box of belongings when she'd been packing up her desk. It was now shattered into a thousand pieces under the rails of the Metro, along with all her other things.

Clutching her purse against her—thank God she'd slung it across her body instead of putting it in the box with her other things—Kinley held the bloody handkerchief to her chin and headed for the escalators.

She had to get out of there. Whoever had tried to kill her could still be watching, waiting for another opportunity to get rid of her.

When Kinley got back onto the street, she didn't hesitate before hailing a cab. Thankfully, one appeared right after she'd exited the station. She climbed in gratefully and gave him her address.

When she was on her way, Kinley still didn't relax. Someone could cause her taxi to crash, or run into them on purpose.

Her mind was spinning with all the ways someone could kill her. A botched robbery, carjacking, home invasion. She wasn't safe, and she knew it.

She was more sure now than ever that what she'd seen in Paris was exactly what she'd feared.

Drake Stryker, the president's choice to represent the

United States in its dealings with France, was The Alleyway Strangler.

And evidence was pointing to the fact that her boss—ex-boss—either knew it or was in on it.

She knew she hadn't sent any emails leaking his schedule, but she had no way of proving that. Just as she had no proof of what she'd seen in that alley in France.

Well, that wasn't true. She'd seen the girl. Knew what she was wearing and could describe her shoes. But she knew it would be hard for the police to believe the girl had spent the evening with the US Ambassador to France.

Kinley's head hurt, and she suddenly felt even more alone in the world than she had an hour ago.

Then she thought of her smashed phone again—and suddenly gasped. *Her phone!* Normally she wouldn't care that it was destroyed; it wasn't as if she needed it to talk to friends or anything. But...

Gage.

He'd sent a quick text to let her know he'd arrived back in Texas, and said he'd be in touch soon.

But now her phone was gone. She could get a new one and reply to his text, but as soon as she had the thought, she dismissed it. If Stryker and Brown had someone who could plant evidence in her email and get her fired, surely they could hack her previous phone too. Could find the text from Gage.

Closing her eyes in pure relief that she hadn't answered Gage's message, Kinley knew she couldn't tie herself to him electronically. The very last thing she wanted was to get him in trouble.

He had a highly sensitive and secret job. If Stryker set his sights on Gage, he'd probably be able to plant something that would get *him* fired too. It was bad enough she was unemployed and allegedly had a serial killer who wanted her dead because of what she'd seen...but if she got Gage involved in this mess, she'd never forgive herself.

Kinley knew what she had to do. She had to leave. Get the hell out of Washington, DC, until she figured out what to do next.

She didn't even think about staying silent. That girl in Paris had only been fourteen. She'd probably been scared out of her mind. Or maybe she'd been like Kinley...alone and desperate for some sort of affection.

But Kinley needed some time to figure out what her next step would be. How could she expose Stryker, and possibly her former boss, without dying in the process?

She had no answers by the time her cab driver pulled up in front of her apartment. Kinley paid him with the little cash she had in her purse and climbed out. She hurried into the small foyer and raced up the stairs, not willing to be trapped inside the elevator with someone who may or may not want her dead.

Even after shutting her door behind her, Kinley didn't feel safe.

Not even bothering to look around, she raced into her bedroom and pulled a large duffle bag out of her closet.

Some things didn't change. Even though she'd been on her own and out of the foster care system for over ten years, she still made sure to always have a bag ready to be filled at a moment's notice. There had been too many homes where, out of the blue, she was told she'd be leaving. She could only pack what she could carry, so having a sturdy duffle bag was imperative.

Kinley had learned not to get attached to physical belongings. She'd had to leave way too many behind over the years. With that in mind, she packed what she could and tamped down any sentimental feelings about pillows, towels, and other household items that could easily be replaced.

When she was done packing, she wrote a note for her landlord and put it, and another month's rent, in an envelope to mail. She hoped she'd be back before the end of the following month, but she honestly wasn't sure.

When that was done, Kinley put her back to the refrigerator and slid down until her butt was resting on the floor.

She wrapped her arms around her updrawn knees and put her head down. She realized she was shaking. Fear and adrenaline. It wasn't even noon yet, but she wanted to wait until it was dark outside before she snuck out. Her car was parked in a garage about two blocks away. She didn't use it much, as it was easier to use public transportation because of the awful traffic in the city, but she'd never been as thankful for her reliable Toyota Corolla as she was right this minute.

She'd made a colossal mistake in calling Brown the night she'd gotten back to town and seen that news clip, but at the time, she'd thought it was the best course of action. She should've known she couldn't trust him. Hadn't she been shown time and time again that she couldn't trust anyone?

You can trust Gage.

The words instantly popped into her head.

She wanted to deny them, tell her silly psyche that she didn't even know the man. There was no way she could literally trust him with her life.

But hadn't she already done that? In Africa, she'd thought she was two minutes away from being raped and killed by the protestors, but then he was there, taking her to safety. Two seconds in his company and Kinley had felt a comfort she'd never known in her life.

That was part of the reason she'd not responded when he'd contacted her after that trip. She'd been scared of how much she liked him. Respected him. If he ended up being like all the other people in her life who had blown her off, it would be excruciating.

But he'd proven in Paris that he was a good man. That he could be a good friend...if she let him in. But was it fair to bring this to his doorstep? To show up and be like, "Hi! I saw a serial killer with his latest victim and now he wants to kill me."

No, it wasn't fair in the least.

She'd head north, then west. Go to South Dakota maybe, it seemed to be in the middle of nowhere, and that's what she needed right now, to hide out until she could contact the FBI or someone. Small-town cops wouldn't believe her, but maybe someone in the FBI would. Or at the very least, they would investigate her accusation that Drake Stryker and Walter Brown were somehow involved in The Alleyway Strangler case.

Shaking her head, Kinley knew her situation was next to impossible. *No one* would believe her. Hell, she could hardly believe it herself.

The longer Kinley sat on her kitchen floor, waiting for the sun to set so she could escape under the cover of darkness, the more fearful she got. Whoever had tried to kill her would try again. He probably knew where she lived, and Brown clearly had contacts who were skilled with computers. What chance did she have?

Not much of one, but she hadn't survived what life had thrown at her thus far only to give up now. For the most part, her foster homes weren't abusive, but there had been one or two that had made her think she might not make it out. But she had.

She's survived those, and hopefully, she could survive this too.

Taking a deep breath, Kinley slowly found her resolve. She'd never liked Walter Brown much. Had overlooked the affairs he had while on trips, had put up with his arrogance and bad temper and taking credit for her research and ideas.

But she *never* would've thought he could stoop as low as this.

Slowly getting to her feet, Kinley went into the bathroom and cleaned up the gash on her chin. It had stopped bleeding long ago, and she'd been so intent on packing and getting ready to leave she'd forgotten about it until now. The cut itself wasn't too bad, and she didn't think she needed stitches...not that she'd be able to take the time to visit an emergency room even if she did. She put a butterfly bandage on her chin, and even though it looked strange, she didn't care.

She went back into her kitchen and methodically emptied out her fridge of anything that might spoil. Thankful that she'd decided to go to the grocery store later that week, so she didn't have too much to waste, Kinley cooked the chicken she'd planned to eat for dinner that evening.

Now that her initial fear had faded, she could actually think a little rationally. She'd take as much food as she could carry, along with her duffle bag, and stop by an ATM on the way out of town. She wouldn't be able to get out a ton of cash, but tomorrow, she'd stop by a branch of her bank and empty her savings.

Then she'd drive as long and as far as she could, using only cash for food and gas. When she got to a town where she felt she was relatively safe, she'd consider contacting someone in law enforcement about what she'd seen. She'd pick up one of those throwaway phones that couldn't be traced.

For just a moment, Kinley thought once more about getting in touch with Gage. She'd memorized his email, phone, and even his address, as if she was an adolescent girl with her first crush.

Gage would know how to help her, she had no doubt, but the last thing she wanted was the person who'd tried to kill her going after him.

She *hated* that if he contacted her, she wouldn't be responding—again. He'd think she was ghosting him once more, even when she'd promised not to.

But not getting in touch was for his own safety. She wouldn't knowingly put him in danger. Maybe after she'd been gone from DC for a while, and felt safer, she could reach out. Apologize for not responding. Again. She could tell him she'd lost her phone, which wouldn't exactly be a lie.

Feeling as if she'd lost something precious, Kinley pushed the thought down and concentrated on cleaning out her kitchen. Gage Haskins was better off without her.

Once the weird foster kid, always the weird foster kid.

* * *

Lefty sighed when he looked at his phone and didn't see any messages from Kinley. He knew Grover had told him to give Kinley time, to not give up on her, but he didn't like the way her ghosting him, again, made him feel. It had been a week, and he still hadn't heard from her. She'd told him that it might take her a while to respond, but a week seemed excessive. He was trying to be patient, but it was difficult. Lefty had tried to call her a few times but the phone didn't even ring, just went straight to voice mail. He'd texted and emailed, asking how she was and letting her know he was thinking about her, to no avail.

And to top off his shitty week, he'd just found out that he and the rest of the team were being sent on a mission. He desperately wanted to let Kinley know that he'd be out of pocket for a while...but it seemed as if she'd ghosted him once again. It was frustrating and irritating at the same time.

He'd thought he'd broken through the shields she had up, but apparently not. Maybe working in DC and around politicians had made her a better liar than he'd expected.

"What's wrong?" Trigger asked as they packed the last of the gear into the plane they'd be leaving on in a matter of hours.

"Nothing."

"She hasn't returned your messages?"

Lefty sighed. "No."

"Maybe she—"

Lefty held up a hand, stopping his friend's words. "Once, I can forgive. Twice? When she swore that she wouldn't ghost me again?" He shook his head. "I'm done. I can't do this. Long-distance friendships are hard enough without me having to do all the work. She should've just told me she wasn't interested in being my friend. I can take a hint."

"Kinley didn't strike me as the kind of woman to be so heartless."

"Me either," Lefty said with a shrug. Her silence hurt. A lot. After their day spent together in Paris, he'd thought for sure he'd hear from her. That they might be able to start some sort of relationship, even an unconventional long-distance one. But her silence spoke volumes.

"Come on," Trigger said, slapping him on the back. "Once we're knee deep in this mission, you'll forget about her."

Lefty nodded. A hard, dangerous mission was just what he needed to put Kinley out of his mind...for good.

CHAPTER SIX

Kinley sat in her car and stared up at the apartment building and debated whether or not to go up to Gage's door and knock.

Again.

She'd been sitting in the parking lot of his apartment complex for two days.

When she'd left Washington, DC, ten days ago, she'd planned on heading to South Dakota or somewhere in the northwest. She got five thousand dollars out of her bank account, and headed west. She stopped at crappy motels along the way, feeling unsafe and on the edge. Then one day, after making it all the way to Colorado, she found herself turning south. She spent the night in Denver. Then Pueblo. Then Santa Fe, and before she knew it, she was driving back east. Toward Texas. Killeen, Texas, specifically.

Being here was stupid.

It was crazy.

And yet, here she was.

She hadn't been able to get Gage out of her mind, and the more she thought about it, the more she realized that he'd probably have connections who could help her. She knew going to him would put him in danger, because if someone was following her, or found out where she was, they'd assume she'd told him what was going on. So she needed to either leave right now and do what she'd originally planned, or suck it up and trust Gage.

She was going to go out on a limb and tell him everything.

But she hadn't expected him to be gone. She should've at least considered the possibility. She knew he was Delta Force. Knew he was sent out on a moment's notice. He'd told her as much. Kinley wondered if he'd messaged her again. If he'd tried to let her know.

Guilt crept in once more. She hated not knowing if he'd tried to get in touch, but hated even more knowing that, if he had, he probably thought she was a colossal bitch for not returning his messages.

And now she was sitting in the parking lot of his apartment complex like a stalker. But she literally had nowhere else to go. She'd slept in her car for most of the last ten days, and she was dirty and smelly. Her belly gurgled, protesting the lack of food Kinley had given it lately. It was nine in the morning, and Kinley had hoped that she'd be able to catch Gage, but that hadn't been the case. He still wasn't home.

She could easily start driving aimlessly again, but her resolve had grown. She didn't want to let Stryker—or Brown, if he was involved—get away with what he'd done. If he truly was The Alleyway Strangler, he needed to be stopped. And right now, she was in the best position to make that happen.

She didn't want anyone else to suffer at his hands.

But she was also scared. She could still feel that hand on her back, trying to push her into the path of the oncoming train. She'd been lucky to come out of that with only a cut on her chin.

Kinley was deep in thought, so when someone knocked

on her driver's-side window unexpectedly, she let out a screech and did her best to crawl into the passenger seat and away from the person she knew was about to come through her window and kill her.

She had her butt on the other seat and was readying to open the door and run when she looked up and met a pair of remorseful green eyes. The blonde woman on the other side of the door took a giant step back and held up her hands, showing her she was unarmed.

"I'm sorry, so sorry!" the woman said. "I didn't mean to scare you. I was just worried about you and wanted to make sure you were all right."

Feeling her heart beating a million miles an hour, Kinley forced herself to take a deep breath. Shit, she was going to die of a heart attack before Stryker's goon could find her to finish her off.

Embarrassed at her over-the-top reaction, Kinley scooted the rest of the way into the passenger seat, then opened the door and climbed out. She might be flustered by the woman showing up out of the blue like she had, but she wasn't an idiot. She wasn't going to step right into the woman's clutches if she was up to no good.

"I really am sorry," the other woman said. "I thought you saw me walk up. My name is Gillian. Gillian Romano, and I live in this complex with my boyfriend. I saw you parked here yesterday too, but I didn't think anything about it until I saw you knocking on our friend's door this morning. Lefty's not here."

Kinley was confused for a second. Who was Lefty? Then she remembered that it was Gage's silly nickname.

Her stomach dropped. She knew he wasn't there, but for some reason, hearing it confirmed made her shitty situation all the more awful. "Do you know when he'll be back?" Kinley asked.

Gillian shrugged apologetically. "Sorry, no. I also couldn't help but notice that you slept out here last night. Do you...do you want to come up and have some breakfast with me?"

Kinley could only stare at the other woman in disbelief. She was pretty. Her blonde hair was squeaky clean and shining. She wore a pair of jeans, as well as a T-shirt with a basset hound wearing sunglasses.

"You don't know me," Kinley blurted. "Why in the world would you invite me into your apartment? Is your boyfriend there?" she asked suspiciously. She'd heard about women luring other females into a trap, allowing their significant others to then rob and sometimes do even worse things to the victims.

"No, Walker's not here. He's with Lefty."

"Does your boyfriend have a nickname?" Kinley asked, realization dawning.

Gillian tilted her head and studied her, as if she was contemplating whether or not to answer. Finally, she said, "Trigger."

"I know him," Kinley told Gillian with a small smile, feeling relieved.

"You do?"

Kinley nodded. "Tall. Black hair. Swimmer's shoulders."

"That's Walker. I'm sorry, what was your name?" Gillian asked, sounding a bit suspicious herself now.

"Kinley."

"Kinley...? Oh! Walker told me that Lefty's been talking about a woman named Kinley. That must be you!"

It was Kinley's turn to be surprised. "He's talked about me?"

"Well, not to me, but if you met Lefty and my boyfriend, then you know how close they are. You don't know me, but I assure you, I'm completely harmless."

"Oh...um...okay." Kinley wasn't sure what to think of the

other woman. She seemed to be sincere, and she did seem to know Gage, but she wasn't sure she should really trust anyone. Anyone but Gage, that was.

"After you knocked on Lefty's door, then slept out here in your car, I had to come down," Gillian said. "To be honest, Walker wouldn't be happy with me; he doesn't even like me taking an Uber. But I'm a pretty good judge of character...one recent misjudgment notwithstanding. I saw you down here yesterday, and last night, and I felt bad. As I said, I don't know when Lefty will get back, but I can offer you an ear over breakfast if you want."

Kinley wanted to refuse. Wanted to politely decline and be on her way. But something about the other woman made it almost impossible. Gillian was open and friendly, and that was something Kinley hadn't experienced much of in the last two weeks.

She nodded tentatively.

"Great! Grab whatever you need. I work from home, and honestly, I'm going a bit stir crazy. I like being by myself, but I'm also used to being around people too...which I realize makes no sense. I'm an event planner, and I'm between events right now, and I'd be happy for the company."

Kinley had never met someone like Gillian. She was outgoing and welcoming and made her long for something she'd never had...someone to talk to about her troubles.

She reached into the backseat and pulled out her duffle bag. She wasn't going to leave it behind, just in case Gillian had ulterior motives. She grabbed her keys and locked her Corolla and followed Gillian up the stairs.

"I moved into this complex with Walker a few months ago," Gillian said. "He had a small apartment that didn't really fit all our stuff. Now I feel absolutely spoiled by three bedrooms. Of course, Walker's already talking about finding a house, but I'm not ready for that yet. We found this place because Lefty already lived here. He talked to the manager when a place opened up, and I think he and Walker have really enjoyed living near each other. Of course, it gives me some space as well. When Walker overwhelms me with his protectiveness, I tell him to go visit with Lefty and give me some peace and quiet."

Gillian chuckled, and Kinley couldn't help but return her smile.

They walked up the stairs together, and Gillian opened her door and led the way inside. For a second, Kinley considered wildly if this could be a trap. The person who was hired to kill her might've somehow followed her, and was using Gillian as a lure...but she dismissed the thought immediately. She had a feeling whoever had pushed her in DC wouldn't bother with such elaborate subterfuge. He'd simply pull out a gun and shoot next time.

Besides, if anyone was following her, they'd had ample opportunity to kill her during the long drive, anytime she'd been forced to pull over and rest for a few hours before hitting the road again.

Kinley placed her bag by the sofa Gillian gestured to before she sat.

"Can I get you something to drink? I put biscuits in the oven before I went downstairs to see if you wanted to join me. I can whip up some eggs too, if you want. Or I've got oatmeal and fruit."

Kinley felt her eyes fill with tears, and she desperately tried to hold them back. After ten days of being on the run and sleeping in her car and doing whatever she could to stay under the radar so she wouldn't be found, the simple offer of something to eat and drink had pushed her over the edge.

She turned her head and bit her lip to try to control herself, but it didn't work. Two tears rolled down her cheeks.

"Kinley? If none of those options sound good, I can—oh!"

Gillian's words abruptly cut off as she finally realized how upset her houseguest was.

Without a word, the other woman came over to the sofa, sat down, and pulled Kinley into her embrace.

Kinley wasn't a cuddler. Wasn't used to being touched. She couldn't even remember the last time someone had given her a hug. But this stranger, a woman she'd only met a few minutes ago, was showing her more compassion and genuine affection than she'd experienced in a very long time.

It was too much for Kinley to take. Normally, she could've gotten herself under control and managed to stop her tears, but not now.

She held on to Gillian as if they'd been friends forever and cried. Cried because she was scared. Cried because someone had tried to kill her. Cried because she'd lost the job she'd had for years. Cried because she had no idea what she was going to do next. Cried for the poor teenager in Paris who'd been killed.

And she cried because she knew, deep down, that Gage had been upset and probably pissed when he hadn't heard from her after she'd promised to keep in touch.

She had no idea how long she clung to Gillian, but eventually, she realized that she was bawling in the arms of a woman who was probably seriously regretting inviting her into her home right about now.

"Feel better?" Gillian asked, not shying away from looking Kinley in the eyes.

Kinley shook her head. She didn't, not really. Her face felt swollen, and she knew she needed a shower. She'd been wearing the same clothes for days, and she was still scared out of her mind. She had no idea what kind of reception she'd get from Gage, but she literally had nowhere else to go. No one else to turn to. She wouldn't be surprised if he refused to get involved in her problem at all.

"Come on," Gillian said gently, pulling at Kinley's hand.

She allowed the other woman to pull her to her feet.

"A shower will make you feel a hundred percent better. Then when you're done, we'll put your clothes in the washer. I'm taller than you, but I've got a T-shirt and some fat pants you can wear if you want."

Once again, Kinley was struck by how generous this woman was. "Are you always this accommodating to random strange women you meet?" she asked.

Gillian chuckled. "No," she said firmly. She stopped walking and dropped Kinley's hand and turned to face her. She eyed her for a long moment before she said, "Here's the thing. You know Lefty. You know Walker...er, Trigger. That means you probably know the rest of the guys on the team as well. And knowing the guys means you probably met them while they were in their official capacity...if you know what I mean. And you showing up here knocking on Lefty's door, in a car with a Washington, DC, license plate, tells me that you need his help.

"And I've been in your shoes. Boy, have I. If I turned a blind eye to you, that would make me no better than the people who my boyfriend and his team spend their lives trying to eradicate."

Kinley was well aware that Gage and his friends were Delta Force. And obviously this woman was too. "I know who and what they are," she told Gillian.

"Right. So you have a good reason to be here wanting to talk to Lefty. He and the others left on a mission about a week ago. I don't know when they'll be back."

Kinley sighed. She really should leave. Being here put Gillian in danger. Hell, it would put Gage in danger too. But she'd already decided to talk to Gage—she literally had *no one* else to turn to—and Gillian's generosity was a gift she couldn't pass up. "I'd love a shower," she said quietly.

Gillian smiled. "Come on. I'll find you something to wear for afterward and we'll get your laundry done."

"Thanks."

Gillian waved her hand. "Of course."

Fifteen minutes later, Kinley was enjoying what had to be the best shower of her life. The water was hot, the water pressure was perfect...and, yet she wasn't relaxed.

Would she ever feel safe again?

Closing her eyes, she remembered with perfect clarity how that hand had felt on her back. For less than a second, she'd simply thought someone was being rude and was trying to push past her. But when she'd started to fall, she knew immediately that it wasn't an accident.

She also couldn't keep the shoes of that teenager out of her mind. She'd been so enamored of those damn sparkly heels. At the time, she'd wished she knew where the woman had bought them so she could see if they had them in flats. Kinley didn't wear heels, ever, but she sure wished she could.

To see them still on the girl's feet, still sparkling while the rest of her body was covered in a tarp, was still extremely jarring.

Kinley knew she should just call the FBI and talk to someone, but she was paranoid now. If Drake Stryker was a serial killer, and her ex-boss was most likely somehow involved in the whole sordid affair, who knew who else in the upper echelons of government was involved? Did the president himself know the man he'd appointed as the ambassador to France was a killer? Know that he was consorting with minors? If he did, maybe the FBI knew too?

Kinley had too many questions; there were too many unknowns to just blindly call someone who worked for the FBI to let them know what she'd witnessed. She was still terrified that Walter was right, that no one would believe her.

Gage will.

The thought popped into her head immediately. And that was the reason Kinley was in Texas. She knew Gage wouldn't doubt her. They hadn't known each other very long, but she knew that much about him.

Kinley had no idea where she was going to sleep that night, or how long it might take for Gage to return from whatever mission he was on, but she'd stay in Texas until she had a chance to talk to him. He'd help her figure out what to do next.

She climbed out of the shower, not exactly feeling great about her situation but definitely feeling cleaner, which went a long way toward clearing her head. She put on the elastic-waist pants—which were too long, but Kinley didn't really care at the moment—and the T-shirt and brushed her hair. Then, taking a deep breath, she headed out of the bathroom.

The air in the apartment smelled amazing. Like freshly baked bread and eggs. Kinley's stomach growled.

"The washer and dryer are next to the bathroom in the hall," Gillian said when she saw Kinley standing at the edge of the room. "Help yourself."

Kinley nodded and headed to where her new friend had pointed. She filled the washer with her dirty clothes and started it up. It was amazing how a shower and the prospect of clean clothes could make her feel so much better.

Breakfast was as good as it smelled. The biscuits were a bit too brown on the bottom, but Kinley figured that was her fault for distracting Gillian. The eggs were perfectly cooked and even the honeydew melon tasted absolutely perfect.

After breakfast, Kinley had cleaned their dishes, and now she and Gillian were sitting on the couch once again as they waited for her clothes to dry.

"Can you tell me what's going on?" Gillian asked.

Kinley shook her head. "No."

The other woman didn't get upset, she simply nodded. "If Lefty doesn't get back today, where will you stay?"

"I'll find a place. Do you think they'll be gone for much longer?"

The look of sympathy on Gillian's face almost did Kinley in. "I honestly don't know. It's the worst thing about dating a Delta. They could be gone for three days, or three months. Walker can't tell me where he's going or anything about what happened when he gets home. I admit, it's hard. *Really* hard. But not because I can't live on my own. I managed just fine as a single woman for over ten years after high school. It's more that I worry about him and just miss being with him."

Kinley understood. She worried about Gage, and they really didn't even know each other.

Gillian went on. "But I trust that Lefty and the others will have Walker's back. Those guys would die for each other, and that gives me comfort."

For the millionth time, Kinley thought about the fact if she confided in Gage, she'd be putting him in danger. And not only him, his entire team too.

The room suddenly began to feel extremely small and closed in.

Kinley stood abruptly. "I need to go."

"Stay," Gillian countered, standing as well. "When Lefty gets back, he'll help you figure out whatever's wrong."

"It's not that easy," Kinley said.

"It never is. Did Lefty tell you how he and the rest of the guys met me?"

Kinley wanted to leave. Wanted to take her clothes, whether or not they were dry yet, and get the hell out of Texas. But she stood rooted to the spot. Whether she wanted to admit it or not, she was curious as hell about Gillian. She shook her head.

"Come on, sit. This is too long a story to be told standing."

Kinley sat on the very edge of the couch, ready to hop up and go as soon as the dryer buzzed, letting her know her clothes were dry.

"I was on a plane that was hijacked and flown to Venezuela."

Gillian's words shook Kinley out of her own head. "What?"

"I was on a plane that was hijacked and flown to Venezuela," Gillian repeated.

"Shit," Kinley breathed. Suddenly her own issues didn't seem quite so big and scary anymore.

"Yup. They made me talk to the negotiators, and lucky me, Walker eventually arrived on the scene and started talking to me."

For the next twenty minutes, Kinley sat quietly, enthralled with the story Gillian was telling. It was full of drug dealers, kidnappings, and even a shooting. It was crazy, but the other woman was recounting the story calmly, as if it had been no big deal.

"I think you're the strongest person I've ever met," Kinley told Gillian honestly when she was finally done telling her story.

Gillian shook her head. "I'm really not. I mean, I'm an event planner, for God's sake. I spend my life planning parties and celebrations. I'm no hero; I've never even held a gun. I like people, but I also like sitting at home reading a book. Though...it's my belief that *everyone* is stronger than they think. We never know how strong we can be until it's our only option. If you had told me that I would someday be in the middle of a hostage situation, I wouldn't have believed you. If you'd told me I would've been able to stand in front of a woman holding a gun on me, refusing to get into her car, I would've laughed in your face. I'm a people pleaser. I do what I'm told. But at that moment, I knew if I got in that car, I would've ended up dead."

"I wish I was stronger," Kinley admitted.

"I don't know you, but I have a feeling you're a hell of a lot stronger than you're giving yourself credit for. Again, no one asks for shit to happen to them in life. No one wants to have a chronic disease. Or to have their child die. Or have their lover killed in battle. No one asks to grow up in poverty or to be homeless. No one wants to be born with a disability that makes them struggle every day of their life. We learn how to be strong because we have no other choice.

"And when we're put in situations where we have to be strong, we downplay what we did and how awesome we were. You might not feel as if you're brave or strong, but I have a feeling you're probably on the top of the heap when it comes to strength."

Kinley was speechless. She wasn't sure what to say to that. First, it was the best compliment she'd ever received. She thought about her life, about how hard it had been, and realized that Gillian might be right. It wasn't easy growing up without parents or affection, but somehow she'd managed. It hadn't been easy working in Washington, DC, but she'd done that too.

She had no idea if she'd make it out of the mess she'd somehow found herself in just because she'd looked out her hotel window at the wrong time (or was it the right time?), but she had to have faith that she would. "Thank you," she said after a long moment.

"You're welcome," Gillian said easily. "I know you said you have to go, but maybe you wouldn't mind sticking around for a while? It's been lonely with Walker gone. I have to make some calls this morning still, I'm planning a two-year-cancer-free celebration for an Army spouse, and I'd love some company."

Kinley knew she should say no, that she had to get going, but she found herself nodding instead.

"Great!" Gillian said with enthusiasm.

Three hours later, Kinley looked up from the book she'd been reading and blinked in surprise. Gillian had told her to help herself to whatever she wanted to read from her book-shelves, and after finding a romance that looked interesting, Kinley had settled onto the couch to start it.

She'd only gotten up once—to fold her laundry and change back into clothes of her own—and then she'd dived back into the book.

Looking to her left, Kinley saw Gillian sitting on the other end of the sofa, reading her own book.

Kinley couldn't help the smile that crossed her face.

"What?" Gillian asked after looking up and seeing it.

"I...we're just sitting here next to each other, reading. Not talking."

"Oh. Sorry, are you bored?" Gillian asked, closing her book.

"No!" Kinley exclaimed. "It's not that at all. I just...this is perfect. All my life I've been made fun of for being able to tune everything out around me while I'm reading. The foster parents I had made it seem like I was being rude, and when I did have friends and we hung out, I always felt as if I had to *talk*."

"Oh my God, me too," Gillian said with a smile. "I mean, I admit that I like to talk, but I'm also happy to sit and just be. Besides, I've been binging this one author's books. I forced myself to get some work done first, but I'm happy to get the chance to just sit here and read. It's nice to have you here, even if we don't talk."

Kinley smiled at the other woman. She looked at her

watch and realized that it was past time for her to go. She put the book down and stood.

"You're going?" Gillian asked.

"Yeah."

"Okay. But you'll come back tomorrow, right?"

Kinley blinked in surprise.

"I mean, I don't know when Walker and the others will be back, so you need to come back and see if Lefty's here, right? I'd love to hang out again."

"I...I'd like that," Kinley told her.

"Great. It's a plan. Do you have a phone? I can call you if I hear from Walker."

Kinley shook her head. "No. I had one, but I lost it." That wasn't exactly true, but it was as close to the truth as she was willing to admit to Gillian at this point. She had a throwaway phone, but she still didn't want to have an electronic tie to anyone Stryker and Brown could use against her.

"That's okay. Feel free to take the book you were reading with you," Gillian offered.

Once again, Kinley felt like she was going to cry. She'd known this woman for only a few hours, and she'd treated her better than any of her so-called friends had over the years. "Thanks," she said. "I promise not to mess it up."

Gillian waved her hand. "You can't mess it up," she said breezily. "I mean, it's a book. The pages might get dirty and the cover torn, but it doesn't change what's inside."

And that right there seemed to be a metaphor for Kinley's own life. From the outside looking in, she was a hot mess. Small, odd, standoffish...but inside, she was a good person, longing to show the world she could be the best partner and friend if she was just given a chance.

"Be safe out there, okay?" Gillian said as Kinley picked up her duffle bag and headed for the door.

"I will," Kinley said. She had no problem with Gillian not

asking her to stay. She *was* a stranger, after all. It wouldn't be smart or safe to ask her to spend the night. It was crazy enough that she'd invited her inside her apartment in the first place. But Kinley would never forget Gillian's kindness.

Before she left the apartment complex, Kinley knocked on Gage's door, not expecting him to answer. When he didn't, she walked to her car and put her bag in the backseat. She had nowhere to go, but at least she was clean and wasn't hungry anymore.

She just had to bide her time. Gage would eventually return, and she would talk to him and get his advice.

Things might not work out the way she wanted, he might say he couldn't help her and she'd be on her own again, but for now, she felt good. She'd made a new friend, and she'd do whatever she could to keep Gillian safe from the danger she felt was right on her heels.

Eventually, whoever had tried to kill her would find her, and the last thing Kinley wanted was to put anyone else in danger.

CHAPTER SEVEN

Lefty ran a hand over his face. He was dirty, tired, and feeling off kilter by the intense mission he and the team had just completed. They'd been sent to Iran to try to rescue an American citizen, a Federal judge's son, who thought it would be fun to climb Mount Damavand. It was over eighteen thousand feet high and apparently on the man's bucket list. But he'd ignored the fact that Iran didn't take kindly to people, especially Americans, crossing their borders illegally. The man hadn't been able to get permission for the climb, and had decided to do it anyway.

Much of their time had been spent planning for the rescue mission. They'd had to go deep undercover, and when diplomatic avenues had failed to get the man released, the Deltas had been given permission to break him out of the Iranian jail by force if necessary.

In the end, unfortunately, that hadn't been necessary. The man had decided he was done waiting to be freed and had tried to break out on his own. That choice had ended in his death.

All the Deltas' planning and subterfuge had been in vain.

It had taken four days for the team to sneak back out of Iran after their failed rescue attempt, and Lefty was exhausted.

He was upset at the man for thinking climbing a mountain was more important than staying at home with his wife and young daughter. He was pissed at the Iranian government for not deciding the man was just young and dumb and releasing him with a fine and a stern warning.

Not helping Lefty's mood was the fact that as soon as they'd landed in Europe to catch their plane home, he'd checked his messages...and hadn't had even one from Kinley.

She'd promised to keep in touch with him, and Lefty had believed her. One week he could make excuses for why she hadn't texted or called him. But two weeks with no contact was less likely to be an accident or oversight. He felt like an idiot. *Fool me once, shame on you, fool me twice, shame on me.* He should've learned his lesson the first time. Kinley seemed like a good person. Someone he wanted to get to know better. But long-distance relationships were hard enough. If she wasn't willing to even meet him halfway, Lefty knew there couldn't be anything between them. It sucked. Bad.

The trip back to the States was long, but Lefty couldn't sleep. He hadn't been able to stop thinking about Kinley and why she might've decided to ghost him a second time. It made no sense, and he had to wonder if maybe something was wrong.

After they landed, the team waited to be dismissed before heading to their respective homes. Lefty planned to go back to his apartment and sleep for twenty-four hours straight. When he was rested, he'd be in a better place to put things with Kinley in perspective. He needed to put her out of his mind once and for all, which he knew would be easier said than done.

Lefty had come to the base with Trigger, because they lived in the same apartment complex now. It was late, after ten at night, and Trigger had just hung up after talking with Gillian.

"She good?" Lefty asked.

Trigger nodded. "Yeah."

The answer was short, but Lefty had overheard some of his friend's conversation. It was clear that Gillian was thrilled he was home, and the feeling was mutual.

"Seriously?" Grover asked from nearby, the surprise and confusion easy to hear in his tone.

Lefty was immediately on alert. "What?" he asked.

The other men on the team were also tense as they waited to hear what had surprised their friend so much.

"Devyn's planning on moving here."

"Devyn?" Lucky asked. "Who's that?"

"My sister," Grover told him, staring at his phone. "She left a message on my voice mail, saying that she's quit her job and she's moving to Texas."

"That's your youngest sister, right?" Oz asked.

"Yeah. She's the baby in the family."

"She okay?" Brain asked.

"I don't know. I mean, I thought she loved her job. She's a veterinary assistant, and every time I've talked to her, she's had nothing but good things to say about it," Grover replied, the worry easy to hear in his tone.

"You gonna call her back?" Lucky asked.

"I tried. She's not answering. It's late though, it could be she's just sleeping."

"Let us know if you need anything," Lefty said, clapping a hand on his friend's shoulder. "You know we're here."

"I will. I have no idea what plans she's made, but she might need help unloading a moving truck or something," Grover said.

"Anything you need, we're there," Lucky reiterated.

They were interrupted by their commanding officer

dismissing them, and soon after, Lefty was sitting in Trigger's Chevy Blazer. Resting his head on the seat back, Lefty closed his eyes.

"You okay?" Trigger asked.

"Yeah."

"Still nothing from her?"

"No. But it's fine. I mean, it's not like we were ever really gonna have any kind of relationship. Not with her being in DC and me here. Lord knows having a regular relationship is already difficult; a long-distance one would never work out," Lefty said, trying to convince himself.

"But you're still worried about her," Trigger said with uncanny insight.

Lefty sighed. "I spent six hours with her, Trigger," Lefty said. "We clicked. I called my *mom* when she was with me, for God's sake. She promised to talk to me. I don't know what to think anymore."

"Maybe tomorrow you can call Winkler, see if he can make some inquiries. I know we were just his bodyguard detail, but he seemed pretty down to earth...for a politician. He and Brown work in the same building, so at least you might know if she's okay if you talked to him."

It was a good suggestion, but at the moment, Lefty wasn't ready to do much of anything when it came to Kinley. "Yeah, I might."

Several minutes went by as Trigger drove toward their apartment complex.

"So, Gillian's good?" Lefty asked.

"Yeah. Said she's been busy planning and reading."

"Does she sit still long enough to read?" Lefty asked. "I swear I can picture her flitting all over the place, talking on the phone, typing out an email, and reading at the same time."

Trigger laughed. "It's funny because I thought the same

thing when I first met her. But you'd be surprised. She loves to sit around and veg. And if she's reading a book? Forget talking to her."

"I'm happy for you," Lefty told his friend. "I mean it. Gillian's awesome. She's one of the nicest people I've ever met. She'd give the shirt off her back if she thought someone needed it. That's pretty rare nowadays. People only think about themselves."

"It's pretty awesome, but it's also scary as fuck," Trigger admitted. "She's always wanting to buy meals and shit for people she sees on the street. One of these days, I'm going to come home and she'll have invited someone down on their luck to stay with us."

Lefty shuddered. "Yeah, that's not good," he admitted. But he couldn't stop thinking about the moment when Kinley had bought a meal for the homeless man in Paris, and how, in Africa, she'd bought out the woman's entire stall of food.

"But I wouldn't change Gillian for the world," Trigger said. "I don't ever want her to harden up. I want her to keep that empathy she has for others forever. I just wish she'd be a bit more aware of her own safety at the same time."

"You've gotten her to stop using Ubers, though, right?" Lefty asked.

"Yeah. But that's just the tip of the iceberg."

They pulled into the parking lot at the apartment complex and, after they'd exited the vehicle, Lefty gave Trigger a chin lift. "Thanks for the ride."

"Of course. There's no point in both of us taking our cars to the base. Thanks again for helping Gillian and me get the apartment here."

"No problem. Any luck on finding a house?"

Trigger shrugged. "We've been looking, but Gillian says she's content where she is for now."

"A woman who doesn't care about material shit is pretty fucking amazing," Lefty observed.

"Oh, I know, and believe me, I'm thankful for it. She couldn't care less about the size of our apartment or designer clothes and stuff like that. But somehow that makes me want to give them to her all the more," Trigger said dryly.

"Go on," Lefty said, playfully shoving his friend. "Go home to your woman."

"She's an idiot," Trigger said after taking three steps toward his apartment. "Kinley, I mean. You're one of the best men I've ever known. She doesn't know what she's losing by ghosting you."

"Thanks," Lefty said. The words didn't really make him feel better, but he liked them all the same. "I'll talk to you later."

"Later," Trigger said, then turned and bounded up the stairs.

Lefty walked to his own apartment a little slower. He knew what was waiting for him. A dark, empty apartment that smelled slightly musty from being closed up for two weeks. He'd thrown away what he thought might go bad in his fridge before he'd left, but he always forgot something.

Sighing, he straightened his shoulders. This was his life, no matter what he might've thought would happen with Kinley.

He opened his apartment door and dropped his bag on the floor just inside. He'd deal with laundry later. Right now, all he wanted was a shower and bed.

* * *

Lefty groaned when his phone rang the next morning. Opening one eye, he saw it was eleven o'clock. He'd slept hard, but he felt as if he could still sleep for another twelve hours.

He fumbled with his phone as it continued ringing and finally found the button to click to answer it.

"'Lo?"

"It's Trigger. You need to come over to my apartment. Pronto."

Lefty was immediately awake. "What's wrong? Is Gillian all right?"

"She's fine. But she needs to tell you something you're going to want to hear."

It took Lefty a moment to let his heart rate settle. "God, don't scare me like that, Trigger. Shit, I thought something was really wrong."

"It *might* be. Get your ass over here, Lefty. I'm not kidding." Then Trigger hung up.

Lefty grumbled about what a pain in the ass his friend was as he dropped his head back down to his pillow. If he went over to the other apartment only to find Gillian throwing them a welcome-home breakfast party, he was gonna be pissed. The food would be nice, because Lefty knew he didn't have a damn thing to eat at his place...but still.

He climbed out of bed and went into the bathroom. He quickly used the facilities and brushed his teeth, not bothering to shave, then threw on a pair of jeans and a T-shirt. He grabbed his keys and put them in his pocket before heading out of his apartment and over to Trigger's place.

He lifted his hand to knock, but the door opened before he could. Trigger stood there with a worried look on his face.

The tension on his friend's face made Lefty finally realize that this wasn't a surprise welcome-home party or anything of the sort. He followed Trigger inside and saw Gillian pacing back and forth in front of the couch.

"Lefty!" she said when she saw him. "Thank God you're here."

Frowning, Lefty couldn't figure out what the hell was going on. "What's wrong?"

"Well, maybe nothing—but maybe lots. And I'm *so* sorry! I was...distracted last night when Walker got home, and I forgot until this morning," Gillian explained, blushing and looking slightly guilty.

"Take a breath, Di," Trigger said, using the nickname he'd given her in Venezuela. He went to her and pulled her into his embrace.

Lefty couldn't help but feel a pang of...jealousy? It wasn't that he didn't want Trigger to have what he had with Gillian... it was just that he wanted it too. And after meeting Kinley, he'd thought maybe there was a tiny chance he might get it, but that was looking less and less likely.

"Okay?" Trigger asked, looking down at Gillian.

She nodded and turned to Lefty. "I think Kinley might still be in town."

Those eight words turned Lefty's world on its axis. "*What?*"

"I know, it's crazy. But she was here looking for you."

When she didn't immediately explain, Lefty ordered, "Start from the beginning, and don't leave anything out."

"Right. It was about a week after you guys left. I'd noticed this woman the day before, but didn't think much about it. She was knocking on your door, and you obviously weren't home. But then she came back the next day. And then the *next* day, she was sitting in a car in the parking lot. I noticed her parked there the evening before...then in the morning, her car was in the same spot, and she was still in it. She looked rough, Lefty. I felt bad for her. So I went down to the parking lot to talk to her."

"See what I mean?" Trigger said, meeting Lefty's gaze with exasperation. "We're still working on personal safety."

Gillian shoved Trigger's chest, but he didn't move, only pulled her closer.

"Anyway, she said her name was Kinley, and I remembered Walker telling me briefly about someone with that name who you'd spent time with in Paris. I mean, I don't know any details or anything, but I felt better that you actually knew her. So I invited her up to have breakfast. As I said, she looked rough."

"What does that mean?" Lefty clipped.

"Easy, man," Trigger warned.

Lefty took a deep breath and nodded.

"Just that it looked like she'd been sleeping in her car. Her hair needing washing and her clothes were super wrinkled. And..." Gillian hesitated, but then went on. "She didn't smell all that great. Not awful, but like she hadn't showered in a while. So I convinced her to come up here—which wasn't easy, by the way—and we ate and she showered. I let her wash her clothes and we hung out."

"You hung out?" Lefty asked, perplexed.

"Yeah. It was pretty awesome, I have to admit. I did some work, she read. Then when I was done, I sat down and read too."

Trigger's lips twitched. "So you two sat on the couch and didn't talk, but you read?"

Gillian smiled. "Yeah. You know how hard it is to find someone who's comfortable just sitting next to you reading and not worrying about carrying on a conversation? I mean, I love Wendy, Ann, and Clarissa, but those three can *talk*. Kinley didn't feel the need to talk just for the sake of hearing her own voice."

"What happened then?" Lefty asked, wanting her to get

on with it so he could figure out why Kinley was there—and where she might be now.

"She left," Gillian said with a shrug. "I didn't know when you guys would be back, so I invited her to come back in the morning so we could hang out again. And she did. I saw her every morning for three days—but I haven't seen her for the last two. She said she didn't have a phone, so I couldn't call her to find out if everything's all right. I'm worried about her. She seemed almost desperate to talk to you, and now you're back, but suddenly she's not here. I don't like it."

Lefty didn't like it either. He couldn't figure out what Kinley was doing in Texas in the first place. Not when her job was in DC. And why the hell was she sleeping in her car? And where was her phone?

Nothing made sense...and that had Lefty's internal oh-shit meter pinging left and right. "What's she driving?"

"A tan Toyota Corolla."

Lefty winced. They were a dime a dozen, and it would make finding her all the more difficult.

"I'll call the other guys," Trigger said, letting go of Gillian.

Lefty wanted to protest. He knew everyone was as tired as he was, but he'd be grateful for the help.

"You want me to call the police?" Gillian asked.

"No," Lefty said immediately.

She lifted an eyebrow in question.

Taking a deep breath, Lefty tried to explain. "Something's wrong. Kinley shouldn't be in Texas. She lives and works in DC. And I definitely don't like the fact that you think she's been sleeping in her car. The police would be able to put out a BOLO on her car, but if she's in trouble, that could make matters worse."

"How so?" Gillian asked. "Do you think she's wanted by the law?"

Lefty wanted to chuckle at her wording, but nothing was

funny about this situation. Nothing at all. "No, but I don't know *what's* going on. I thought she wasn't answering my messages and texts because she didn't want to talk to me, but what if it's something else?"

"She could be trying to stay under the radar," Trigger said.

"Exactly. So I don't want to get the police involved just yet. Believe me, if too much time goes by, I might not have a choice, but for now, I want to see if we can find her on our own. Killeen isn't too big, so maybe we'll get lucky," Lefty said.

"I can call Ann, Wendy, and Clarissa to help."

"Thanks, but let's keep this on the down-low for now," Lefty told her. Then he walked over to Gillian and put his hands on her shoulders. "Thank you for befriending her." He hesitated, then continued. "She doesn't seem to have any friends, so I appreciate you reaching out."

"That's just stupid," Gillian said heatedly. "I don't even know her very well, but I like her a lot. She's...calming. That's not really the right word, but it'll do for now. I didn't once feel like I had to entertain her. She was perfectly happy just sitting on the couch and reading. But she could also hold a conversation. We talked about one of my upcoming events, and she had some great ideas for me. And one day I was having trouble finding anything in my client's budget, and she was able to give me some hints and tricks to negotiate a better rate with the venue. I like her, Lefty. I hope she's all right."

"Me too," Lefty said. He let go of her shoulders and looked at Trigger. They shared a glance, and Trigger motioned to the front door with his head. Understanding that he wanted to talk about their plan of action away from Gillian, Lefty nodded.

"Thanks again for letting me know," Lefty told her.

"I'm so sorry I didn't think to call you last night. I was just so excited that Walker was home."

Lefty snorted a laugh. "I know. You hadn't seen Trigger in a while."

Gillian nodded, but was still frowning. "I feel horrible about it. I'm a terrible person for not thinking about it immediately. I should've told you last night."

"It's okay. Seriously," Lefty told her. He would've liked to have known last night, but he'd been tired. He wouldn't have slept if he'd known Kinley had been in town looking for him, and there was a good chance he needed to be on top of his game when he found her. She wouldn't be here if something hadn't happened.

Determination rose within him. Kinley was here. She'd come to him. *Him.* It was bad timing that he'd been on a mission, but he was going to find her and figure out what she was doing in Texas. He knew she wouldn't have come if whatever she needed wasn't important.

Within thirty minutes, Lefty was standing in the parking lot of his apartment complex surrounded by all six members of his team. No one had bitched about having to come over on their day off.

Trigger had just finished telling the guys what Gillian had told him and Lefty.

"She's here somewhere," Lefty said. "I know it. We just need to find her. I don't know her plate number, but it'll be a Washington, DC, license plate. If she's really been sleeping in her car, she'll probably have looked for a safe place. A parking lot of a business that's open twenty-four hours, or some other place that's not too desolate. There's a chance she's not even in town anymore...but for some reason, I think she is. She came all this way to see me and she's very determined. I can't see her leaving before she accomplishes what she set out to do. If you find her, don't approach. Call me and watch her. Okay?"

Everyone nodded.

Lefty loved his team. They didn't worry about who was in charge or who was calling the shots. Their egos were checked at the door before they started a mission. And this *was* a mission, even if it wasn't being assigned by their country.

Lefty gave them all different areas of the town to search and immediately after, they all headed for their cars.

Brain held back as the others left. "You okay?" he asked.

Lefty shrugged. "I'll be better when I find out what the hell is going on."

"You want me to see what I can find on the computer?"

Lefty hesitated then shook his head. "My gut is telling me to wait. To find out what's going on before we do anything that might alert someone else that she's in the area and we're looking for her."

Brain examined Lefty's face for a long moment. "You think she's being electronically tracked?"

Lefty shrugged. "Honestly? I have no clue. But I do know this isn't like her. She isn't the kind of woman to up and leave her job, sleep in her car, and be all mysterious. She's smart, Brain. Frugal with her money. There's no reason she can't rent a hotel while she's waiting for me. I thought she wasn't answering my messages because she didn't want to talk to me, but what if there's more to it than that? She told Gillian that she doesn't have a phone. I know she does, or *did*—but what if she doesn't want to use it? At this point, I have more questions than answers, and it's not sitting right."

"You want me to talk to Winkler?"

"No!" Lefty exclaimed. Then he took a breath to try to calm down. "I'm not saying the man won't have information, because we all know how small the political community is in DC. But what if she's running from someone there? What if she doesn't want anyone to know where she is? If we start asking questions, it could get around and bring someone to our doorstep who she doesn't want to see."

"Understandable," Brain agreed. "But if you need anything, all you gotta do is say the word and you know I'll bend over backward to get whatever info you need."

"Appreciate it. Right now, I just need to find Kinley and make sure she's okay. We'll figure out where to go after that. I'm hoping she just got an opportunity to take an overdue vacation and nothing's wrong. I'm conceited enough to hope she wanted to spend that vacation with me, but my gut's screaming that something's wrong."

"We'll find her," Brain said, clapping a hand on Lefty's shoulder. "And for the record, not that it matters, I like her. I don't really know her all that well, but from what I've seen of her, she seems as if she's down to earth, just happy to sit and enjoy the day, if that makes sense."

Lefty nodded. It made perfect sense. He remembered how she'd been perfectly happy to sit on a bench and stare up at the Eiffel Tower. She hadn't needed to talk about it, and didn't take a million selfies of herself in front of it. She just took it in and enjoyed being in the moment. He liked that. A lot.

Brain gave Lefty a chin lift and headed for his car. Taking a deep breath, Lefty headed to his own pickup truck. With every minute that passed, his anxiety increased. He needed to find Kinley, and find her fast.

CHAPTER EIGHT

"Found her," Lucky said when Lefty answered his phone an hour later.

That was the thing about Lucky, and how he'd gotten his nickname. The man was extraordinarily lucky in just about everything he did. From narrowly missing being hurt on missions, to finding obscure information needed to complete a job. And Lefty had never been so thankful for his teammate's luck as he was now.

He got the address where Lucky had found her car and turned his own truck around. Lucky had promised to call the rest of the team as well, and Lefty knew they would all race to get to her.

Lucky hadn't said much else, just that he'd found her car and drove by once to see if she was inside. He saw her in the driver's seat, but he hadn't approached. One part of Lefty had wanted him to immediately go to her to make sure she was all right, but the other part of him wanted to be the one she saw first.

She'd met Lucky, but if she wasn't expecting him, she

might be scared when he knocked on her window out of the blue.

Lefty drove faster.

Within seven and a half minutes, he pulled his truck up beside Lucky's. They were in the parking lot of a local factory. It was a smart choice on Kinley's part. The lot was full of cars all day and night because of the various shifts, and while someone might notice her sitting there, they wouldn't necessarily think it was too odd.

Grover, Lucky, Doc, and Brain were already there, and Trigger and Oz were on their way. Not wanting to wait on the rest of his team, Lefty approached Kinley's door and saw her eyes were closed and her head was resting on the headrest behind her. With each step, his heart rate increased. He could feel the adrenaline coursing through his body.

He tried to quietly open the door, but it was locked. He hated to knock on the window and scare her, but he didn't have a choice.

Lefty rapped twice on the window—and he began to sweat when Kinley didn't even move. Maybe she wasn't merely sleeping. Maybe something was really wrong.

"Fuck," he muttered and knocked again, louder this time.

He held his breath—and when he saw her head move a fraction, he let it out. She was alive. God, for a second he'd thought he was too late. He'd lost his chance with her for good.

"Kinley?" he called out. "Unlock the door."

He saw her eyes squint open, then shut again.

He knocked on the window once more. "Kinley!" he shouted louder. "Unlock the door."

Her eyes opened again, and he saw her mouth his name.

"Yeah, it's me, Gage. Unlock the door, sweetheart. Let me in." Lefty held his breath as he watched her hand come up and fumble at the buttons on the armrest in the door. She seemed to be extraordinarily uncoordinated, which wasn't like her. Yeah, she might be out of it because she'd been sleeping, but this seemed different. "That's it, baby, come on, open up," he whispered.

Finally, just when he was afraid they'd have to break a window to get to her, he heard the locks disengage.

Lefty had the door open and was on his knees on the ground at her side in two seconds.

Kinley had closed her eyes again, and her head was resting on the seat. Lefty reached up and touched her arm, wincing at how hot she was. "She's burning up," he told Doc, along with the rest of his team, then turned back to Kinley.

"Hey, Kins."

"Gage," she whispered.

"I'm here."

"Cold," she mumbled, shivering.

"Shit." Lefty heard Doc say from behind him. "We need to get her to a doctor."

As if his friend's words were some sort of magic elixir, Kinley's eyes popped open. "No doctor!" she exclaimed frantically.

Lefty reached out and grabbed hold of her shoulders. "Easy, Kins,"

He knew he'd never forget the look in her eyes as she stared at him. It was panic mixed with terror. "No doctor," she repeated. "He'll find me...and *you*."

"Who will find you, Kins?"

But she closed her eyes and sagged against him. "No doctor..." she said for the third time.

Realizing she was in no condition to answer any of his questions, Lefty relented. "Okay, no doctor."

"Promise," she said without opening her eyes. One hand came up and gripped his biceps with a surprisingly strong hold. He could feel her fingernails digging into his skin.

111

"Promise," he said firmly.

Every muscle in her body relaxed. So much so, Lefty got concerned. "Kinley?"

She didn't answer.

"Shit," he muttered before scooting a bit closer and putting two fingers on the pulse in her neck. "It's fast, but steady," he told his teammates, who were gathered close behind him now, watching.

"Are you seriously not going to take her to a doctor?" Grover asked. "She looks bad, man."

Lefty looked back at his team. "I'm not. I'm taking her home with me. If she gets worse, I'll call Doc."

Everyone looked at the other man. He'd gotten his nickname because before he'd decided to join the military, he'd been in medical school. They were all licensed EMTs, thanks to their training, but the name had stuck.

"I'll drive her car back to your place," Lucky volunteered.

"We'll figure out the car situation," Trigger said. "Just get her home. If you need Gillian's help, she'll be glad to be of assistance. In fact, I have a feeling she's gonna insist on it."

Lefty nodded. He hadn't thought past finding Kinley and getting her back to his apartment, so he was thankful his friends were figuring out logistics. "Thanks, guys. Brain, can you help me get her out?"

Brain stepped to his side and helped Lefty stand so he didn't have to let go of Kinley. He stumbled a bit when he finally stood with Kinley in his arms, but Brain and Doc were there to steady him. She was burning up, and she'd hardly moved except to snuggle into him further after he stood.

She moaned a bit when he started walking for Trigger's Blazer, but didn't protest. She was scaring the shit out of him, but Lefty didn't let any of his concern show in his voice when he said, "I've got you, Kins."

Goose bumps broke out on his arms when her lips

brushed against the sensitive skin under his ear. She wasn't doing a damn thing to try to turn him on, but his body reacted to her closeness anyway.

"Cold," she mumbled.

Lefty tightened his hold on her and, once again, his friends helped steady him as he climbed into the back of Trigger's car. He knew he should let her go, should strap her into a seat belt, but he literally couldn't make himself let go of her. Not to mention every time he loosened his hold, she did her best to meld her body with his.

Being this close to her, Lefty couldn't miss the fact that it had been a couple days since she'd showered. She didn't smell bad, exactly, but neither did she have the fresh, clean scent he'd noticed when they'd hung out together in Paris.

He could feel her shivering against him, which wasn't good, considering it wasn't the least bit cold outside. Trigger drove quickly but safely back to the apartment complex, and Lefty waited until he'd opened the door to try to get out with Kinley in his arms. He walked swiftly up the stairs to his apartment.

"I came by," Kinley mumbled into his neck.

"I know. I'm sorry I wasn't here."

"You were off saving the world. I'm not important."

Lefty frowned. "If I'd known you were here, I would've sent someone to help you. One of my other Delta Force friends."

Kinley shook her head weakly. "No...only wanted you."

Trigger got his door open, and then Lefty had other things to concentrate on than how great her words made him feel. He headed straight for his bedroom and leaned over to put her on his bed.

She clung to him, not letting go.

Hunched over her, Lefty braced himself on his hands. "You need to let go, Kins."

"No," she protested.

Lefty didn't want to be amused, but he still was. Not able to stop himself, he leaned down and brushed his lips across her cheek. "Let go, sweetheart. I need to make sure you're all right."

Her eyes had been closed, but at the feel of his lips against her skin, she pried them open. "Gage?"

"Yeah?"

"Did you message me?"

Lefty frowned in confusion. "Yeah, you didn't get them?"

"My phone was smashed into a million pieces," she informed him. "I wasn't ghosting you."

Even though she was sick and had a fever, Lefty could see the worry and sincerity in her gaze. He put a hand on her cheek, and she relaxed her neck muscles until he was holding the weight of her head in his palm. "Okay, Kins," he told her.

"But I'm glad my phone was smashed because it kept you safe."

Lefty was confused as hell. "How?" he asked.

Kinley sighed and closed her eyes once more. "Thanks for getting me to the hotel. I'll talk to you tomorrow when I'm feeling better," she muttered.

"You want me to bring Gillian over to help get her changed?" Trigger asked, ignoring her hotel comment. She was obviously out of it and confused.

Lefty reluctantly stood and pulled his comforter up and over Kinley.

She was shivering again. He turned to his friend. "No, don't bring Gillian over yet. If Kinley's contagious, the last thing you need is Gillian getting sick too. She's wearing a T-shirt and leggings, she should be comfortable enough in those."

"If you need us, call." It wasn't an offer, it was a demand.

Lefty nodded. "I will. Thanks for helping rally the troops."

Trigger ignored his thanks. "I'll come over in a few hours to check on you guys. Are you going to bring her to the ER if she gets worse?"

"I can't," Lefty says. "Not unless it looks like I have no choice. I have to honor her wishes. Something's wrong. *Really* wrong, Trigger. If she doesn't want to go to a doctor, I have to believe she's got a very good reason."

"For the record, she seems more concerned about *you* than herself."

"I thought the same thing, which doesn't make any sense," Lefty said.

"She's safe here for now," Trigger said quietly. "You'll make sure she gets better, then you can find out the answers to all your questions. Just don't forget that you aren't a one-man band here. You've got your team waiting to help. And Gillian. You heard for yourself, she really likes Kinley. I don't know what it is about your woman that makes people want to bend over backward to help her, but there it is."

"She's not my woman," Lefty protested, the words tasting like ash on his tongue.

"Isn't she?" Trigger asked, but he didn't give him time to answer. "I'll let myself out. See you later."

Lefty watched his friend turn and leave his room. He heard the front door shut behind him, and knew Trigger would've made sure the doorknob was locked on his way out. Making a mental note to go and secure the deadbolt and chain in a bit, Lefty looked back down at Kinley.

Her black hair was dirty and knotted. Her cheeks were flushed and her pulse beat heavily in her neck.

Taking a deep breath, he turned and headed for his bathroom to get a cool washcloth. He needed to cool her down and break the fever that had taken hold, but he also wanted to clean her up. She'd hate feeling or looking dirty when she woke, and he vowed to do whatever it took to make her as comfortable as possible.

Four hours later, Kinley's fever still hadn't broken. She thrashed and moaned on his bed and, even though she was burning up, clutched the covers to her as if she were lying naked in Alaska in the middle of winter.

"I need to get you cooled down," Lefty murmured, more to himself than her. She hadn't really said anything coherent in a while, and he was getting more concerned that he was going to have to break down and take her to the emergency room.

"Leave him alone!" she yelled out of the blue, scaring the shit out of Lefty. "He has nothing to do with this!"

"Kinley, you're safe."

"Gage?" she asked, clearly confused.

"Yeah, it's me."

Her eyes popped open, and she stared up at him without the cloudy look of confusion she'd had for the last four hours. "Sparkly shoes," she said urgently.

"What?"

"It was the shoes," she muttered, closing her eyes.

Lefty sighed in frustration. She wasn't making any sense.

He knew he had to act.

He left her on the bed, going into the bathroom. He turned on the taps until the water was on the cool side. He wasn't heartless enough to dump her into a freezing-cold bath, but she still wasn't going to like being forced into water just on the edge of being lukewarm. To her overheated body, it would seem as if it was an ice bath.

He went back into his bedroom as the tub filled and steeled himself. This was going to be harder on him than it was on her, but it had to be done. Lefty had no idea if Kinley would hate him when she was more coherent, but he'd deal with that later. He'd much rather have an embarrassed woman on his hands than a dead one.

He sat next to her and tried to assess her state of mind. "Kinley, we need to get your clothes off so we can get you in the tub."

No response.

"Kins?"

She groaned.

Deciding that maybe it was better if she was completely out of it, Lefty pulled back the covers and ignored the moan that escaped Kinley's mouth at losing the warmth of the blankets. Working as quickly and clinically as possible, he stripped off her T-shirt and leggings. He left her underwear and bra on, not quite able to make himself remove them. It seemed a huge breech of her trust to disrobe her as much as he had, even if it was for her own good.

Lefty knew he could've called Gillian over to help, but he felt a deep-seated need to take care of Kinley himself. He had a feeling that she was somehow protecting him. From what or who, he had no idea, but from what little she'd said, it was clear she was scared to death and on the run.

He bent over and picked up a nearly naked Kinley, loving the feel of her in his arms. Her skin was too hot and she was too pale, but she fit him like a glove. Her five-five frame was tiny compared to his six-foot-one, but she was curvy in all the right places. He kept his gaze off her tits and concentrated on how smooth her skin was under his hands. She buried her nose into his neck again, and Lefty knew he'd never get tired of how that felt.

Knowing there was no good way to get her in the water, and that he'd made a mistake in not taking his own jeans and shirt off before he'd picked her up, Lefty stepped over the rim of the tub, thankful he'd taken off his shoes and socks earlier.

The water immediately soaked into his jeans, but he barely even noticed.

"This is gonna suck," he murmured to Kinley. "Hold on to me, Kins."

She moaned, whether in agreement or dismay, he wasn't sure. Being very careful, he slowly sat down in the water. He shivered at the temperature—but the second Kinley's skin touched it, she shrieked and arched her back, trying to get away.

"I know," Lefty commiserated, "but you need this. It's important."

"S-S-S-So cold!" she complained, and continued trying to sit up and get away from both him and the cool water.

Wishing the tub was deeper, Lefty shifted her in his grip until she was sitting on the bottom of the tub. He kneeled over her and lay her back into the water as gently as he could. It wasn't easy, as she fought him every second of the way. Water splashed all around them as she tried to kick and fight to get out of the tub.

Within a minute, she was too exhausted to do anything but lie in the water. Her breasts heaved up and down in her agitation, and Lefty knew if she wasn't feeling as horrible as she did, he never would've been able to hold her still. For a woman of her height, she was amazingly strong.

"I know it's cold, but your body's too hot, Kins. I have to get you cooled off."

"I'll be good," she said in a scarily flat, emotionless tone. "I won't sneak into the kitchen for food again. I promise."

Lefty's body went rigid. What was she talking about?

"Please. Let me up and you won't hear a peep from me again. I won't bother you. *Please*."

"Kinley, you're with me, Gage. You're safe. You're sick, and I'm trying to get your body temperature down."

"Don't hold me under! I'll be good. I'll be good!" Now she was whimpering, begging.

Lefty felt sick at what he was hearing. He didn't know who had punished her by holding her underwater, but there was no way he could continue to hold her down now. No way in hell.

He pulled her up on top of him and lay down in the water. This wasn't as conducive to getting her temperature down, as the water was only lapping at her sides instead of covering her entire body, but he didn't want her reliving even a second of whatever torture she'd already lived through in her past.

"Shhhh, you're safe, Kinley. I've got you, hang on to me. That's it."

She shoved her arms under his body and clung to his back as she lay on his chest and trembled. Lefty scooped water up with his hands and did his best to cool her down. He did that for about five minutes, then couldn't stand the shaking any longer, and he simply wrapped his arms around her and held her against his body. She was practically naked, and he was still fully dressed, but all he felt was gentle affection and worry for the woman in his arms.

"If I could trade places with you, I would," he whispered.

To his surprise, she shook her head. "No. I wouldn't wish my life on anyone."

He forced himself to stay in the tub for another five minutes or so. When Kinley's body finally stopped shivering, and she lay quietly on his chest, he took a deep breath, knowing he needed to move.

Getting out of the tub was harder than getting in. Kinley was no help, she was practically comatose, but her skin felt cooler. He gently placed her on the rug on the floor after he'd climbed out of the tub with her in his arms. He quickly stripped off his soaking-wet clothes, leaving them in a heap on the floor. Striding naked back into his room, he pulled on a pair of boxers and a T-shirt, and then grabbed one of his gray Army shirts from a drawer for Kinley.

He took the time to strip the bed and change the sheets. Now that she was a little cleaner than she'd been when he'd first brought her into his room, he wanted her to go back to sleep on freshly laundered sheets.

When he returned to the bathroom, Kinley hadn't moved from where he'd left her, and the sight of her lying completely still wasn't a good one. He knelt next to her and felt for her pulse, relieved when he felt it, slow and strong. He towel-dried her as best he could, then awkwardly got his shirt over her head. He quickly removed her bra before it could soak the shirt he'd just gotten on her.

Knowing he needed to remove her wet underwear, he closed his eyes and gently tugged the cotton over her hips and thighs. In any other circumstance, it might've been sensual; when she was sick and hurting, it was anything but.

That done, he pulled his shirt down, covering her, then he knelt and picked Kinley up once more. She helped a little this time, putting her arms around his neck and holding on when he stood.

Lefty gently placed her on his bed and pulled the covers back up and over her. She sighed and turned onto her side, pulling her legs up into a fetal position.

How long Lefty sat on the side of the bed and watched her sleep, he had no idea. All he knew was that it felt right having her there. He hated that she was so sick, but he couldn't deny that he liked having her in his bed.

Knowing he needed to get some food into her—he had no idea when she'd last eaten—Lefty forced himself to stand. Before he left the room, he ran the backs of his fingers down her cheek and whispered, "Whatever's wrong, I'm gonna fix it, Kins. I'm sorry I wasn't here when you needed me, but I'm here now."

The woman on the bed didn't respond, but that was all right. He was really talking more to himself anyway.

* * *

Kinley swallowed, and it felt as if she'd been sucking on cotton balls. She didn't understand why her mouth was so dry and why every muscle in her body hurt. Without opening her eyes, she tried to remember why she felt so crappy, but came up empty.

She'd obviously been sick, she recalled not feeling that great, but couldn't pinpoint exactly what had happened recently.

Opening her eyes, she froze.

She didn't recognize where she was. It wasn't her apartment back in DC, that was for sure.

And just like that, her memory kicked in.

She'd left DC because someone had tried to push her in front of the Metro. She'd driven to Texas, only to find that Gage wasn't there. She'd been sleeping in her car, waiting for him to get back from whatever mission he'd been on, and... and nothing. Everything after was a blank.

She did remember meeting Gillian, and spending a few days hanging out with her, but one morning, she'd felt so bad that she hadn't gone over to the apartment complex. She'd decided to just stay in her car in the parking lot of the factory she'd found.

And now...now what? Where was she? What day was it?

Rubbing her forehead, Kinley tried to remember something, anything, with no luck.

Hearing a noise, she sat up and scooted back on the bed. The quick movement left her swaying where she sat. The room spun, and she thought for a second she was going to pass out. By sheer force of will, she made herself stay upright and kept her eyes glued on the door across the room.

Taking a deep breath, she realized she recognized the underlying smell in the air seconds before the door opened quietly and Gage appeared. He was wearing a pair of sweat-pants and an old T-shirt. He hadn't shaved for several days and his eyes were bloodshot. He was carrying a bowl and concentrating on not spilling it as he walked toward the bed.

He stopped when he finally looked up and realized she was staring at him.

"Kins?" he asked gently.

Kinley swallowed hard and nodded.

"Are you awake? *Really* awake?"

It was an odd question. She was sitting up and looking at him. "Yes."

Gage carefully walked over and set the bowl on the table next to the bed. Then he brought a hand up and placed it on her forehead. She shivered at the feel of him touching her.

"You feel cooler."

"Cooler than what?" she asked in confusion. Then other things slowly sank into her consciousness. She was in what had to be his room, in *his* bed...and she wasn't wearing anything but a T-shirt. The covers on the bed were in abso-lute disarray and the room was a disaster. There was random clothing all over the floor, and she saw a few towels here and there. A couple of mugs sat on the table next to the bowl he'd just put down.

She licked her dry lips. "What am I doing here?"

He frowned. "You don't remember?"

Kinley shook her head.

"What *do* you remember?"

"Being in my car," she told him.

His frown deepened. "That's it?"

"Yeah. When did you get back?"

"Three days ago."

"*What?*"

"I got back three days ago," he repeated. "I came home, slept for about eight hours straight, got a call from Trigger, and I spoke with Gillian, who was worried sick about you since she hadn't seen you in two days. The guys and I fanned out, found you in your car, and I brought you back here. You've been sick with a fever for forty-eight hours. This is the first time I think you've actually been coherent."

Kinley stared at him in disbelief. "You took care of me?" she asked.

Misunderstanding why she was asking, Gage looked uncomfortable. "Gillian came over a couple of times, but you were pretty out of it. I'm sorry about...um..." He gestured to her body with his hand. "I had to undress you because you were burning up with fever, and I had to get it down. Then you threw up. I wasn't quick enough to get you to the bathroom, so I had to change your shirt. But I *swear* I was more interested in getting you warm and covered than in checking out your naked bits."

Kinley stared at Gage with wide eyes. It was impossible to process everything she was hearing. "You took care of me?" she said again.

"Yeah," Gage said, looking worried, probably because she was repeating herself. "You were adamant that you didn't want to go to the doctor. Trigger told me I was being stupid, that you could get brain damage if your fever didn't break, but I knew you had to have a good reason not to want to go to the emergency room. But I have to tell you, Kins, if your fever hadn't broken last night, I was going to take you, and we'd have dealt with the consequences later. You scared me, sweetheart."

Kinley's head was spinning. She had a lot to tell Gage about why she was there in the first place. What she'd witnessed in Paris, and why she didn't want to leave any kind of electronic trail Drake Stryker or Walter Brown could use to find her...but at the moment, she couldn't get the fact that Gage had actually taken care of her when she was sick out of her mind.

Tears formed in her eyes and spilled over her cheeks. She didn't make a move to wipe them away, kept her gaze on Gage. "I can't believe you took care of me."

He sat on the bed, his brow furrowed. "You were sick, Kins. *Really* sick."

"No one's taken care of me when I've been sick before."

"Well, other than being puked on, it wasn't exactly a hardship," he said with a smile.

Kinley shook her head. "You don't understand. No one's *ever* taken care of me when I've been sick." She knew she was repeating herself, but she wasn't sure how to make him understand. "The first time I remember being really sick, I was in elementary school. I think I had the flu. My foster mom freaked out and told me that she didn't have time to deal with a houseful of sick kids, so she told me to stay in my room and not come out until I was better. She brought me some crackers and water, but otherwise I was on my own."

A muscle in Gage's jaw ticked. He reached out and put a hand on the side of her face, brushing away a tear with his thumb, but he didn't speak.

"When I was a teenager, I remember being sick again, and just like before, I had to deal with it myself. My foster family was going on vacation, and they didn't want to cancel because I was sick, so they left me home while they continued with their plans."

"They left you home alone when you were sick to go on *vacation?*"

Kinley shrugged. "I wasn't really a member of their family

and was old enough to take care of myself. They'd been planning the trip for months. I understood."

"Well, I don't. That's bullshit! It was abuse." He looked like he wanted to say something else, but he pressed his lips together unhappily.

"What?"

"You gave me the impression that you weren't abused when you were in foster care."

"I wasn't," Kinley said, reaching up to wipe her tears away. "Not really. Not like a lot of kids were."

Gage caught her hand in his and brought it up to his mouth and kissed the palm before lowering it. Kinley's heart leapt in her chest but she kept her gaze on his.

"You truly don't remember anything from the last few days?"

Kinley shrugged. "Flashes here and there."

"Like what?" Gage pressed.

Kinley took a deep breath and closed her eyes, trying to remember. "Being really cold. Then hot. Being thirsty, and how much my stomach hurt when I was throwing up."

"Look at me, Kinley."

She opened her eyes and stared into his dark brown gaze. She felt guilty all over again when she really noticed how tired Gage looked.

"You aren't alone anymore," he said firmly. "I'm sorry you had such shitty examples of parenting. Even though you were a foster kid, those families did wrong by you. Leaving you alone, locking you in your room, excluding you from their family activities...it *was* abuse." He shook his head when she opened her mouth to protest. "You are an amazing woman, and now that I know some of what you've overcome, I'm even more impressed. But your time of being on your own is done. It might've taken twenty-nine years for you to find your people, but you have now."

Kinley frowned at him. She didn't understand.

"*I'm* your people," Gage told her. "And Gillian. Trigger, Brain, Oz, Lucky, Doc, and Grover too. You came to Texas for a reason, one we'll get to after you've eaten, maybe showered, and when you feel comfortable. You will *never* suffer through being sick alone again. I don't care if it's just a cold. You've got people here to care about you, who'll bend over backward to make sure you're all right. Understand?"

Kinley shook her head. No, she didn't understand. Not at all. "I don't even know them."

"They know *you*. Who you are in here," Gage said, resting his hand on her upper chest.

She knew he'd be able to feel her heart beating wildly in her chest, but she didn't pull away. It was as if they were in an intimate little bubble and nothing between them was awkward or weird.

"Gillian was distraught when she didn't see you for so long. She loved hanging out with you, said you even helped her out a lot with her business and haggling over price."

"It wasn't a big deal," Kinley protested.

"To her it was."

"Honestly, Gage. We didn't really do anything. I just sat on her couch and read one of her books she let me borrow. We didn't even talk much."

"Don't you get it?" Gage asked. "That's *why* she likes you. Because you're calming. Because you came into her life and just fit. Did it feel awkward to sit next to each other for hours without talking? Just reading?"

Kinley shook her head.

"Right. Because you were being yourself, and you let Gillian be herself. And Trigger already knew a lot about you from me, but after hearing how much Gillian liked you, your place in his life is solidified. The other guys have been calling and messaging nonstop asking how you are, if you're better, if we need anything. You didn't get any of my texts or emails, did you?"

Kinley blinked at the change of subject. She frowned and shook her head.

"Right. The guys all knew how upset I was when I'd thought you'd blown me off again, but the second they heard that your phone had been destroyed, they all understood you probably didn't even *get* most of my messages. Not to mention the fact that it's obvious you're in trouble, and by not answering any of my texts, you did what you could to keep that trouble from showing up on my doorstep."

At his uncanny insight, Kinley blanched.

"No, don't freak," Gage ordered, reading her reaction correctly. "Breathe, Kins," Gage said, bringing his hands up to her face and forcing her to look at him. "You said a lot of stuff that didn't make sense during your fever, but the mere fact that you're here and sleeping in your car said a lot without you having to say a word. Why did you come to Texas, Kinley?"

"It was on my way?"

"Wrong. Try again," Gage said sternly.

Kinley closed her eyes. She felt off kilter and naked, and not just because she was sitting in Gage's bed wearing only one of his T-shirts.

"Look at me, Kins."

She reluctantly opened her eyes.

"Why'd you come to me?"

And that was the crux of the issue. She'd come to Texas, but more than that, she'd gone straight to Gage. She knew he'd help her. Even though her being near him was putting him in danger, she'd still run straight to him. She'd already decided to trust him, and she needed to suck it up and be brave for once in her life. "Because you're my only friend, and I knew you'd help me."

"Damn straight," Gage said with an odd tone in his voice. "Whatever's wrong, I'm going to fix it. But I'm not your only friend. You've got Gillian and the rest of my team. I know this will be a hard thing to get used to, but you're not alone anymore. You get the sniffles and need some tissues and don't feel like going to the store, you call one of us. Your toilet overflows and you need a plunger, call. You simply want someone to sit quietly in the same room while you read a book, *call*. Understand?"

Kinley licked her lips and shook her head.

Gage smiled. "You will. I brought you some soup in the hopes that I could somehow get you to eat. But it's even better that you're coherent again. You hungry?"

"I think I want to know what I said when I was out of it."

He shook his head. "It doesn't matter what you said when you were out of your mind with a fever. What matters is that you're here. You came to me for help, and for a man like me, that says more than words ever could."

"A man like you?" Kinley asked.

"Yeah. Now, you want to go to the bathroom before you eat?"

Kinley was frustrated. She needed Gage to understand that her being here was putting him in danger. It seemed like a good idea to come to Texas when she'd been driving aimlessly across the country, but she was having second thoughts now.

"Kinley, concentrate. Bathroom or food?"

"Bathroom," she said automatically.

Gage smiled. "Come on, then. I'll get you a clean T-shirt to put on and while you're in the bathroom, I'll change the sheets. Your fever finally broke last night and you sweated all over everything. No—don't get embarrassed. I was fucking thrilled because it meant you were getting better, and I wouldn't have to resort to the emergency room."

He pulled back the covers and Kinley awkwardly pulled down the T-shirt she was wearing to cover her private bits. But like a gentleman, Gage turned his head, not looking until he was sure she was standing. Then he walked with her to the bathroom.

"Give me just a second," he said as he left her standing with one hand on the counter for balance. He was back with a T-shirt in his hand before she could move.

"Don't try showering yet. I know you probably feel gross, but I'm thinking you're still a bit too unsteady on your feet. After you eat and take a nap, we'll see how you're feeling, and we'll get you in there later, okay?"

Kinley nodded. It felt odd to have someone take care of her like Gage was, but she couldn't deny it felt good too.

He put the T-shirt on the counter, and then leaned down and kissed her forehead. His lips pressed against her skin for a long moment. He murmured, "I'm glad you're feeling better, Kins," then he was gone.

Looking into the mirror, Kinley almost shrieked in fright. Lord, she looked awful. Her skin was pale and she had dark bags under her eyes. Her black hair literally looked like a bird's nest, it was so matted and crazy around her skull.

Groaning, she leaned on the counter with both hands and her head drooped in defeat.

She'd never been pretty. She knew that. But for once in her life, she wished she was different. Wished she was witty and knew how to flirt. She wanted Gage to be bowled over by how beautiful she was. But instead, she'd apparently puked on him, had been out of her head with a fever, and was a pathetic mess.

"Kinley?" Gage called out from the other side of the door.

"Yeah?" she replied.

"Stop thinking. Do what you gotta do, change, and get back out here before your soup gets too cold."

Kinley couldn't stop herself from smiling. She had no idea how Gage knew she was in here overthinking everything, but she was. "Keep your pants on. I'm moving as fast as I can."

She had no idea how he'd done it, but somehow with one sentence, he'd pulled her head out of her ass and made her smile at the same time. She was in big trouble. She wasn't sure she'd be able to leave. Gage made her feel more than she'd ever felt about anyone. It was as if her life went from black and white to Technicolor simply because she was near him.

Thirty minutes later, Kinley's belly was full and she was sitting on the couch in Gage's living room. He'd hovered while she'd eaten, making sure she didn't feel sick and that she was going to be able to keep the bland soup down. He'd also brought her a bottle of Pedialyte, and when she'd raised an eyebrow at him, he'd told her it had everything she needed so she didn't get dehydrated.

Then he'd asked if she wanted to sit out in the other room while he called his friends to update them on her condition. Not wanting to be alone, Kinley had agreed.

Now she was sitting on his couch, half asleep, burrowed under a very soft, fluffy blanket. She'd listened with half an ear as Gage called Trigger, then Brain. She'd gotten the impression that his friends were going to contact the rest of the guys to pass on the word about how she was doing.

Gage came toward the couch, and Kinley was only half aware of what he was doing—until he sat right next to her, then lifted her so she was sitting across his lap.

"What are you doing?"

"Relaxing," he said on a sigh.

Kinley held herself stiffly over him. She wasn't used to being touched by anyone, certainly not sitting on a guy's lap. She wasn't sure where to put her hands or what she was supposed to do.

"I'm not going to hurt you, Kins," Gage said gently. "I'm exhausted. I haven't slept that well in two days because I was so worried about you."

She immediately relaxed slightly. "I'm sorry," she whispered.

"Don't be. There's nowhere I would rather be than by your side. Besides, you should be used to this...it's one of the only positions where you seemed to settle."

Kinley looked up at him. "Really?"

"Really."

Kinley had put on a pair of underwear Gage had pulled out of a stack of freshly washed clothes. She'd also donned the now-clean leggings Gillian had let her borrow last week that she'd never returned. She was more than aware that the only thing separating her from Gage was a few layers of cotton. She couldn't even think about what the situation had been while she was sick.

"You're thinking again," Gage accused, not opening his eyes. One arm was around her back, holding her, and the other was resting over her thighs. The weight of his arms was comforting rather than stifling.

"I just...you saw me naked," she blurted.

Gage didn't even tense. "Yup. But honestly, I was more concerned with how hot your skin was and if your brain was going to boil to really even notice anything else."

Kinley breathed out a sigh of relief.

Until he spoke again.

"But I can say with one hundred percent certainty that the fact you're still a virgin is a fucking miracle. You're beautiful, Kins. Every curve and inch of you is perfection. Don't doubt my attraction to you simply because I was able to take care of you without copping a feel. Any man who would try anything while you're out of your head with a fever is not only a douchebag, he's a predator who should be locked up forever."

His words made goose bumps break out on her arms. And he was right. If he'd said it had been hard to keep his hands off her while he'd been caring for her, she would've been weirded out. But the fact that he'd found her attractive, went a long way toward making her feel less like a scary troll who'd just crawled out of a hole in the ground.

She forced her muscles to relax, and she leaned against him.

"That's it," Gage murmured. "You're safe here. Relax. We'll both take a nap, then figure out what's next."

Sleeping on top of Gage was comfortable. Very comfortable. She closed her eyes—and the last thing she thought was how amazing it would be to fall asleep with Gage's arms around her every night.

Lefty was exhausted. Between the stress of worrying about Kinley and the sheer fact he hadn't gotten much sleep in the last four days, he was ready to drop on his feet. But he couldn't stop thinking about what Kinley had admitted.

She'd said a lot when she'd been out of her head with a fever. Not much made sense, but he understood that she was scared out of her fucking mind. That she'd fled Washington, DC, in terror. And that she'd come to him.

They might not have spent a lot of time together, but they'd connected, just as he'd thought. She hadn't ghosted him by not responding to his emails and texts; she simply hadn't received them. And now she was here, in his arms, safe. He'd do whatever it took to keep her that way.

They needed to talk. He needed to know what the hell was going on and what she was so afraid of. But first, he had to rest. Kinley was going to be all right, and if he was going to be able to think straight so he could figure out how to fix whatever was bothering her, he needed some sleep.

Holding Kinley when she'd been sick had been nice, but it had been tinged with worry. He'd slept in fits and starts, jerking awake every time she moved, hyper-aware of her needs. But having her relaxed and healthy in his arms felt even better.

Turning his head, Lefty kissed her forehead. She curled even more into him, and that small movement made his heart soar.

Whether she knew it or not, Kinley Taylor was his.

Anyone who tried to hurt her or take what was his would find that Lefty might be an easygoing guy in general, but when someone he cared about was threatened, all bets were off.

CHAPTER NINE

Kinley sat at Gage's small table next to his kitchen and tried not to freak about the conversation she knew was coming.

After they'd awoken from their nap on his couch, he'd brought her back into his bathroom and hovered outside while she'd showered. When she'd managed not to fall over and kill herself, and had gotten dressed, he'd come in and helped her with her hair. It took him a while to comb through it, but he didn't seem irritated by the job. Kinley had almost fallen asleep again as she sat on the chair he'd brought into the bathroom for her to sit on while he worked on her tangles.

She'd snuggled back on the couch while he'd showered and shaved. He'd made them a healthy dinner of baked chicken with green beans, which she barely made a dent in.

Then, when she'd thought he was going to ask her to explain what she was doing there, he'd surprised her by calling his mom.

He'd talked to her for a while before letting her know Kinley was visiting. Molly hadn't seemed surprised, just over-joyed to talk to her for a while. She'd told her how sorry she was that she'd been sick, and then proceeded to share a bunch of embarrassing stories about Gage when he was little.

Then they'd watched TV until Kinley had fallen asleep on the couch. Gage had carried her into his room, got her settled in his bed, and left her there. She'd been both relieved and disappointed, which made no sense whatsoever, but she'd been so tired she hadn't been able to stay awake long enough to try to figure out what her problem was.

Now it was morning, and her respite was over. It had been over two weeks since someone had tried to kill her, and she knew the guy was probably out there looking for her. She had no idea what to do next, or whether Drake Stryker or her ex-boss had actually ordered a hit on her.

Gage had made a big breakfast of waffles and eggs, and while she hadn't been able to eat much of either, she'd done her best. He was now sitting across from her sipping a cup of coffee.

"We need to talk," he said, and as nervous as she was, Kinley was still almost relieved it was finally time to share the burden of what she'd seen with someone else. She felt bad because she knew as soon as she told Gage, he'd be in danger too, but keeping the secret was hell on her psyche.

And realistically, she knew she'd put him in danger the moment she'd come to Texas.

She couldn't stop thinking about that poor girl who'd probably been excited and nervous about her upcoming evening when she'd put on those sparkly shoes, and then ended up dead in an alley. No one deserved that. Especially not a kid who hadn't even had a chance to start living her life.

A knock on the door startled Kinley, and she saw Gage sigh. "I'm guessing that's Gillian and Trigger. He said he would try to keep her from coming over, but I guess he wasn't successful. You want me to ignore them?"

Kinley frowned. "That would be rude," she said.

Gage grinned, but merely shrugged.

"I wouldn't mind seeing her," Kinley admitted.

Without a word, Gage pushed back his chair. He walked around the table to her, leaned over and kissed her temple gently, then headed for the front door.

Kinley loved the gesture, and she'd just stood up when Gillian came bursting into the room.

"Oh my God, you look so much better!" she exclaimed. "I'm so glad you're all right!" She dropped a bag she had in her hand on the floor and rushed right up to Kinley and gave her a huge hug.

Startled by the show of affection, Kinley could only stand there and return the other woman's hug awkwardly.

"You're smothering her, Gilly," Trigger said, the love and humor easy to hear in his tone.

"Whatever," Gillian said, but she took a step back anyway. "Seriously, you look great. Lefty's been taking good care of you. I wanted to come over and help more, but he said that he didn't want me getting sick and that he had it covered."

Alarmed, because she hadn't even thought about the fact that she could've gotten Gage sick, she turned to him. "Are you feeling all right?"

"I'm fine, Kins."

Now she was worried not only about some hitman coming after Gage, but that she might've gotten him sick in the process.

"I'm *fine*," Gage said again.

"I brought you some more books to read," Gillian said, bringing Kinley's attention back to her. "I wasn't sure if you'd finished the one you borrowed before. And I know I hate running out of new books to read. I've got plenty, so anytime you want to come over and browse yourself, feel free. You're always welcome at our place. Are you going to be staying here with Lefty? Because that'd be great!"

Trigger came up beside his girlfriend and put his hand over her mouth, stopping her from saying anything else. "What she means is...we're glad you're feeling better and if you need anything, all you have to do is ask."

But her words were already sinking in. Kinley hadn't thought too much about what she was going to do next. She'd been perfectly happy staying with Gage, but now she realized it might look...awkward. They weren't dating, even if he *was* the only man who'd ever seen her naked. She had to figure out where she was going to go next. Right after she told Gage her story and why she was there, she'd need to find a place to stay and figure out what her plans were.

"Breathe, Kinley," Gage said, putting his arm around her shoulders. "You're on the mend, but I'd feel a lot better if you weren't gallivanting around the city. You could have a relapse."

"I can't stay, Gage," she told him quietly.

"We'll talk about it," he said smoothly.

"I didn't mean to make you uncomfortable," Gillian said with remorse. "I just thought...I don't know what I thought. But if you need a place to stay, you can always stay with me and Walker. I feel as if you're a friend now, and I'd feel horrible if you went back to sleeping in your car when we have a perfectly good guest room you could stay in."

"She's not sleeping in her car *ever* again," Gage said firmly.

"Okay. Good."

There was another knock at the door, and Kinley looked up at Gage questionably.

"I'll get it," Trigger said. "Be good," he admonished Gillian playfully before he headed for the door.

Within seconds, the room was full of Gage's team.

"You look a lot better than the last time I saw you," Brain said.

"Definitely," Oz echoed.

"Good to see you up and about," Lucky added.

"I brought her keys," Doc told Gage, putting her keychain down on the counter.

Grover didn't say anything, but gave her a small chin lift in greeting.

The room was downright crowded now, but surprisingly, Kinley didn't feel hemmed in at all. She was the shortest person there, by a long shot, but Gage had put his arm back around her shoulders and, at his side, she felt safe and comfortable. It was an odd feeling, one she'd never experienced when in a group of people before. Usually she parked herself against a wall and did her best to fade into the background.

"Um...hi?" Kinley said uncertainly. She'd met the men before while in Paris and Africa, but wasn't sure why they were all there now.

"What did we miss?" Lucky asked. "Did you start without us?"

"No," Gage said. "Gillian wanted to come over and say hi first."

"Start what?" Kinley asked, looking up at Gage.

His arm tightened around her shoulder, but he didn't respond.

"That's my cue to leave," Gillian said with reluctance. "I don't know what's going on, but I hope you know that I'm ready to help too," she told Kinley. "If you need anything, I'm here for you."

Kinley could only nod. Gillian smiled at her, then went up on her tiptoes to kiss Trigger before she headed for the door.

No one said anything until she was gone. The second the door shut behind her, Gage said, "If anyone wants coffee, help yourself." Then he steered Kinley into the living room and set her down in the corner of the couch. He took a seat right next to her, not giving her any extra room. His thick thigh touched hers, and even though she was tucked into the corner, Kinley didn't feel threatened.

The other guys eventually got settled around the room and everyone looked at her expectantly.

"Kins, it's time to tell us everything," Gage said gently.

Feeling like an idiot because she hadn't seen this coming, she shook her head. "No, just you, Gage."

"That's not how this works," he said seriously. "I know you're scared, it's obvious. But these men have our backs. You know we're a team. We have no secrets from each other, and there's no one I trust more than them to help me make sure you're safe."

Kinley didn't like this. She'd planned to tell Gage what she'd seen but still hoped to minimize the number of people in danger. She should've known better. She'd been on her own her entire life; she hadn't even thought that he might want to share her problems with his friends.

"It's not that I don't trust them, it's just..." She trailed off, not sure how to say what she felt without offending the big alpha men around her.

"It's just what?" Gage asked.

Knowing she was going to have to spit out what she was thinking, Kinley took a deep breath and just went for it. "It's bad enough I'm putting *your* life in danger. I don't want anyone else to get hurt because of me. And the more people who know, the more lives are at risk."

The room was silent for a beat before Brain asked, "Is she serious? Are you serious, Kinley?"

She couldn't read his tone, so she just nodded.

"Fuck me," Oz said under his breath.

"Kinley, look at me," Gage said.

She turned her head—and saw he was looking at her with amusement. "You know what we do. What we're sent around the world to do. Are you seriously trying to protect *us*?"

"You don't understand. It's bad," she whispered.

"Then tell us, so we can help you figure out whatever it is," he urged.

Kinley looked around the room at the six other men. They were all focused on her, and she could read compassion and genuine affection in their gazes. They weren't pretending to be patient with her, they actually were. She had a feeling they'd sit there all day if that's what it took for her to get up the guts to tell them why she was there.

The thought of any of them getting hurt or dying because of what she was about to say made her extremely uncomfortable.

"I saw something I shouldn't have," she said after a moment.

When she didn't elaborate, Doc asked, "What did you see?"

This was it. Right now, there were only a couple of people who knew what she'd seen in that alley. Her ex-boss, probably Stryker, and her. She doubted either of the men had told the hitman why he was supposed to kill her, but it was possible. If she told these men sitting in Gage's living room, it would more than double the people who knew. Was that a bad thing? She truly had no idea.

Taking a deep breath, she made her decision. "Two weeks ago, right before we left Paris, The Alleyway Strangler killed another victim."

The men around her all looked confused, but they nodded.

"I remember seeing that on the news," Grover said. "The girl was found in an alley on the other side of the city from where the conference was being held, right?"

Kinley nodded. "I saw the story on the news when I got back to DC. And I..." This was it. If no one believed her, she wouldn't really be surprised. She could hardly believe it herself, and if she hadn't gotten fired and someone hadn't tried to flatten her, she might've gone on thinking she was imagining things.

Gage reached over and took her hand in his. He twined their fingers and squeezed. His actions gave her just enough courage to continue.

"I wasn't very tired that last night in Paris, and I was awake in the middle of the night. I was looking out my window, wishing I had a better view than just an alley next to the hotel. A car pulled up...it had diplomatic plates...and a man came out of a door in the hotel, holding on to a woman. She was obviously drunk or something because she could barely walk. I recognized him. It was Drake Stryker."

"The US Ambassador to France?" Brain clarified.

"Yes."

"You're sure it was him?" Doc questioned.

"One hundred percent. He looked up for just a second, and I saw his face as clear as day," Kinley said firmly. "He got into his car with the woman and they drove away." She paused, trying to get her thoughts together.

None of the men interrupted her. No one told her to hurry up and get on with her story. They patiently sat, silent, waiting for her to continue.

"When I got back to my apartment in DC, it was late, and as I said, I turned on the TV for some background noise. The news was on. They were talking about another victim killed by The Alleyway Strangler. It was her. The woman from the alley."

She heard someone inhale sharply but wasn't sure who it was.

"How do you know?" Trigger asked gently. He didn't sound doubtful, just curious.

"Her shoes," Kinley breathed.

"Sparkly wedges," Gage said from next to her.

She looked up at him in surprise. "Yes, how did you know?"

"You talked about them when you were sick," he said. "Sorry, I didn't mean to interrupt. Go on."

Feeling off kilter, wondering what else she'd blabbed when she was out of it with fever, Kinley continued. "Right, she had on a pair of sparkly high heels. I remember thinking when I saw her in the alley how much I liked them, feeling sad because I'd never be able to wear them. High heels hurt my feet. But they were so pretty, and they made me think of Cinderella." She laughed, but it wasn't a humorous sound. "When the news ran a clip from the crime scene, they showed a body covered in a tarp, but her feet were sticking out. She still had on those same sparkly high-heel shoes. Then I found out she wasn't a woman at all—she was a kid. She was fourteen years old. I kinda freaked out."

"Rightly so," Oz muttered.

"I know what I saw. That didn't mean the ambassador was a serial killer, of course. But I couldn't get it out of my mind. He was supposed to spend the evening with my boss, and I didn't know if he'd picked up the girl after their meeting and then dropped her off somewhere, and The Alleyway Strangler found her after *that* and killed her, or what. So I called Walter to talk to him about it. The last thing I wanted to do was accuse the ambassador when I had no proof."

"Shit," Brain said.

"Yeah. Shit," Kinley echoed. "He talked me down, told me he'd never seen the girl and that I was imagining everything. He told me the police wouldn't believe me, that there were probably thousands of women who had those same shoes. I started doubting myself."

When she didn't say anything for a while, Grover asked, "Then what happened?"

Kinley sighed. "I was fired."

"What? Why?" Gage asked.

It felt good that he sounded pissed on her behalf, but it didn't change how she felt about being fired. "I was called into HR two days later and informed that I was being fired on suspicion of treason."

"Treason?" Lucky exclaimed. "That's bullshit!"

Kinley smiled at him. "Thanks for the vote of confidence. But HR had proof that I'd emailed Walter's schedule to an unsecured Gmail address—some reporter's—three days before we left for Paris. And that sort of thing is definitely against all protocol, for obvious reasons. That's how politicians get assassinated. They said that since I couldn't be trusted, my employment was terminated immediately."

"Did you see the email?" Brain asked.

Kinley nodded. "Yeah. It was just the itinerary and a note, supposedly from me, saying that everything was going on as planned. But I *didn't* write or send it. I swear."

"No one thinks you did," Gage soothed.

But Kinley wasn't done. "Right. Well, I had to clear my desk out right then. They had a security guard watching over me the whole time, making sure I didn't steal anything, I guess. It was extremely humiliating, and I was so confused, because I was accused of something I didn't do and didn't even get a chance to defend myself.

"I was on my way home, with my things in a cardboard box—so cliché—and wasn't really paying attention to everything around me. I was waiting for the Metro when someone pushed me. Hard. I had just decided to go back and try to plead my case and...suddenly my things went flying. The box I was carrying fell onto the tracks. Luckily, I caught myself right at the edge of the platform—and two seconds later, the Metro went flying by. I remember my hair blowing in the wind from the train. When I looked around, I didn't see anyone who looked like they might be trying to kill me, but I *knew* that's what had just happened."

No one said a word for a moment, but Brain got up and began pacing the room.

"I went back to my apartment and grabbed my go-bag. I always keep one packed with some of my important stuff. I learned that as a foster kid. A lot of times, I didn't get a chance to pack all my things. Anyway, I threw in some clothes and left a note for my landlord, plus the next month's rent, but I'm guessing by the time I've figured this out, he'll have cleared out my stuff and rented the apartment to someone else." She shrugged. "I waited until it got dark and snuck out to my car in a parking garage a few blocks away. I got five thousand dollars out of my savings account the next day, and I haven't used any credit cards since then."

"Smart," Brain said as he continued to pace. "If someone was able to plant a fake email in your account, they'd probably easily be able to track where and when you're using your credit cards."

"That's what I thought," Kinley admitted.

Then she took a deep breath. She'd done it. Told them what happened. No one said she was crazy for suggesting the ambassador might be a serial killer or thinking someone had pushed her on that train platform.

All her life, people had second-guessed her. It felt really good to be believed now.

"Why'd you come here?" Trigger asked.

Kinley looked down at her hand clasped in Gage's. She was embarrassed to admit her real reason, but she'd been honest so far, she didn't want to start lying now. "I hadn't planned on it. I was going to go northwest. To North Dakota or somewhere. And I did. I drove around aimlessly for a while, but then I found myself heading south toward Texas. I didn't want to put anyone else in danger. I know what I felt on that train platform, but I also knew that if I was going to get someone to listen to me, to believe me, I needed help. I figured Gage would maybe know someone in the FBI who was trustworthy."

She felt fingers under her chin, and she turned her face toward Gage. He caressed her cheek with his thumb before he said, "You did the right thing. My team and I are going to help you. If the ambassador is a pedophile and a murderer, he's not going to get away with it. Not to mention, I'd bet any amount of money that your ass of a boss is in this up to his eyeballs. I'm sorry I wasn't home when you got here."

Kinley shrugged. "I should've known you might be on a mission."

"I'm gonna keep you safe, Kins," Gage said tenderly, staring into her eyes.

"You can't promise that."

"I can, and I am," he swore.

Kinley knew if Stryker or Brown really wanted her dead, they had the money to hire someone to make sure that happened, but it still felt good that Gage was willing to do what he could to keep her safe. She wasn't sure she'd done the right thing in confiding in him and his team, but what was done was done. She'd have to live with the consequences of her actions.

She just hoped those consequences wouldn't be the death of the man sitting next to her...or his friends.

CHAPTER TEN

Lefty wanted to lash out. Throw things. Fucking kill whoever it was who'd *dared* lay a hand on Kinley. But he had to control himself. Kinley needed him to be calm and rational. They needed a plan.

"Brain?" he asked as he watched his teammate pace back and forth. He was the smartest man on the team, and when he got like this, it was a sure sign his mind was working overtime.

"Unfortunately, Brown was correct in that it'll be hard to prove Stryker is a serial killer based only on shoes. Especially considering it was the middle of the night, and thus dark, and she was a couple stories above the alley. But the hotel surely has video cameras, and it should be easy enough to at least prove the girl was with him that night, and possibly Brown too. Phone and email traffic between the two men—including anything that might look fishy—should be relatively easy as well."

"'Fishy' like child porn," Trigger suggested.

"Exactly. That girl was fourteen. And if I'm remembering right, The Alleyway Strangler's other victims were also underage. The police can track the ambassador's movements compared to where the girls were last seen. But ultimately, Kinley's right, she can't just go to the local cops with her suspicions. They won't take her seriously, and it'll be her word against that of a friend of the fucking president's. Not to mention, these crimes took place in France. Any accusations made will be up to Paris police to follow up on. Brown can be investigated here in the States for the child porn thing, but ultimately, this is France's case."

"Unless he killed before he was stationed overseas," Lefty said.

"Very true. It's doubtful his desire for underage girls manifested itself only after he got to France."

"What about Cruz Livingston?" Trigger asked suddenly.

"Who?" Kinley asked with a tilt of her head.

"Cruz Livingston," Lefty answered. "He's an FBI agent who works out of San Antonio. We know him through a friend of a friend. We could ask him to come up and keep things unofficial until we hear what he thinks. Maybe he could look into murders in DC involving underage girls, as well as start a child porn investigation. It's possible he can also clear you of treason charges. You didn't send those emails, and I'm sure with his connections, he can somehow prove it. The last thing we want is that shit being brought up in court by a defending attorney."

"I can do some digging," Brain said. "Anything I come up with won't be official, but if I can pass it on to Livingston and give him a head start, it won't be a bad thing. Honestly, if the only thing the prosecutors have is shoes, it's likely the case won't go anywhere. But if there's video, and other evidence..." His voice trailed off.

Lefty turned back to Kinley. "You're staying here."

She blinked. "I can't."

"You can," he countered. "And you will. If you think I'm

gonna let you go stay in a hotel, or your fucking car, or be flitting around when someone's already tried to kill you once, you're insane."

"I could've imagined it," she said weakly.

"You don't believe that any more than I do. If you did, you wouldn't be here right now," Lefty countered.

She bit her lip and refused to meet his eyes.

"Look at me, Kins," Lefty said.

He waited until she met his gaze. "This isn't going to be over anytime soon. Because of Stryker's political connections, he's got a lot of power. He's going to hire the most expensive and successful lawyer he can find. The prosecutors are going to have to have all their ducks in a row before they accuse him of anything. In the meantime, you aren't safe. Especially since it seems Stryker has already set the ball in motion to shut you up. You came to me for a reason. It was the right thing to do, and I'm going to do everything I can to protect you."

"I appreciate it, but part of me still questions why you'd agree to help some nobody. And now I realize I've put your careers in jeopardy. I mean, I'm not sure you guys can fight two career politicians who know the president personally. I obviously didn't think this out as well as I should've."

"You're not a nobody," Gage said firmly. He leaned forward and wouldn't let her drop his gaze. "You're *not* nobody. You're Kinley Taylor. You're funny and smart, and I haven't been able to stop thinking about you since I first met you in Africa. You're considerate and kind, and while I'm not happy about the reasons behind you being here, I can't deny I'm fucking thrilled to see you."

He didn't think Kinley was even breathing, but he kept going, not caring that his friends were listening. "I'm not worried about my job, because I believe in you. If you say that you saw the ambassador to France with The Alleyway Strangler's last victim, I believe you. And we're going to find a way to nail his ass so he can't hurt anyone else."

"He's personal friends with the *president*," Kinley said softly. "You don't know the kind of power that exists in Washington, DC. I should've just kept my mouth shut."

"What was her name?" Lefty asked.

"Émilie Arseneault," Kinley told him, knowing exactly who he was talking about.

"You think Émilie's not worth fighting for?"

Kinley was shaking her head before he'd finished asking the question.

"Right. Someone has to stand up for those who can't stand up for themselves. Émilie certainly can't talk about what happened to her. I won't lie and say this will be easy, because it won't be. But if you were the kind of woman who could ignore a girl being murdered, I wouldn't be so attracted to you."

Kinley flushed.

"I think that's our cue to head out," Doc said, the humor easy to hear in his voice.

"I'll be in touch with anything I find out," Brain said. "I'm going to start with some basic internet searches. I won't get too crazy into this because the last thing I want to do is lead a hitman straight to Texas."

"When you're ready to talk to Cruz, let me know and I'll reach out to him," Oz offered.

"My sister's coming into town tomorrow, but you know I'm here if you need anything," Grover said.

"You need help moving her in?" Lucky asked Grover.

Grover eyed Lucky for a moment before nodding. "That'd be great. I don't know how much stuff she's brought. I got the impression she left pretty quickly, but she's not telling me much."

"She in trouble?" Lucky asked, his brows furrowing.

"With Devyn, there's no telling," Grover said honestly.

"I'll come over to your place in the morning, we can head to her apartment together."

"Sounds good."

Trigger waited until everyone had left before turning to Kinley. "I second what Gillian said, you're welcome at our place whenever you want. You don't need to call ahead of time. Although if we don't answer right away, we might be busy." His eyebrows waggled up and down suggestively, making Kinley laugh.

"I think I'll call, if that's all right with you," she said with a grin.

Trigger smiled, but then he sobered. "Gillian's friendly. Very friendly. People like her. But she's picky about who she decides to be friends with. Especially with everything that happened down in Venezuela and after."

"Um...okay?" Kinley said.

"What I'm trying to say is, it's rare that she clicks with someone as easily as she has with you. She's got three friends she's had forever, and as long as I've known her, she hasn't really tried very hard to get close to anyone else. Inviting someone into our apartment so they can eat, shower, and do their laundry is—unfortunately, for my peace of mind—just like something she'd do. *But*, she wouldn't invite them to stay, and she certainly doesn't lend them her precious books. She likes you, Kinley. When she said she'd love to spend more time with you, she was serious. She already thinks of you as her friend."

Lefty had his hand on Kinley's back, so he felt her muscles tighten. He moved without thought, pulling her into his side. She stood stiffly in his half embrace and stared at Trigger as he continued.

"Not only that, but *I* like you too. I've known Lefty a long time, and I've never seen him so worked up over a woman.

Worked up in a good way, that is. Trust him, and trust us, to help you through this. I'm guessing it won't be easy, and there won't be a fast solution, but we'll do everything in our power to keep you safe from whoever wants to silence you."

Kinley studied Trigger for a long moment before nodding. "Thank you."

"You're welcome." Trigger then gave Lefty a chin lift and turned and left the apartment.

Lefty moved to lock the door behind his friend and when he turned back to Kinley, she was staring at the door. "Come on, Kins," he said, pulling her into his side again and leading her back to the couch. "How do you feel? Do you want something to eat? Some orange juice?"

She shook her head.

"Talk to me," he begged. "What's going through your head?"

She turned and met his gaze. He could see the confusion and how overwhelmed she was just by looking at her. How he'd come to know her so well in such a short amount of time, he had no idea, but there it was.

"I don't understand."

"What don't you understand, sweetheart?" he asked gently.

She shrugged. "I'm just me. I've never really had friends. I told you that I'm weird. I don't understand how your friends can decide so quickly that they like me. They should be leery. I've brought *danger* straight to your doorstep. And all of your careers could be over just like that." She snapped her fingers, demonstrating her point. "Stryker or Brown could easily ruin your careers with one word to the right person. You should be pushing me as far away as you can."

"That's not going to happen," Lefty told her. He needed her to hear him, so he did something he'd never done before —he used his size and strength to overwhelm a woman. He eased Kinley back until she was half lying on the couch, and he sat at her hip with his hands on either side of her, effectively trapping her.

"I need you to listen to me, Kins. Really hear me. Are you listening?"

She nodded, her eyes wide, and he felt her fingers grab ahold of his forearms and her nails dig into his skin.

He wanted to look down, see her hands on him, but he forced himself to look her in the eyes. "I don't know what it is about you that has me wanting to slay all your dragons. I'm furious that Brown broke your trust so badly. And before you defend him, there's no other explanation for that email being found so soon after you'd confided in him. I'm guessing he immediately called Stryker and blabbed, and one or both of them decided you had to be taken out, and they hired someone to do their dirty deeds."

She nodded slightly and licked her lips. Lefty was distracted for a second by the sheen her tongue left behind. He wanted so badly to lean down and taste her, but he refrained...barely.

"Trigger wasn't lying, I've been talking to him about you for months. I like you, Kinley. A lot. The last thing I want to do is take advantage of this situation, but I have to admit, I'm not upset that you need a place to stay. I'm not going to overstep my bounds with you, you can sleep in my bed and I'll stay out here."

"Gage, no!" she exclaimed, her fingers flexing on his arm. "That's not fair."

"You ready to let me sleep with you?" he asked. "And I truly do mean sleep, nothing else...yet."

She bit her lip, and he lost her gaze.

Lefty held her chin until she looked at him again. "That's what I thought. Me sleeping on the couch puts me between you and the door, and it makes it easier to protect you," he told her. "I want you to get used to me. See that I'm not like the other clueless assholes you've obviously known your whole life. I want you to get to know me, faults and all.

"When you invite me into your bed...or *my* bed, as the case may be...I want you to be one hundred percent confident in the fact that I want to be there. That you're an amazing woman who deserves the best from her man. He should cherish you and encourage your so-called weirdness, not try to change it *out* of you. I want you to want me as much as I want you, to the point that you'd do just about anything to have me."

She blinked but didn't respond.

"This situation isn't ideal," Lefty said, stating the obvious. "But that doesn't mean we can't get to know each other like any other man and woman who are dating. You can find out my quirks just as I'll find out yours. I already know when you're sick, it guts me. It makes me crazy, and it was impossible for me to leave your side. Gillian offered to sit with you so I could get some sleep, but I refused. There's just something about you that calls to me, Kinley. I want to see where that can go. But...and this is the important part..." he said solemnly.

Kinley licked her lips again, and once again, Lefty had to force himself not to move. Not to lean down and cover those lips with his own. "What's that?"

"You are under no obligation whatsoever to do anything you don't want to."

Her brows furrowed.

"I like you, I'm not lying about that. But if you don't feel the same about me, I'm not going to freak out or get violent. I'd no sooner touch you in anger than I would my mother or anyone else I love. I'll be upset, and sad, but you're allowed to feel however you feel. Do *not* feel as if you have to enter into a relationship with me if you don't think you could one day love me. I'd much rather be your friend and have you in my life in some capacity, than have you date me when you don't feel the way I do."

The words popped out without Lefty thinking about them.

"Don't panic," he said when he saw her doing just that. "I'm *not* saying I love you. I don't know you well enough to be able to feel that yet. But, I can honestly say that I've never been as intrigued about a woman as I am you. And I feel as if it'll take years for me to find out all your secrets, and I'm actually looking forward to it. Every piece of you I uncover feels like a victory. All I'm saying is that you have a safe place to stay here with me, and it comes with no strings. I'll help you no matter what our personal relationship is because it's the right thing to do. For you and for Émilie, and for all the other victims of The Alleyway Strangler. Understand?"

She nodded, but said, "You're going to be disappointed in me."

"Not possible," Lefty told her without hesitation. "If anything, *you're* the one who'll be disappointed. I didn't have the strength to let Gillian help you when you were sick, despite knowing it would've been the right thing to do. I might be strong physically, but when it comes to you, I'm as weak as a kitten."

One of her hands came up to his face, and Lefty felt his heart rate increase when she palmed his cheek. "You're the only man who's ever seen me that way. Am I...do you think... Shit." Her eyes closed, and she started to drop her hand.

Lefty moved quickly, placing his hand over hers, keeping the connection between them. "What? You can ask me anything, sweetheart."

She looked him in the eye and asked, "Did I look okay?"

He blinked. "What?" he asked, uncertain what she meant.

"Never mind," she mumbled.

"If you're asking me if I liked what I saw when I held you in my arms, the answer is no."

She stiffened, but Lefty kept going. "I didn't like that you were burning up with fever. I didn't like the way your body seemed as if it was roasting from the inside out. I didn't like how you looked *through* me instead of at me. I didn't like that you thrashed in my arms because you were scared I was going to hold you under the water in that tub. And I didn't enjoy taking your clothes off to bathe you, changing your shirt when you threw up on the one you were wearing, or using a cool washcloth to wipe you down while trying to get your fever to abate.

"I was wholly focused on getting you better, not on what your body looked like. I'm a man, Kinley, but not an asshole. I wasn't going to ogle you when you were completely out of it and helpless.

"But if you're asking if I find you attractive, the answer is a resounding yes. Now that you're better, and I know I'm not going to have to break your trust and bring you to a doctor when you clearly didn't want that—for good reason, I might add—I've been fighting a damn erection all morning. Watching you eat, drink...hell, even just sitting here watching you bite your lip has my cock standing up and begging to touch you. You have absolutely no worries when it comes to your body, Kins."

She was blushing now, but he liked that she didn't have the embarrassed look on her face that he'd seen earlier.

"I like your body too," she said shyly.

Lefty smiled. "Good. Now, I'm gonna get up and find something to do in the kitchen. I don't know what, but I'll figure it out when I get there. If I sit here with you looking all soft and cuddly under me for too much longer, I might forget all my chivalrous words and do something that will make you think I'm a louse."

"A louse?" she said, chuckling.

"Yup. You okay after everything that's happened today?"

She thought about it for a second, then shrugged. "Do I have a choice to be anything but?"

"Yeah, sweetheart, you do. What's happened to you throughout your life sucks. It's not fair, and you deserve a hell of a lot more. If I was a better man, I'd let you go, so you can find someone who doesn't have to be gone for weeks at a time. Who lives in a big house and works a regular nine-to-five job."

"What if that's not what I want?" she asked.

"What *do* you want?" he retorted.

"To be loved just as I am," she said immediately. "All my life, that's all I've *ever* wanted. I don't need fancy clothes, jewelry, or a huge house. I just want someone to want *me*."

Lefty felt his heart lurch in his chest. She asked for so little, but she also asked for everything. He wanted to be the man who could give her what her heart desired—but it also scared the shit out of him. "Don't ever settle," he ordered.

"I won't," she whispered.

Lefty couldn't stop himself from leaning down and kissing her forehead. Then he stood up and went into the kitchen to find something to keep him busy before his desires overwhelmed his good sense.

* * *

Kinley lay on the couch right where Gage had left her in a daze. It had been an emotional few hours. Nothing in her life had changed from when she'd left DC, but somehow it felt as if *everything* had changed. Gillian seemed to genuinely like her, which was crazy because all she'd done was mooch off her and sit on her couch and read a book, but Kinley was going to roll with it.

Gage's friends believed her, even though doing so could seriously hurt their own careers. They were already trying to think of ways to help her and, amazingly, they even knew an FBI agent who might be willing to listen to what she had to say.

And then there was Gage.

She couldn't help but feel overwhelmed with everything he'd said, but in a good way. All her life she'd been looked through as if she were invisible. But Gage *saw* her. Moreover, he seemed to like what he saw. It was crazy. Insane. But it also felt right.

From the first time she'd talked to him in Africa, Kinley had felt a connection with him. It made no sense, and she'd never held even a scrap of hope that he might feel something back, which was part of the reason why she hadn't messaged him after Africa. She'd been trying to protect herself from another heartbreak in a long line of them throughout her life.

But now here she was. In his apartment. And he'd said she'd be sleeping in his bed. It was almost surreal. She wanted to be confident enough to tell him he could sleep with her. To do *more* than sleep. But she knew if she had sex with him, and he walked away afterward, it would destroy her.

She wasn't a tease, at least not on purpose, but she'd never met a man—or woman, for that matter—who she'd felt as if she could trust both her body and heart to. And until she did, she'd stay a virgin.

Thinking about Gage and sex made her uncomfortable... but not in a bad way. She felt as if she was finally coming awake after being asleep for a very long time. She shifted on the couch and her thighs rubbed together, reminding her how long it had been since she'd given herself relief.

Closing her eyes, she suddenly felt exhausted.

It could've been a minute later or an hour, but she felt

Gage drape a blanket over her. Snuggling into the warmth, Kinley smiled when she felt his lips against her temple.

"Sleep, Kins."

"I'm so tired," she mumbled.

"You were really sick. Your body's still recovering. Just relax."

"Gage?"

"Yeah?"

"Thanks for believing me."

"I'll always believe you, Kinley," he said firmly. "Believe you and believe *in* you."

With those beautiful words floating in her head, she slept.

"This is bullshit. She needs to be silenced!" Drake Stryker barked into the burner phone he was going to get rid of after this phone call.

"She's smart," replied Simon King, a man known for being willing to take on dirty jobs no one else wanted to do.

"She's a chick; she's not *that* smart," Stryker scoffed. "I can't believe you fucked up a simple job."

"Don't piss me off," Simon said gruffly. "You want her dead, you can come to the States and take care of shit yourself."

Stryker took a deep breath. He couldn't afford to lose King. He needed him to take care of his huge problem. There was no way he was going to spend the rest of his life in jail. *No fucking way*. Especially not because of some nosey bitch. He had to make sure she kept her mouth shut about what she'd seen. "Sorry. I'm just frustrated," he told the hitman he'd hired to find and kill Kinley Taylor.

"Right. She just got lucky on that Metro platform. She was just starting to turn when I pushed her, and the angle was wrong when she fell. I hadn't really planned on doing the job right then, but figured I might as well when I had the chance. Anyway, I followed her home, and when I broke into her apartment that night it was obvious she'd already taken off. I watched her place for a while and she never returned. Do you have any other information for me to go on?"

Stryker frowned. He *hated* this. He'd had to bring someone else into this mess, which wasn't good. The fewer people who were involved, the better, but he and Brown had needed someone to plant the email in her account, and the same man was watching her bank accounts and trying to track her electronically. "She took out most of her money not too long after your attempted hit. She filled up her gas tank in DC and hasn't used her credit card since."

"Are you tracking her license plate?"

Stryker ground his teeth. "Yes, but it's not that easy. She's avoided any toll roads, and my guy doesn't have the time to look through every traffic cam in the country to try to find her."

"What about friends? Family?"

"She's got no one."

"Well, that makes things harder," King said without any kind of emotion. "She could be literally anywhere in the world then."

That lack of emotion was what made him such a good hitman. He didn't get all worked up about who he was being paid to kill. It didn't matter to him. Women, teenagers, old men...he'd whack anyone if the price was right.

"She hasn't left the country, we know that," Stryker said. "Because her phone was destroyed on the tracks—thanks to you—we don't even have *that* to go on." He tried not to sound pissed, but it irked him that one of the best ways they had to track her had literally been smashed to pieces in King's assassination attempt.

Stryker'd had nothing but bad luck when it came to Kinley Taylor, and it was beginning to unsettle him. It was as if the universe was on *her* side rather than his.

"You hired me to kill her, not keep track of her fucking belongings," King growled.

"Whatever. Anyway, my guy took a look at her phone records from the last six months or so, and the only person outside of her job who called or messaged her was a guy who lives in Texas."

"And?" King asked.

"She never responded, but it sounds like he wanted to be more than friends, if you know what I mean. But there's a problem."

"What?"

"He's Army. Delta Force."

"What's the connection?" King asked, not sounding worried in the least.

Crazy motherfucker, Stryker thought. "Nothing that we know of. But he was in Paris a few weeks ago. He and his team were assigned to guard Johnathan Winkler. And the same team guarded Kinley Taylor's boss in Africa months ago. They could've met then."

"I don't know or care who the fuck Winkler is, but if that's all you've got, give me the details and I'll head down to Texas to check things out."

Stryker was starting to hate this asshole, but he gave him the info on Gage Haskins that their contact had managed to ferret out.

"I'm going to need cash to get down there," King informed him.

Biting back the bitter response, Stryker agreed.

"And my fee for this job is now two million instead of one."

"What? No fucking way!" Stryker exclaimed. "We agreed on one. You can't change the terms now!"

"I can't? Seems to me that I'm holding all the cards here. You gonna fly back to the States and find her yourself? *You* gonna kill her?"

"I could," Stryker bit out. "She wouldn't be the first bitch I fucking choked. It's not as hard as you think."

King chuckled, but it wasn't a humorous sound. "Seems to me two million's not a very high price to pay if it keeps your hands clean. I don't know why you want this chick dead so badly...but I can find out."

Stryker was so furious, he wanted to reach through the phone and fucking kill the asshole on the other end. "Fine. Two million. I'll have the money for getting to Texas wired. But you're not getting a dime of the millions until I have proof she's dead. If she's not breathing, she can't tell anyone what she saw."

"Done," King told the ambassador. Then clicked off the connection.

Stryker wanted this bitch dead. He didn't care when it happened. Tomorrow, next week, ten years from now. She'd dared to accuse him. *Him.* He was the fucking ambassador to France. He'd had dinner with the president. Hell, he'd fucked the man's wife in one of the bedrooms in the White House while her husband had been on some humanitarian trip.

If Kinley Taylor thought she could narc on him, she was wrong. Dead wrong.

No one cared about the teenagers he'd killed. They were runaways or prostitutes. Trash. Throwaway human beings that were as important as the gum people spit on the ground.

Still, he had no choice but to agree with all of King's terms. Of *course* he couldn't fly to the States undetected and do the deed himself. The man had him by the short hairs, and they both knew it.

"Fucking asshole," Stryker muttered before dropping the phone to the ground and stomping on it. When it was nothing more than a pile of tiny plastic pieces, he headed back down the alley toward his car and driver.

He needed to call Walter and find out if he'd heard anything about the missing assistant. And to make sure the man had kept his own mouth shut about the entire situation. Though, he wasn't so worried about that. Brown was as involved in this mess as he was. He might not've killed the bitch that night a few weeks ago, but he'd certainly had his fun with her. Including taking a few videos for his personal collection.

Brown had also done him a solid by immediately letting him know what his assistant had told him.

He needed Walter Brown to be his eyes and ears in Washington, DC. If even a whisper of this got back to the president, Stryker knew he'd be fired in a heartbeat. The president would do whatever it took to cover his own ass, and if that meant throwing his friends under the bus, so be it.

"I'm going to find you, Kinley Taylor," Stryker said softly as he sat against the expensive leather in the backseat of his government-provided car. "You're going to regret not keeping your mouth shut."

CHAPTER ELEVEN

The last few days had been weird for Kinley. She hadn't felt hemmed in at all in Gage's apartment. She didn't mind being by herself, and it hadn't been hard to promise Gage that she wouldn't go anywhere, not even stick her toe outside the door, when he had to leave to go to work. He'd wanted to take time off to stay with her, but she'd shooed him away after promising not to go outside for any reason.

His apartment was surprisingly comfortable. Kinley usually felt uneasy being in someone else's space. She didn't want to touch anything or mess it up. She knew that was a byproduct of being a foster kid for so long. All the homes she'd lived in hadn't been hers, and she'd gotten yelled at so many times for touching things that didn't belong to her, she'd learned to keep her hands to herself.

But Gage's place was cozy. He didn't have any expensive knickknacks sitting around and all the books on his book-shelves were well worn, as if he'd read them many times over. He had blankets and pillows on his couch and, since he'd been sleeping there, they smelled like him.

More often than not, Kinley found herself napping on his

couch after he left, loving being surrounded by his earthy scent. Because she'd never slept—or done anything else—with a man before, she hadn't realized how comforting it could be to fall asleep with the masculine smell in her nostrils. But maybe it was just Gage's scent that had the ability to soothe her.

One day, when she'd been bored, she'd rearranged his kitchen. Only afterward had she been afraid he'd get pissed at her, but he'd merely smiled and pulled her into a hug and thanked her.

They talked for hours, from the time he got home until they went to bed. She'd found herself opening up and telling him things she'd never told anyone before. In return, he told her stories about his own childhood. And instead of it making her feel sad that she hadn't had a stable upbringing for herself, she loved that *he* did. She'd already liked his mom, but hearing what a wonderful mother she actually was, now she liked her more.

Living with a man was an eye opener, for sure. She hadn't thought she'd be comfortable in the least, but something about Gage made the experience...easy. She'd thought they'd be tripping over each other and she'd constantly be saying embarrassing things. But the reality was that they'd fallen into a routine quickly. And it just seemed to work.

He'd get his clothes ready in the evening before they went to bed, and in the mornings, he'd sneak into the bathroom in the master bedroom and shower. The sound of the water would inevitably wake Kinley, and she'd wander into the kitchen and turn on the coffee before snuggling under the still-warm blanket on the couch where he'd slept.

Gage would apologize for waking her up, get a cup of coffee, and he'd sit at her feet on the couch as they talked about what his schedule was like for the day. He'd warn her not to go outside, and then he'd leave. Kinley would nap for a while then get up and shower. Gage would return home in the afternoon and they'd decide whether to order out or make something together. Her choice was always to cook, because she loved puttering around his small kitchen with him.

Today was Saturday, and Gage had the day off. Because she was a creature of habit, Kinley woke at the same time she had been for the last few days. She lay awake on Gage's bed and thought about him sleeping on the couch in the other room. She'd tried again to get him to take his bed, but he'd refused, saying the day he made her sleep on the uncomfortable couch while he was in the bed was the day he'd quit the Army and give up his man-card...whatever that meant.

Quietly, Kinley slipped out of bed and picked up her pillow. She padded into the living room and watched Gage sleeping for a moment. He had one arm thrown over his head and one foot was sticking out of the blanket covering him. She hadn't previously thought about what he wore to bed, but from her vantage point, it looked like he was completely naked.

She could see his muscular chest where the blanket had slipped down...and she had an intense urge to investigate the tattoos she could see. She wasn't seeing anymore skin than she might if they were at the beach or pool, and he was in a bathing suit, but because he was sleeping, it seemed a lot more intimate.

The decision to join him on the couch hadn't seemed all that odd a second ago, but now she was undecided. She should return to his room and go back to sleep there. She didn't want to wake him on one of the few days he had to sleep in.

"Kins? What's wrong? Are you all right?" he asked sleepily.

Dang. She must've made some sort of sound to wake him.

"I'm good," she told him softly. "I'll just..." She gestured to the hallway behind her.

"Come 'ere," Gage said, holding out his hand.

Biting her lip, Kinley was undecided. She wanted to bolt back to the safety of his room, but another part of her wanted to stay. Wanted to take his hand and see what would happen.

He didn't say anything else. Didn't pressure her in any way. Just lay there looking mussed, sleepy, and oh so sexy.

Kinley stepped toward him, putting her hand in his.

The satisfaction on his face was easy to see, but he didn't say anything. He pulled her down so she was sitting in front of him. "Drop the pillow, you won't need it. Lie down, sweetheart."

As if in a trance, Kinley lifted her feet and brought them up to the couch. Gage put his arm around her waist and pulled her into him until they were spooning so tightly, she didn't know where she stopped and he started.

She lay stiff in his arms, wondering what the hell she was supposed to say.

"Go to sleep," he whispered, and she shivered when his hot breath wafted over the sensitive skin of her neck.

Sleep? Was he serious?

She felt his nose nuzzle against her hair for a second, and he said, "You always smell so good."

"I think that's my line," she blurted.

He chuckled and squeezed her waist. "Are you comfortable?"

She thought about it for a second before nodding.

"We've got another hour and a half before we need to get up and start getting ready," he told her.

Kinley nodded. They were going over to Grover's sister's new apartment. Something had happened with the delivery of her things, and they'd been held up somewhere. They were supposed to finally arrive that morning, and everyone was going over to help her move in.

Kinley wasn't thrilled. She liked hiding out in Gage's apartment. She felt safer here than she'd felt in a very long time. Besides, she never made the best first impression, so she wasn't all fired up to meet Devyn. She knew the other woman was tall, blonde, and beautiful, and Kinley hadn't had the best experiences with women like that. But she'd rather have her fingernails pulled out one by one than admit it to Gage...or Grover.

"You aren't going to be out of my sight," Gage said, misreading her tension.

"I'm not worried about that," Kinley admitted.

"Good. Because as long as you're with me, you're safe."

He'd said that over and over in the last few days, and Kinley didn't doubt it for a second. "I know," she told him.

"Then what's bothering you?"

"Nothing really. I was just thinking about today. And... um...are you comfortable?" she asked, wanting to change the subject.

He stilled behind her, then his arm lifted off her waist and he somehow managed to put a few inches of space between them. "Shit," he muttered. "I didn't think. I'm sorry. I didn't mean to haul you into me like that or pressure you. Go on back to bed, we don't have to get up yet."

Kinley's heart dropped. She hadn't meant to make him think she didn't like being next to him. She was such a dork. She always seemed to say the wrong thing at the wrong time.

Not thinking about it, she turned onto her other side until she was facing him. She scooted forward and shoved one arm under his body and the other around his waist. Then she wiggled until her nose was pressed against his neck. She held on to him as if he were a giant teddy bear.

"Kinley?" he asked uncertainly.

"I don't want to go back to bed," she said mulishly. "I'm comfortable here."

"Thank Christ," Gage muttered before she felt his arms clamp back around her. He shifted until he was on his back and she was pressed against his side, half lying on top of him and half next to him. It was a tight squeeze on the couch, but Kinley didn't care.

He shifted some more, until she felt the blanket he'd been using settle over both of them. Now she was cocooned against him. His scent surrounded her and the warmth from his body seeped into her own. He was naked except for a pair of boxers...and she'd never felt anything she liked more.

"Better?" he asked when she sighed in contentment.

She nodded against his shoulder. Kinley wanted to memorize the moment, but being held by him was like a drug. Her eyes closed and she felt exhausted.

"Sleep, Kins."

"*Ummm*," she mumbled deep in her throat.

She thought she heard him chuckle, but she was asleep before she could think about it.

* * *

Lefty was wide awake.

He was tired. He hadn't been getting enough sleep. Every little noise made him sit up in alarm, just in case someone was trying to break into his apartment to get to Kinley.

Brain was being very careful in searching for answers, and so far hadn't been all that successful. Cruz Livingston, the FBI agent, was driving up to Killeen from San Antonio in a few days to hear Kinley's story firsthand. Lefty had no idea what the next steps would be, but he vowed to stay by Kinley's side every step of the way.

Lefty had never lived with a woman before. Had never

had the desire to. But he had to admit, coming home after working all day was a hell of a lot better with Kinley in his apartment. Her shy, welcoming smile made all his aches and pains from working out with the team disappear. He loved puttering around his kitchen with her. She wasn't the best cook, but then again, neither was he.

She'd sworn that she was perfectly happy hiding out in his place, and he hadn't seen any signs that she was lying.

Kinley didn't seem to care about anything most women did. She hadn't mentioned needing to buy anymore clothes; she'd only brought a few outfits with her, but seemed to enjoy wearing his oversize T-shirts with her leggings. And, of course, he wasn't going to complain. He loved seeing her in his clothes. Maybe it was the caveman in him, but seeing his too-big T-shirt swimming on her made something deep inside him growl in approval.

She was perfectly content to sit in his apartment all day and amuse herself. She didn't seem to be going stir crazy in the least. She was a woman who was happy being by herself, and that was something he hadn't experienced before. He liked it.

The more he was around her, the more Lefty was intrigued, and the more the connection he'd felt in Africa and Paris grew. He loved talking with her about everything and nothing. She'd opened up about her childhood, and hearing more details had made his heart hurt. If ever there was a girl who'd been begging for someone to love her, it had been Kinley.

When she'd insisted, he'd told her some stories about his own family, and while it made him feel guilty that he'd been so blessed and spoiled, she'd told him that it made her heart feel good to hear how happy his childhood had been.

It had only been a few days, but Lefty had no idea how

he'd lived without seeing her every day of his life. She made him laugh, but she also calmed something deep within him.

But any calm he'd felt over the last few days was thrown out the window the second he pulled her into his arms on his couch.

He'd touched her plenty. Hugs, an arm around her shoulder, putting his hands on her waist as he moved her out of his way in the cramped kitchen, but nothing compared to this.

She was wearing another one of his shirts, but her legs were bare. He felt them entangled with his own, and it was all he could do not to shove them apart and press his hard-as-nails cock between her legs.

Virgin, he thought to himself. He couldn't do anything that might scare her. Besides, he'd promised to behave.

Kinley's slow, even breaths were warm against his chest and he tightened his hold on her. He felt more satisfied and content simply holding her like this than he'd felt after fucking any of the other women he'd been with.

Lefty didn't understand it, but he decided not to overanalyze. He hadn't meant to rush her, to pull her into his arms, but now that she was there, he had no idea how the hell he'd manage to ever sleep again without holding her.

The hour and a half they had before they needed to get up went by way too fast. Lefty had stayed awake the entire time, wishing the clock would stop and he could hold her this way forever.

The alarm on his phone sounded, and Lefty leaned over to grab it from the table next to the couch and turn it off. Kinley groaned and snuggled deeper into him.

"Not a morning person?" he asked.

She shrugged.

"But you've been getting up with me every day this week."

"And then going right back to sleep on the couch after you leave," she mumbled.

Lefty chuckled. "The couch? When you have a perfectly good bed?" he teased.

"Smells like you," she said softly.

Lefty closed his eyes briefly, and it took everything in him not to turn and trap her under him.

Virgin, virgin, virgin, he chanted to himself. "I admit that I like how my bedroom now smells like you," he told her.

She picked up her head, and he smiled. Her hair was a mess, flattened on one side and sticking up wildly on the other. She had a crease on her cheek from lying on him and her eyes were unfocused from sleepiness. "I'm not ready for... you know. But I definitely liked this," she said, nodding to his chest.

He smiled. She wasn't very articulate when she just woke up. He'd have to remember that. Hell, who was he kidding? There was no way he'd forget anything about her. "I like this too," he said. "But whatever we do or don't do, it's up to you."

He watched as her eyes cleared and she stared at him. "I... Do you think we can try the bed tonight? I mean, if you don't like it, or if it's too uncomfortable for you, it's okay, I just—"

Lefty put his finger over her lips. "I'd like that. A lot."

"I'm not a tease," she said seriously after pulling her mouth away from his finger.

"I know you're not. I can control myself, Kins. Are you gonna freak out if you feel my erection against you? Because I might be able to control where I put my hands and what we do in bed, but I can't exactly control my reaction to you."

She blushed, but she didn't break eye contact. "I'm not going to freak," she told him. "I might be a virgin, but I've... um...seen pictures and videos and stuff. I know how sex works. And I've had orgasms and used toys."

Lefty inhaled deeply and closed his eyes again. Thinking about the woman in his arms playing with herself and using a vibrator almost pushed him over the edge. He wasn't a porn man, didn't find it exciting in the least, but watching it with Kinley? Yeah, he could definitely get on board with that.

"Gage?" she asked, pulling back a little.

He tightened his arm and stopped her from moving any farther away from him. He opened his eyes and knew they were probably dilated. His dick was hard and ready to fuck, but he did his best to ignore it for now. "Good," he told her. "I can handle you being a virgin, but the thought of having to teach you *everything* is a little daunting."

She smiled shyly.

"I need to get up and shower if we're going to get to Devyn's apartment on time this morning," he said.

Her grin faltered. "Oh...okay."

Lefty leaned forward and nuzzled a spot behind her ear, going so far as to lick her skin before nipping her earlobe. "I'm gonna need some extra time in the shower this morning to take care of...things. Having you in my arms for the last hour and a half was the sweetest kind of torture."

He picked up his head and looked at Kinley.

She was still blushing, but she said, "I think an extra-long shower for myself is necessary too. You know...just to make sure I'm clean before I meet Grover's sister."

Lefty groaned, and another vision of her standing in his shower, dripping wet, with her hand between her legs was enough to make his cock weep in excitement.

"Up, woman. Start the coffee. Relax for a while. And Devyn's gonna love you. Wanna know how I know?"

"How?"

"Because you're you." Lefty then sat up with Kinley in his arms and plopped her on the cushion next to him. His cock was still hard, but he did his best to ignore the way her eyes took him in from chest to knees. He stood there for a moment, enjoying the way her own pupils dilated as she drank him in.

"Like what you see?" he asked. He wasn't usually self-conscious about his body, but this was Kinley. Her opinion mattered.

She licked her lips and nodded.

Lefty couldn't resist reaching out to touch her once more before he retreated to his bathroom to take care of his needs. He ran his knuckles down her cheek then gripped the back of her neck. He leaned down and kissed her forehead, then brushed his lips against her cheek.

"Be back soon," he told her, then strode out of the room, doing his best to think about anything other than how soft Kinley's skin was, and how badly he needed her in his life on a permanent basis.

* * *

Kinley wasn't sure how she'd survived the morning. First there was sleeping in Gage's arms. She'd never slept better and had never been so comfortable. She'd had no idea sleeping with a man could feel so good. Except she had a feeling it was simply because it was Gage's arms she was in that made it so comfortable.

Then there was the embarrassing admission about masturbating. She could've died right then and there, but somehow Gage had made it not so embarrassing, especially when he'd admitted he was going to get himself off in the shower.

She'd seen his erection—how could she not—behind the boxers he'd been wearing, and it had both impressed and scared the shit out of her. She wasn't an expert, but his size was daunting. She'd kinda hoped to lose her virginity to someone with a smaller-than-average penis, but Gage definitely wasn't small by any stretch of the imagination.

In the end, she'd been too embarrassed to masturbate in

his shower, but she'd definitely thought about it. And Gage, being Gage, hadn't made things awkward after they'd both gotten dressed. They'd sipped their coffee and he'd toasted her a bagel and put extra cream cheese on it, just how she liked it.

They'd arrived at Devyn's apartment and stepped into the middle of World War Three. At least that's what it felt like. Grover wasn't happy with his sister's choice of apartment complexes, saying it wasn't safe. Devyn, in turn, told her brother he was being high-handed and ridiculous and she was twenty-nine and could take care of herself.

The bickering back and forth between brother and sister was pretty humorous. And the longer Kinley was around them, the more envious she became. She would've given anything to have a brother or a sister. Especially a brother like Grover. He was overprotective, and his concern for Devyn was obviously coming from a place of love. She'd had plenty of foster brothers and sisters over the years, but no one had cared for her like Grover obviously cared about Devyn.

Gillian had shown up to help as well, and Gage had ordered both women to stay inside and assist in the placement of boxes. Kinley was perfectly okay with that, as it would keep her out of sight of anyone who might want to do her harm. There were large chunks of time that she was able to forget that someone was probably out there trying to find her—*and kill her*—because of what she'd seen, but being outside the safety of Gage's apartment made her wary, and she was hyper-alert for anything that seemed out of the ordinary.

She was currently sitting on a chair in the corner of the small living area, staying out of the way and watching as Devyn ordered the guys about, telling them where to put her things.

If she hadn't been looking at the other woman at the exact moment she reached up to grab a box off a stack that Grover had carried in, she would've missed it.

But there was no mistaking the large bruise on Devyn's side.

It was yellow and obviously almost healed, but Kinley knew that whatever caused it had to have hurt like a son of a bitch.

She inhaled sharply. Devyn and Grover didn't hear her as they disappeared into a room, still bickering.

But Lucky did. "What's wrong?" he asked.

"What happened to Devyn?"

Lucky's eyes narrowed. "What do you mean?"

Kinley hesitated at the tone of his voice. "Um...it's not my business, really. I was just surprised by the size of the bruise on her side. It's huge."

Kinley couldn't miss the hardness that crept over Lucky's face. "Which side?"

"Her right one. It looks mostly healed now, but it's pretty big."

"I'll ask her about it and make sure she's okay," Lucky said.

Kinley wasn't sure that was the best idea, as it truly wasn't *his* business either, but she appreciated that he seemed worried about her. "I haven't had a lot of opportunity to talk to her today, but I like her."

Lucky looked distracted now, but he said, "I'm sure she likes you too," before he stalked away.

"Hey, Kinley, wanna help me in here?" Gillian asked. "I swear Devyn has eight thousand cups and like two plates."

Kinley nodded and stood, still worried about the bruise she saw on Devyn's side. She'd been kicked once in one of her foster homes, and it had hurt like hell, even weeks later. The other woman wasn't moving as if she was in pain, but she had a feeling there was a lot more to Devyn than the breezy person she was pretending to be. She'd already heard from Gage about how she'd suffered leukemia as a child, and that would make a lasting impression on anyone.

Two hours later, Kinley was sitting on the couch with both Devyn and Gillian, all the guys elsewhere. Brain, Oz, and Doc had called it a day, heading home. Grover and Gage were taking the broken down boxes to the recycling center, Trigger was picking up some food, and Lucky was sitting in his car out in the parking lot, keeping an eye on the building, just in case. Gage hadn't wanted to leave her without protection, so Lucky had volunteered to stay and keep watch over the apartment. When he'd planted himself in a chair in the corner of the living room, Devyn had glared at him and pointed to the door.

Amazingly, Lucky hadn't protested—but he'd shot a look at Devyn that Kinley couldn't interpret before leaving without complaint.

Kinley had been nervous to meet Devyn, but the other woman turned out to be very down to earth. She was indeed gorgeous, but she didn't act like any of the popular girls she'd known back in high school. At five-eleven, Devyn was tall, and definitely pretty enough, to be a model, but she didn't seem bothered that she'd worked up a sweat and her hair was up in a messy bun.

Kinley felt guilty that she'd judged Devyn before knowing her. She'd been nothing but welcoming and friendly since they'd been introduced.

"Want to tell us what's up between you and Lucky?" Gillian asked, settling back on the couch cushions.

"No," Devyn said grumpily.

"I know we just met, but I've known Lucky for a while now, and he's normally the happiest of all the guys. It's hard to rattle him. But he definitely seems rattled."

"He cornered me and asked me some uncomfortable questions," Devyn reluctantly admitted.

Gillian sat up in alarm. "He was harassing you?" she asked.

Devyn sighed and shook her head. "No, not like that."

"I'm sorry," Kinley blurted, figuring she knew what Devyn was talking about. "I didn't mean to make you uncomfortable. I told him about the bruise on your side."

Devyn turned to her, and Kinley did her best not to shrink back. "*You* told him? How'd you even know?"

"I saw it when you reached for a box. I mean, it's none of my business. I just remembered that when I was around fifteen, one of the kids in the foster home I was in didn't like me. He got his friends to hold me down and he kicked me, really hard. He would've hurt me more, but my foster dad arrived home and he had to let me go. I didn't say anything about it because that would've made my life even worse, but I had a bruise just like that, and it hurt like hell for a really long time." Kinley knew she was babbling, but the last thing she wanted was for this woman to dislike her.

"I was worried about you. You've been lifting boxes and stuff all day. I didn't tell Grover because he's your brother, and he probably wouldn't've been happy at all. I didn't think Lucky would react like he obviously did. I'm *really* sorry."

She held her breath as Devyn stared at her for a long moment. "What happened to your foster brother?"

Kinley wrinkled her nose. "What do you mean?"

"I mean, he and his friends assaulted you. What happened to them?"

"Nothing. I didn't tell anyone, but I talked to my case manager and begged her to move me to a different home. Of course there *were* no other homes, because not a lot of people want to foster teenagers. I told her I'd rather be in a group home than go back to the one with that kid who hated me. She agreed, and I moved out that week."

Kinley heard Gillian say under her breath, "Jesus," but she kept her eyes on Devyn.

"I'm all right," Devyn said quietly. "Thank you for not telling Fred. He would've freaked."

Kinley was confused for a second, then realized Fred must be her brother. "And Lucky *didn't?*"

Devyn chuckled. "He did. But in a more subdued way than my brother would've."

"What happened?" Gillian asked.

When Devyn didn't say anything, Gillian tried again. "I know you don't know us, but nothing you say will make *us* freak. Hell, I was held hostage and almost shot, and Kinley's on the run after witnessing a serial killer's last moment with his latest victim."

Devyn's eyes almost bugged out of her head. "Are you serious?"

"Unfortunately, yes. Now spill before the guys get back with the food."

Devyn sighed, then said, "It's not a big deal. My boss back in Missouri decided he liked me. And when I turned down his numerous offers to take me out, he got pissed. Was a dick at work. Then one day, when I didn't move fast enough for him, he pushed me. I hit an exam table and fell. Then he kicked a little stool with wheels on it, which hit me in the same place the table did. I'm fine though. I quit right then and there, and now I'm here."

Kinley winced in sympathy.

"What an asshole," Gillian muttered.

"Yeah," Devyn agreed.

Kinley had a hundred questions she wanted to ask. Starting with, why had Devyn come to Texas? Sure, her brother was here, but she was twenty-nine, old enough to not hide behind a big brother. She also had another older brother who lived in the same town in Missouri where she had. And why didn't she press charges against her boss? From every-thing Grover had said today, Devyn was a damn good vet assistant, so she could've gotten a job anywhere, including another in Missouri.

But instead of asking the questions swirling around in her head, she kept quiet. She and Gillian were strangers to Devyn, it was unlikely she'd open up to them. It was amazing enough she'd told them how she got the bruise.

"Well, I'm sorry. But I think you'll really like this area. I've found people in Texas are generally nicer than in other parts of the country. Of course, we have our assholes and problems, but more often than not, you'll find people want to help rather than hurt. And it goes without saying that me and Kinley are here if you want to talk or just hang out."

"Thanks, I appreciate that," Devyn said.

Just then, they heard the front door opening. Kinley tensed until she heard Gage's voice call out, "We're back!"

As much as she liked Gillian, and now Devyn, it was somewhat worrisome spending time with them because Kinley knew she was putting them in danger. Whoever had tried to kill her was still out there. And the more time went by, and the longer she stayed in one place, the easier it would be for him to find her...if he hadn't already done so.

The absolute last thing she wanted was for anyone to get hurt because of what she'd seen. The sooner she talked to the FBI friend of Gage's, the better. She just wanted this to be over, but she knew in her gut it would be a long time before she would have her nice boring life back.

* * *

That evening, Lefty watched Kinley carefully. Something was bothering her, and he hoped like hell it wasn't that she was nervous about the upcoming night. She didn't seem worried that morning when she'd asked him to sleep in his bed with her, but she could be having second thoughts.

"You all right?" he asked when she'd sat back down on the couch after getting up for the tenth time. "You seem...unsettled. If you've changed your mind about our sleeping arrangements, I'm not going to get upset."

"It's not that. I just...I'm both anxious and nervous to talk to your FBI friend."

Lefty sighed. "I wish I could make this better for you. Make it disappear."

"I know. But you can't. I can't unsee what I saw, and I can't just forget about it either. Especially when, while in foster care, no one ever saw *me*."

"If I knew you, I would've," Lefty said firmly.

Kinley smiled at him and shook her head sadly. "You wouldn't've. And that's okay. I'm weird, but I was even weirder back then. Besides, I'm not telling you this for sympathy, I'm trying to explain how I feel."

"Sorry, go ahead," Lefty said. "But do you think maybe I can hold you while you do it? I'm guessing I'm not going to like this story."

Without hesitation, Kinley scooted over and leaned into him. Lefty put his arm around her shoulders and pulled her into his side.

"I was picked on a lot," Kinley started. "I mean, I was the quirky foster kid with no one to stand up for me. I had no friends and no family. I was an easy target. I got picked on every day for twelve years. I didn't get any less odd in college, so the teasing continued there, but not as bad, as people were generally more interested in passing their classes or getting laid. Anyway, when I was in the tenth grade, there was this guy who was especially mean. Every day, he'd knock my books out of my hands or find something about me to make fun of.

My shoes, my hair, my clothes, something. It was miserable, but I put up with it.

"One day, the boy shoved me so hard I fell against the wall and banged my head. He laughed about it before turning his back on me and leaving with his group of friends. There were at least a dozen people who witnessed me getting hurt. No one offered to help. No one went to the principal about that boy. No one wanted to get involved and possibly have him turn his attention on them.

"I don't ever want to be like those people. It would be easier if I just ignored what I saw in Paris and went on with my life. But then I'd be just like those kids back in high school. I can't help Émilie, or the other victims, it's too late for them, but I *can* help the next girl. I'm scared, Gage. I don't want to do this...but I have to."

Lefty had never been prouder of someone in his life. "It's not easy doing the right thing," he told her softly, kissing her temple. "It's fucking hard. But I'd never ask you to keep quiet. Even if it meant keeping you safe. Because I know it would harm you mentally. I hate that you're involved, but I'm as proud as I can be that you're standing your ground. I'll do whatever it takes to help you through this journey. One day at a time, sweetheart. That's what we'll do. Okay?"

"Okay," she said softly.

"I think Cruz will be here the day after tomorrow. You'll tell him what you saw, and we'll figure out what our next steps will be from there."

"I don't want you to be my babysitter," she said.

"You're a grown woman, you don't need a babysitter," Lefty told her.

"Right, and yet you're spending all your free time locked in here with me. I know this can't be your idea of a good time."

"Look at me," Lefty said sternly. He waited until she'd picked her head up and he had her attention before continuing. "I *like* being in my apartment with you. I know you don't see yourself this way, but you're interesting and funny. You're calming. I've never looked forward to coming home after work before, simply because my place always seemed dark and cold. But now I can't wait to be released for the day because I get to come home to *you*. I don't need you to have dinner waiting for me, or for you to do my laundry and clean the place. You just sitting on my couch, smiling as I come through the door, is enough to make me thankful that you found your way to me in Texas."

She eyed him skeptically.

Lefty chuckled. "I'm not lying, Kins. I *like* having you in my space."

"I don't want to be afraid of leaving your apartment, and yet I still am."

Lefty's stomach lurched. He hated that for her. He urged her to rest her head against him once more. "You're not a prisoner here. I just need you to be very careful. We've parked your car a few blocks over in another apartment complex, just to be safe. But if you want to go out, I'm not going to tell you no. As I said earlier, you're an adult. And you got yourself out of DC and to Texas safely."

"But that's just it, the longer I'm in one place, the greater the chance whoever tried to kill me will find me."

Lefty nodded. "I know." And he did. A part of him *wanted* to lock her in his apartment and never let her go. But he couldn't do that. "I wish I could stay with you twenty-four-seven. Although, then you'd probably start hating my guts because you'd get very sick of me staring at you like a lovesick puppy and following you around." He squeezed her shoulders, letting her know he was kidding... sort of. "But I have a job that I have to do. My boss is pretty understanding, but I'm not sure he'd let me sit at home like a slug until this whole thing with the ambassador is figured out."

"I'd never ask that of you," Kinley said.

"I know you wouldn't. But the time's gonna come when I have to go on a mission. You'll be on your own, and you'll have to go out to get food and other necessities."

"I also need to figure out what I'm going to do money-wise," she said.

"For now, you don't need to worry about it," Lefty said firmly.

"How can you say that?" she asked, pulling away from him once again. "I have to eat. And I can't sleep in your bed forever."

"Why not?" The two words popped out without thought. Lefty sighed. "Look, you already know how much I like having you here. It's not exactly a hardship. And it's not as if you're eating me out of house and home. I've got plenty of money, Kins. Enough for you to hunker down here until this shit gets figured out. In the meantime, Gillian's said that you've been helping her make some phone calls and negotiate. Maybe she can hire you part-time."

Kinley blinked, then frowned. "I'd never ask her for money for helping her out."

"Which is why she'll probably insist on paying you," Lefty retorted. "Listen, all I'm saying is that you don't have to figure this all out right this second. Stay here with me. No strings attached."

"The second you get sick of me, you have to tell me," Kinley said sternly.

Lefty couldn't help it, he laughed.

"Don't make fun of me," Kinley said.

"I'm not," Lefty told her. "I'd *never* do that. But the thought of *me* getting sick of *you* is hilarious. You're so unob-trusive, it's not even funny. I'd say there are times I forget you're here, but that would be a lie. Even when you read your books and we don't say a word to each other for hours, I'm still well aware that you're here with me."

Kinley licked her lips. "I feel the same about you. For someone who's been alone all her life, I thought it would be hard to live with someone else. But it's not. I like looking up from my book and seeing you sitting next to me."

"Good. You tired?" Lefty knew the question was abrupt, but suddenly he couldn't think of anything he wanted more than to lie in his bed and hold her.

"A little."

"Why don't you go in and get ready. I'll clean up out here and lock up. You still okay with me being in there with you?"

She nodded shyly. "But, I'm still not ready for…"

"I know. Neither am I. Believe it or not, I don't sleep with women simply because they're available."

"Okay."

"Okay," he echoed.

She smiled at him then stood and headed for his bedroom.

As Lefty put away the dishes they'd used that night, he had the thought that this was what his life could be like in the future. Cozy. Homey. Relaxed. And looking forward to joining Kinley in their bed.

His cock twitched in his pants and he adjusted himself firmly. "Down boy," he muttered before heading to the door to make sure it was locked up tight. While he might've told Kinley that he respected her decision to speak up about what she'd seen in Paris, that didn't mean he liked it. She was putting herself in danger, and he hated that. But he'd do whatever he could to make sure he had her back.

Giving her ten minutes to make sure she'd had enough time to change and get into bed, Lefty eased open his bedroom door. Kinley had left the light on in the bathroom so he wouldn't trip over anything as he came in.

Smiling at her thoughtfulness, he did his thing in the bathroom and stripped down to his boxers. He contemplated putting on a pair of sweats, but decided even though it would be torture, he wanted to hold her against him. Skin on skin.

He pulled back the covers and inhaled deeply, loving the faint scent of vanilla that entered his nostrils. Kinley didn't wear perfume, but the lotion she liked to wear put off just enough of a subtle scent that he knew he'd never be able to smell vanilla again and not think of her.

Without hesitation, he reached out and pulled Kinley into his side. He smiled when she immediately snuggled into him, putting her arm over his stomach.

"Comfortable?" he asked.

"Yeah."

"Good," he said with satisfaction. "If I crowd you too much, don't feel bad about pulling away."

"You aren't crowding me. You remind me of a teddy bear I had once. I slept with it every night, and it comforted me."

"What happened to it?" he asked before thinking.

Kinley shrugged against him. "No clue. I got transferred to another home and it wouldn't fit in the trash bag I was given to pack my stuff."

"A trash bag?" he echoed in shock.

"Yeah. I didn't get a real duffle bag until I was in middle school."

Lefty took a deep breath and reined in his temper. "Well, if you want to think of me as a big ol' teddy bear, I'm okay with that."

She giggled lightly, and Lefty memorized the sound. She didn't laugh a lot, and she certainly didn't giggle. "What's so funny?" he asked, attempting to sound hurt.

She laughed again. "Don't get offended. I mean, yes,

you're comforting, but you also make my stomach swirl and when you tangle your fingers in the hair at my nape, goose bumps break out on my arms. My teddy never did any of *that*."

Hearing about her reactions to him made Lefty sigh in relief. He wasn't the only one affected by their closeness. That somehow made it easier to simply enjoy the moment and not get sucked down into the lust he could feel just under the surface of his skin.

"Go to sleep, sweetheart. One day at a time."

"One day at a time," she echoed.

Surprisingly, this time, Lefty fell asleep fairly quickly. Maybe he was getting used to holding her, or maybe he was just exhausted from a long day. Whatever the reason, he knew in the morning he'd probably feel more rested than he had in a very long time. Maybe forever.

CHAPTER TWELVE

Kinley sat nervously across from Cruz Livingston, the FBI agent who Gage knew through friends of friends. He was tall, even taller than Gage and the rest of the guys on his team. He was at least a foot taller than her own five-five, and that in itself made her very nervous.

His black hair was cut short...and he was currently frowning at her.

"Ease up, Cruz," Gage said in a near deadly tone.

"We aren't exactly getting together for a cup of tea," Cruz replied.

Kinley couldn't help but smile at that.

When Cruz smiled back, she relaxed just a little bit. She was very glad he'd agreed to meet here, in Gage's apartment. Just thinking about having to go down to San Antonio stressed her out. She felt safe here. Driving around Texas, especially in a big city, would make her feel like she had a huge bullseye on her back.

"I understand you've got a hell of a story to tell," Cruz said.

Kinley nodded.

"Okay. Take your time. Don't leave anything out, no matter how small or inconsequential you think it might be. I'm not saying the FBI will take this on, but if the little bit I already know is true, then I'm thinking this is very serious."

It *was* serious. Kinley knew that. She took a deep breath and began telling the man across from her everything she'd seen.

It took a couple hours, especially since Cruz kept interrupting her, repeatedly asking for clarification or more information. When she was done, Kinley was exhausted. As if she'd just run a marathon or something.

Throughout the recounting of her tale, Gage sat next to her with a heavy hand on her thigh. She was comforted by his steady presence. He didn't interrupt her, didn't butt in to add something he thought she might've missed. He was just there. She'd never had anyone support her like Gage did. Without judgment and with no reservations.

"You understand that, since The Alleyway Strangler's murders happened in Paris, the FBI has no jurisdiction over that, right?" Cruz asked.

Kinley nodded. "I know. But I figured maybe you could work with the police over there. I'm willing to testify to what I saw, but I don't know how to go about getting in touch with anyone in France."

"We can help with that," Cruz said, but it was obvious he was still deep in thought.

"What are you thinking?" Gage asked.

"That we can't get Stryker for killing that girl...but what if that wasn't his first kill?"

"That's what the team and I thought too," Gage said with a nod.

"He might've honed his craft, so to speak, here in the States before he was appointed as ambassador to France. And the child porn could be another avenue to get to him, and to Brown as well."

Gage nodded.

Kinley's head swiveled back and forth between the two men as they spoke.

"I need to talk to my supervisor, but I think it's very likely we have a good case," Cruz said.

She sagged in her seat, relieved that he'd not only believed her, but was going to help.

"But—and you're not going to like this, Kinley—based on what you've told me about someone trying to hurt you, I highly suggest that you enter WITSEC."

"No. Fuck no!" Gage exclaimed.

Kinley frowned. "What's WITSEC?"

"The Witness Security Program," Gage said between clenched teeth as he continued to glare at Cruz.

"It's not ideal, I get it," Cruz started, but Gage interrupted him.

"Not ideal?" he bit out. "What a joke. First of all, Kinley hasn't done anything wrong. You know as well as I do that most of the protected witnesses in the program are criminals themselves who've turned on someone in order to reduce their own culpability."

"I never said she's in the wrong," Cruz said easily.

"Second," Gage continued as if the agent hadn't spoken, "hiding her would take her away from all her friends. Her support network. There's a ton of corruption in DC and all it would take is one word to the wrong person, and she'd be a sitting duck. *No*, it's a bad idea."

"How long?" Kinley asked. She felt Gage's eyes on her, but she didn't turn her head.

Cruz shrugged. "It depends on how fast the case moves forward. It sounds like we have a lot of work to do to research both Brown and Stryker. Months at the least. Most likely years."

Kinley shivered. She didn't want to hide out for years. She may not have been so reluctant before she'd come to Texas, but in the short time she'd been staying with Gage, she finally understood what it meant to have friends. She'd never missed what she hadn't had, but she knew without a doubt that if she left now, went into the witness protection program, she'd miss Gillian, Trigger, and all the other guys horribly.

She turned to look at Gage. And it was impossible to imagine not seeing or talking to him for years. She'd always thought she was perfectly fine on her own. She enjoyed her own company and hadn't ever felt as if she was missing anything. But now? It was both a blessing and a curse that she'd met Gage. She found herself missing him while he was at work. It was hard to picture her going back to her old life, doing everything on her own.

"Can I think about it?" she asked.

She knew Gage was frowning at her, but she'd turned her attention back to Cruz.

"Of course. But every day that goes by is another day that whoever was hired to shut you up has a chance to get to you."

She knew he was being extra cautious, maybe even trying to scare her...and it was working.

"No one's going to get to her," Gage growled.

"Really? And are you watching her twenty-four-seven?" Cruz asked. "Are you by her side every minute of the day? What about when you're deployed? Who's going to watch her then? You can't keep her prisoner in your apartment, Lefty. At least in WITSEC, she could lead a relatively normal life. She could have a job. She could go out with friends...could date."

Kinley felt Gage tense at that, but Cruz kept talking.

"Here, she's a sitting duck. We're talking about a friend of the *president*," Cruz said in a low tone. "If I thought this was going to be an open-and-shut case, I'd never suggest something like WITSEC, but I think you know as well as I do that this is gonna drag on and on. They'll do whatever they can to protect their asses, which means they'll plaster Kinley's name all over the place. They'll dig up whatever dirt they can find on her, including the accusation of treason. She won't be able to go anywhere without being recognized. The press will camp out in the parking lot outside. And when you get called on a job, she'll be here alone."

"She won't be alone," Gage insisted.

Cruz's voice gentled a bit. "You know what I mean. Someone already tried to kill her once. When the investigation is done, and Stryker and possibly Brown are arrested, then the shit's *really* gonna hit the fan. Whoever tried to kill her before will be even more desperate to take her out before she can testify."

Kinley hadn't realized it, but she'd begun to shake. Listening to the hell that her life was about to become wasn't fun. She was an introvert. She didn't want to be the subject of gossip for the press.

Gage shifted closer and put his arm around her shoulders, pulling her into his side. It was awkward, as they were both still sitting in the chairs at his table, but she felt better simply because he was there.

"What if she doesn't testify?" Gage asked.

Cruz shrugged. "I'd say the odds of someone coming after her would still be fifty-fifty."

"Fuck," Gage muttered.

"I'm testifying," Kinley said firmly. "You know why I have to," she told Gage. "You *know*."

"You guys don't have to decide right this second," Cruz said after a moment. "I need to get back to San Antonio and make some calls. We need to check into Kinley's accusations, see how much merit they have before we decide on anything.

It's not very likely Stryker will be convicted on just her testimony, we'll need to find more. The agency will need to contact our counterparts in Paris and get some details on The Alleyway Strangler. Look for evidence, videos, digital footprints, things like that. Once that's done, if it's determined that Kinley might be called as a witness, we can talk again."

"How long?" Gage asked.

"A couple of weeks. Maybe more, maybe less," Cruz said.

Kinley inwardly relaxed. For some reason, she thought she'd have to leave right that minute. That she'd walk out the door with Cruz and that would be that. Anything she might've thought she could have with Gage would be over in the blink of an eye.

Cruz turned to her. "You did the right thing," he said.

Kinley snorted. "Yeah. But the right thing doesn't feel very good right about now."

"I know," Cruz echoed sympathetically. "Once upon a time, I worked undercover. It was hell. Every day felt as if I lost a piece of my soul. I knew I was doing the right thing, but it was the hardest job I'd ever done. I didn't like being someone else. But when the dust settled, we got the bad guys, and they won't ever hurt anyone else again." Cruz turned his gaze to Gage as he continued. "And I thought that job would be the end of me and the woman I knew I wanted to be with for the rest of my life. And while it certainly made things more difficult, in the end, we became closer as a result."

"Being undercover, and being fucking hidden away somewhere that we can't talk or see each other isn't exactly the same thing, Cruz."

"You're right. It's not. I'm just trying to say...I understand sacrifice. Asking Kinley to consider WITSEC isn't high on my list of fun things to do." Cruz then reached into his pocket and pulled out a business card. He placed it on the table in front of Kinley. "If anything comes up, no matter how inconsequential you think it might be, that's my contact info. You have a burner phone?"

"Yes," Gage answered for her.

"Good. It's probably best not to get a new cell in your own name for now. You've done a good job of staying under the radar, but with all the texts and emails Lefty sent you before you got here, if someone hacks into your accounts, they'll assume he has a connection to you."

Kinley had been afraid of that. "But I didn't answer him."

"True. But that doesn't mean someone won't come looking for him to see if he's had contact with you. It's another danger of staying here with him."

Kinley ground her teeth together. She'd known coming to Gage could be dangerous for him, but she trusted him to keep them both safe. Anything else was too difficult to contemplate.

When neither Kinley nor Gage commented, Cruz stood, and Gage and Kinley followed suit.

They all walked to the front door together. Cruz reached for one of her hands and squeezed it gently. "For the record, I think what you're doing is amazing. It's not easy to stand up to bullies. And from the little I know about Stryker, he's definitely a bully. I'll be in touch soon."

She nodded and thanked him again for coming all the way up to Killeen. Then he was gone, and Gage had shut the door behind him.

Jerking in surprise when Gage abruptly grabbed her hand and started towing her back into the apartment, Kinley couldn't do anything but stumble along behind him.

He sat on the end of the couch and tugged on her hand. Kinley landed on his lap. One hand went behind her neck to hold her in place, the other clamped over her legs.

"I can keep you safe," he growled.

Instead of being scared of him, or irritated at the way he

was manhandling her, Kinley felt her nipples peak in excitement and she got wet between her legs. No one had ever dared treat her this way before. They either kept their distance because they thought she was strange, or they barely touched her.

Gage was handling her as if it was his right. As if touching her was a normal part of their relationship...which she realized it kind of was. He'd touched her more than anyone ever had before.

From the time she could remember, she'd always been on the outside looking in when it came to affection. She didn't really get kisses or hugs from her foster parents. And the older she got, the fewer the rare affectionate touches.

Some people would be pissed if they were dragged down a hall and forced to sit on someone's lap. They'd *really* be upset if they were held in a grip so firm, they had no choice but to look into the extremely emotional face of the person holding them so tightly.

Maybe Kinley was more messed up than she realized, because she liked the way Gage was holding her. She liked it a lot. It was forceful, but not painful in the least. It reminded her of how he held her in bed; of how, even asleep, he held her close, as if he'd never let anyone snatch her away from him.

She held onto his biceps with one hand, the other clenching a handful of T-shirt at his side.

"Did you hear me, Kinley?" he asked. "I can keep you safe."

"I know," she told him.

"Do you?"

She nodded as best she could with his hand holding her nape. "But Cruz was right, you can't be with me all day, every day. You have a job. You're gonna get called to go sooner or later."

She could tell he wasn't sure what to say to argue that point. A muscle in his jaw ticked as he stared at her.

Feeling bolder and more feminine than she'd ever felt in her life, Kinley moved a hand up to his cheek. "I knew when I saw that news show about that murdered girl that my life had changed. I just didn't know it would lead me to you."

Her words did what she hoped, lessened a lot of the torture she saw in his eyes. "I can't lose you when I just found you," he said softly.

Kinley's throat closed up, and she couldn't respond if her life depended on it. She'd told this man over and over that she was nothing special. She had no idea what in the world he saw in her that no one else in her entire life had. But she felt the same way about him.

"We aren't making any decisions right this second," she said when she'd gained her composure. "The FBI might decide what I saw was nothing. That there's no way Stryker can be a killer. I might've imagined someone pushing me; I wasn't exactly in a good frame of mind after being fired."

"You saw what you saw," Gage said firmly. "Don't downplay it. And if you said you were pushed, you were pushed. I'm not a big believer of coincidence," he told her. "The timing for everything that happened is just too perfect."

That's exactly what Kinley believed as well. It felt good to hear him validate her thoughts.

"I don't want you going into WITSEC," he said after a moment. "Everything in me rebels against it. You'd be on your own, and whoever is after you could still find you, making you a sitting duck. At least here with me, you've got friends and people who have your back. It's not ideal, I know that, but I can talk to Ghost, a friend of mine who used to be on another Delta team. He's still in the Army, but he and his team retired from Delta. They can help keep you safe when I'm deployed."

Kinley didn't want to be pawned off on someone else, but at the same time, Gage was trying to think of anything he could do to keep her safe when he wasn't around. How could she not appreciate that?

Without thought, Kinley leaned forward and touched her lips to Gage's.

She stilled when she heard him growl.

For a second, she thought she'd gone too far, overstepped her bounds. But when she tried to pull back, the hand on the back of her neck tightened, and he held her in place. Gage's lips opened under hers, and he tilted his head, giving them both a better angle.

With her hand still on his cheek, and his at her nape, she couldn't help but feel surrounded by Gage.

His kiss was nothing like she'd ever experienced before. She'd kissed other men, more out of curiosity as to what the fuss was about than anything else. But *nothing* prepared her for the rush of feelings that coursed through her body when Gage's tongue slipped past her lips and joined with hers.

Kinley gripped his shirt even tighter and leaned into him, wanting more. And Gage gladly gave her exactly what she needed.

How long they sat on his couch and made out, she had no idea, but when he finally pulled back, Kinley moaned and tried to follow his lips. She didn't want to stop. Didn't *ever* want to stop.

"Kins," he whispered. "As much as I love this, we have to stop."

She opened her eyes and saw he was inches from her face. His pupils were huge and his lips were pink and slightly swollen. She imagined she probably looked the same way.

She whimpered.

The smile that spread across his face was almost enough to make her okay with him stopping their kiss. Almost.

"I know, believe me, I don't want to stop either."

"Then why are we?" she whined.

He leaned forward and kissed her forehead before saying, "Because if I don't stop now, I'm going to end up taking you right here on this couch."

"And that's bad because...?" she asked.

"Because your first time will *not* be on my couch, right after a hard morning talking with the FBI about putting a serial killer behind bars," he said firmly.

Kinley could only stare at him. She'd known Gage was a good man. How could she not? But the more time she spent with him, the more she realized just how amazing he really was. "Most men wouldn't care," she blurted.

"I'm not most men," he retorted without missing a beat.

"I know. You're the kind of man who worries about a woman he's never met who walked into danger even though she didn't know it at the time. You're the kind of man who keeps his word, even if the woman he's trying to communicate with doesn't. The kind who would welcome a sick woman into his apartment and take care of her for two days, even when she's out of her mind with fever and pukes all over the place. You're the kind who would give up your bed to said woman even when she's not sick anymore. And you're the kind of man who sees something in me no one has ever seen before."

"No," he said with a shake of his head. "I'm the kind of man who has no idea what the fuck is wrong with every other guy in the world who's ever met you...and who's staking his claim."

"Is that what you're doing?"

"Yes," he said firmly. "I want to date you, Kinley. I want us to be exclusive."

She chuckled a bit at that. "Gage, it's not as if there are

any other guys who're remotely interested in going out with me."

"Good," he said succinctly. "I know this is out of the ordinary," he went on. "I mean, we're living together, but I don't want to take advantage of you. I want to continue to get to know you. Watch movies, cook, read...and this is one of the stranger things about our arrangement, but I want to continue to go to sleep with you in my arms and wake up to you in the mornings."

His hand was still on her neck, but he'd loosened his hold, and his thumb was caressing the sensitive skin on her nape, making goose bumps break out all over. "I'm afraid the longer you spend time with me, the more you'll realize that I wasn't lying about being weird," she said.

"And *I'm* afraid the more time you spend with *me*, you'll figure out that I'm not the man you've made me out to be in your mind. I'm not a superhero, Kins. I'm just a guy. I've got flaws like everyone else. I'm bossy, overprotective, and I love watching sports a bit too much. I'm not going to be able to stomach watching any of those stupid reality shows on TV, even for you. I have a job that's unpredictable, and I'll have to leave you behind to deal with whatever shit crops up more than I'd like. I want to say I'll put you first in my life, but the reality is that the Army comes first...at least until I retire."

He paused as if waiting for her negative reaction. Kinley shrugged. "And?"

"And what?"

"Is that it? Those are all your flaws?"

He grinned and shook his head. "No. That's just the tip of the iceberg."

"Gage, I don't expect you to be perfect."

"It's a good thing," he said quickly.

"Let me talk," she huffed.

"Sorry, add interrupting to the list," he said with a smile.

She wanted to be annoyed with him, but couldn't be. Not when he was so damn cute. "My entire life...I've tried to figure out what's wrong with me. Why I wasn't loveable. Why no one wanted to keep me. I came to the conclusion that it was my lot in life to be alone. And I was okay with that, Gage. Then you came along and made me feel...normal. You didn't hesitate to help me out in Africa, and you treated me as if I was just another woman. No, that's not true. You made me feel special.

"I already told you that it freaked me out. That you must've been delusional or something, and that's why I didn't write you back. But then you were just as amazing in Paris. When I had no one else to turn to, I immediately thought of you. I prayed the entire way to Texas that you wouldn't take one look at me and ask me what the hell I was doing here. I didn't mean to get sick, but I guess with all the stress and me not eating right and sleeping in my car, it was too much. And you took care of me. I know you don't understand what that meant to me, but suffice it to say, no one's ever done that for me before. And you didn't even know me."

"I knew you," Gage said.

Kinley shook her head. "You know what I mean."

"I know what *you* mean, but I don't email and text every woman I meet while on a job, Kinley. You're the one and only person I've felt that immediate connection to."

She swallowed hard and finished her thought. "I can't promise not to embarrass you, because I say the wrong thing all the time. I can't promise to be super social; more often than not I'll want to stay in rather than go out and hang with others. But I *can* promise to always treat you with respect. To never cheat on you. To be there when you need to talk about work, and to be there when you *don't* want to talk about work. I know I'm not the best catch, but I swear that I'll do everything in my power to make your life easy."

"Ah, sweetheart," Gage said softly, but he didn't elaborate.

He pulled her into him, and she went gladly, melting into his chest, curling her arm around him and holding him as tightly as he was holding her.

"I'm not a fortune teller," he said after a moment. "I have no idea what's going to happen with Stryker or the case. And I'm appalled that no one has seen what a gem you are, but that's their loss and my gain. How about we continue taking things one day at a time? We'll date, you'll stay hunkered down here until we have more information, and we'll just see how things go. All right?"

Kinley nodded. "Okay."

Silence surrounded them for a minute or two before Kinley said, "Gage?"

"Yeah?"

"I might be a virgin, but I liked our kiss. A lot."

She felt more than heard him chuckle. "Me too, sweetheart."

"Dating means we'll do more of that, right?"

This time his laugh was louder. "Oh, yeah, we're gonna do more of that. I know you said that you've used toys and gotten off before, but exactly how much of a virgin are you?"

Kinley sat up and looked at him in confusion. "I think there's only one kind of virgin, Gage."

He was grinning, but the look in his eyes was tender. "This is a hard conversation for me to have because the thought of anyone else touching you makes me want to hurt them, but...have you seen a cock? Like, in person? Has anyone ever touched your pussy? Made you come? Sucked your tits? I know I'm being crude, but I'm trying to find out exactly how innocent you are."

Kinley knew her face was probably flaming, but if Gage could be an adult while talking about this, so could she. "I've French kissed before, although what *we* just did was, hands down, better than anything I've ever experienced. A guy put his hand up my shirt, but he squeezed my breast too hard so I kneed him in the groin. Needless to say, he called me a prude and that was the last time I went out with him."

At the grim look in Gage's eyes, she went on quickly. "I had a guy flash me before, does that count as seeing a real dick?"

"No," Gage said, then closed his eyes and shook his head.

"What about dick pics through social media? Do those count?"

He opened his eyes. "You're fucking with me now, aren't you?"

She shook her head. "Actually, no. I'm trying to answer your question but not seem like a total loser at the same time."

"You aren't a loser if you haven't seen or touched a man's dick, Kinley."

"I'm twenty-nine and still a virgin. That's pathetic," she told him.

"It's beautiful," Gage countered.

"I've masturbated," she said, wanting this conversation over with. "I've used a dildo on myself, but didn't understand what the big deal was. It hurt, and it really did nothing for me. I like my vibrator, though."

"Birth control?" Gage asked in a tight voice.

Kinley shook her head. "No need. My periods are regular, and it's not like I was gonna need to be on the pill for any reason anytime soon."

"Are you allergic to latex?" he asked.

Kinley shrugged. "I don't know."

Gage nodded. "All right, we'll check back in on that after our first time. But all that gives me something to go on."

"You...do you still want to go out with me?" she asked shyly.

"If you think me having to use condoms when we make love, and the fact that I'll be the first man to touch you, taste you, get inside you, is going to turn me off, you're insane," he said, completely seriously. "Kinley, the more I get to know you, the more interested I am. We'll go slowly when it comes to being intimate, but you need to know that I want you. I've thought about you for months, ever since I met you in Africa, and getting to know you in Paris and over the last few weeks has only increased my desire to know more."

"Okay," she whispered.

"Just okay?" he asked.

Kinley nodded.

"And for the record...you can touch me anytime and in any way you want. Nothing's off limits to you."

She blinked in surprise. "Even your..." She couldn't say it, using her eyes to gesture to his lap instead.

He burst out laughing. "Yeah, even my dick," Gage confirmed. "I want you to be completely comfortable with me before we go all the way."

"Are you going to touch me too?" she asked.

It was a few seconds before he answered. "Eventually."

Kinley pouted. A hand-to-God pout. And she didn't even care. "That's not fair."

"I'm trying to be a gentleman," he said.

"This isn't the eighteenth century."

"I'm aware. But you haven't had good examples or role models when it comes to relationships. I want to show you what it's like to be the center of attention for once."

Kinley didn't know what to say to that.

"As much as I don't want to change the subject, I need to," Gage said after a moment. "Cruz is right in that you have to be very, very careful. We have no idea how long this case will take, and you could be in danger every minute of every day. You can't ever take your safety for granted. Okay?"

Kinley nodded.

"You aren't a prisoner in this apartment. You're free to come and go. I would ask, however, that you take my truck instead of your car. Wear a hat, and don't talk to anyone you don't know. If you can take Gillian or someone else with you, that's ideal. There might be a case without you, but it won't be as strong, and the more time that goes by, the more desperate Stryker is gonna get." He touched his lips to her temple and continued to speak. "I was serious. I just found you, Kinley. I can't lose you."

"I'll be careful," she said.

"Okay."

How long they sat together on his couch, Kinley wasn't sure. All she knew was that she loved having his hands on her and feeling his hard thighs under her. She might be a virgin, but she wasn't a nun. She wanted to know how good sex could be. And she wanted Gage to teach her.

When he finally stood, Kinley had her libido under control. She listened as he called Trigger and told him what Cruz had said. Then he'd passed the phone to her, and she'd talked to Gillian for a while. Afterward, he proceeded to call everyone else on his team, informing them that the FBI was now involved and hopefully they'd hear before too long whether they thought there was any kind of case against Stryker and Brown, and if the French authorities wanted to talk to her and prosecute.

They spent the rest of the day holed up in Gage's apartment. He ordered a couple of security cameras for the inside of his apartment, just in case, and Kinley did her best to lose herself in another book that Gillian had lent her.

As far as days went, it had been intense, but by the time Gage crawled into bed with her that night, Kinley was surprisingly relaxed. She should be fretting, her mind in overdrive about witness protection, worrying about whether the

FBI would believe her—and what Stryker would do when he found out he was under investigation. But instead, she couldn't think about anything other than how nice it felt to have Gage's arm around her and to snuggle into him.

"Gage?" she asked when they were plastered together under his covers, and he'd turned off the light.

"Yeah?"

"If this is out of the ordinary, I don't care."

"Me either," he responded, tightening his arm around her for a moment.

Then she closed her eyes and promptly fell into a dreamless sleep, content in the knowledge that she was safe in Gage's arms and that, by some miracle, he saw something in her that he liked and wanted to protect. It was a heady feeling, and Kinley knew if he ever decided he was wrong and broke up with her, she'd never be the same again.

* * *

"I found her," Simon King told Stryker.

"Where?"

"Texas. She's staying with that Gage guy, just as we suspected. But it's not going to be easy to get to her."

"Why not?" Stryker demanded.

"Because she doesn't leave his apartment much at all. She's holed up. And Gage isn't your average Joe."

"Shit. So how long?"

"I don't know," King said. "I'm not going to do anything that will risk my own freedom. Eventually, she'll fuck up, and I'll be there to grab her when she does. You have another problem, though."

"What now?"

"She met with a Fed today."

"Fuck!" Stryker exclaimed. "How do you know?"

"Well, he wasn't wearing a sign, but if you think I don't know a fucking FBI agent when I see one, you're an idiot," Simon said. "He came to the apartment and was up there for hours. If you'd hoped she'd keep her mouth shut, I'd say you're shit out of luck."

"I want this bitch to suffer," Stryker growled.

Simon wasn't a man who cared much about anyone. He'd lived a hard life, had learned the only person he could count on was himself. He was a loner who took high-paying jobs when his money ran low. He normally would've turned this job down, as getting involved in anything related to politics was just asking to be double-crossed, but he couldn't pass up the million-dollar payroll. Now two million. And he was willing to be patient, to wait to strike until the moment was right. And he didn't care if she suffered either. His job was to kill her. Period. In whatever manner the client requested.

"She will," Simon told the man confidently on the other end of the phone line.

"I mean it. Don't just shoot her in the head and be done with it. I want her to know why she's getting the shit beat out of her, and why she's dying a long, slow death."

Simon chuckled. "You're a little bloodthirsty, aren't ya?"

"Screw you," Stryker said. "My entire *life* is on the line here, and if that bitch thinks she can take me down, she's mistaken. I've kissed a lot of ass to get where I am, and some little fucking nobody isn't going to ruin it!"

"Fine. But you're going to have to be patient. I need to watch and learn her boyfriend's schedule. Figure out the best time to snatch her."

"Let me know when it's done," Stryker said.

"I will."

"And only call me again if you've got good news for me."

"I'm gonna need another five thousand to tide me over."

The ambassador was silent on the other end of the line for a moment. "You're a motherfucker," he finally seethed.

"Hey, I'm not sleeping in my car," Simon told him. "No fucking way. And I need to eat. And it's not easy blending into the background down here. I'm a big guy, and this Delta and his friend are gonna notice me sooner or later. Now that the Feds are involved, I need to lie low. And in order to do that, I need some fuckin' cake. Since I'm here because *you* want me to be, you'll provide me with what I need to stay under their radar. I could leave tomorrow and it'd be no skin off my back."

"Fine. Five thousand, but no more," Stryker warned. "You need to get this shit done."

"I will. In a few weeks, when she's let down her guard a bit, and after I know there will be little to no chance I'll get caught. Nice talking to you," Simon said, then hung up without warning.

He hated Drake Stryker, but he loved money more than he disliked working for the guy.

He felt nothing for Kinley Taylor. She was just a mark. It wasn't personal, it was business.

He'd watch her for a while longer, maybe figure out her weakness. Everyone had one. Then he'd get her out of that apartment and finish the job.

He was actually looking forward to having a little fun with her. It had been a while since he'd gotten to take his time with a mark. Most customers wanted him to kill their enemies quickly. Make it look like an accident or a random crime.

He smiled, making a mental note to go to the home improvement store and pick up some duct tape. Yeah, teaching Ms. Taylor she should've minded her own business was going to be fun...for him.

CHAPTER THIRTEEN

Kinley had no idea how in the world she'd found herself sitting in a chain restaurant a few miles from Gage's apartment, laughing her ass off with Devyn, Gillian, and Gillian's three friends, Wendy, Ann, and Clarissa.

She'd never clicked with other women, hadn't ever had much in common with them. But over the last week, she'd found herself hanging out with Gillian almost every day. Kinley had been helping her with research for places to hold events, and for new and exciting options to offer her clients.

One day when she'd arrived at Gillian and Trigger's apartment, Devyn had been there. At first she'd been self-conscious, as she didn't really know the other woman, and there was the awkward fact that she'd pointed out her bruise to Lucky. But Devyn hadn't mentioned that day, or anything about why she'd decided to move to Killeen, instead telling funny stories about Grover and how he'd been protective and a bit of a badass, even growing up.

With every day that went by, and no boogieman jumped out from behind the bushes to ambush her, Kinley was feeling braver about going about her daily business. She wasn't being stupid, though. She always went outside the apartment with someone else, mostly Gage, sometimes Gillian, and she never answered when someone knocked on Gage's apartment door during the day when he was at work—at least not when she didn't know who might be there.

She was also fielding calls from the FBI almost every day. Cruz had called a few times, as had other agents who were also working on the case. They were always polite and vigilant, giving their names and requesting that she call the San Antonio field office to verify their identities before speaking to them about the case. It made her feel better that they were so concerned for her safety.

A district attorney from DC had also called—and told her they were moving forward with the case against Brown and Stryker as soon as they had enough information. Search warrants were being secured for their electronics, and he'd told her he had little doubt they could, at the least, be charged with child pornography.

The French police were *extremely* interested in talking with her, excited that they might finally have a lead in The Alleyway Strangler case. Kinley wasn't happy about the possibility of having to go back to Paris to be interrogated about what she'd seen, but Gage had reassured her that if that happened, he'd do whatever he could to be right there with her.

Cruz had informed her things were actually moving along very quickly, at least as fast as the federal government could move. He had high hopes that both Stryker and Brown would be arrested in a few weeks to a month. And while they were doing their best to keep the investigations on the down-low, it was possible information would leak. When and if that happened, she'd have to be even more careful about her safety.

While she was happy the cases against Stryker and Brown were definitely moving along, she was happier still that it seemed she might've made some true friends.

Gillian had mentioned recently that she and her other friends hadn't been out in a while, so they'd all decided to meet up. And it had been *Gage* who'd pressed her to agree to dinner, which surprised her. He'd told her that she needed to get out and show the world she wasn't going to hide away as if she'd done something wrong.

It wasn't until he'd said that he, Trigger, and Lucky would be there, watching over them, that she'd let herself be talked into attending.

And she was having a great time. She felt normal. Like a woman who was out with her friends without a care in the world. Devyn told them about her job-hunting adventure, which apparently wasn't going as well as she'd hoped. Most of the vet clinics in the area weren't hiring, and because she didn't have any references, the ones in need of staff were leery to take her on without having anyone vouching for her.

Ann, Wendy, and Clarissa were hilarious in a way only friends who'd known each other for years could be. Kinley had thought maybe she'd feel like an outsider, but they'd gone out of their way to include her. It felt amazing.

"Wendy, how are things with you and Wyatt?" Ann asked. "Have you talked about the M word yet?"

"Money? Ménage? Mommy?" Wendy quipped.

Ann rolled her eyes. "Marriage, dummy," she said.

"We've only been dating for about six months, it's a bit early for that. We can't all be like Gillian and Walker."

"Hey, don't bring me into this!" Gillian said with a laugh.

"You guys were living together and engaged in like three seconds," Clarissa said.

It was easy to tell Gillian's friends were just teasing her, but the conversation still made Kinley uncomfortable.

"When the man you can't keep out of your mind moves you in to keep you safe, are you gonna say no?" Gillian asked with a smile. She didn't wait for an answer and kept talking. "No. You're gonna agree and take the opportunity to get to know him better in the hopes that he's just as amazing as you thought he was. And when you find out he *is* just as amazing, you aren't going to hesitate to say yes when he shows you the most perfect engagement ring and asks you to spend the rest of your life by his side."

"So when's the big day?" Ann asked.

Gillian smiled. "I'm not sure. I just know it's going to be super low-key. I don't want a big, fancy party. I already told Walker that I'm *not* planning it. I do enough of that shit for my day job. One day, we'll probably just go to the courthouse and get it done."

"I'm never moving in with a guy," Devyn said out of the blue.

Everyone turned curious eyes on her.

"I mean, on the outside, they look like they have their shit together. They're nice to old ladies in the store and say all the right things. But when you least expect it, bam! They turn on you. Say hurtful things, lie, steal, and only care about themselves. There's no way I'm going to risk falling in love with someone, only to have them pull a bait-and-switch on me. No thank you. I'm going to be single for the foreseeable future. It's just easier."

Silence followed her little speech, and even Kinley was a little taken aback.

"Jeez, Devyn. What happened?" Gillian asked.

The other woman sighed. "It doesn't matter. I *am* happy for you and Trigger. He really seems like a nice guy. But nope. No men for me."

"Does Lucky know that?" Ann asked, gesturing with her head toward the men sitting at the bar.

"Lucky?" Devyn asked, a blush spreading over her cheeks.

"You know he's been extra attentive lately," Gillian said. "I heard him asking Grover about you the other day."

"What'd he say?" Devyn asked.

Everyone grinned at her interest. "He just wanted to know how you were settling in and if you'd had any luck in your job search."

Devyn shrugged. "Oh. Whatever. He's Grover's friend. That's all."

"I'm not sure that's it," Gillian insisted. "Walker says he's never seen Lucky so focused on a woman before."

Devyn snorted. "Yeah, right. With a name like Lucky, I'm sure he's not hurting for women."

"He doesn't have that nickname because he's lucky with the ladies," Gillian said. "At least not from what I understand. I guess he's super lucky on missions. Like, he's always at the right place at the right time. He's just missed being shot more times than they can count, and he always seems to be the one to find whatever evidence they're looking for."

"Whatever," Devyn said again. "I'm not interested."

"*Hmmm*," Clarissa hummed.

"I'm not," Devyn insisted. "Anyway, I don't know why you're all gossiping about *me*. We should all be grilling Kinley on what's going on with her and Lefty."

"Duh. You just gave us a long anti-men speech. Why *wouldn't* we try to change your mind?" Gillian smiled.

Everyone laughed.

"But now that you mention it...what's up with you and Lefty?" Clarissa asked not so innocently.

Kinley had just taken a sip of her margarita when five pairs of eyes turned to her, and she nearly choked on her drink. "Me?" she asked, wracking her brain for a way to change the topic, and coming up empty.

"Yeah, you. You're shacking up with Lefty. Are the rumors

true? Are left-handed men better in bed than their right-handed counterparts?" Wendy asked with a smile.

Everyone giggled, but Kinley was suddenly flushed with embarrassment. She wasn't ready for this kind of banter. She'd never had a girlfriend to gossip with. And she didn't have the knowledge to talk about sex in a way that would make these women think she was more experienced than she was.

Gillian put her hand over Kinley's. "We're not making fun of you," she said quietly.

"I know," Kinley said. "I just...I don't know."

There was silence around the table for a moment.

"You don't know what?" Clarissa asked.

"I don't know if Gage is better in bed than other men because I've never had sex."

Kinley hadn't meant to just blurt out that she was a virgin, but it seemed to be her new habit.

She was *so* a weirdo. Why had she admitted that?

"Seriously?" Ann asked.

Kinley took a big gulp of her drink and nodded.

"I think that's kinda cool," Wendy said. "I mean, I lost my virginity when I was fifteen and regretted it immediately. I wish I would've held out longer."

"Right?" Clarissa agreed. "The older you are when you give it up, the better you know yourself and what you like."

"Exactly," Ann agreed. "My first time was *horrible*. It hurt so bad, I thought I was being split in half. And the boy didn't give a shit. Just kept thrusting inside me, trying to get off. He didn't care that I was writhing in pain under him."

"Guys," Gillian said, but Ann was on a roll.

"I didn't even orgasm until I was like twenty, and even then I had to take care of myself because the guy had no idea what a clitoris was."

"Did you guys bleed a lot your first time?" Wendy asked.

"I didn't, and I thought that was so odd, and my boyfriend at the time didn't believe that I was a virgin."

"Guys!" Gillian tried again, but her friends didn't pay any attention.

"Oh my God, I bled all over the place," Ann said. "It wasn't until the guy was done and pulled out that he looked down. I swear he thought he'd broken something inside me. Instead of him comforting *me*, I had to do all the reassuring. He was ready to bring me to the hospital."

"Enough!" Gillian practically shouted. "You're freaking Kinley out!"

The other four women turned to look at Kinley, and she knew her horror was showing on her face.

"Shit, sorry, Kinley. It really wasn't that bad," Ann said lamely.

Kinley couldn't help it. She laughed. And once she'd started laughing, she couldn't stop. Between the alcohol she'd consumed and her embarrassment, she just kept giggling. Then the others joined her, until all six of them were crying, they were laughing so hard.

"S-Sorry," Kinley said when she could talk again. "Ann just got done saying how she thought she was going to die, and then she's all like, 'It wasn't that bad,'" Kinley managed to choke out. And that set everyone off again.

When they'd finally settled down, Gillian turned to Kinley. "I admire the fact that you haven't given in and had sex just to have it."

Kinley held up a hand to stop her. "I would've had it a long time ago if there had been anyone who was interested." No one had anything to say to that, and Kinley knew she'd just made things awkward again. "I'm not like you guys," she said quietly. "I'm not pretty. I don't wear makeup. I can't wear high heels because they hurt my feet, and I'd fall on my face if

I tried to walk in them. I'm an extreme introvert. Not many guys have ever really taken the time to get to know me, and the few who have realized pretty quickly that I was boring and not worth their effort."

"Listen to me," Devyn said, leaning forward and grabbing Kinley's hand from across the table. "Fuck those guys. It's better to wait for the one man who gets you, *truly* gets you, than to learn the hard way that they're all douchebags. And believe me, most men *are* douchebags. You're quirky, Kinley, and if others can't see how cool quirky can be, it's their loss, not yours."

Kinley didn't want to get all emotional about the other woman's words, but she couldn't help it.

"Lefty's one of the good men out there," Gillian told her. "I'm guessing you can't go wrong with letting him introduce you to sex."

"I know he is," Kinley said. "He's probably *too* good for me."

"Fuck that," Wendy said. "That's someone else talking for you. I don't know your backstory, but you need to own your uniqueness. You should be thinking *you're* too good for most men out there, not the other way around."

"Exactly," Ann agreed. "Why should you give yourself to just anyone? No, they need to work for it. Prove to you that they're worth *your* time."

Kinley smiled. She liked that. She wasn't completely on board with it, but she liked the idea.

"Now, tell us how living with Lefty is going," Gillian said. "I know you're there because of the danger you're in, but talk to us about *him*."

"Wait—you're in danger?" Wendy asked, sitting up straight.

"What can we do to help?" Clarissa asked.

"Seriously? What's up?" Ann piped in.

Kinley's eyes filled with tears. These women didn't really know her, and yet they were still concerned. "Thanks, guys, but Gage has it covered," Kinley told them.

"If you need anything, we're here," Wendy told her.

"All right, all right," Gillian said with a wave of her hand. "Tell us about living with Lefty."

"We're sleeping together."

When all five women's eyebrows shot up, Kinley shook her head. "*Sleeping*. That's it. He was on the couch for a while, but one morning, after I went out to the living room and fell asleep with him, we decided to try sharing the bed."

"You and Lefty are sharing a bed, but just sleeping in it?" Ann asked incredulously.

Kinley nodded. "He told me that I could touch him however and wherever I want."

"Awesome," Clarissa breathed.

"And have you?" Wendy asked.

Kinley was embarrassed yet again, but somehow these women were making it easy to talk to them. Or maybe it was the tequila in the drinks. She shook her head.

"Why not?" Ann asked.

"I just...I don't want to make things weird," Kinley said. "Well, weirder than they already are. I love sleeping in his arms, and the last thing I want to do is make him *not* want to be there anymore."

"How would you touching him make him *not* want to sleep with you anymore?" Wendy asked, sounding genuinely confused.

"I don't know. I guess I'm just scared."

"Kinley," Gillian said earnestly, "if Lefty says it's okay for you to touch him, it's *okay for you to touch him*."

For the next ten minutes, the other women gave Kinley all sorts of advice on how and where to touch Gage. She was blushing bright red by the time they were done, but their advice helped.

She couldn't help but blush anew when Gage, Trigger, and Lucky wandered over to their table.

"Looks like you guys are having a good time," Trigger said.

"Definitely," Gillian agreed. "But we're ready to go, aren't we, ladies?" she asked, winking at Kinley.

"Yup, definitely ready," Wendy agreed.

"Tom's probably anxiously waiting for me," Ann said.

"And Johnathan doesn't know he's anxious for me to get home...but he is," Clarissa said with a smile.

The guys just looked confused, but Kinley shared a knowing look with Gillian.

"I'll get the bill this time," Ann said, but Gage shook his head.

"I already got it," he said.

"Asshole," Trigger mumbled. "When you went to the bathroom, right?"

Gage simply smirked.

"Far be it from me to complain over someone else paying for food and drinks," Ann said with a smile. "Thanks!"

"Of course," Gage told her.

Lucky hadn't said anything, but when the women started to climb out of the booth, he was there to lend a hand to Devyn. Kinley wondered if there was more between the two than Devyn had let on, but she didn't think about it long—because the second she stood up, she swayed dangerously.

Gage was there immediately. He put his arm around her waist and leaned down. "How many margaritas did you have?" he asked.

Kinley shrugged. "Two. Wait...maybe three?"

He chuckled. "Come on, you lush. Let's get you home."

Home. Kinley loved the sound of that.

She said goodbye to the others and let Gage lead her to

his truck. He helped her inside before walking around to the driver's side. She watched him, his head seemingly on a swivel, looking for danger. His attentiveness made her feel all the more safe.

The ride back to his apartment went by quickly and before she knew it, she was standing in his living room. "You gonna be able to get ready for bed without falling over?"

Kinley smiled up at him. She was drunk, but still cognizant of everything going on around her. "Yup."

"Fuck, you're cute. Go on then. I'll be in after I lock up."

Kinley nodded and headed down the hall to his bedroom. She didn't worry about where she was throwing her clothes as she stripped, but took the time to brush her teeth before she climbed into bed wearing another one of Gage's T-shirts.

She watched as he came in and disappeared into the bathroom. He reemerged not too much later wearing a pair of sweatpants.

He got into bed as he did every night, but for once, Kinley wasn't content to snuggle up to him and fall asleep. Maybe it was the alcohol running through her veins. Maybe it was all the advice she'd gotten from the other ladies about how to touch him. But she wanted more than sleep tonight.

When he lay on his back and put his arm around her, Kinley put one of her legs up and over his thigh, her hand resting on his bare stomach. She felt it contract under her palm—and he stiffened when her fingers brushed against his waistband.

"Kins?"

"*Hmmm?*"

"Aren't you tired?"

She looked up at him and said succinctly, "No."

"Fuck me," he swore as his head fell back against the pillows, and he shut his eyes.

Kinley hesitated for a beat but when he didn't grab her hand and push it away, she smiled and let her fingers roam.

She traced his six pack and the muscles alongside his hips that pointed right to his groin. Those muscles tensed under her touch, but when he groaned and shifted, she kept going.

Slipping her fingers under the waistband of his sweats, she realized immediately that he wasn't wearing underwear. The coarse hair between his legs tickled her fingers, but she stilled when she brushed his hard cock.

"Don't stop," he whispered.

It was all the encouragement she needed.

Moving slowly, Kinley wrapped her hand around him and explored.

His skin was soft, yet his dick itself was so hard. She could feel him pulsing in her hand, and when she ran her palm to the tip and down again, his excitement spread along his shaft, making it easier for her hand to move.

Groaning, Gage shifted up on one hip, pushing his sweats down until they were below his ass, freeing his dick from the confines of his clothes. Wanting to see him, Kinley pushed the covers away.

She could feel her nipples peak under her shirt and wetness coated her thighs. She'd left off her underwear, feeling brave, and for the first time, she was beginning to comprehend how exciting sex might be. She'd never felt this eager with anyone else. Even watching porn, she hadn't been so aroused. But feeling Gage's dick in her hand, and seeing for herself how much he liked what she was doing to him, was a huge turn-on.

Shifting so she was up on one elbow, Kinley concentrated on putting all of the advice she'd gotten earlier to good use.

It wasn't too long before Gage's hips began thrusting upward as her hand stroked down. They got into a rhythm, and when she glanced at Gage's face, she lost all interest in watching what her hand was doing.

His eyes were closed, and he was breathing in and out harshly through his nose. His hands were clenched in the sheet at his hips, and she could see his nipples were tight and hard. Everything about him was heartbreakingly beautiful.

Kinley felt more powerful than she'd ever felt before. *She* was giving this to him. Her. The oddball kid who never had any friends. She realized that he'd probably react like this to any woman who had their hand around his dick, but she pushed that to the back of her mind. *She* was here right now, and it was her giving him this pleasure.

Just then, his eyes popped open, as if he could feel her looking at him. She could barely see the brown of his irises as his pupils were so far dilated. He licked his lips, and before she knew what he was going to do, he'd reached up and snagged her behind the neck. Her rhythm faltered as he pulled her down and latched onto her lips with his own.

When his tongue began thrusting in and out of her mouth erotically, she regained her former rhythm with her hand.

Gage pulled his mouth away from hers and gasped, "I'm gonna come, sweetheart."

It was a warning Kinley didn't need. She'd felt his balls pull up against his body. She tore her gaze from his and looked down. Every muscle in his stomach was taut and his hips jerked spasmodically as he got close to his release.

"Kins!" he moaned as he thrust up once more.

She was fascinated as cum shot out of the tip of his cock. She kept caressing him, and soon her hand was covered in his fluids. She couldn't help the smile that crossed her face, and when he groaned and nudged her hand out of the way and began to caress himself the way he liked, she sighed in satisfaction.

The entire thing, from the time she'd put her fingers

under his sweats until the time he came, couldn't have been more than six minutes or so, but she didn't care how fast it happened. She was thrilled he'd let her touch him, and that he hadn't been embarrassed to orgasm in front of her.

Looking down at her hand, covered in his cum, she had the sudden need to know what he tasted like. Before she'd thought about what she was doing, she brought her hand up to her mouth and hesitantly licked her index finger.

He was a little salty and bitter, and nothing like what she'd imagined.

When Gage groaned, she looked down and saw he was watching her.

Blushing, she looked away, embarrassed for the first time. Before she could move away from him to go wash her hand, Gage rolled over, taking her with him.

Kinley looked up at him in surprise. Her T-shirt had ridden up, and she felt his wet length against her thigh. He wasn't hard, but she couldn't help spreading her legs to give him room.

He was still breathing hard, and she couldn't interpret the look in his eyes. For just a second, she was scared. She was as vulnerable as a woman could be. Gage was bigger than her, and she'd made it very easy for him to take what he wanted.

Cursing herself for not putting on panties, she stared up at him uneasily.

"Don't be scared of me," he said softly.

And just like that, Kinley relaxed. This was Gage. He wouldn't hurt her.

She wasn't sure what to do with her sticky hand, so she held it out to the side. But Gage wasn't having that. He reached out, twined his fingers with hers, and brought their hands together between them.

"Gage, I need to wash my hand."

"Sex is messy," he said.

She tilted her head. "What?"

"Sex is messy," he repeated. "It's nothing to be embarrassed about."

"Um...okay."

"And nothing's off limits between us. *Nothing*."

Kinley relaxed a bit more. "All right."

"And I have to say, that was fucking phenomenal. I didn't last near as long as I wanted to. I mean, the second your hand closed around me, I was ready to explode. I'll be better next time."

Kinley licked her lips and nodded.

"Thank you, sweetheart. Did you enjoy that?"

"Yeah."

"Good. And you like how I taste?"

She closed her eyes for a second, then tried to remember that he'd said she didn't have to be embarrassed with him. She opened her eyes and met his gaze. "I just wondered what it tasted like. It's not terrible, but I'm not sure it's all that good either."

He chuckled. "Noted. But for the record, I can't fucking *wait* to taste you."

Now Kinley knew she was blushing.

As if knowing he'd pushed as far as he could, Gage rolled over onto his back and pulled her against his side. He shifted and hauled his sweats back up and grabbed the covers while he was at it.

"Don't you want to clean up?" she asked.

"Not particularly," he mumbled. "I just had the most amazing orgasm, and I'm tired. I've got you in my arms and I'm enjoying the feel of you against me. I like drunk Kinley, but, take note, I'm going to want you to do that again when you aren't three sheets to the wind. Okay?"

Kinley nodded against him. She closed her eyes. Her body hummed with lust, but it felt good knowing Gage wasn't putting any pressure on her to let him touch her back, or do anything else. She liked making him feel good. Liked knowing she'd been able to make him come within minutes.

Just as she was nodding off, Gage moved under her and leaned over to the table next to the bed.

"What's wrong?" she asked.

"Nothing," he said calmly. "I just forgot to give this to you earlier. I ordered it online. It's from a company called FLATOUTbear. They're based in Australia. It's made out of Australian sheepskin, and it's the softest thing I've ever felt in my life. The body doesn't have any stuffing in it, it's just leather covered by the sheepskin. I thought you might like it."

Kinley stared at the teddy bear he was holding out to her. It was dark brown and looked a bit strange. The body was completely flat, as the name implied, and it had a slightly poofy head. It was a remarkably sweet gesture...and she wasn't sure what to say. She reached for it with her clean hand.

The second she touched the stuffed animal, she was in love. It *was* the softest thing she'd ever touched.

"After you told me about the teddy bear that was lost when you were little, I felt bad and wanted to replace it. I won't always be here for you to cuddle, particularly when I'm deployed or have to work late, so I thought you might like it."

No one had ever done something like this for her before. Oh, she'd been given gifts, but none had been as meaningful as this one. Not wanting to get the bear dirty, she placed it on Gage's chest and rubbed her cheek against it. "I love it," she whispered.

"I'm glad," he whispered back.

A tear escaped her eye, but she didn't move. She was over-whelmed with feelings.

She had friends.

She'd touched Gage and it hadn't been weird.

And now Gage had given her the most thoughtful gift she'd ever received.

Her life might look awful to someone on the outside, on the run from a killer and the possibility of having to testify against some pretty powerful politicians, but Kinley had honestly never been happier.

CHAPTER FOURTEEN

Another week had gone by, and Lefty was feeling cautiously optimistic. Cruz had been in constant contact, letting them know that Brown would most likely be taken in for questioning either today or tomorrow. Stryker was under surveillance in France, and Cruz was hopeful the Parisian detectives would be talking to him in the very near future.

He also hadn't seen anyone suspicious hanging around his apartment complex. He hadn't felt anyone watching them, and he hadn't seen anyone who looked out of place. All of that didn't mean someone wasn't there, but the more time that passed, the greater the chance that whoever had been after her either hadn't figured out where she'd gone, or was no longer interested in finding her.

Kinley had started to go out without him by her side a little more. She wasn't crazy enough to go gallivanting around by herself—that was a sure way to invite trouble—but she'd gone shopping with Gillian, as well as accompanied Devyn to an interview.

Lefty loved seeing her blossom as her friendships with the

other women deepened. If ever there had been someone who needed and deserved friends, it was Kinley.

But it was their one-on-one time that had him feeling the best. Kinley was inquisitive, and after the first night when she'd gotten him off, hadn't been reticent about touching him. Of course, while that made nights pleasurable for him, they were frustrating too. He wanted to take Kinley the way he'd dreamed, but he was still trying to move at her speed. The last thing he wanted was to make her feel uncomfortable in any way.

Last night, she'd asked if she could try oral sex on him. He wasn't about to say no to that. The second she'd wrapped her mouth around his cock, he'd had to grab himself and recite baseball stats in order not to explode in her mouth. He knew how she felt about swallowing, and while he'd enjoyed having her mouth on him, he didn't want to do anything that would turn her off oral in the future.

She'd finished him off with her hand...and then had tentatively asked if he might want to touch *her*.

He'd been waiting for her to ask for a very long week. It had been torture for him not to reach out for her. He hated not giving back the same pleasure she'd been giving him. But he'd promised that he wouldn't do anything she wasn't ready for.

Two-point-one seconds after the words had left her mouth, his fingers were between her legs and he'd felt her for the first time. She'd been soaked, and it hadn't taken very long at all for him to get *her* to orgasm.

Gage wasn't normally a patient man. As a single child, he'd been given pretty much whatever he wanted, when he wanted it. But he knew without a shadow of a doubt that waiting for Kinley to give herself to him would be one of the best gifts he'd ever get in his life. And he'd wait however long it took for her to be comfortable with letting him take her virginity.

He'd never wanted the pressure of being with a virgin. Even when he was in high school and college, he'd steered away from the inexperienced girls. But he couldn't think about anything other than how beautiful their coming together would be.

It was lunchtime, and he'd just gotten off the phone with Kinley. She was going to go to the grocery store with Gillian in about an hour. She said she had a surprise dinner planned for him, and he couldn't wait. She wasn't the best cook, said she'd never had the desire to learn or had anyone interested enough to teach her, but now that she was living with him, she wanted him to come home to nutritious meals every night.

He'd just hung up after telling her to be careful when he turned around to see his team all watching him.

"What?" he asked.

"Looks like things between you and Kinley are going well," Brain said.

Lefty couldn't read his tone. "They are, but I'm not sure how that's your business."

"It's our business because you're our friend, and we like her," Oz chimed in.

"She's been living with you for a few weeks now. We know her case is moving quickly, with people being questioned and the surveillance and all, but still... We don't see you outside of work too often these days. Just want to know she's okay," Grover said.

Lefty wasn't sure whether to be pissed that his friends might think she *wasn't* okay, or pleased they cared enough about Kinley to ask. "Kinley is... She's different," Lefty said, trying to find the words to explain their relationship.

"We know that," Lucky said. "That's why we're wondering what's going on between you guys. We're worried about her too, you know."

"What do you guys think? I'm pretending to care about the fact she witnessed a girl's last moments on earth just to get some pussy?"

No one said anything for a long moment, and Lefty's words seemed to echo in the small break room they were using to eat their lunch.

Then Trigger said, "I think they're just concerned about you both. It was obvious to all of us how much you liked her, and then she showed up here, and you moved her into your apartment and got involved in her issues without a second thought. And you're updating us on the case, but not your relationship. We're just trying to figure out where things between you guys stand."

Trigger was right. He *hadn't* talked much about Kinley simply because it felt rude, and the last thing he'd wanted to do was talk behind her back. Especially once she'd moved in. He'd never been *that* guy, and he wasn't about to start now.

He decided to set things straight in the bluntest way he could. "I'm not having sex with her."

The looks on his friends' faces ranged from surprise to confusion.

"You aren't?" Brain asked.

"No."

"Why not?"

Lucky's question was a little offensive, but Lefty knew he wasn't trying to be a dick.

"Because she's not like other women. She's been hurt in the past. A *lot*. Imagine you're six years old and you're living with a family. You like them, and they're nice. The nicest people you've ever lived with. They don't beat you or starve you or ignore you. Then one day, you get home from school and they hand you a garbage bag filled with your clothes and tell you that they're sorry, but they're moving and can't take you with them. That you'll have to go live with another family. How would that make you feel?"

When Kinley had told him that story, Lefty had been pissed. How someone could be so callous toward a child was beyond him.

He went on. "She's been let down again and again, until she learned to trust no one but herself. By the time she got to high school, she was known as the 'poor foster kid' no one wanted. She kept to herself and her classmates gave her a wide berth—when they weren't bullying her. She somehow managed to make it through college and get herself a great job. But that job was in Washington, DC, and you all know as well as I do how fake and horrible people in politics can be. She's never had any true friends," Lefty said.

"Before she showed up here in Texas, I was intrigued by her. In Africa, she kept her head in the middle of that mob. Then we talked, and I realized she was smart and I really liked being around her. When we were in Paris, we connected even more. The bottom line is that we're friends first. The last thing I want to do is rush her into any kind of relationship. But—and it pisses me off that I'm telling *you* this before I talk to *her* about it—I want her to stay here. I want to continue to get to know her better. And yes, I can see myself being with her for a very long time, but I'm moving slowly. I don't want to freak her out and have her decide I'm not a good prospect for a boyfriend."

Lefty knew he was talking too much. That he wasn't letting his friends get a word in edgewise, but he couldn't stop. He took a deep breath, then admitted something else.

"She's never had a real boyfriend. She's never *been* with anyone...if you know what I mean. At first it concerned me, but the more I'm around her, the more shocked I am. Someone should've snatched her up by now. She's amazing. Generous, kind, and has a core of steel. She has to in order to have survived her childhood without becoming a homicidal maniac.

"Yes, she's living with me. Yes, we're sleeping together, but we're not having sex. I haven't touched her...much. I want her to want me as much as I want her. Every night I fall asleep thinking I'm the luckiest bastard in the world to have her by my side, and I want to kill every single person in her life who made her feel like a piece of dirt on their shoe. I hate that she's scared. I hate not knowing whether someone is still after her, and I *really* hate that eventually, the time will come when we get called on a mission and I have to leave her on her own. But I'd hate even more separating myself from you guys because you can't or won't understand how special she is to me."

He was practically panting when he was done, but Lefty didn't care. His friends had to understand how important Kinley was to him, and if they did anything to make her feel uncomfortable, they'd have him to answer to.

But instead of being pissed, all his friends were smiling.

"I can't believe you've found yourself an honest-to-goodness virgin," Doc teased.

Lefty didn't even crack a smile.

Doc realized that he'd probably stepped in it and quickly backpedaled. "I mean, that's great, man. It doesn't matter, not to us."

"Not a word about that leaves this room," Lefty said between clenched teeth. "You know what? I've led a charmed life. My parents are still together and happily married. I had an amazing childhood. I was spoiled, I admit it. I enjoyed high school and had a lot of friends. I joined the Army and was strong enough to make the teams and now I've got awesome friends in all of you. Kinley's life has been *anything* but easy. She was passed around from home to home without a single family being interesting in keeping her forever. Her school years were hell, and even when she got a job in DC, she was still alone. But I know deep inside that she's one hundred percent stronger than I am. What she's been through would've broken most everyone else. But instead, she's kind, compassionate, friendly, and by some miracle...she seems to like *me*.

"Being around her makes me realize just how much I've missed out on. We have a connection. One that's real. I love hanging with you guys, but there's just something about knowing she's waiting for me back at my apartment that completes me. I can't explain it."

"I get it," Trigger said with a nod. "It's hard to explain until you have a woman you love, who loves you back."

"I'm not sure about love," Lefty said.

Trigger chuckled and rolled his eyes. "You love her," he said with conviction. "If you didn't, you wouldn't be standing here defending her. You'd take some ribbing from us and be done with it."

Lefty thought about that for a long moment. Instead of being weirded out by the idea, it felt right.

"Our asking about her wasn't because we were being nosey," Brain told him. "It's because we like Kinley. And it's obvious that she looks at you with stars in her eyes."

That felt good.

"What's the latest on her case?" Oz asked.

Lefty was glad to have the subject changed from his relationship with Kinley to something they were all experts in. He told them about his latest phone call with Cruz.

"So they're picking up Brown today?" Grover asked.

"That's the plan," Lefty said with a nod.

"And Stryker's being watched? Are his phone calls monitored?" Lucky asked.

"Yes."

"How's Kinley taking everything?" Doc asked.

"As well as can be expected. She was really jumpy there for a while, didn't want to leave the apartment at all. But I think she feels a lot better, now that others know what she saw, and they believe her."

"She still needs to be careful," Brain warned.

"I know, and she is. *We* are. But she's an adult. I can't be by her side every minute of the day, and she knows that. I've told her what to be on the lookout for. She doesn't answer the door if I'm not home if she doesn't expect anyone. And she never leaves the house by herself. We're being as careful as we can be while not making her a prisoner. Cruz had talked to us about WITSEC, and we decided against it."

As soon as the words were out of his mouth, he knew he wasn't exactly being truthful. They never did have a conversation about her going into the witness protection program after Cruz had left. He'd told her he didn't want her doing it, and she'd kissed him and that was that. The thought of her being hidden away somewhere, once again without friends and not knowing who she could trust, was abhorrent. He hated that for her, especially now that she'd experienced how important having true friends was.

"WITSEC, huh?" Brain asked. "That's some serious shit."

Lefty nodded. "Stryker is a personal friend of the president. I'm guessing a lot of people won't be happy to have his particular dirty laundry aired in public, especially if it includes him being a murderer."

"So she's going to testify?" Oz asked.

"Yes. The selfish part of me wishes she wouldn't, because doing so puts her straight in the crosshairs of who knows how many people, but she won't budge on that. It's just another way she amazes me every damn day. She could easily forget what she saw or claim she was mistaken; instead, she's determined to stand up for what's right. For those murdered kids in France, and all the others who might've been hurt by Stryker and Brown."

The men were silent for a second, then Brain said, "If you need anything, anything at all, you know all you have to do is say the word, right?"

Lefty nodded. He might not always agree with his friends, but he knew without question that he could call on them day or night and they'd be there. For him *and* Kinley, especially now that they knew where things stood between them. "I appreciate that. Seriously."

Trigger sighed. "Now that we have that out of the way, are we ready to go back in and figure out what the fuck the terrorists are up to lately?"

Everyone nodded and began to file out of the break room. Grover brought up the rear and paused in front of Lefty, who was holding the door for everyone. "I'm happy for you and Kinley," he said.

"Don't be too happy yet," Lefty told him. "We're still muddling our way through things. I'm not sure where I stand with her, and there's the whole testifying thing we need to get through."

"You'll figure it out," Grover said without hesitation. "She's good for you, and you're definitely good for her."

"Thanks, man."

Grover nodded.

"Have you found out anything more about Devyn's situation back in Missouri?" Lefty asked quietly.

Grover shook his head. "No, and it's driving me crazy. All she'll tell me is that she's an adult and she has it under control. But I can't help but worry. You know she had leukemia when she was little, and it's made all of us extremely protective of her."

"She had *leukemia*?"

Lefty looked over at Lucky. Neither he nor Grover had

seen him hanging back, and he'd obviously overheard their conversation.

"Yeah. It was touch and go there for a while, but she pulled through, and even though she's almost thirty, me and my other sisters still feel the need to watch over her. I'm not sure Spencer, my brother, cares about anyone but himself, but that's a story for another time. Anyway, then boom, one day I got that voice mail, with her telling me she's moving here to Killeen. It doesn't make sense, I know she loves adventure and she's impulsive, but I don't think she would've quit her job without a second thought. Something's up, and she won't talk to me. It's maddening," Grover said as he ran a hand through his hair.

Lefty couldn't take his eyes from Lucky. The other man looked extremely agitated at hearing the news about Devyn. Overly so. They'd all gotten to know Grover's sister over the last couple of weeks, but Lucky's reaction seemed a little peculiar.

"Anyway, I'll keep asking. She called this morning, and said she got the last job she applied for, so that's good. Means she'll hopefully be sticking around for a while. I've got time to work on her and report back to the rest of the family."

"She'll talk to you eventually," Lefty said reassuringly.

"I hope so."

And with that, the two men left the room, following behind Lucky as they headed back into the meeting they were having before they'd broken for lunch.

* * *

Kinley smiled at Gillian as they made their way out of the grocery store toward her Rav4. She felt a little silly making such a big deal out of the dinner she'd planned for Gage, but Gillian hadn't laughed at her.

Kinley knew Gage tried to eat healthy because he had to keep his body in the best shape possible. He could be called out on a mission at any time, and even putting ten pounds of fat on his frame could mean the difference between being able to fight effectively and being a liability for his team.

So she'd looked online for different recipes for chicken. It was lean and full of protein, and while she didn't want to slather it with something fattening, she also wanted to do more than just bake it plain.

She'd found a recipe for a parmesan-crusted chicken that looked amazing, and best of all, the recipe wasn't overly complicated. This was good, as Kinley had discovered she was a horrible cook. Gage could eyeball something and throw ingredients together and make a tasty meal, but when she'd tried that, it tasted like something a three-year-old had made out in the yard with mud and sticks.

She'd checked Gage's cabinets and realized she needed to get some ingredients to make the dish, and Gillian had offered to go with her. Kinley had spent the morning with the other woman, helping her brainstorm some things a group of nine year olds could do at a pirate-themed birthday party that were fun and not too cheesy, then they'd headed out to the store after lunch.

"You're sure it's no big deal to come over and help me?" Kinley asked Gillian.

"Not at all. I'm happy to. I mean, I'm no professional chef, but surely with the two of us, we can figure the recipe out and not burn the place down."

They both chuckled. Then Gillian said, "I wasn't going to ask...but I have to. Things are still going okay with you and Lefty?"

Kinley blushed and nodded. "We haven't...you know, but we're getting there. I'm honestly surprised at how much I enjoy what we do together. I thought it would be awkward, but instead it feels completely natural, and I get the appeal now."

"The appeal of sex?" Gillian asked with a snort. "Oh, yeah, there's definitely an appeal," she said with a smile.

And for the first time, Kinley understood the look of satisfaction that crossed her friend's face. In the past, she always just pretended to know what the fuss was all about, but after the last couple nights, when she'd gathered up the courage to let Gage touch her...she had a feeling she'd been missing out on a hell of a lot. But then again, she figured she wouldn't feel the same if it was anyone *other* than Gage touching her. He just did something for her. The second she'd met him, she'd felt...at home.

Which was a huge deal, since she'd never really had a home. Not a real one. Her apartments had all been places to sleep. But Gage's was a place of refuge. Safety. And when he was there with her, even sitting next to him and reading was more satisfying than any relationship she'd had before.

Yes, it was safe to say Gage Haskins was the best thing that had ever happened to her. It was scary as hell, because she'd always lost everything that had meant anything to her. From that long-lost teddy bear, to the foster parents she'd thought she could love.

If she lost Gage, she'd never recover. Kinley knew that down to her toes. She loved him and was scared to death of him at the same time. He had the power to destroy her if he decided he couldn't deal with her problems or her weirdness. So her plan was to keep quiet about her feelings and see where the future went.

If Gage wanted her, if he by some miracle could love her, she'd never do anything to make him want to change his mind.

They were approaching Gillian's small SUV when Kinley noticed a man walking toward them. He had on a pair of black pants and a white long-sleeve shirt. His dark tie matched his pants, and she had the thought that he was probably one of the many religious pilgrims that frequented the area.

Annoyed that they'd have to deal with him—because Kinley always tried to be polite, even if she had no desire to listen to a speech on being saved—she was surprised when the man said her name as he approached.

"Kinley Taylor, I'm so glad I found you."

Gillian stopped their cart and took a step in front of Kinley. "Who are you? What do you want?"

"Sorry!" the man exclaimed, taking a step back. "My name is Robert Turner. I'm with the FBI. There's been some developments in Ms. Taylor's case, and we believe she could be in danger. I've been instructed to take her to the nearest field office, in Austin until Mr. Haskins can be notified and can join her."

Kinley's heart started beating overtime. "What's happened?"

The man turned sympathetic eyes to her. "Walter Brown's been arrested, and Drake Stryker is currently being interrogated in Paris. We really do need to get you somewhere safe, Ms. Taylor."

Gillian held out her hand and said, "If you're really FBI, let me see your ID."

The man didn't hesitate. He reached into his back pocket and pulled out a leather wallet. He flicked it open and held it up. On one side was a silver badge, and on the other were the words FBI, his picture, and name.

"Good job on asking for proof. You can never be too safe, especially in your situation, Ms. Taylor."

The fact that he'd immediately produced his ID and that he praised them for being cautious went a long way toward making Kinley feel better.

Robert Turner was clean-cut and fairly good-looking. He was probably not quite six feet tall. His face was clean-shaven and his blue eyes looked directly into her own without hesitation.

"You're not safe standing out here in the open," he coaxed.

"Did Cruz send you?" Kinley asked.

"Cruz? Oh, yes. Of course. He would've been here himself, but he's busy trying to get as much information as possible from the French authorities," Robert said. Then he turned and gestured toward a black four-door sedan. "My car is right here."

Gillian turned to look at Kinley, then back at the FBI agent. Her brow was furrowed, and she looked worried. "How'd you track Kinley down here at the grocery store?"

"I went to her apartment first and your neighbor told me where you were headed. I came here hoping I could catch you," Robert said smoothly.

That made sense. Kinley *had* seen one of Lefty's neighbors when she was headed out. She'd exchanged pleasantries with the older woman and had asked if she needed anything from the grocery store as that's where she was headed.

"I think we should call Cruz and make sure this is all legit," Gillian said.

Kinley nodded and pulled out her phone. She clicked on Cruz's number, which she'd memorized. The phone rang, but no one picked up on the other end. "He's not answering," Kinley said.

"Because he's neck deep in everything that's happening," the FBI agent explained. "I'm sure he'll call you as soon as he can get a minute or two to himself."

Kinley immediately felt guilty. "You're right," she said. Making her decision, and feeling relieved that both Walter and Drake were in custody, she turned to Gillian. "I'm sorry," she apologized. "I had no idea everything would happen today. I never would've brought you out in public if I'd known."

"It's okay," Gillian soothed.

"I hate to ask, but can you take my groceries up to your apartment until I can get home? I'm not sure when I'll be back."

"Of course. Don't worry about that at all."

"Rain check on helping me make that chicken?" Kinley asked.

"You know it."

"Thanks." Kinley looked at the FBI agent. He didn't look impatient, which she appreciated. His head kept turning, as if he was constantly looking for danger. It reminded her of something Gage would do. She gave Gillian a hug and thanked her again.

"Stop thanking me," Gillian scolded. "You'd do this for me in a heartbeat, and it's not a big deal. I'll just stick your stuff in my fridge until you get home."

"Okay. I'll call as soon as I can to update you on what's happening."

"You better," Gillian mock threatened. "Go on. I'll see you soon."

Kinley turned to Robert. "Okay, I'm ready."

The FBI agent nodded and gestured for her to precede him as they headed toward his car. He opened the passenger-side door and waited until she was seated before closing the door and jogging around to the other side. He didn't look at her as he started the engine and pulled out of the parking spot.

Kinley looked back at Gillian and saw her still standing in the middle of the lot. She waved, but Gillian apparently didn't see her, as she didn't wave back.

Turning back around, Kinley took a deep breath. She'd

been afraid this would happen, but last she'd heard it was going to be a few days before Stryker was confronted by the Parisian police. She wondered what had happened to make them move on him already. Frankly, it was a relief.

They'd been driving for a while and were headed south toward Austin on the interstate when Kinley leaned over to grab her purse.

"What are you doing?" Robert asked.

"Calling Gage. I know you said that he would be on his way, but I'm sure he'll be worried about me."

"I'm afraid you can't do that," Robert said.

"What? Why not?"

"Because your phone could be tapped."

"It's a throwaway," Kinley informed him. "Just like Cruz told me to use."

She saw Robert's jaw tick.

"What?" Kinley asked, suddenly feeling very nervous.

Robert looked over at her—and she shivered at the look in his eyes. "I'm almost sorry I have to do this...but not really," Robert said.

Kinley frowned. "Do what?"

"This," Robert said.

Before she knew what was happening, his arm flew out and he punched her in the face.

Kinley's head bounced backward and smacked against the glass window on her side. She dropped her purse and both hands came up to cradle her throbbing cheek.

Before she could do anything more than wonder what the hell was happening, he hit her again. Then again.

"Stop!" she screamed, trying to hold up her hands to protect her face, but Robert—or whatever his name was—just laughed.

"Stryker said I could take my time and have some fun

with you...and I hadn't decided whether to kill you and be done with it quickly or not. I think I just decided to play."

His words barely had time to register before his fist was once more moving toward her.

She tried to move out of the way, to grab his arm, but he was too fast. His fist made contact with her already throbbing cheekbone, and this time the pain was too much for her to endure. She lost consciousness to the sound of evil laughter ringing in her ears.

CHAPTER FIFTEEN

When Kinley came to, it took her a moment to figure out where she was and why her face hurt so badly. Her eyes opened—well, one of them did, the other was already swollen shut—and she realized she was in some sort of warehouse.

"You're awake finally, huh?" someone asked.

Kinley turned to see the obviously fake FBI agent smacking a wooden baseball bat into his palm over and over as he came toward her. He'd changed into a pair of jeans and a black T-shirt. The tie and white shirt were gone, and he looked positively evil.

"Not gonna talk to me? That's okay," he said. "I prefer my women to be silent, actually."

"Who are you?" Kinley croaked, wanting to stall him. If she could just get her brain to work, maybe she could find a way out of this.

Hell, who was she kidding? She was in deep shit, and she knew it.

He stopped about five feet from her and bowed, as if he were a gentleman in a bygone era. "Simon King, at your service," he said with a smirk. "And to clear things up, in case you're entertaining thoughts of living to see tomorrow... Stryker hired me to kill you."

Kinley inhaled sharply. Shit.

"I have to admit, you're making me earn the two million bucks I'm getting paid for this job. I thought it would be easy to take you out, but somehow you got lucky back in DC. It would've been quicker if you'd have just fallen in front of that train." He shook his head and *tsked*. "But you ran and made me hunt you down. You've also been smarter than I would've thought, especially for a woman. I've been watching you for *weeks*. Trying to figure out your schedule and come up with a plan for getting ahold of you. I was beginning to think I was going to have to take out that boyfriend of yours. Or that pretty little filly you were with today. I usually try not to have any collateral damage, but in your case, I would've made an exception."

Kinley's blood ran cold, and she stared up at the man sent to kill her. This was why she'd hesitated to come to Texas in the first place, because she didn't want to involve anyone else in her problems. Didn't want anyone else to get hurt on account of her.

Simon squatted down and stared into her one good eye. "This isn't personal. It's business," he said almost conversationally. "I was hired to kill you, and that's what I'm gonna do. As I said, there's two million dollars waiting for me when you're dead."

"Killing me makes you no better than him," Kinley said, doing her best not to cry.

Simon snorted out a laugh. "I. Don't. Care," he enunciated. "I've been in this profession for as long as I can remember. And no one's caught me yet. I'm good. The best. All I care about is the money. You're nothing to me. No one. Killing you isn't even a blip on my give-a-shit meter."

He stood, and Kinley saw his fingers tighten around the handle of the bat.

"You ready?"

"Fuck you," she whispered.

He grinned. "Nah, that's not my kink. I get off on pain, sweetheart. And you're about to experience just how good I am at dishing it out."

Before she could leap up and try to escape, Simon swung the bat in his hands.

Kinley screamed as it hit her in the side. She felt something snap, and knew it was one of her ribs. Then he did it again. And again.

Despite the pain, she could tell he wasn't putting all his strength behind his blows. He was playing with her, just as he warned he would.

When he got sick of beating her with the bat, he began to use his feet. He kicked her over and over, laughing all the while.

When Kinley didn't think she could withstand anything else, he dropped to his knees and hauled her almost unresisting body under him. He straddled her chest and wrapped his hands around her neck.

Kinley reached up and tried to claw his face, but he held himself just out of her reach. She did manage to rake her nails down his neck, but he tightened his hold on her, and soon all she could think about was getting air into her lungs.

She had no choice but to stare up at his grinning face. "Don't worry, sweetheart. I'm not going to kill you yet. I'm just getting started."

* * *

Lefty was tired. His work days had been long recently, as they were ramping up for another mission. They'd been researching terrorist groups in the Middle East, and it looked like the government was going to have another High-Value Target for them to go after soon.

He was worried about leaving Kinley, especially when the FBI and the Parisian authorities were going to move on both Brown and Stryker soon. It seemed as if the better things got between him and Kinley, the more uncertain everything around them became.

He'd been in meetings all day—some bullshit political stuff, and others that were more interesting, involving possible future cases he and his Delta team might be involved in. Now, he was looking forward to going home and hanging out with Kinley.

Looking down at his phone, Lefty saw that he'd missed a call from Gillian, which was a little odd. He didn't know why Trigger's girlfriend would be calling him.

He clicked on the message—and froze as he heard what Gillian had to say.

Hey, Lefty, it's Gillian. Kinley and I went to the grocery store and an FBI agent stopped us on the way out, said he'd been sent to pick up Kinley and take her to Austin. He said Walter Brown had been arrested and Drake was being questioned in Paris. His name is Robert Turner, and he showed us his FBI badge and everything. Kinley tried to call Cruz, but he didn't answer. It all seemed to be on the level, but after messing up and not telling Walker or you that Kinley had been in town before, I didn't want to mess up again by not letting you know right away. I'm sure it's nothing, and everything is fine, but I wanted to call. I'll talk to you later. Oh, and I've got the groceries Kinley bought here in our apartment, so you can come over and get them anytime. Bye.

· · ·

Lefty immediately felt sick. "Fuck," he swore, running as fast as he could toward his car. He needed more information, and he needed it now. And the best way to get that information was to talk to Gillian.

Driving as fast as he dared, Lefty dialed Cruz's number.

As soon as the other man answered, he said, "Cruz, this is Lefty. Please tell me the FBI arranged to have Kinley picked up today and brought to Austin for safekeeping."

He could tell he'd caught the FBI agent off guard, but Cruz barely missed a beat. "Fuck. No. Not that I know of. Talk to me."

Lefty told him everything he knew, which wasn't much. "I'm just now getting to my apartment complex. Hang on, I'm headed up to talk to Gillian." He ran up the stairs toward Trigger and Gillian's apartment. The door was opened almost immediately after Lefty began banging on it.

Lefty pushed past his friend without a word, looking for Gillian. She was standing in the middle of the living room, her eyes wide and concerned.

"Tell me everything about the man who said he was an FBI agent."

"He wasn't...was he?" she asked.

"I doubt it," Lefty told her.

"I was just about to call you," Trigger said. "Gillian told me what happened as soon as I got home."

"I've got Cruz on speaker," Lefty said. "Gillian, tell us everything you remember."

She did. She told them what the car looked like, a description of the man posing as an agent, what he said his name was, and everything he'd told them.

"As far as I know, Brown was discreetly picked up in DC today," Cruz told them. "He's being charged with several things, the most serious being the child porn charge. His work computer was clean, but he used his government-issued cell phone to download videos, and his personal laptop at home was full of that shit. As far as I know, Stryker is under surveillance. The Parisian authorities are still investigating and trying to collect evidence against him. They don't want to tip him off and have him flee before they're ready to arrest him."

"And without Kinley, their case is a hell of a lot weaker," Lefty said. It wasn't a question, and Cruz didn't even attempt to blow smoke up his ass. "He got to her," Lefty whispered. "If we don't find her...she's as good as dead."

"Don't think that," Cruz ordered. "I'm gonna call in the troops. Gillian said they were headed to Austin, so we'll put out a BOLO on his car and make sure every cop in the area has their eyes and ears open."

Lefty appreciated Cruz's immediate call for action, but he knew in his gut it wouldn't be enough. He didn't want to think it, but he had a feeling his Kinley was already dead. If Stryker's hitman was efficient, he would've put a bullet in her head as soon as he got her away from the grocery store.

"Oh! Lefty!" Gillian exclaimed. "I almost forgot, I wrote down the guy's license plate number. Right before he got too far away, I thought it might be a good idea."

"Give it to me," Cruz ordered, obviously having overheard Gillian.

Lefty read the numbers and letters off Gillian's phone, where she'd noted them.

"This is a big deal," Cruz said. "It's good."

Lefty wanted to be excited, but he knew it was still a long shot that anyone would be able to find the car before it was too late. His head dropped, and he thanked Cruz. "Keep me in the loop," he begged.

"Of course. I need to hang up and make some calls," Cruz said apologetically.

"Okay. Thanks for all your help. It means a lot."

"I know it doesn't feel good right now, but I've had some very close friends who've been in your shoes. They thought all hope was lost, but they got a miracle. Don't stop believing in miracles, Gage."

Hearing his given name made Lefty flinch. The only person who called him Gage was his mom…and Kinley. "Later," he said and clicked off the phone. He appreciated Cruz's attempt at giving him hope, but it was very hard at the moment to believe a professional hitman would somehow make a mistake. It was likely Kinley had already been dead for hours.

"I've texted Doc and he's calling the others," Trigger said. "We'll head out and search for her."

"Where?" Lefty asked in agitation. "She could be anywhere by now. It's been hours since she was taken. You know as well as I do that the Hill Country around Austin is incredibly vast. He's probably already dumped her body somewhere. Not to mention, he probably didn't even go south, since that's what he *said* he was going to do. He's probably on a plane headed back to DC by now. *Fuck!*"

Without thought, Lefty turned and threw his phone as hard as he could. It flew across the room and smashed into a hundred pieces when it hit the wall. He heard Gillian shriek, but he couldn't get the picture out of his head of a broken and bleeding Kinley lying helplessly in the dirt somewhere. Dying or dead. And he couldn't do a damn thing about it.

For once, Trigger didn't have anything to say. He was always the one who was giving pep talks to the team and telling them to hang on, that everything would be all right. But Lefty didn't think this time things *would* be all right.

"Well, we aren't going to just sit around here and wait," Trigger finally decided.

Lefty took a deep breath and nodded. He tried to pull

himself together. Kinley needed him, and he'd be damned if he let her down now.

* * *

Kinley had no idea what time it was. All she knew was that she'd been in the trunk of Simon's car for what seemed like forever. She was pretty sure he was lost, which would've been funny if she wasn't so scared and if she didn't hurt so badly.

It turned out, Simon liked to choke her until she passed out, then let go and let her regain consciousness. He'd done it at least three times, and every time she'd thought that was it. That she was dead. But she'd realized the last time he'd strangled her that as soon as she stopped fighting him and went limp, he let her go. She figured maybe she could use that against him later. If she had a later, that was.

She literally had no way of fighting him. The last time she'd regained consciousness, she realized Simon had duct-taped her hands together in front of her, then he'd wound tape around her torso and legs. She was basically a mummy; she couldn't move her arms to protect her face and throat and couldn't kick him now either.

He'd picked her up without too much difficulty and dropped her in the trunk of his car, laughing when she turned her head and puked because the motion hurt her ribs so much. Both her eyes were swollen so badly, she could only see through slits, but somehow she was still alive.

As she rolled around in the trunk, listening to Simon swear and do a bunch of U-turns, she thought back to something Gillian had told her once. She'd said that people generally had no idea how strong they could be until they had no choice. Kinley had never felt strong. She'd lived a hellish life and had somehow muddled through, but had never thought of herself as particularly strong.

Lying there, she realized that if she was going to live through this, she *had* to be strong. Simon hadn't simply shot her, like most executioners would've. No, he'd decided to inflict as much pain on her as he could. And he'd done a hell of a job. She hurt. Bad. But the thought of how Gage would feel when he realized she and Gillian had been tricked hurt even more.

Kinley decided that she'd do whatever she had to in order to survive. She'd watched true crime shows and read books. Some victims played dead and others fought back. Well, fighting back was out of the question. She'd tried and failed at that. Her only other option was to make Simon think he'd succeeded at killing her.

Of course, that might not work, and there was a high probability that she'd never see the light of day again, especially if he just shot her in the head.

Kinley also knew she was on her own. She knew Lefty and his friends would do their damnedest to find her...but they'd fail. Hell, Simon obviously had no idea where he was, how could Lefty find her? And judging by the twists and turns of the roads they were on, Kinley suspected they weren't in the Killeen area anymore. Her best estimate was probably somewhere in the hills around Austin. Her stomach rolled with every dip the vehicle made, and she was definitely carsick, something that only happened when she was in the mountains.

Kinley wanted Simon to both stop and keep going at the same time. Her breaths came out in short pants because it hurt to breathe deeply and every movement of her body rolling around the trunk was excruciating. But she knew when he stopped, her nightmare was going to continue. Simon had definitely broken some bones, and she'd never forget the look of excitement on his face as he hovered over her with his hands around her neck.

It could've been ten minutes or an hour later when she heard Simon swear again, and the car finally began to slow.

Doing her best to brace herself, Kinley still flinched when the trunk opened.

Simon stood over her. It was completely dark outside.

"Time to die," Simon said calmly, as if he was telling her something as inane as the time. He leaned over and grabbed hold of her shoulders, pulling her out of the trunk and letting her fall to the ground. The movement was enough to make black spots dance in front of Kinley's eyes. He might as well have stabbed her in the side with a knife.

She tried to lift her head, but it hurt too much, so she turned it instead. She saw they were in the middle of a narrow country road, and she heard what sounded like water from somewhere nearby. But she heard no other sounds. No other cars, no birds, no sounds of civilization. There were even weeds growing up through the asphalt, as if the road wasn't very well traveled, which made Kinley's stomach drop.

Simon was obviously in a hurry because he didn't take the time to taunt her and tell her exactly what he had planned, something he'd done previously. He just bent over her legs and began wrapping something around them.

Kinley tried to kick out at him, but her attempt was weak, and Simon merely laughed at her. When he finished whatever he was doing, he grunted in satisfaction, then straddled her chest again. "You've been fun to fuck with," he said as he wrapped his hands around her neck once more. "But I've got two million bucks waiting for me, and I need to figure out where the hell I am and how to get out of here. This wasn't exactly what I'd planned, but I need to get this shit done while it's dark. Any last words?"

"Karma's a bitch," Kinley croaked. There was more she wanted to say, but she barely had time to take a deep breath before Simon's hands tightened.

She fought him on instinct, because she really, *really* didn't want to die, but it was no use. Simon outweighed her, her hands and arms were completely immobile, and there was absolutely nothing she could do to protect herself.

Remembering what she'd thought about in the trunk, she forced herself to relax her body and go limp.

She internally panicked when he didn't immediately remove his hands this time.

He really *was* going to kill her now. He wasn't playing around anymore.

Kinley's last thought before her world went black was how devastated Gage was going to be when someone, some-day, found her bones.

* * *

Simon King drove east, away from the random fucking bridge he'd found, and called the contact number he had for Drake Stryker. It rang and rang, and eventually went to voice mail.

Swearing at how shitty his luck had been, and ready to be done with this fucking job, he left a message.

"This is King. It's done. I've sent a photo for proof. If I don't have the money we agreed on in my account in twenty-four hours, I'm comin' for you. Don't fuck me over, Stryker. I'm not a man you want to piss off."

He clicked off the phone and threw it onto the seat next to him.

This job had been nothing but a pain in the ass since the beginning. He'd had to hang around fucking Killeen, Texas, for way longer than he'd wanted. There were too many soldiers and everyone was so damn friendly. It made it harder to blend in, to not blow his cover. He hadn't wanted to approach his mark in the middle of the day, and in public, but she'd given him no other choice.

She'd been too smart. Too wary. And of course, her living with that fucking Delta Force guy hadn't helped.

Simon smiled. But he'd shown her. It had been fun to beat on her. He loved hearing her scream and cry. He didn't always get the chance to play when he took out a mark. Excitement filled him every time her body went limp under him, when his hands were around her throat. He could've fucked with her for days...but he wanted his money more than he wanted to deal with her crying and pleading.

He'd scoped out a perfect place to dump her in the Colorado River, but then he'd gone and gotten lost. The roads all looked completely different in the dark. In the end, he'd had to make do with the fucking bridge he'd stumbled upon. He'd taken a picture with his phone after he'd strangled her, proof of her death. He had no idea how far down it was to the water, but it *sounded* pretty far when he'd thrown a rock over the bridge. He'd then tied the cinderblock to the bitch's ankles to weigh her down and dumped her over.

The sound her body made when it splashed was satisfying in a way Simon could never explain.

He felt good about another job well done and was dreaming of what he'd spend all his money on when he saw blue lights in his rearview mirror.

"Shit. *Fuck*. God *damn* it!" he swore. Taking a deep breath, he mumbled, "Just play it cool, King. They don't know shit."

He immediately put on his blinker and pulled over to the shoulder of the road. It seemed to take forever before the state trooper got out of his car.

But instead of coming up to his door, Simon watched as he pulled his sidearm.

"Let me see your hands!" the officer yelled.

Simon's stomach lurched.

"Shit!" he swore again. Not only had this job been a pain

in his ass from day one, it looked like his bad luck hadn't changed now that he'd completed his assignment.

There was only one reason the cop would be drawing down on him before he'd even walked up to his vehicle to talk to him. If the cops wanted to take him in, they were going to find that Simon King didn't go down easily.

He opened his door and bolted into the wilderness alongside the road without looking back.

* * *

Lefty was riding shotgun in Brain's 2008 Dodge Challenger, trying to stay positive. It was the hardest thing he'd ever had to do in his life. Everything within him was screaming at him to fix this. But he couldn't. No one could.

They were headed south toward Austin to aimlessly drive around, but Lefty didn't have the heart to tell his team that it most likely wasn't going to be of any use. He figured they already knew it as well as he did.

Brain's phone rang, and Lefty answered. His own phone was currently smashed into a hundred pieces with no hope of being fixed, and so he had to rely on his friends to get information. Lefty regretted his outburst, especially because now Kinley couldn't call him if she miraculously escaped, but he couldn't change what he'd done.

"Hello?"

"Lefty, it's Oz. State Troopers have stopped a car matching the description Gillian gave. Same plate and everything."

Lefty's adrenaline spiked. "Seriously?"

"Yeah."

"Where?"

"On State Road 1431, headed east back toward Round Rock."

"And?" Lefty asked impatiently.

"That's all we know right now."

"Is Kinley in the car?"

"Negative, at least from what they can see. They haven't checked the trunk yet though."

That thought made Lefty want to throw up, but he controlled himself. "Brain, we gotta get on 1431. It's to the west," Lefty said.

"Well, shit, could you be any more vague?" Brain complained, immediately slowing and putting on his blinker to get off on the next exit.

"I'm not sure it's a good idea for you to go there," Oz said. "If he managed to kill Kinley..." His friend's voice trailed off.

"Fuck that. If that's where this asshole is, then he either dumped Kinley somewhere in that direction, or she's with him. Either way, I have to be there. No matter what."

"All right. Be safe. You and Brain getting in an accident won't help Kinley. We're all headed in that direction too."

"Thanks."

"Anytime. You know that," Oz said. "Later."

Lefty clicked off the call and immediately pulled up a map. "Okay, get off here and turn right. I'll get you to 1431."

Brain didn't comment, just pushed his car a little too fast as he roared down the exit ramp.

Twenty-five minutes later, flashing red and blue lights could be seen ahead of them. They really were in the middle of nowhere, and it didn't exactly make Lefty feel all warm and fuzzy about what the hitman had been doing out here. He held his breath as they approached the cars. Brain pulled over, and Lefty was out and moving toward the closest trooper before Brain had even turned his car off.

"Wait," a trooper said, holding out his hand. "Stop right there."

"What's the situation? That man kidnapped my girl-friend," Lefty said urgently.

His words didn't seem to have any effect on the officer. "I'm going to have to ask you to move along," he said sternly.

Lefty did his best to look around the man, and his heart sank when he saw the open trunk and no Kinley standing nearby.

Brain had arrived behind him by then, and he did his best to explain to the trooper who they were and why they were there. It took some fast talking on Brain's part—Lefty couldn't get a coherent word out to save his life—but eventually the trooper called over a supervisor to talk to them.

"I'm sorry, but no one was in the car but the driver," he told them.

"What happened? Where is he? What'd he say about Kinley?" Lefty shot the questions at the poor man without giving him a chance to answer.

"He ran. The second his car stopped, he bolted. The trooper gave chase but wasn't able to catch up to him before he disappeared."

"Did you bring a dog in?"

"We're working on it," the trooper said.

Lefty's head dropped, and he put a hand over his face. He couldn't believe this. They couldn't have gotten this close, only to fail now. Not only was Kinley not there, but the man who'd kidnapped her, most likely a hired killer, had escaped.

"What about the car? Any clues?" Brain asked.

The trooper looked uncomfortable now. "There was a burner on the passenger seat, and there's evidence that someone was in the trunk at some point."

"What evidence?" Lefty asked, dreading the answer.

"Blood. And a roll of duct tape."

"That's it?" Brain asked.

The trooper shrugged. "There might be more, but we

didn't want to contaminate the evidence so we backed off and are waiting for a tow truck. We'll take the car back to the station and get the crime lab to look it over with a fine-tooth comb. Same with the phone."

That was all well and good, but it wouldn't help find Kinley.

Hearing a commotion behind him, Lefty turned to see the rest of the team had arrived. He headed for them without saying another word to the trooper. He heard Brain thanking the man for his time.

"What's going on?" Trigger asked.

"It's the car, she was in the trunk, but she's not anymore. The driver bolted and is in the wind," Lefty summarized.

"Any ideas on where he stashed Kinley?" Grover asked.

"No. But she's out there somewhere. He wouldn't have been on this road if she wasn't," Lefty said with conviction.

"So we go out and find her," Lucky said matter-of-factly.

Brain stepped forward. "We need to coordinate this. We can't just drive around willy-nilly."

Lefty nodded, but he stepped away from his friends and stared out into the darkness surrounding him. He closed his eyes. He could hear his team making plans on who was going to search where, as well as the state troopers talking in the distance.

He hoped somehow in their search for Kinley, he ran across the man who'd taken her. He'd kill him without a second thought.

The cicadas were loud in the night, and the sound soothed him. It was the same sound he and Kinley had heard from his bed when they'd opened the window after a rare evening storm the other night. He'd just eaten her to an orgasm, and she'd reciprocated before finishing him off with her hand. They were relaxed and happy, and she'd made some comment about how they were being serenaded by the insects.

It seemed like a lifetime ago, when he knew it was only a few days. The thought of never hearing her little giggle or holding her in his arms again made him almost physically ill.

"Hang on, Kins. Wherever you are, just hold on. I'm comin' for you."

His words seemed to echo back at him, mocking in their futility.

"Ready, Lefty?" Brain called.

Lefty had no idea how long he'd been standing at the side of the road staring off into the darkness, but he mentally gave himself a shake. "Ready," he called, and turned to rejoin his friends. If anyone could find Kinley, it was his team.

CHAPTER SIXTEEN

Kinley lay in the wet mud and stayed as still as she could. She'd turned her head so she could breathe, but she was afraid to move just in case Simon was watching from the road above.

She didn't remember what happened after he'd choked her the last time, but with the way her body hurt, she knew he must've thrown her over the side of the bridge.

She was lying in the cold, squishy mud of a fast-moving stream. By some miracle, she hadn't landed on the multitude of rocks and debris not four feet from where she was lying. Nor had she been thrown into the actual deep part of the water.

It was pitch black, Kinley could barely see the water she heard rushing nearby. She assumed that Simon had been in such a hurry, he'd thought the stream was wider than it was. That it was as wide as the bridge. But, lucky for her, it wasn't. Even luckier, Simon hadn't bothered to make sure she was dead before he'd thrown her body off the side.

He was a shitty hitman, not that she was complaining.

Hell, maybe she *had* been dead, or at least not breathing,

but when she'd hit the ground, her body was somehow shocked into breathing again. She had no idea what happened. All she knew was that, by some miracle, she was alive.

But Kinley knew she wasn't out of danger. Not by a long shot. Simon could return. There could be a flash flood. She could bleed to death internally—because something was definitely not right inside. She couldn't take a deep breath, and every inhale felt like someone was stabbing her.

Her head hurt and she felt nauseous, which meant she probably had a concussion. Not to mention, her right ankle was throbbing and was probably broken. The mud had saved her life, but that didn't mean the fall from the bridge hadn't done some serious damage.

After what seemed like hours, Kinley knew she had to do *something*. She couldn't just lie there and hope someone would happen to look over the bridge when they were driving by at sixty miles an hour...not that she'd heard more than two cars in all the time she'd been lying in the mud.

And each time she'd heard a car, she'd thought that was it. That Simon was coming back to finish what he'd started. But when the cars had passed without slowing, Kinley began to realize she was in deep trouble. She needed help.

And the only way to get it was to get out of this stream and up to the road.

But it might as well be a hundred miles from here to there. Kinley tried to move, and quickly realized she had something tied around her ankles, weighing her down.

Simon truly had planned on her landing in the water, and if she'd somehow managed to survive everything else he'd done to her, she'd have drowned.

Tears leaked out of her eyes, and Kinley felt such despair, she wasn't sure she'd be able to get herself out of this.

Using what seemed like all her energy, she rolled onto her

back. She wanted to scream with how the movement made her injuries seem even worse than two seconds before, but then she heard something over the sound of the water rushing nearby.

Cicadas. They were loud, as if they were calling to her. Yelling at her to get a move on. To not just lie there like a useless lump of flesh.

She remembered when she and Gage had heard them while they'd been lying in his bed after one of the most mind-blowing experiences of her life.

Just thinking about Gage gave her the boost she needed.

She wasn't dead. Simon had failed. She refused to think about the fact that he'd most certainly try again. Not only because she could still testify against Stryker if she was alive, but because he'd be pissed he'd failed the first time. And Kinley knew if he had a second chance, he'd make sure he didn't fail. She'd have a bullet, or two or twenty, in her head before she knew what was happening.

First things first. She had to get the tape off her body. She couldn't wiggle up and out of the ravine and stream bed like a worm.

It hurt to move. A lot. She'd never felt pain like this in her entire life. But if she was going to get back to Gage, she had to endure it.

She got lost in her head, wondering if Gage and his friends had ever been hurt while they were on a mission.

Of course they had, they were Delta Force operatives. They didn't just skip around the desert telling people to "be good."

She used that humorous image to keep her going. She rubbed the tape around her torso against the few rocks under her, wiggling and contorting her body as best she could. It was excruciating, but she didn't stop.

It took a while. A *long* while. The wet mud under her

seemed to help loosen the tape, or at least make her slippery enough to move easier. When she'd gotten the tape pushed down around her waist, it was easier to move her arms, and getting free from the miles of tape around her hands didn't take as long.

She was about to throw the tape she'd removed as far away from her as she could, when something struck her. It probably had DNA on it. She'd seen Simon use his teeth to tear it off the roll. She had to keep it. Protect it from further contamination.

Her body protesting, she balled up as much of the tape as she could, making sure the end where Simon had used his teeth was on the inside of the ball, protected from the elements.

Now she had to work on the tape around her thighs and legs. She couldn't sit up, the pain in her ribs was just too great, and breathing was almost impossible, so it was slow going yet again. But eventually, she managed to remove that too.

By now, the tape ball was a pretty good size, and Kinley had second thoughts about taking it with her. But it would give her something to do. She could throw it ahead of her and use it as incentive to crawl forward.

The only thing she had left to remove before she could start the trek up to the road was the cinderblock still tied to her ankles. She couldn't reach the rope without sitting up, and she could only stand that searing pain for ten seconds at a time before she had to lie back down and take a breath.

"I can't," she said out loud after what seemed like the hundredth time she'd sat up to try to unknot the rope. She lay on her back in the mud and cried. Cried for how badly she hurt and how much she needed Gage.

She cried for quite a while...

But then she swore she heard his voice calling to her.

"Gage?" she yelled, but got no answer.

After several more attempts to gain his attention, she realized that she was hallucinating. Gage wasn't there. No one was. It was just her. And the only person who was going to save her was herself.

You never know how strong you are until being strong is the only choice you have.

The words ran through her head over and over. She had no choice but to do this. No matter how much it hurt. No matter how long it took. No one was going to see her down here in the mud. She had to save herself.

Hadn't she survived a shitty childhood?

Hadn't she survived being a loner?

Hadn't she survived working in Washington, DC, for as long as she had?

This was a piece of cake compared to all that.

Okay, not really, but she pushed the doubts out of her mind and went back to work on the knot attaching the cinderblock to her body.

It took about twenty more times pulling at it, but finally, *finally*, the rope fell to the mud on either side of her feet.

Smiling, then moaning at how even *that* hurt, Kinley lay back once more, but in triumph this time rather than despair. She'd done it! She'd gotten herself out of the tape and removed that fucking rock attached to her ankles.

It was still pitch black outside, but somehow Kinley felt ten times lighter than she had just ten seconds ago. Moving ever so slowly, she rolled onto her stomach—and immediately realized that was immensely painful. She got up on her hands and knees and panted as pain coursed through her body. *God.*

She went from feeling triumphant to being in the pits of despair once again. How in the hell was she going to climb out of this fucking stream when even *thinking* about moving hurt? Hell, even the hair on her head felt as if it weighed a ton and was too much to carry.

Blood dripped from a gash in her head and down her face, but because her eyes were so swollen, she barely even noticed. Gritting her teeth, Kinley reached for the ball of tape she'd removed earlier. She tossed it with a weak throw toward the bank. It probably landed only eight feet away, and even that looked way too far for her to go. But she tentatively moved one hand, then a knee, and shuffled forward.

The mud squished under her fingers and her body sank into the soft ground, but she stayed upright.

She moved her other hand and knee forward, and almost doubled over at the pain that shot through her pelvis at the movement. The tears were falling from her eyes nonstop now, but since she could barely see anyway, she didn't really notice.

It took her probably fifteen minutes to move the eight feet to the ball of tape—but she'd done it.

Kinley turned and lowered herself down to her back to rest. She could see stars in the sky overhead. She must be in the middle of nowhere, because there was no light pollution to distort the view of the Milky Way.

She stared upward for a long time, before the sound of the cicadas penetrated once more. It was if they were taunting her. Daring her to keep going. So Kinley again struggled to her hands and knees and picked up the ball of tape. She tossed it in front of her once again and slowly and painfully crawled toward it.

She did this again and again. And when the ravine got too steep to throw the ball of tape upward, she kept nudging it with her head. It felt as if she were climbing Mount Everest. There were times she thought for sure she wasn't going to make it. She couldn't breathe very well at all now, and every inhale felt like an elephant was sitting on her chest.

At one point, she lay on her back and took a nap, or

passed out, whichever the case might've been. She didn't know how much time had passed when she woke up, as it was still dark, but she didn't feel any better for the break. Her tears had dried up for now, and she would've killed for a drink out of the stream she'd long since left behind.

The only thing keeping her going was Gage. She kept his brown eyes in her mind and every inch she moved forward was for him. She wanted to see him again. Wanted to feel his hands on her body. Wanted to feel him *inside* her body. She hadn't gone through everything she had in her life to lose him now.

But more than that, she didn't want him to beat himself up about her being stupid enough to get into a car with a stranger. Especially when she knew someone was trying to kill her. Even if he'd said all the right things and had that ID, she should've known better. She should've continued trying to reach Cruz to verify the guy's identity.

Gage would take the blame for her being taken. Even though he wasn't there, he'd still feel guilty. She had to live, if only to tell him it wasn't his fault.

So she kept going. Inch by painful inch. Her hands and knees were bleeding from the rocks beneath her, but she barely felt them over all the other hurts.

When she finally emerged at the top of the ravine, she could scarcely believe it.

She'd made it.

Now all she had to do was crawl to the road. "All" she had to do...right. But compared to what she'd just done, it was a piece of cake. She just had to make sure she didn't crawl right back into Simon's clutches. She'd have to be careful, only show herself when she was sure the car wasn't a dark sedan. But with how slowly she was moving, it wasn't going to be easy to try to see what make and color a car was, then hide if it seemed it might be the hitman.

But first things first...she had to make it to the road.

Picking up the ball of tape, she tossed it in front of her once more, then again, very slowly crawling toward it.

Gage, Gage, Gage, she mentally chanted, over and over. He was going to be her reward for all the pain and suffering she was feeling right now.

Time had no meaning. All Kinley could focus on was the ball of tape. She ignored everything else. Her strength was fading and she was beginning to think she wasn't going to make it to the road. After everything she'd been through, that would be the ultimate slap in the face. She couldn't stop now.

It took a moment for her to realize the ground under her hands and knees had changed.

It wasn't soft anymore.

Looking up—she realized she'd done it! She was kneeling on the asphalt on the side of a road!

For a second, she panicked. If she was in sight, Simon could see her. He would finish what he'd thought he'd accomplished...namely, killing her.

Kinley shook her head. She was going to have to take the chance. Hopefully he was long gone, thinking she was dead at the bottom of the ravine in the stream. If she wasn't found, she'd be dead in a few hours. She knew that down to the bottom of her soul.

The task of getting herself up and out of the ravine had overtaken her mind, blocking everything else out. But now that she'd made it to the road, she was suddenly exhausted. She carefully lowered herself to the ground and turned over onto her back.

It hurt to move. It hurt to breathe. Even her skin hurt. It was still dark outside, but she could tell that the sky was just a little bit lighter. It had taken her all night to get out of the stream and up to the road.

Her breaths were shallow, and each one was more painful

than the last. Her fingers tingled, maybe because of lack of oxygen, she had no idea. But the longer she lay there at the side of the road, the more she relaxed.

Her eyes closed, and she felt as if she were floating. Suddenly, she didn't hurt anymore. She wanted to take a nap. If she could only rest for a second, she'd feel better.

DON'T GO TO SLEEP!

The voice was loud in her head, and she jerked in surprise, then moaned at how the movement jarred her bruised and battered body.

For just a moment, she had no idea where she was and why she hurt so much, then it all came back to her. She turned her head and saw the ball of tape next to her. If someone didn't drive by soon, this was going to be her death bed.

In the distance, she heard a sound.

As if her inner thoughts had conjured the vehicle, headlights appeared in the distance. It didn't sound like a sedan, and the lights looked to be higher off the ground than the car Simon drove. At least she hoped so.

Knowing if she dragged herself to the middle of the road, she'd probably get run over, and also realizing there was no way she could even stand up to try to attract the driver's attention, Kinley did her best to wave her arm in the air.

The lights got closer and closer, but they weren't slowing down. The car was going to go right by her.

Kinley's stomach dropped. Her arm was throbbing, but she didn't stop waving.

One second the car was approaching, and the next it was flying past her.

"No!" Kinley croaked in despair.

But the moment it passed her, she saw its brake lights come on and heard the tires screech a little as the driver tried to stop.

Thank God.

"Please don't be a serial killer," she whispered. "That's all I need right now."

She couldn't move from her position on her back because it hurt too badly, so she turned her head to watch as the car reversed ever so slowly. It stopped, and she saw a man climb out of the driver's seat and jog toward her.

She blinked up at him as he towered over her.

"Holy shit, are you all right?"

It was a stupid question, but Kinley forgave him. After all, he'd probably never seen a bleeding and beaten woman who'd almost been killed lying on the side of the road before.

"No," she whispered.

As if the man's appearance was all she'd been waiting for, her body finally gave out. She'd managed to continue moving by sheer will. Her thoughts of Gage had kept her going. But now that rescue was at hand, it was as if her mind and body shut down.

The last thing she remembered was the man pulling out a phone and putting it to his ear.

* * *

Brain and Lefty had been driving around for hours. They had no idea what they were looking for, but neither wanted to admit defeat and return to Killeen.

Lefty stared out the window and had a hard time thinking clearly. He was exhausted and heartsick. He just wanted to hold Kinley in his arms and tell her how much he loved her and promise he'd never let anyone touch her again. How he was going to accomplish that, he had no idea, but somehow he'd do it.

Brain's phone ringing startled Lefty so badly, he jerked in the seat, but he recovered quickly and grabbed the cell.

"'Lo?"

"It's Trigger. They found her."

For a second, the words didn't penetrate. Then when they did, his entire body locked.

"Is she..." He couldn't make himself say the words.

"She's on her way to The Hospital at Westlake Medical Center. They're probably going to fly her to Fort Worth from there."

Lefty closed his eyes in stunned relief. Kinley was alive. *Holy shit, she was alive!*

"Turn around!" he barked to Brain. "Kinley's alive and headed to Westlake Medical."

"No shit?" Brain gasped, already pulling over to the side of the road.

"No shit," Lefty told him.

"She's in bad shape," Trigger warned.

And just like that, Lefty's relief crashed and burned.

"Bad shape how?" he asked.

"I don't know. The trooper who called me didn't have details. But, Lefty...she's alive. We have to concentrate on that."

Lefty nodded, but he couldn't get his brain to work. "Where was she found?"

Trigger gave him the details about the man who'd been driving on a back road, miles from where they were currently looking, and had seen a woman lying on the side of the road, waving her arm to try to get him to stop.

"You headed to the hospital?" Lefty asked.

"Of course. Don't know how long Kinley will be there, but I'm guessing the docs will want to stabilize her before they put her in a chopper for Fort Worth."

"We'll be there as soon as possible," Lefty told his friend, then hung up. "Go about five more miles, then take a right," he ordered Brain.

"We aren't going straight to the hospital?" Brain asked.

"No. There's something I need to see first."

Brain didn't ask any more questions, simply followed Lefty's directions as he told him where to turn.

Within twenty minutes, they'd arrived at the place where Kinley had been found. It wasn't hard to find when they got close, as there were three state trooper cars parked alongside the road, as well as a crime scene van. Brain parked a little distance away and Lefty got out without saying a word.

It was light enough outside now to see clearly, and Lefty didn't bother to approach any of the troopers or detectives working the scene. He simply stood at the end of the bridge over the ravine and stared down.

He didn't know what happened, but he could imagine it in his mind's eye.

The hitman had most likely thrown his woman off the side of this bridge.

Looking down, it hardly seemed possible that she could've survived. The stream was fast moving, but still somewhat puny from the lack of rain that summer. The right side of the stream was mostly mud—and if the cinderblock with rope attached to it, and the deep indentation in the muck was any indication, that was where Kinley had landed.

It made Lefty sick. But he forced himself to stand there for a few more moments.

He saw where she'd crawled out of the mud and up the steep bank. He saw where her tracks disappeared into some trees. His eyes traced the most likely trail she probably took before arriving on the asphalt on the side of the road. There was a ball of duct tape lying there, with orange cones set up around it.

But it was the blood shining in the morning light on the black asphalt that made his entire body go cold.

That was *Kinley's* blood. She'd been lying there on the side of the road, bleeding, when the bystander had noticed her and called 9-1-1.

Lefty had been in his share of life-threatening situations. He'd seen enough blood to make him immune to the horrors of war. But this wasn't war, and this wasn't a stranger. This was the woman he loved. The woman he'd held in his arms not twenty-four hours ago.

The thought that she'd come so close to dying, could *still* die, was too much.

He turned and puked his guts out right there on the side of the road. Then he stood there, bent over, his hands on his knees, and tried to get his equilibrium back.

Brain came up next to him and put a hand on his shoulder. "She's alive, man. You have to keep that in mind."

Lefty nodded, but he was having a hard time moving.

"Come on. She needs you."

Those three words were what Lefty needed to hear. He stood and wiped his mouth with the back of his hand. He nodded at Brain, and the two of them headed back to the car.

Without another word, Brain headed for Austin.

Lefty would never know why the hitman had chosen this road. This bridge. But he was grateful. If not for the mud, Kinley might've busted her head open on the rocks. Or she might've drowned. He knew there was a chance she might still die due to complications from her ordeal, but deep down, he had a feeling she'd be all right. He'd always thought she had a core of steel, and seeing where she'd fought a brutal battle for her life just solidified that.

Hold on just a little longer, Kins. You got this.

CHAPTER SEVENTEEN

One second Kinley was unconscious, and the next she was wide awake. But she didn't let on. If Simon was still there, she needed to play dead. She knew that as clearly as she knew her name was Kinley Taylor.

But the second she heard Gage's deep, familiar voice, she moaned.

Had Simon kidnapped him too? Was his life in danger?

"Kins?" Gage asked, and she heard his shocked intake of breath.

She tried to talk. Nothing came out but a croak.

"Easy, sweetheart. You're all right. You're safe. Do you understand?"

It was as if he knew exactly what she needed to hear. She nodded, and even that slight movement hurt.

"You've got several broken ribs, a broken ankle, one of your lungs was punctured, and you have a severe concussion. The doctors put you in a medically induced coma for a while to try to let your body heal. But you're okay. You're alive, and I'm here."

His words sounded as if they were floating around her

head, and she desperately wanted to open her eyes and tell him that she loved him, how thoughts of him had helped her stay alive, but she was so incredibly tired.

"Just relax, Kins. I'm here."

She squeezed his hand and fell once more into the blissful land of sleep, where she didn't hurt.

* * *

Lefty had never felt so relieved in all his life.

It had been three long days. When he'd first seen Kinley, after finally being allowed into her room in the hospital up in Fort Worth, it had taken all he had not to throw up again.

She still looked horrible.

Her face was swollen and bruised. Her lips were cracked and split from an obvious beating. The bruises on her throat were horrifying and told their own story. She'd been choked. More than once, if the overlapping finger-shaped bruises were any indication. Her palms and knees had deep cuts on them from where she'd crawled to safety.

One night, when the nurse had come in to bathe her, he'd seen the horrific bruises on her torso, which the police assumed had come from the baseball bat they'd found in the backseat of the hitman's car.

The thought of his Kinley being beaten to within an inch of her life was almost unbearable.

And yet, somehow, she was still here. Alive.

There had to be a reason. The hitman had tried to kill her *twice*, and failed both times.

That just didn't happen.

Sitting by her side, Lefty knew he didn't want to go through his life without her. She was it for him. Everything about her impressed and intrigued him, and he didn't want to go even one day without talking to her. Laughing with her. He needed her in his life.

As he sat there holding Kinley's hand, a knock sounded on the door. He turned and saw his mom poking her head in.

His teammates had all been taking turns visiting as well, making the drive up from Killeen to visit for a few hours and make sure he was all right. It meant the world to him to have his friends by his side, and to see them just as worried about her.

Gillian and Devyn had come up as well. Gillian felt guilty for not stopping Kinley from going with the fake FBI agent, but Lefty had reassured her it wasn't her fault. And he truly believed that. The hitman was a professional. Lefty hadn't even noticed him watching the apartment, and he was trained to notice that shit.

"Can I come in?" his mom asked gently.

Lefty gestured for her to enter. It was just him and Kinley in the room at the moment. His friends had all left for the day.

When his mom had learned what had happened, she'd gotten on a plane and shown up the next day. Lefty had been surprised, but his mom had simply said, "My boy needs me, and a girl needs a mom. And since she doesn't have one, I'm standing in."

Lefty had known his mother liked Kinley when they'd talked in Paris, but he had no idea exactly how much Kinley had impressed her.

Molly Haskins tiptoed up to the bed and kissed Lefty's head. She put a hand on his shoulder and said, "She looks better."

Lefty did his best not to snort. How the hell she could say that, he had no idea. Kinley still looked awful.

"I'm serious," his mom said as if she could read his mind. "She's not as pale and her breathing seems deeper."

Lefty tried to look at the woman he loved objectively, but it was no use.

"You should go shower. Eat something," Molly said.

Lefty shook his head. "I'm not leaving."

"It wasn't a suggestion," his mom said firmly. "I know you're a grown man, but you stink. You won't be any good to her if you drop over in your chair. I promise not to leave her side until you get back. Besides, you know Cruz isn't going to leave either."

Taking a deep breath, Lefty looked back toward the door. He knew the FBI agent felt responsible for what had happened to Kinley, just as he did. He'd personally been standing guard outside the hospital room since Kinley had arrived. He'd only left one time that he knew of, to debrief his superiors and to take a quick three-hour nap. He was concerned because the hitman hadn't yet been found, and Cruz was obviously just as worried as Lefty and his team about Kinley's safety. What the plan was next in regard to Stryker, Brown, and Kinley testifying, Lefty didn't know. Nor did he care. All he cared about was seeing Kinley's beautiful hazel eyes opening and recognizing him.

"All right. I'll only be fifteen minutes or so," he told his mom.

She shook her head. "An hour. If you're back before then, I'm gonna tell Cruz not to let you in."

Lefty pressed his lips together. He wanted to be there in case Kinley woke again. He didn't want to miss it. *Couldn't* miss it.

"I'll call you if I think she's waking up," his mom promised, reading his mind. "Go, son. Take a break."

Sighing, Lefty nodded. He brought Kinley's hand up to his mouth and kissed it. "I'll be back," he whispered. "I love you." Then he stood, kissed his mom's cheek, and headed out of the room.

* * *

Time had no meaning in the hospital. Kinley knew she was there. Knew Gage was at her side. But every time she woke up, it was so hard to stay that way. But this time when she woke, she felt as if she had more energy.

She opened her eyes—and immediately closed them again.

"Close the curtains," Gage ordered someone. "Sorry about that, Kins. Try again. Open your beautiful eyes and look at me."

Not able to resist the order, Kinley squinted...and looked right into Gage's eyes.

"Hey," he said with a smile.

Licking her lips, Kinley croaked, "Hi."

Gage closed his eyes for a moment, then she was once more looking into his intense brown eyes. "How do you feel?"

"Terrible," she said immediately. "But I'm alive, so I'm great."

"Yes, you are," Gage told her.

One of his hands came up and rested against her cheek. It hurt, but Kinley made sure not to let that show, as she loved him touching her. Especially since there was a time very recently when she didn't think it would ever happen again.

"Water?" he asked.

"Please."

He moved his left hand, not taking his right from her face. He brought a cup with a straw up to her mouth and she gratefully took a few sips. It hurt to swallow, but the cool water felt amazing on her sore throat.

"Better?" Gage asked.

"Yeah, thanks," Kinley told him. "How long have I been here?"

"Six days," Gage said.

Kinley blinked in surprise. "Really?"

"Yeah. You're in Fort Worth. You were flown up here from Austin. You were treated for a collapsed lung, and you've got several broken ribs. The doctors put you in a medically induced coma to try to help your body heal. They've been weaning you off the drugs though."

Kinley nodded. "What else?"

"Broken ankle, cuts, scrapes, bruises, concussion," Gage told her without hesitation.

She appreciated him not beating around the bush.

"Simon?"

"What?"

"Simon King. He said that was his name," Kinley told him. She watched Gage's face harden, and he turned and snapped his fingers. "Mom, get Cruz in here."

Kinley jerked, and Gage obviously felt it.

"What?" he asked with concern.

Kinley tried to lean over to see who was in the room with them, but inhaled sharply at the pain that tore through her body at even the slight movement.

"You're safe here," Gage reassured her, misunderstanding her inhale.

Within seconds, Kinley saw the FBI agent standing by Gage's side. "She's awake?" he asked.

"Yeah. Simon King. That's the asshole's name."

Cruz nodded and pulled out a small pad of paper. "What else does she remember?"

"I'm lying right here," Kinley complained. "You can talk to *me*."

Cruz grimaced. "Sorry. Since you've been napping, I'm just used to talking to Lefty here." He winked, letting her know he was teasing. "What else can you tell us?"

Her throat hurt, and sleep was already pulling at her, but Kinley forced herself to concentrate. "Same guy who tried to

kill me in DC," she said. "Said Stryker was paying him two million dollars to kill me."

"He *told* you Stryker hired him?" Cruz asked.

"Yes."

"Anything else?"

"He's been here for weeks. But he couldn't get to me," she continued.

Then Kinley remembered something else Simon had said...

He told her he'd have gone after Gage or Gillian if he hadn't gotten to her soon.

She swallowed hard, and tears came to her eyes, both at the pain swallowing caused and the thought that her friends had been in danger because of her, just as she'd thought might happen.

That was *her* fault.

She didn't say anything though; she knew they'd tell her not to worry about that now.

"Fuck," Gage swore.

"Language," a woman reprimanded from behind him.

"Why is your mom here?" Kinley blurted. "Are you all right?"

For some reason, Gage smiled. "She's here because you got hurt," he said.

Kinley was shocked. "Really?"

"Really," Gage said.

Then Molly Haskins appeared at the other side of the bed. "Why so surprised?" she asked. "You're important to my son, you were hurt, I like you a lot, so here I am."

Kinley was so touched, she wanted to cry. "But you barely know me," she whispered.

"I care about you, Kinley. You're an amazing person, and I'm so glad you came into Gage's life. I know you love Notre Dame as much as I do. I know you're smart and funny and

you need a mom. I mean, Gage is great, but he can't take the place of a mother's loving touch. So I thought I'd come and lend a hand."

Kinley stared at her for a beat, then closed her eyes tightly and really *did* start to cry then.

Molly's hand rested on her forehead and smoothed her hair back. "*Shhh*. Don't cry," she crooned.

Until Gage had taken care of her when she'd been sick, no one had ever gone out of their way to be there when she wasn't feeling well. Not once since she could remember. But here was Gage's mom, treating her as if she was important. Loved. It was overwhelming, and Kinley wanted so badly to be this woman's daughter, it was almost more painful than what Simon had done to her.

"Give us a sec, Mom, Cruz," Gage said.

Kinley didn't open her eyes, but she heard them leaving the room.

"Look at me, Kinley," Gage ordered.

Too tired to fight him, she did as he requested.

"I love you," Gage said as soon as she met his gaze.

Her heart sped up, and the monitors next to her actually beeped in alarm.

Gage smiled, but didn't look concerned. "It's probably not fair of me to spring that on you right now, but I don't care. When I heard you'd been taken, I swear to God my life stopped. I couldn't breathe, and I knew if I didn't get you back, I'd never recover. I'm not telling you to put any kind of pressure on you. We'll continue as we have been. Slowly and steadily. But I couldn't *not* tell you.

"My mom's here because of *you*, Kins. You're incredible, and she knows that. No matter what happens between the two of us, you'll always have her. Understand?"

Kinley nodded.

"You're tired," Gage observed.

She nodded again.

"You in pain?"

"A little."

Gage reached over and pushed the button attached to her IV. "A little morphine should take the edge off. Close your eyes and rest, sweetheart."

"What about Simon? Was he caught?"

She knew what the answer was before Gage said anything, simply by the look on his face. "Unfortunately, no. He was stopped by state troopers the night you were found, but he ran, and the dogs couldn't catch his scent. But don't worry, you're safe," he said quickly. "He made a mistake and left his phone behind. From what I understand, the last number he called was to a burner phone in Paris. There's no question who he was calling. No matter what it takes, I'm gonna make sure he doesn't get to you."

A lump formed in Kinley's throat. Simon was still out there. And he hadn't managed to kill her. He'd be pissed about the two million dollars he probably wouldn't get now, and he'd be back for her. Next time, he'd make sure she was dead. No more "playing" with her. He'd shoot her in the head and be done with it. She knew that as well as she knew her name.

She wouldn't survive a third attempt. But more importantly...who would he go through to get to her?

"Sleep, Kinley. Cruz is here watching over you, and my commander gave me some leave to stay here until you're released. You're safe."

She closed her eyes and tried to relax, but the contentment she'd felt a moment ago at hearing that Gage loved her was gone. She *wasn't* safe. And neither was anyone she came into contact with. How had her life gotten so damn complicated?

CHAPTER EIGHTEEN

Two more days had passed, and when Gage and his mom left to go grab some breakfast—at her insistence—Kinley knew this would be her only chance to talk privately with Cruz.

Gage's friends had been in and out, and she was surprised he'd agreed to leave her alone, but she didn't question it. She had a chance to talk to the FBI agent, and she needed to take it.

She was still in a lot of pain, but the doctors reassured her the pain was normal because broken ribs took a long time to heal. The swelling in her face had finally subsided enough that she could see clearly again. She'd looked in the mirror the first time she'd hobbled to the shower, and had cried. Gage's mom had been helping her, and at first she'd been alarmed, but then she simply held her until she'd gotten control of her emotions again.

She was covered in bruises. Her torso looked bad, and she could remember each and every time Simon had hit her with that damn bat. But it was her neck that horrified her the most. She could clearly remember the excitement in Simon's eyes as he'd kneeled over her helpless body and wrapped his hands around her throat. He'd *enjoyed* strangling her.

But each bruise made her more determined to live. She wouldn't give Simon King or Drake Stryker the satisfaction of knowing they'd killed her.

An idea had formed in her mind at that moment, and she'd spent the last two days trying to talk herself out of it... to no avail.

It was the only way. It sucked, and she didn't want to do it, but Simon wasn't going to disappear. He was going to haunt her forever if she *didn't* do this.

So when Molly and Gage left the room, she called for Cruz. He appeared within seconds, looking immaculate and not as if he'd been watching over her for the last week.

"I want to go into witness protection," she told him without preamble.

His eyes gentled, and he pulled a chair up to the bed. "Why now?" he asked. "Brown's in jail and the Parisian police have picked up Stryker. He's got a good lawyer, but from all accounts, he's going to go down."

"For murder?" Kinley asked.

She saw the answer in Cruz's eyes even before he shook his head. "Not without your testimony. They have surveillance video of him having dinner at the hotel's restaurant with Émilie, but there's not enough proof that he killed her. His DNA was inside her, but he's claiming their sex was consensual. He'll go down for statutory rape, having sex with a minor, but he's claiming she left the hotel on her own, and that was the last he saw of her."

"They need my testimony to tie him to her murder," Kinley said flatly.

Cruz sighed and nodded.

"Simon's not going to stop until I'm dead," she told him.

"The money's already been paid," Cruz informed her.

That surprised Kinley, but it didn't change her mind. "It doesn't matter. If he doesn't already know I survived, he'll be pissed when he finds out. He's going to come for me again. To finish the job."

Cruz stared at her but didn't comment.

"He is," she whispered. "And he's not going to care who stands between him and my death. He threatened Gage. And Gillian. And I know he wouldn't care if he had to hurt any of the others. He watched me for *weeks*, Cruz. He knows who's important to me. He'll go after them just to fuck with me. He *played* with me...his word, not mine. He'll hurt or kill everyone I care about before he finally puts a bullet in my brain. I want Stryker to pay for what he's done. I want Émilie and all the other girls to have justice. But more than that, I need to protect the only person who's ever loved me."

"Lefty," Cruz said.

"Gage," Kinley agreed.

After a moment, he said, "If you do this, you can't contact him at all. No letters. No emails. Nothing."

"I know."

"There's no telling how long Stryker's case will take to go to trial."

Kinley nodded.

"And even then, if what you're saying is true, you still won't be safe. You may not be able to see Lefty again. *Ever.* Are you willing to sacrifice your happiness, and possibly his too?"

"Yes."

"He's not going to agree. He's going to try to talk you out of it," Cruz told her.

"That's why I don't want him to know until I'm gone."

Cruz inhaled sharply. "That's not fair to him."

Kinley's eyes filled with tears. "I *have* to do it that way. Otherwise I'll let him talk me into staying. He has a job,

Cruz. He can't watch over me twenty-four-seven. Simon's gonna get to me sooner or later, and I can't have that on Gage's conscience."

Cruz's jaw ticked with displeasure. Then he finally said, "You can't leave without explaining your reasoning." He held up a hand to stop her protest. "You owe it to him. At *least* leave him a note. He loves you," Cruz said, leaning forward. "Men like Lefty and his teammates don't love easily. They know they live dangerous lives. The last thing they want is to leave a woman or family high and dry if they die while on a mission. If you disappear without a trace, he's going to lose his mind. He won't understand. He won't be able to concentrate on his job. You don't want that, do you?"

She shook her head, and the tears she'd done her best to hold back finally spilled over.

"Think long and hard before you agree to this," Cruz told her. "When you enter the program, you'll be alone, and you can't contact anyone you've met here."

"I've always been alone," Kinley said sadly. "I never expected to find a man like Gage. I don't know how or why he loves me, but I'm doing this for *him*."

Cruz looked sad then. "I know you are. And I think it's the bravest and most honorable thing I've ever witnessed in my life."

"I want to go soon. The sooner the better," Kinley said between sniffles.

"I'm not sure you're well enough to be moved yet. It'll be very stressful, and the last thing you want is to have a relapse."

"I *need* to do this as soon as possible," Kinley argued. "It'll kill me to lie to Gage. And you know as well as I do that Simon's probably heard I survived by now. The fact that a beaten, near-dead woman was picked up on the side of the road has been all over the papers, even if they didn't use my name. He's not stupid. He'll figure it out. He'll be chomping at the bit to get to me."

"All right. You've got some time right now to write your letter. When you're done, give it to me, and I'll make sure Lefty gets it after you're gone. You understand that even I won't know where you are, right?"

She nodded. It was scary as hell to know she'd be taken to some strange city and basically left on her own, but if it meant keeping Gage safe, she'd do it.

Cruz stood and leaned over, kissing her on the forehead.

"Just think," Kinley said with an attempt at a smile. "After I'm gone, you can go home to your family and you won't have to babysit me anymore."

"Mickie knows enough about what I'm doing to be completely okay with me being here as long as it takes."

"She sounds like a good woman."

"She is," Cruz said.

And for a moment, Kinley was jealous as hell. She wanted to be that woman for Gage. But it wasn't meant to be.

"I'll be just outside. I'll knock on the door if I see Lefty and Molly coming back so you can hide the letter. If you finish before they get back, just call out and I'll come get it."

"Thank you."

"Don't thank me," Cruz said gruffly. "I'm not happy about this at all, but that doesn't mean I don't think it's the right thing to do. I'm going to do everything I can to find this Simon King guy for you, Kinley. To make it safe for you to come home to Lefty."

Choked up again, she could only nod. *Home to Lefty*. Three words had never sounded so beautiful. Maybe except for when he'd told her he loved her.

After picking up a pad of paper and a pen from the table across the room and handing them to her, Cruz nodded and headed for the door, leaving Kinley alone with her thoughts.

She thought the letter would be hard to write. But the words flowed from her fingers. She didn't know if she explained herself in a way Gage would understand, but she knew down to the bottom of her heart that she was doing the right thing. If Simon came back for her, he'd find that she was gone, and he'd have no reason to hurt anyone else. At least she hoped that would be the case.

She called out for Cruz, and he pocketed her letter just in time before Gage, his mom, and Brain returned.

"Did you have a good lunch?" she asked. "I didn't know Brain was coming up."

"I didn't either," Gage told her. "And yeah, lunch was good. I brought you a present," Gage said, holding out a cup. "Vanilla milkshake," he said with a smile.

Kinley took it and forced herself not to cry. He'd remembered the story she'd told him about how one of her favorite foster mothers, one of the ones she'd thought might adopt her, had taken her to dinner for her birthday and bought her a vanilla milkshake. She'd loved her ever since, even when that family hadn't worked out.

She savored the shake, and laughed and chatted and tried to forget everything that was about to happen.

Gage's mom left later that afternoon, and Kinley memorized everything about Gage as evening fell. She knew this might be the last time she saw him, and she wanted time to stop. But of course it didn't.

Somehow, between her and Molly, they'd convinced Gage to leave the hospital the night before and go to a hotel to get some sleep. It had done him a lot of good, as he looked less stressed when he'd returned that morning.

All Kinley had to do was convince him to once more leave her for the night, to go back to the hotel. It took a while, but he finally agreed to leave around eight. It helped that Brain volunteered to stay and watch over her.

"If I didn't know better, I'd say you were trying to get rid of me," he teased.

Kinley hoped the guilt she felt wasn't showing on her face. "Never," she said. "In a perfect world, I'd never leave your side. I'd be stuck there like a barnacle. You'd have to hobble around with me affixed to you like a parasite or something."

He chuckled, which was her intention. Even if her words were funny, she meant them one hundred percent. "Kinda like that teddy bear's attached to your side, huh?"

Kinley nodded. Gage had brought the soft teddy he'd gotten for her, and it managed to make the sterile world of the hospital a little more tolerable. "I love this guy. If it wouldn't look out of place for a grown woman to carry a teddy bear around with her, I'd take it with me everywhere."

"You do what you want, sweetheart," Gage told her with a smile. "Anyone gives you shit about your teddy, tell them to fuck off."

She smiled up at him.

"I'll see you bright and early in the morning," Gage said softly. "You want me to bring you anything?"

She shook her head, knowing if she spoke, she'd break down in tears. Kinley so badly wanted to tell Gage she loved him, but she couldn't. For her own sanity, she needed to keep that last inch of distance between them.

Gage leaned down and gently hugged her, and Kinley inhaled deeply, drawing his essence into her nostrils one last time.

"Love you, Kins. Sleep well. You'll be safe with Brain watching over you."

"I know," she lied. She wasn't safe, and neither was anyone around her.

He kissed her on the lips. It wasn't passionate, but it wasn't chaste either. His tongue came out and licked over her still cracked lips gently. "See you tomorrow," he whispered as he straightened.

"Bye," Kinley croaked.

With one last wave, Gage walked out of the room.

Kinley closed her eyes and willed herself not to break down into sobs. Brain was smart. He'd realize something was wrong and would call Gage and tell him to come back in a heartbeat.

"You all right?" Brain asked.

"Just tired," Kinley said with a sigh. That wasn't a lie. Her whole body hurt, and she knew tonight was going to be hard, mentally and physically. Cruz had found a moment to tell her earlier that everything was arranged, and the handlers who'd been assigned to get her out of the hospital would be there around midnight.

She made small talk with Brain for a while and learned more about him. For one, he knew a shitload of languages. He'd simply shrugged and said he had a "knack" for them, which was an understatement. He admitted that he didn't date much simply because he hadn't found a woman in a long time who he'd clicked with.

"And what does it take for you to click with someone?" Kinley asked, genuinely interested in hearing the answer.

Brain shrugged. "Someone who's interested in more than what color nail polish to wear," he said vaguely. "I want someone I can talk to, who understands me."

"So, you're punishing women in general for past girl-friends not understanding you?" she asked, a little surlier than she might've if she wasn't stressed out about the upcoming night.

"I didn't say that," Brain insisted.

"Really? Because that's kinda how it sounded to me," she said. "Not many people are as smart as you, Brain. I mean, I don't remember a damn thing about the pre-calc class I took in high school, and the only thing I know how to say in Spanish is, '¿Dónde está el baño?' According to your high standards, it sounds like you shouldn't even be my friend."

"I don't care that you can only ask where the bathroom is in Spanish," Brain said with a scoff. "You're Lefty's woman, so that means you're my friend too."

"Oh, well, gee, thanks for liking me for who I am," Kinley told him, then winced as she moved the wrong way and her ribs complained.

"Are you all right?"

"Yeah. I still hurt when I move the wrong way." She sighed. "I'm sorry I'm being grumpy. I'm stressed out and worried about everything. But, Brain...I think you're going to miss out on a pretty great woman because you're looking for someone who's on the same academic level as you are, who can understand you intellectually."

"I didn't really say that I wanted her to be smart," Brain said.

"You *kinda* did," Kinley argued. "I'm not one to wear nail polish, but if I was, I'd probably want it to match my outfits. Or at least be a neutral color so it wouldn't clash. Would that mean you wouldn't want to be my friend?"

"No," Brain said.

"Then what *did* you mean?"

"I don't know," he said, sounding a little grumpy himself now.

"Then give us women some slack," Kinley said gently. "Many of us hide who we are from the world for very good reasons. We're afraid of how we'll be treated. Or that we'll be looked down on because of our past, of who we are deep inside. Maybe try to have a little more of an open mind when it comes to women. You might be surprised at who you click with if you do."

Kinley was exhausted by the time she'd finished her little

lecture. She didn't know how she'd expected Brain to respond —but taking a deep breath, letting it out, and hanging his head wasn't it.

"You're right."

"I know," Kinley said with a small smile.

"I just...all my life, I've only been useful for what I know. I love the guys, but even they see me as just a walking brain. Hell, that's how I got my nickname."

"Bullshit," Kinley challenged. "I know Gage doesn't give a shit about how smart you are. I mean, yeah, I'm sure it comes in handy on missions, but you can't let people rely on you for a certain skill, and then turn around and be mad when they can't see past it. They can't see past it if you don't let them in, Brain. It's okay if you don't have all the answers. No one expects you to be perfect."

"Don't they?" he countered.

"No. Because perfect is boring. Just be yourself, and if you're trying to impress women with that big brain of yours, stop. Just be you. And let her be who *she* is. Maybe she won't have an advanced degree or know twenty languages, but that doesn't mean she can't love you with all her heart. You want to know what most women really want?"

"God, yes. Please," he mock begged.

Kinley couldn't help but smile. "We want to be wanted. That's it."

Brain looked skeptical.

"When push comes to shove, we want a man who wants us and *only* us. And isn't afraid to let us know it. We don't need expensive presents and huge houses. We need our man's time. His smiles. Small things like teddy bears and milkshakes to let us know he's thinking about us. That's it, Brain. When you find a woman who you want to give the world to, and all *she* wants is you, that's how you know you've found the one."

Brain studied her, and Kinley didn't look away from his gaze. "You make it sound easy."

She snorted. "It's not. There are a lot of bitches out there. You know that as well as I do. Women who haven't learned that the worst thing in life is to not be loved. You find a woman who needs you exactly how you are, hold on and never let go no matter what happens."

"Kinda like what Lefty's done with you, huh?" Brain asked.

And just like that, the pain at knowing she was going to hurt the man she loved was back. Even knowing she was doing the right thing wasn't enough to temper the pain in her heart. "Yeah," she whispered.

They talked a bit longer, and then Brain turned on the television. They were in the middle of watching a movie—Kinley had no idea what it was, as she wasn't paying attention to anything but the click of the second hand on the clock on the wall, letting her know the time was quickly approaching when she'd have to leave—when a nurse Kinley had never seen before knocked on the door.

"It's time for a shower," she said chirpily.

"And that's my cue to take a walk," Brain said with a smile. "You all right with that?"

"Of course," Kinley told him, her heart hammering in her chest.

This was it. She never took a shower at night, so she knew the nurse must be a part of the plan to sneak her out of the hospital. She might never see Brain again. It didn't hurt as much as saying goodbye to Gage had, but it still stung. She couldn't say anything that would make him suspicious though.

"I'll be back in an hour, that enough time?" he asked.

"More than," the nurse said.

Brain waved at her from the doorway. "Don't be afraid to take the painkillers, Kins," he said.

"I won't," she whispered, then he was gone.

Twenty seconds later, Cruz appeared in the doorway. "You ready?" he asked.

She wasn't. She had about a million second thoughts, but she had to do this. Remembering how evil Simon had looked and the joy in his eyes when he'd tortured her made the decision much easier.

"Help her into the wheelchair," he told the nurse.

"Yes, sir," the woman said, and Kinley realized she wasn't a nurse at all. She must be an agent. Her handler. The person who was going to take her away from Texas and Gage.

"Take this first," the woman said, holding out a pill and a cup of water. "This isn't going to be pleasant, and it'll help with the pain as we get you out of here."

Kinley didn't even ask what it was. She downed the pill and did her best to sit up. Pain shot through her torso but she didn't even wince. She'd made the decision to do this, and she had to suck it up and be gone before Brain returned.

She had no idea what Cruz was going to tell him, and how he was going to keep him from immediately calling Gage, but that wasn't her problem. All she could concentrate on was getting from her bed to the wheelchair. Then from the wheelchair into whatever car the agency was stashing her in. One minute at a time. She'd get through this the same way she'd gotten out of that ravine and up the hill. Thinking about Gage every step of the way.

Right when she was about to be wheeled out of the room, she cried, "Wait!"

Everyone stopped.

"Please, I almost forgot my bear," Kinley whispered.

Cruz walked over to the bed and picked up the already well-loved animal. He placed it in her arms and leaned down and kissed the top of her head. "Good luck, Kinley. As I said before, I'm going to do whatever I can to find Simon King and make sure he isn't a threat to you or the ones you love so you can come home."

"Thank you," she said before the "nurse" began wheeling her out of the room.

She took one look back right before they got into the elevator and saw Cruz watching them. She raised a hand and waved, like a dork, and got a chin lift in return.

Kinley knew it was the last time she'd see anyone from her old life for a very long time, possibly forever. She cried all the way to the car, and on and off for hours after.

CHAPTER NINETEEN

The next morning, Gage walked down the hallway toward Kinley's room with a smile. She was getting better quickly, and soon the doctors would let her go home.

He'd started to make plans for when she got back to his apartment. An alarm system had already been installed, which was a bit overkill for an apartment, but he wasn't going to take any chances with her safety. He'd ordered a tracker for her to wear, so he and his team would always know where she was.

He wouldn't be able to do anything about his job...but when he got back to the base, he'd talk with his commander about the possibility of transitioning off the team.

He hated to do it, as he loved being a Delta Force operative, but he loved Kinley more. And he couldn't keep her safe if he was thousands of miles away in another country. He'd talk to Ghost and see what he thought about Lefty joining his team in a training capacity on the base and go from there.

He was immediately concerned when he noticed Cruz wasn't standing outside Kinley's room. His calm thoughts veered toward fear, and he practically jogged the rest of the way down the hall.

Lefty opened the door—and his heart about stopped in his chest when he saw the room was empty. The bed was freshly made, the bathroom door was open, and Kinley was nowhere to be seen.

He spun on his heels and almost ran into both Brain and Cruz. They'd obviously entered the room behind him. He hadn't even heard them.

"Where's Kinley?" Lefty barked.

"She's gone," Cruz said.

All the blood drained from Lefty's face. "But...but she was fine last night."

Swearing, Cruz shook his head. "Sorry, man, I don't mean *gone*. I mean she left. She's in WITSEC."

It took a moment for the FBI agent's words to penetrate —and when they did, Lefty was angrier than he'd ever been in his life. He lunged toward Cruz and had his arm cocked back when Brain caught it.

"It was her decision!" his teammate told him.

The focus of Lefty's anger switched from Cruz to his teammate. He jerked out of his hold. "What do you know about it?" he bit out.

"I didn't know anything about *anything* until I came back from a walk around midnight to find her room like this. Scared the shit out of me too, and I was ready to call in the troops when Cruz sat me down and explained what was going on. I was going to call you right after he told me what the fuck was happening, but his superiors pulled rank. Took my phone and refused to let me leave the hospital."

"That's bullshit!" Lefty raged. He couldn't believe this was happening. Then he turned to Cruz. "What the *fuck* is going on? We decided no on witness protection. She's not healed enough to leave anyway! Someone needs to start talking.

Now!" Lefty shouted desperately. He couldn't understand what was happening. Kinley was *gone*? Had she been forced into WITSEC? If so, he wouldn't stop until he'd found her and she was back in his arms.

Cruz held out a piece of paper to him, and childishly, Lefty wanted to smack it out of his hands.

"It's a letter. From Kinley to you," Cruz said.

Lefty stared at it and didn't want to touch it. He didn't want to know why she'd left. Had he done something wrong? Had she thought he couldn't protect her? He felt sick.

"Read it, Lefty," Cruz ordered.

Slowly, knowing her words would gut him, Lefty reached for the paper.

He unfolded it and wanted to cry at seeing her handwriting. It was messy, a mixture of cursive and print, and he'd recognize it anywhere.

Gage,

Don't be mad at Cruz, this was my decision, and my decision alone.

We talked about what Simon did to me, but what I didn't tell you was that he told me if he hadn't been able to get his hands on me, he would've gone after you. Or Gillian. Or the other guys on the team.

When I made the decision not to ignore what I saw, I had no idea what the ramifications would be, but even if I did...I still would've spoken up.

But it was my decision. And there's no way I'm going to risk the only people in my entire life who have made me feel loved. When you've never had that, you'll do whatever it takes to keep it. And that means making sure none of you are in danger because of me.

Simon's still out there. He's not going to stop until I'm dead. So in order to protect Gillian, and you...I have to go.

Don't worry about me. I'll be fine. I've spent my entire life alone, this isn't a big deal. But you should know, I'll think about you every day. Every time I hear a cicada, I'll think about you. Every time I hug the teddy bear you gave me, I'll think of you. And every time I watch the news, I'll wonder if you're all right.

Please be careful. I can do this because I know you're out there somewhere. Alive and well. If you weren't, I'm not sure what I'd do.

I love you. I didn't say it before because I was afraid if I did, it would make it impossible to leave. But it's only fair that you know.

I want to tell you to wait for me. To not give up on me coming back. But it could be years before it's safe...if at all. So, don't wait for me, Gage. Live your life. Be happy.

I'll never forget you.

Love, Kins

Lefty could see where the ink was smeared at the end, as if she'd been crying. He wanted to crumple the paper in his hands and throw it against the wall. He'd never regretted his decision to leave for the night more than he did right that second.

Carefully folding the note, Lefty put it in his pocket and took a deep breath. After a few minutes, he turned to Cruz and Brain. "So that's that," he said emotionlessly.

"I promised her that I was going to do whatever I could to find Simon King and make sure he wasn't a danger to her anymore," Cruz told him.

Lefty nodded. "Thank you."

The men looked at each other for a long moment. "I'm sorry, Lefty," Cruz said.

Lefty had nothing to say to that. He simply nodded again.

"If you need a few more days, I can talk to the commander," Brain told him.

"I'm good. I have a feeling getting back to work is the best thing I can do," Lefty said.

Brain just eyed him.

"If you both will excuse me, I need to call my mother and let her know what's going on, and see if I can't get her a flight home. Cruz, I appreciate you being here, and while I'm pissed you didn't at least warn me she was thinking about this, I'm sure I'll come to terms with it eventually." Then he gave both men a chin lift and walked out of the room.

He didn't remember walking through the hospital and going back to his truck, but he found himself sitting behind his wheel before he realized it.

Pulling out the note, Lefty read it once more.

Kinley loved him.

He wanted to scream out his rage at how unfair this situation was. She'd spent her entire life looking for love, and it had been ripped out from under her.

Then he cried. Huge, hulking sobs that shook his frame.

He cried for what she'd been through, and because he was so damn proud of her. He hated that she'd made this decision without him, but he couldn't be mad at her.

When he finally got himself under control, Lefty took a deep breath. He wiped his face with the back of his arm and reached for his new phone. He couldn't be by her side right now, but that didn't mean he wouldn't do everything in his power to look out for her.

He dialed a number that he'd memorized a long time ago. He never thought he'd have any reason to use it, but he couldn't think of a better reason than Kinley.

"Hello?" the man on the other end answered.

"This is Gage Haskins, you might know me as Lefty. I need your help."

"Of course I know who you are, Lefty. What can I do for you?"

It was almost unreal that he was talking to the infamous Tex. The former SEAL who'd been medically retired after losing part of his leg, and who'd become a computer genius who went out of his way to help military personnel all over the country.

"My woman's just entered WITSEC. I need you to keep an eye on her. I'm not asking you to tell me where she is or anything about what she's doing. In fact, I'd prefer it if you didn't. I have a feeling if I knew anything about what she's going through, it would make it impossible for me to do my job and get through each day."

Lefty went on to explain to Tex why she was in witness protection, and a little about her background.

"I love her," he concluded. "I always thought love would be this easy, gentle feeling that would make me content. But it's not. It's made me fierce, and anxious, and I know I'd use everything I've learned over the years to kill for her if necessary. I just need to know that someone other than the government is watching out for her. Making sure she has what she needs to be safe. Can you do that?"

"Yes," Tex said promptly. "I can definitely do that for you. I promise I'll do whatever I can to make sure she's safe until you can be reunited."

"I don't know if that'll be possible," Lefty said honestly. "But knowing she's not completely on her own will make me feel better."

"She won't be alone," Tex swore.

"Thank you."

"Don't thank me," the other man said gruffly. "I know if it was my wife or children, you'd do the same."

"I owe you."

"If you don't stop, I'm gonna get pissed," Tex said.

Lefty would've laughed if he wasn't so sad. Tex's hatred for any kind of thanks was legendary.

"You said the hitman's name is Simon King?" Tex asked.

"Yeah." Just hearing the man's name made him angry. "That's what he told her, at least. It's probably an alias."

"Hmmm. I've got some work to do and some markers to call in. I know some people who will be more than happy to take care of wiping another evil human being off the planet. You have my word that your woman will be looked after. I'll talk to you later." Then Tex hung up.

Lefty clicked off his own phone and threw it onto the seat next to him. He gripped the steering wheel tightly and sat in the parking lot for quite a while. His mind was spinning. He had no problem with Tex finding Simon King and sending people to take him out. The sooner the better, as far as he was concerned.

Then his thoughts turned back to Kinley. He was amazed that, for a woman who'd never known love, and had only experienced loss after loss, she had more love inside her than anyone he'd ever met. She'd sacrificed her own happiness for him. And Gillian. And his team.

Shaking his head, Lefty finally started his truck. He would go to his mom's hotel and talk to her in person. Then he'd go back to Killeen and take things one day at a time. Kinley had made one hell of a sacrifice for him; he wasn't going to spit in her face by wallowing in his grief.

* * *

Two months later

The first month after Kinley left had been hard. Lefty went through each day like a zombie. He kept his emotions closed off, rarely spoke, rarely laughed. He knew his friends had been worried about him, but he just couldn't bring himself to care about anything.

He was eating like shit and barely got enough sleep each night to function.

Things came to a head when he was on a mission in the Middle East. They were supposed to find and eliminate an HVT. Lefty had been reckless, rushing into situations without making sure they were clear. Luckily, no one had been injured or killed, but his team had lit into him when they'd been on their way back to the States.

"You've got to pull yourself together!" Trigger raged. "You're gonna get yourself killed."

"What does it matter?" Lefty yelled.

"It matters!" Trigger shouted as he got into his friend's face. "I know you're hurting. But damn it, Lefty, how do you think Kinley is gonna feel when she comes back after this is all over, only to find that you couldn't get your head out of your ass and got yourself killed?"

"She's not coming back!" Lefty exclaimed, his fists clenching, ready to fight.

"You don't know that!" Trigger yelled right back. Then he took a deep breath. "Call me crazy, but with a love like the two of you have, I don't think there's any way she *won't* be coming back. I don't know how, and I don't know when, but when she *does* come back into your life, do you want to have to tell her that you were a dumbass while she was gone, or do you want to tell her how you honored her sacrifice and her strength by moving forward and being strong for her while she was away?"

That conversation had been a turning point for Lefty. Trigger had been right. He wanted to be the kind of man who was worth the huge sacrifice Kinley had made. She'd left to keep him safe, and if he went and got himself killed because he couldn't deal with her decision, it would disrespect that decision in the worst way.

So while he wasn't exactly happy, he'd been able to push his sorrow down far enough to function.

Going back to his apartment at the end of each day was the toughest part of life without Kinley. Her scent had faded, and more often than not he slept on his couch rather than having to face his empty bed.

The only consolation he had was opening his windows and hearing the cicadas. He hoped that wherever Kinley was, she was also listening to the insects and thinking about him.

Lefty was standing in his kitchen, eating a microwave meal, when his phone rang. Figuring it was Gillian or one of his team calling to check on him, as they were wont to do, he answered and brought the phone up to his ear. "Hello?"

"Lefty, it's Cruz. I've got some news for you."

Lefty's stomach clenched, and the few bites of the cardboard-tasting meal he'd choked down churned in his belly. "Yeah?"

"Simon King is dead."

That wasn't what Lefty was expecting to hear. "Are you sure?"

"Very. There was an incident in Montana. A trooper stopped to check on an abandoned car on the side of the road. A man was found in the driver's seat, dead. It wasn't until they did an autopsy that they realized someone had killed him. Jabbed him with a needle and filled him with enough morphine to stop his heart in minutes. He had no ID on him, so his DNA was put into the nationwide database to see if they could figure out who he was. You know the ball of tape Kinley had so painstakingly pushed up that ravine? There was DNA on it, just as she thought there would be. Saliva from where Simon had torn it with his teeth. It matched the dead man in Montana."

Everything within Lefty sagged in relief. "Is Kinley in Montana?" he asked.

"Not from what I've been told," Cruz said.

Lefty mentally thanked Tex for having the kinds of connections he did. No one else could have found King.

Then something occurred to him. "So she can come home. Now that the hitman is dead, she'll be safe."

"You know as well as I do that she's not safe," Cruz countered. "Stryker might be in custody in France, but that doesn't mean he can't hire someone else to go after Kinley. Until she testifies, and he's put away for good, she's safer in WITSEC."

Lefty *did* know that, but he'd held on to a small bit of hope that maybe, just maybe, he'd get her back. The ache in his heart from missing her was constant. He'd come to terms with it, but that didn't mean he wouldn't do whatever it took to have her back.

"Any news on when his trial will happen?" Lefty asked.

"Unfortunately, no. But the FBI is working closely with French inspectors to get as much evidence against Stryker as possible."

"Will Brown's suicide make a difference? Will it hurt the case?"

Kinley's old boss had been found dead in his cell a week and a half ago. It had been ruled a suicide, but Lefty had his doubts. He didn't have the details, but it seemed awfully coincidental that he'd killed himself hours before he was supposed to meet with detectives. Rumor had it he was going to spill his guts and throw Stryker under the bus to try to lessen his own sentence.

"It shouldn't. The FBI has correspondence between him and Stryker that included videos of young girls. They also texted the night Émilie Arseneault was killed, making plans to meet up for dinner and drinks in Brown's room. It ties them together with the girl. Both of their DNA were also found on her body, as well."

"But it doesn't counter Stryker's claim that the last time he saw Émilie was when she left the room around midnight."

"No. Only Kinley's testimony does that," Cruz said.

Lefty sighed. "I appreciate you letting me know about King," he told Cruz.

"Of course. I'll be in touch when I hear anything about the case."

"Appreciate it."

"This is gonna end sooner or later," Cruz said solemnly.

"I know." And Lefty did. He just hoped that when the time came, the outcome was that Kinley returned to Texas and they could pick up where they'd left off.

He hung up the phone after saying goodbye and threw away the rest of his uneaten dinner. He went over to his couch and ran a hand over his face.

Lefty was exhausted. Mentally and physically. But he'd keep going. One day at a time. It was the least he could do for his Kinley. She'd somehow been able to crawl out of that ravine with injuries that should've killed her. Comparatively, what he was going through was child's play.

I'll wait as long as it takes, he silently vowed.

Three months later, Lefty had just let himself into his apartment when there was a loud knocking on his door. He'd hoped to have three days of solitude to miss Kinley in peace, and to recover from the intense mission he and his team had just returned from. They'd been in South America this time, and Lefty never thought he'd admit it, but he much preferred the desert to the jungle.

He opened his door and saw Trigger standing there. He'd literally last seen his teammate less than a minute ago when they'd parted to go to their respective apartments.

"My place, now!" Trigger barked.

Scared that something had happened to Gillian, Lefty didn't think twice, he bolted out the door and followed Trigger. They went into his apartment, and Lefty was relieved to see Gillian sitting on the couch looking healthy and whole.

But he didn't have time to even greet her before Trigger pointed at the television and said, "Look."

Confused, Lefty turned his attention to the news. Gillian was holding a remote, and when he was paying attention, she pushed the button to unpause the program.

The trial of US Ambassador to France Drake Stryker started today in Paris. He's accused of being The Alleyway Strangler and killing not only Émilie Arseneault, but at least five other teenagers as well.

Seen entering the courthouse was the mysterious witness for the prosecution, Ms. Kinley Taylor. Because no press was allowed in the courtroom, no one knows exactly what she saw and what kind of witness she is, but her testimony is said to be crucial to the prosecution's case.

The president has no comment on the case except to say that Mr. Stryker was replaced as the ambassador after he was arrested. We'll be watching this case closely and will bring you more information as it becomes available.

Gillian pushed the pause button again.

Lefty was confused. He was glad the trial was finally getting underway, and he loved being able to see Kinley, but was that really why Trigger had almost given him a coronary? "And?" he asked his friends.

"Watch it again," Trigger ordered.

And even though it was torture to see Kinley, and not be able to touch her or speak to her, he watched the news clip again. She looked relatively healthy, if a few pounds lighter. He ached to take her into his arms and wanted more than anything to buy a plane ticket to Paris just to try to get a glimpse of her.

When Lefty still wasn't sure what Trigger wanted him to see, he turned to him with a confused look.

"Fuck. Right—watch it *again*, and pay attention to the person who's walking *next* to her," Trigger said.

This time, when the clip played, instead of staring at Kinley, Lefty focused his attention on the man at her side. He inhaled sharply and turned to Trigger. "Is that...?"

Trigger nodded.

Just then, Lefty's phone rang. The number said unavailable, and he clicked it on. "Hello?"

"It's Merlin," the man on the other end of the line said.

"I'm staring at you on TV right this second," Lefty said.

"Damn. I was hoping to get ahold of you before you saw that," the other Delta operative said. "Turns out we were sent on a special mission to Paris to guard a very valuable witness in an ugly trial. All five of us are here, and we're keeping an extremely close eye on the witness. From what we understand, strings were pulled for us to get the job."

Lefty closed his eyes and swayed on his feet. He felt Trigger take hold of his elbow and steer him to the couch. He sagged onto it. "Is she...damn." He didn't know what to ask.

"She's amazing," Merlin said. "Right now, she's sitting in the hotel room playing Go Fish with Woof, Zip, and Jangles... and kicking their asses, I might add. Earlier, she actually made Duff smile too, can you believe that? We didn't think it was possible.

"And a funny thing...after this job, we're all being transferred to Texas. If I didn't know better, I'd say someone had a hand in getting us out of DC. Which, don't get me wrong, we're very glad for. After everything we've seen and heard, guarding politicians isn't high on our list of fun things to do."

"You're coming to Texas on a permanent change of station?" Lefty asked.

"Yup."

Tex. It had to have been him. Not only had he somehow found Simon and had the son of a bitch taken out, and gotten the other Delta team assigned to guard Kinley, he'd *also* arranged for them to PCS to Texas.

Fuck, he owed Tex. Huge.

Not that the man would ever admit he'd done anything.

"She doesn't know I'm calling," Merlin said. "But if you want to talk to her..." His voice trailed off.

Did he want to talk to the woman he loved more than life itself? Fuck yeah.

But he wouldn't.

Lefty's shoulders sagged. It sounded like she was doing well. Merlin and his team would keep her safe and look out for her. The last thing she needed was to deal with the emotional upheaval of talking to him in the middle of the damn trial. Lefty felt stupid feeling insecure when it came to Kinley, but he didn't want to create more drama in her life. It was better to let things play out the way they had to play.

"I want to, but I can't," Lefty croaked. "If I hear her voice, it'll gut me. But, please...keep her safe for me."

"You don't even have to ask. We know her story, it was in the info packet we got. She's why we do what we do. Protect the innocent and all that. I swear to you as a Delta, she's coming home safe and sound."

Lefty wanted to ask what that meant. Coming home to him, or back to the home she'd made for herself, with the help of the WITSEC program? But he was too chicken to ask. "Is she all right?" he asked quietly.

"She's a bit too skinny for my taste, and she's obviously

stressed out, but she's hanging in there. Joked the other day about what the judge would think if she brought this weird flat stuffed-bear thing with her into the courtroom for emotional support."

Lefty smiled at that. She still had the teddy bear he'd gotten her. It was a little thing, but it meant the world to him. For the first time in months, he felt lighter.

Maybe, just maybe, there was hope for them.

"I'm looking forward to you assholes getting here to Texas. It'll be fun to kick your ass in PT."

"As if," Merlin said with a snort.

Then Lefty got serious again. "Anything you need, all you have to do is ask. Keep Kinley safe for me, and I'll be forever in your debt."

"We *will* keep her safe, and I'm offended that you think you need to do a damn thing for us to do our job."

"She's more than a job," Lefty countered. "She's my entire life."

"All the more reason for us to make sure she's safe," Merlin said.

Lefty heard someone say something in the background but couldn't quite understand it.

"I need to go. The witness is hungry, and it's my turn to go out and find us some macarons and espresso."

"The vanilla ones are her favorite," Lefty whispered.

"Got it. Lefty?"

"Yeah?"

"Hang in there. This will be over soon."

"I hope so," Lefty said. "Bye."

"Later," Merlin said.

He sat on the couch in shock and had a hard time wrapping his mind around what he'd just heard.

"So Jangles and his team are coming to Texas?" Trigger asked.

Lefty nodded.

"Awesome. It'll be good to have another team we know and trust here on base with us."

"Lefty?" Gillian asked, and he felt her hand on his arm. "Are you all right?"

He took a deep breath and nodded. "Yeah. I think so." And as soon as the words were out of his mouth, Lefty realized that he *was* okay. He still missed Kinley like crazy and worried about her every second of every day. But knowing the trial was finally happening, and that she had five men making sure she was safe, went a long way toward easing his mind. Knowing where she was, and that she wasn't alone, made him feel so much better.

"Thanks for showing me the clip," Lefty said as he stood.

"Do you want to stay?" Gillian asked.

Lefty chuckled. It felt rusty, but good. "I'm not staying with you guys the first night we're back from a mission."

Gillian blushed, and Trigger merely grinned.

Lefty walked to the door, his teammate at his heels. "Thanks again for coming over to get me," he told him.

"Of course. You really all right?"

"Surprisingly, yes. I've had the same nightmare every day since Kinley left. She's in a room and crying because she's all alone. With Merlin and his team with her now, I know she's *not* alone. That sounds stupid, but..."

"It's not stupid," Trigger reassured him. "Hopefully she'll be home soon. Now that Simon is dead and her testimony is done, there will be no reason for anyone to want her dead."

"Unless Stryker is a sore loser," Lefty said with a shrug.

"Honestly? I think he's got enough on his plate right now. He'd have to pay someone a pretty penny to kill her, and I'm not sure, after losing two million dollars to Simon, he'd be willing to go that route again. Not only that, but between the divorce he's going through and paying lawyer fees, I'm betting he doesn't even *have* the money he'd need to hire someone to go after her again. I'm not a psychic, but I'm guessing after this is over, it's over."

"I hope so."

"She'll be back," Trigger said confidently.

"Again, I hope so," Lefty repeated. "I'm gonna go crash."

"Let me know if you hear anything else," Trigger said.

"I will. Later."

"Later."

Lefty headed back to his apartment, feeling a tiny bit lighter than he had when he'd left. With any luck, he'd have Kinley back in his life, and arms, soon. All he could do was wait, and hope she'd find her way home to him.

CHAPTER TWENTY

Kinley felt like she was going to throw up.

It had been over seven months since she'd seen or talked to Gage. Two hundred and fifteen days, to be exact. And she'd thought about him every last one of those two hundred and fifteen days. Went to sleep with him on her mind and woke up missing him.

She hadn't made any friends while she'd been living in New York City. Not only that, but she hadn't been able to sleep with the windows open, listening to the sounds of the cicadas. All she'd heard was horns, sirens, and people. She'd missed Texas and couldn't wait to get out of the city.

As part of her relocation, she'd been given a job at the New York Public Library on Fifty-Third Street, and had spent most of her days stocking shelves. A perk of the job was that she could read as much as she wanted, but that only made her miss Gillian and everyone else all the more.

Her studio apartment was stark and bare, and completely fit her mood most days. When she'd heard Simon had been killed, she'd had the fleeting hope that she could go back to

Texas, but her handlers had quashed that hope by telling her she was still in danger.

Testifying in Stryker's trial had been terrifying, but having Merlin, Woof, Jangles, Zip, and even the dour Duff at her side every step of the way, went a long way toward making her feel better. She knew them from her old life, and even that small connection was enough to calm her.

Stryker had been found guilty on charges of child pornography but, more importantly, he'd been convicted of killing Émilie Arseneault. He wasn't charged with the murders of the other teenagers who detectives believe The Alleyway Strangler had killed, because there wasn't enough evidence, but his sentence of sixty years without parole might as well have been a death sentence. He wasn't ever going to get out of the French prison, and Kinley couldn't have been more relieved.

While in Paris, she'd met Émilie's parents, and while she couldn't understand them, or vice versa, they'd still somehow clicked. It had felt good to make a difference at that trial. Her testifying wouldn't bring their daughter back, but it had prevented another family from suffering as they had.

Kinley had thought maybe she'd leave Paris and go straight to Texas, but that wasn't the case. Apparently, the government moved very slowly, even when it came to letting someone go back to their old life.

Her handlers had suggested that maybe she stay in New York and not try to reintegrate back into the life she'd left behind, for her own safety, but Kinley knew she had to try. Gage might not be able to forgive her for leaving like she had. It had been cowardly of her to not talk to him about her decision, but at the time, it had felt like her only choice.

It had taken a while for her to heal from her injuries, but just as she'd done in that ravine, she'd taken things one minute at a time. One day at a time. One week at a time.

And now she was here in Killeen.

Merlin had told her that he and his team would be moving to Texas, and he'd given her his number. Kinley knew she could've called Trigger, or anyone else on Gage's team, but she was too scared.

Merlin was safe. He'd stayed up with her one night and listened to her entire sob story. From being an unwanted foster kid who'd never been adopted, to when she'd decided to enter witness protection. He hadn't interrupted or told her she was crazy. He'd simply listened. Then he'd given her a hug and said Gage was one lucky man. He'd given her his number and told her to call him when she was ready to return to Killeen.

So she had.

And he'd managed to set up this meeting tonight.

Standing outside the bar, Kinley was having second, and third, thoughts. This was a stupid idea. What if she went inside and saw Gage flirting with someone else? What if he'd found another girlfriend by now? Her return would make things awkward for everyone.

Then she took a deep breath. She wasn't the same person she'd been seven months ago. Or even nine months ago. Living what she'd lived through and loving Gage had changed her. She felt stronger. She no longer cared that she was weird. She was who she was, and if someone didn't like her, it didn't matter.

Gage had shown her that there wasn't anything wrong with her. He and his mother had done what no one had been able to do in twenty-nine years...shown her that she was love-able exactly as she was. Made her *like* herself.

She straightened her shoulders and took a deep breath. What was the worst that could happen? Gage could've been so mad that he'd fallen out of love with her and found someone else. Right?

Of course, that would devastate her, but no matter what,

she'd be all right. She'd lived through everything else life had thrown at her, she'd survive this too.

She marched up to the door of the bar and opened it before she chickened out.

The noise level inside was insanely loud, and Kinley's head immediately began to pound. Ever since her concussion, she'd found that she was much more sensitive to loud noises, but she refused to back down now.

The room was dim and the flashing lights on the dance floor made it hard to recognize anyone, but she pushed forward toward the bar area. Merlin had texted and told her that's where everyone was hanging out. Kinley had waited seven long months for this day, and she was more than ready to get it over with. Whatever happened, happened.

But the second she caught sight of Gage, her bravado disappeared as if it had never been there. She felt like she was seven years old again, and she was waiting to hear from her case worker on whether the current family she was living with wanted to adopt her (they hadn't).

One by one, the men standing around Gage saw her and stilled. It would've been comical if it wasn't her life. Trigger elbowed Brain, who nudged Oz. Slowly but surely, Gage's entire team had turned to stare at her.

Then Zip saw her, and he got Merlin's attention. Then Jangles and Woof smiled huge when they noticed her. But it was Duff who made the first move. He walked up to her, leaned down and kissed her cheek.

"'Bout time you got here," he said gruffly as he curled his arm around hers and turned them to face the group.

"Kinley!" Gillian gasped, tears already coursing down her cheeks.

Kinley barely noticed Devyn, Ann, Wendy, and Clarissa standing there...

Her eyes were glued to Gage's.

But then he turned his back to her, placed his drink on the bar, rested his hands on the oak, and dropped his head.

Kinley's stomach plunged.

She hadn't known *what* to expect as a reaction from Gage, but that wasn't it.

She tore her arm from Duff's and turned to stumble blindly for the door.

She'd been wrong. She *couldn't* handle Gage's rejection. Not after everything she'd sacrificed. All her pep talks about accepting whatever happened were bullshit. It was hard to breathe, and she knew if she didn't get out of there, she was going to seriously embarrass herself by bursting into tears.

She'd barely gone a few steps when someone took hold of her arm. She was spun around, and the next thing she knew, her face was planted in Gage's chest.

For a second, she stood there stock still, frozen, but at the first inhale of his familiar woodsy scent, she melted.

She felt his arms tighten, and hers did the same to him. She pressed against him harder, wanting to fuse her body with his. They stood there, in the middle of a crowded bar, music blaring and people bumping into them, without saying a word. Simply clinging to each other. Kinley couldn't make herself let go.

After several deeply emotional moments, Kinley finally realized the jostling against her wasn't other people...but Gage's body heaving with sobs.

Feeling him lose it made her lose her own battle against tears.

After a few more moments, Gage whispered into her ear, "You came back."

Kinley nodded. "It was my plan all along. I was going to come back as soon as you were safe."

"Don't leave me again!" he pleaded. "I can't go through that again."

She pulled back until they were looking at each other eye to eye. "I won't," she told him.

"Promise me," he ordered.

"I promise," she repeated.

"Marry me," Gage blurted.

"*What?*"

"Marry me," he said again. "If we're married, no one can separate us ever again. Not without a hell of a fight."

Kinley's stomach rolled. "Is that the only reason?"

"Fuck no!" Gage said without hesitation. "I love you. I think I love you more today than I did the last time I saw you. I've had a lot of time to think about what you did, and your strength amazes me more with every passing day, Kinley. I'm not nearly as strong as you, but I'm hoping you might rub off on me even just a little bit."

Kinley snorted and shook her head.

He brought his hands up to her face and held her still as he leaned down and gently kissed her forehead. Then her nose. Then her cheeks. Then finally he brushed his lips against hers. "I love you, Kins. I didn't ever expect to feel this way about someone. You leaving made me realize how much I'd come to rely on having you in my life. Even after only a few short weeks. Make an honest man out of me?"

As wedding proposals went, it wasn't exactly the most romantic. They were standing in the middle of a crowded bar with a nineties boy band playing in the background. But as far as Kinley was concerned, it was the most romantic thing that had ever happened to her.

"I don't think I can answer that until I find out what kind of lover you are," she teased, feeling brave and happier than she'd ever been in her life. "I mean, what if we aren't compatible in bed? I love you and all, but that would make getting married awkward and extremely disappointing in the long run."

Without a word, Gage wiped away the tears on his cheeks, and Kinley had never seen such a carnal look on a man's face before. Not one aimed at *her*, at least. He didn't turn to say goodbye to his friends, he just took her hand in his and started towing her toward the door.

Kinley managed to wave at everyone, and saw Gillian holding her thumb and pinky finger up as if she were talking into a phone as she mouthed "call me."

The eleven men standing at the bar were all grinning and giving each other high-fives and clinking their beer glasses together.

She was thrilled they were happy for her and Gage, but at the moment, all she could think about was what Gage was going to do to her when they got back to his apartment.

She'd dreamed about this moment and wondered what and when it would finally happen, but she couldn't have imagined anything better than Gage losing his iron control and taking her as if he couldn't stand one more second of being apart.

* * *

Lefty had no memory of driving back to his apartment. All he could think about was the woman sitting next to him. She had her hand on his thigh, and it felt as if it was burning a hole in his jeans. He needed her. *Now.*

Kinley loved him. He'd read her words, but hadn't heard them until a few minutes ago. And if she wanted to make sure they were compatible before accepting his marriage proposal, he was more than happy to oblige.

His conscience tried to tell him to slow down. That he needed to talk to her, find out where she'd been for the last half a year. Get to know her again before rushing her into something she might not be ready for. But when her fingers moved not so innocently down the inside of his thigh and brushed against his already rock-hard cock, any thoughts of waiting were thrown out the window.

She seemed different somehow. More sure of herself. He'd loved who she was before, but he had a feeling this new Kinley would blow him out of the water.

After parking, he hauled her across the seat and didn't even give her time to step out of his truck. He swept her into his arms and closed the door with his hip. Then he was striding up the stairs toward his apartment as if she weighed no more than a child.

Between the two of them, they managed to unlock his door and get inside before he completely lost his control and took her against the wall outside his apartment.

But the second the door shut behind them, and he'd turned off the fancy security system he'd bought to keep her safe, something inside Lefty relaxed. She was here. Home. Inside their apartment. Some of the urgency he'd felt at seeing her faded.

He let her legs fall to the floor, and she stood there, gazing up at him with a look of absolute love in her eyes.

"Be sure," he told her.

"I am," she replied without hesitation. "I've thought about nothing but you for months. Well, okay, that's a small lie. I didn't think about sex until my broken ribs had healed, because that shit hurts, but once they did, and I could manage to orgasm again without being in pain, I couldn't help but think of you."

Lefty tilted his head and studied the woman in front of him. "You're different," he said.

Her brow furrowed. "Is that bad?"

"Not at all. It's just an observation."

"I had a lot of time to think," she told him. "All my life, I've let what other people think about me define what I thought about myself. I didn't think I was strong, not at all. But when the shit hit the fan, I proved to myself that I *was* strong. And while I'll never regret going into witness protection, you have to know it was the hardest thing I've ever done in my life. Leaving you behind, and not knowing if you'd ever want to see me again, haunted me every day. I thought when you saw me that you were disappointed. That you were sorry to see me again."

"Never," Lefty breathed. "I just couldn't believe what I was seeing. That you were really there. I needed a second to regain my composure. And when I turned around, you were leaving! No way was I gonna let that happen. No way in hell. You came back to me, and I'm not letting you go ever again. You promised. Any threats in the future, we'll face together. Got it?"

Kinley smiled. "Got it."

"Now...I think we need to talk more about these orgasms you gave yourself...in great detail," he said with a smirk, slowly walking backward, pulling her with him as he headed for the hallway to their bedroom.

"Less talk, more action," Kinley quipped.

Lefty laughed, feeling happier than he had in months. "Whatever you want," he vowed, then grabbed her hand and turned, walking faster now. He pushed open the bedroom door and towed her to the side of the bed.

Without words, his hands went to the hem of her tight-fitting black shirt, and he began lifting it over her head. She didn't protest and dutifully raised her arms, making his task easier. He didn't stop to ogle her, but immediately went to work on the button of her jeans.

She reciprocated, and they both shoved their pants down and off. Lefty ripped his T-shirt over his head before slowing down, staring at the most beautiful woman he'd ever seen in his life. Her bra and panties were simple black cotton, but he'd never been as turned on as he was right that moment.

"You're going to have to take the lead this first time," Kinley told him nervously. "I mean, I know how things work, but since I've never done it, I'm a bit out of my element."

"I'm gonna take care of you, Kins," Lefty told her, not feeling nervous in the least. He hadn't ever been with a virgin, but this was Kinley. He'd never hurt her. Ever. He reached down and pulled her into his body, loving the feel of skin-on-skin contact. He hugged her hard and closed his eyes, more thankful than he could admit that she was home.

* * *

Kinley was nervous, but it was an excited nervousness. She loved the feel of Gage against her, but she wanted, needed, more.

Just when she opened her mouth to tell him to get on with it, he pulled back. He reached behind her and undid her bra clasp. Shyly, she lowered her arms, letting the garment fall to the floor at their feet. He didn't ogle her, but moved his hands to her hips, pushing her underwear down and off as well. Then he pulled back the sheets and gestured for her to climb onto the bed. As she did so, Gage removed his own boxers.

She caught a glimpse of his long, hard cock before he climbed onto the mattress with her. Before she could worry about where to put her hands and what was going to happen, Gage's mouth was on hers. He didn't ease into the kiss. He poured seven months of worry and missing her into it, and she did the same.

One of her hands grabbed his back, and the other his bicep, and she held on to him as they kissed as if their lives depended on it. His tongue was demanding, and she immediately complied, letting him in as if she'd been doing so all her life. One of his hands moved down her body until he cupped her breast. His fingers played with her nipple, pinching and tugging until she gasped and arched her back.

His mouth moved down her throat, sucking and licking until he reached her chest. His lips took over where his fingers had been, kissing and torturing her turgid nipple until Kinley swore she could feel her heartbeat in the small nub.

When he'd sucked on both nipples, and left a few hickies on her breasts, Gage moved down her body. He nudged her thighs open and settled between her legs. He'd done this before, but not when she'd been completely naked, and somehow it felt way more intimate at the moment. Maybe it was because she knew what was coming afterward. He'd finally make love to her the way she'd dreamed of for so long.

Instead of the lazy licking he'd done the last time he'd gone down on her, Gage latched onto her pussy as if he were a starving man. She cried out and held on to his head as he feasted between her legs. His tongue lapped at her, and when he sucked her clit over and over, it was almost painful. But Kinley wasn't about to complain. No way in hell.

She loved Gage, and she'd never dreamed a man could enjoy going down on a woman as much as he seemed to like it.

When he moved a hand up and entered her virgin body with one of his fingers, all she could do was moan. He sucked on her clit as he added another finger. The dual assault sent Kinley over the edge.

She came with a small scream and felt Gage moan with his own excitement. By the time he lifted his head, his five o'clock shadow was covered in her juices. He brought his hand up and stuck his finger in his mouth, licking off every drop of her excitement.

Then he rose to his knees and walked forward, pushing her legs apart as he did so.

Kinley figured she'd be embarrassed to have her legs spread for a man for the first time, but this was Gage. Besides, she couldn't take her eyes away from the very large erection in his hand. He stroked himself, groaning as he did so.

"I want to fuck you bare," he croaked. "I'm clean. I swear. I haven't been with anyone for almost two years. Way before I met you."

"Yes," Kinley hissed, wanting him inside her more than she wanted her next breath.

"I don't want to get you pregnant though," he went on. "As much as I can't wait to see your belly round with our child, I want you all to myself for a while."

Kinley sighed deeply. She liked that thought. More than liked it. "I'm on the pill," she admitted.

Gage's gaze focused on her, and he tilted his head in question.

"I knew I was going to come back. And that I wanted you to make love to me. And just in case it all worked out, I wanted to be prepared."

His eyes clouded over with lust once more. "Thank fuck," he said softly. Then he leaned over and grabbed a pillow, shoving it under her hips. He brushed the tip of his dick against her soaking-wet folds, but didn't enter her. He did this for so long, Kinley got impatient. She reached between them and closed her hand around his erection. She gently pulled him toward her. "Stop messing around and make me yours, Gage," she told him.

"You *are* mine," he told her. Then, without taking his eyes away from between her legs, he notched himself at her opening and gently began to push. "Tell me if I'm hurting you," he said between clenched teeth.

He wasn't. Kinley had given her newly purchased vibrator a good workout over the last few months. She'd used it on herself, trying to pretend it was Gage. She was pretty sure he wouldn't hurt her, and he certainly felt a hell of a lot better than the piece of silicone she'd been using.

"More," she moaned when he was halfway inside.

"Are you sure?" he asked.

"Very," Kinley reassured him. She grabbed hold of his butt cheeks when he leaned over her and tried to pull him inside.

"All right, here I come," he whispered as he slowly but steadily pushed his hard length all the way inside her.

It pinched a little, as he was longer than her vibrator, but his penetration didn't hurt. She definitely knew the difference between a little discomfort and true pain.

He stayed stock still inside her, and they both breathed harshly, absorbing the feel of each other.

"Damn," he said after a moment. "I've seriously never felt anything so good in my life. And I'm not blowing smoke up your ass when I say that either. You're hot and wet and strangling my cock so tight, it's all I can do not to explode right this second."

Kinley had thought dirty talk during sex would be awkward, but it was sexy as hell. She squeezed her inner muscles even tighter and smiled when he groaned.

"You like torturing me?" he asked, but didn't give her a chance to respond. He pulled out, then slid back inside slowly.

It was Kinley's turn to moan.

"You like that?"

"Duh," she gasped.

Gage chuckled. "I'm gonna speed up, but tell me if this hurts."

Kinley nodded and held on to Gage's biceps as he began to move his hips faster. He impaled her over and over again, and all Kinley could do was moan and gasp. She dug her fingernails into his skin and did her best to spread her legs even wider. She couldn't believe how good he felt. Her own sexy times by herself felt nothing like this. *Nothing.*

"Harder!" she begged.

"Touch yourself," Gage ordered.

She looked up at him in confusion.

"I know you know how. Reach between us and get yourself off. I want to feel you go over while I'm inside you."

He smiled when all her muscles clenched at the thought.

"You like that, don't you? Like knowing that it'll throw me over the edge."

She did. A hell of a lot. She didn't reply verbally, but she immediately brought a hand between them and fondled herself. His belly hit her hand with every thrust, and the angle wasn't very good, but none of that mattered. All that mattered was Gage and the fact that they were finally making love. It felt like the biggest reward after everything they'd been through.

"Faster, sweetheart," he panted. "I'm right on the edge, and feeling your hot, wet virgin pussy squeezing me, knowing I'm the only man who's ever been in here, and *will* ever be in here, isn't helping."

Kinley wanted to roll her eyes at his over-the-top caveman attitude, but she couldn't. She was on the edge herself, and she wanted to orgasm with him inside her more than she wanted anything. Her fingers moved faster, as did his hips. Gage pounded his dick inside her, and after a few more thrusts, she knew she was there.

"I'm coming!" she warned before throwing back her head, arching her back, and thrusting her hips into him.

"Fuck yeah," he moaned. He scooted upward, pulling her ass onto the cradle of his thighs and holding her to him as he went over the edge himself. Kinley felt a rush of wetness between her legs but couldn't do anything but remain in his grasp and try to breathe.

Without dislodging himself from inside her, Gage fell over and hauled her on top of him. She lay atop his sweaty chest, still trying to catch her breath. She was sore in the most delicious way, and she felt completely wrung out.

"Well?" Gage said after a moment.

Kinley managed to open her eyes and prop herself up to look at him. "Well, what?"

"You've tested out the merchandise, so to speak. Will you marry me now?"

Kinley couldn't help it, she giggled. Then she was laughing so hard she couldn't stop. She felt Gage slip out of her body and wanted to complain about that, but couldn't because of her giggles.

Before she knew it, she was on her back once more with Gage looming over her. He was smiling.

"What?" she asked when she could breathe again.

"I've never seen anything more beautiful than you naked and laughing in my bed," he said seriously.

Kinley melted. "Yes, Gage."

"Yes, you'll marry me?"

She nodded.

"My dad's gonna want to walk you down the aisle. And my mom's gonna want to go with you to find a dress. But that doesn't mean I'm waiting months to make things official between us. You need to figure that shit out quickly."

Kinley's eyes filled with tears. "Really?"

He knew what she was emotional about. "Really. My mom would adopt you if she could, but that would be way too out there. My family is your family, sweetheart. You'll find my mom will probably start nagging you for grandkids way too soon, just ignore her. I wasn't kidding about wanting you to myself for a while. Maybe five years or so. It won't be safe for you to have kids if we wait much longer than that, but I *do* want to put it off for a while. That all right?"

Kinley nodded. She hadn't thought she'd ever have kids. Hell, she had to have sex for that to be a possibility, and that hadn't been on her radar at all.

"I don't have a ring, but I'll get one soon. Whatever you want."

"Nothing big," she said immediately.

He nodded.

"I mean it," Kinley warned. "The bigger the ring, the bigger target I'll be for thieves."

His face fell but he nodded. "True. Okay, sweetheart. I'll get you something tasteful and unique, just like you."

"I love you," Kinley blurted.

"I love you too," he returned.

She closed her eyes and let his words sink in. When she opened them, he was right there, still gazing down at her. "I never thought I'd hear those words in my life. I didn't think I *was* loveable. Then I met you."

"Then you met me," Gage agreed.

He shifted his hips, and Kinley felt his cock brush against her still soaking-wet folds. "Are you sore?" he asked.

She was, but not enough to deny either of them what they needed. She shook her head.

As if knowing she was full of shit, Gage entered her slowly and gently. Then he proceeded to make love to her as if she were a fragile piece of glass. Their lovemaking didn't have the desperate edge it did before, but it was no less beautiful.

She didn't orgasm this time, but it was almost as exciting to see Gage lose it as he held himself deep inside her body. He rolled over, pulling her on top of him once more. They hadn't slept like this previously; usually, she only partly rested on him. She started to shift, but he held her in place.

"Stay," he murmured.

Kinley complied and snuggled deeper into the man she loved. She knew their life wouldn't always be sunshine and roses, but they'd already survived absolute hell. Dealing with his job, and whatever else life threw at them, would be a piece of cake comparatively.

EPILOGUE

Brain was happy for his teammates, but Trigger and Lefty also annoyed the crap out of him with their constant discussions about how great their girlfriends were. And now they were both torturing the rest of the team with their wedding plans.

Gillian and Trigger were planning on going to the courthouse soon and having a laid-back party afterward. And Lefty and Kinley were actually going to tie the knot in San Francisco. His mother was throwing a huge-ass party for the two of them, and they figured they might as well do the deed there.

Brain loved his friends, but the thought that he'd never have what they had was weighing heavily on him lately.

He was the smart guy. The tech guy. The go-to guy when they needed research.

He was also the last one hit on when they went out.

It never used to bother him, but witnessing Trigger and Lefty's happiness every day made him realize how much he wanted a woman of his own.

But wanting someone to love and knowing how to find them were two completely different things.

When they'd first been stationed in Texas, Brain had bought a house. It seemed like a good investment. The housing market at the time favored buyers, and if the Army changed his duty station, he could always rent it out. But living in the three-bedroom house in a nice neighborhood only made him feel even *more* lonely.

Brain sighed. He'd put off heading to the bar to hang with the guys long enough. Not really in the mood to be social, but knowing if he didn't go, he'd just sit in his house and wallow about shit he couldn't control, Brain grabbed his wallet, slipping it into his back pocket and headed to his garage.

He climbed into his Dodge and backed out of his driveway.

Brain arrived at the bar and took a deep breath before forcing himself to get out of his car. He was already mentally going over what he'd use as an excuse to leave early as he opened the door.

One second he was standing just inside the bar, looking around for the guys, and the next, a woman was walking straight toward him with a determined—and nervous?—look on her face.

He had time to appreciate the fact that she was almost as tall as he was, around five-nine or so, and was probably around his age, as well. She wore black jeans that clung to her body in intriguing ways. A pair of Converse sneakers and a T-shirt that said "Will give medical advice for tacos" completed her outfit. Her brown gaze seemed to pierce his own as she continued toward him.

Brain smiled at her—and was shocked when she walked right into his personal space and put her arms around his neck.

"I'll give you twenty bucks if you kiss me right now like you mean it."

Her voice was husky, and Brain could swear he heard

desperation. He didn't have time to tell her that he'd happily kiss her, but not for money, when she put her hand on the back of his head and leaned forward.

At first their kiss was awkward, merely a brushing of their lips. Then Brain wrapped an arm around the woman's waist and took a step forward, bending her backward.

She gasped in surprise and switched her hold from around his neck to latch onto his biceps.

Brain took advantage of her mouth opening, and he changed their angle just slightly...and kissed her like he hadn't kissed a woman in a *very* long time. Slow and deep.

The little moans she made weren't encouraging him to stop anytime soon. He could tell she was muscular and strong, but at the moment, tilted backward, she was completely helpless in his arms.

And he liked it a hell of a lot.

Hearing a few catcalls around them, Brain knew he had to stop, but it took a moment for his brain to communicate with his mouth and limbs. Finally, he eased his mouth from hers and brought her upright once more. They stared at each other for a long, intense second.

Brain registered that they were both panting, and he really liked how her lips looked, all swollen and pink. He couldn't help but notice that her nipples had puckered under her shirt and bra.

"All you had to do was tell me you'd moved on, Aspen," an irritated voice said from behind her.

The woman licked her lips and sighed in frustration. Brain saw her mouth "sorry" to him before she cleared all emotion from her face and turned toward the man behind her. She wrapped an arm around Brain's waist, and he had no problem tugging her into his side.

"I *did* tell you, Derek. I told you a month and a half ago when I broke up with you. I told you at least three times in texts. And I told you *again* tonight, when you showed up here begging me to get back together. I've moved on. It's time you do the same."

The man looked to be in his mid-thirties, and the pout on his face definitely wasn't doing him any favors. But it was the glimmer of pure, unadulterated anger in his eyes that had Brain concerned.

"When did you meet *him*? I mean, you're training with the rangers every day."

"We've known each other a while," Aspen said.

Knowing things could get awkward very quickly, Brain held out his hand toward the other man. "Name's Kane Temple. But people call me Brain."

Derek looked in disgust at the hand Brain was holding out to him then frowned at Aspen. "Brain? Seriously?"

She merely shrugged.

"Fine. Don't come crawling back to me when he breaks your heart," Derek bit out.

"I won't," Aspen assured him perkily.

"I think it's time you ran along," Brain said, annoyed that the other man wasn't taking the hint.

When Derek opened his mouth to say something he'd probably regret, Brain was done. "Come on, baby. I see my friends. I'm sure they've saved us some seats." He walked them away from the heartbroken, angry man and steered Aspen toward his teammates.

She looked back once, and Brain assumed Derek had left because she stopped in her tracks, and he had no choice but to do the same.

"Thank you so much, and I'm so sorry for involving you in that. But he wouldn't leave me alone, and the only thing I could think to do was give him concrete evidence that I'd moved on." She started to reach for the small purse strung across her body.

"If you even *try* to pay me for that kiss, I'm gonna be pissed," Brain told her.

She froze and looked at him with wide eyes.

"How about we start over?" Brain suggested. He took a step back and held out his hand. "I'm Brain."

"Aspen Mesmer," she said as she placed her hand in his.

Brain shook it, then brought it up to his lips and kissed the back.

"You really don't have to hang out with me, I'm sure he's gone," Aspen said. "My friends just left, and I should be going too."

"Don't be scared of me," Brain ordered, not liking the nervous look in her eyes.

Her shoulders straightened, and she stood taller. "I'm *not* scared of you."

"Good. I wasn't lying. My friends are here waiting for me. And Trigger and Lefty's fiancées are too. You won't be the only woman in our group, and everyone will get a huge kick out of what just happened."

She hesitated.

"At the risk of sounding like the nerd I am, it's been a *very* long time since my toes have curled when I've kissed a woman. And letting you leave without getting to know you will make me feel like I've been used."

Her lips twitched. "Well, I *did* kind of use you, didn't I?" she asked. "I suppose the least I could do is buy you a beer."

"Good, it's decided," Brain said, feeling more excited than he'd felt in a very long time. "And since we're now dating, I suppose it's only fair that you meet my friends."

"We aren't dating," she argued, but she didn't pull away when he reached for her hand.

"But you just told poor Derek that we were. It wouldn't look good if he was hanging around waiting to talk to you in the parking lot and we didn't leave together, would it?"

"You think you're pretty smart, don't you?" she asked.

Brain shrugged. "I didn't get the nickname Brain because I'm stupid."

"Lord save me from conceited soldiers," Aspen said, rolling her eyes.

"How'd you know we were soldiers?" Brain asked.

"I deal with people like you enough in my line of work."

"And what's that?" Brain asked.

"I'm a combat medic," Aspen told him.

Brain tilted his head as he studied the woman next to him. That was the last thing he'd expected her to say, and he couldn't deny it intrigued him. But before he could ask her more about it, he heard his name being called.

"Yo, Brain, 'bout time you got here!" Oz called out.

"Who's your friend?" Doc asked as they neared.

"Everyone, this is Aspen. My girlfriend."

"No, I'm not," she countered.

Brain couldn't help but laugh at the confused looks on his friends' faces. This was going to be fun.

*

Gotta love a man who's not sure about his appeal...find out how Brain and Aspen get along in the next book in the series, *Shielding Aspen*.

And...as a treat...you know the other Delta Team our guys were friends with and who helped Kinley?

Woof, Zip, Merlin, Duff, & Jangles get their Happily Ever Afters in the Delta Team Three series!

I convinced some of my author friends to write their stories! And you can get them NOW!

Delta Team Three

Book 1: *Nori's Delta* by Lori Ryan

Book 2: *Destiny's Delta* by Becca Jameson

Book 3: *Gwen's Delta* by Lynne St James
Book 4: *Ivy's Delta* by Elle James
Book 5: *Hope's Delta* by Riley Edwards

Want to talk to other Susan Stoker fans? Join my reader group, Susan Stoker's Stalkers, on Facebook!

JOIN my Newsletter and find out about sales, free books, contests and new releases before anyone else!! Click HERE

Want to know when my books go on sale? Follow me on Bookbub HERE!

Also by Susan Stoker

Delta Team Two Series
Shielding Gillian
Shielding Kinley
Shielding Aspen (Oct 2020)
Shielding Jayme (novella) (Jan 2021)
Shielding Riley (Jan 2021)
Shielding Devyn (May 2021)
Shielding Ember (Sep 2021)
Shielding Sierra (TBA)

SEAL of Protection Series
Protecting Caroline
Protecting Alabama
Protecting Fiona
Marrying Caroline (novella)
Protecting Summer
Protecting Cheyenne
Protecting Jessyka
Protecting Julie (novella)
Protecting Melody
Protecting the Future
Protecting Kiera (novella)
Protecting Alabama's Kids (novella)
Protecting Dakota

SEAL of Protection: Legacy Series
Securing Caite
Securing Brenae (novella)
Securing Sidney
Securing Piper
Securing Zoey

Securing Avery
Securing Kalee (Sept 2020)
Securing Jane (Feb 2021)

SEAL Team Hawaii Series
Finding Elodie (Apr 2021)
Finding Lexie (Aug 2021)
Finding Kenna (Oct 2021)
Finding Monica (TBA)
Finding Carly (TBA)
Finding Ashlyn (TBA)
Finding Jodelle (TBA)

Delta Force Heroes Series
Rescuing Rayne
Rescuing Aimee (novella)
Rescuing Emily
Rescuing Harley
Marrying Emily (novella)
Rescuing Kassie
Rescuing Bryn
Rescuing Casey
Rescuing Sadie (novella)
Rescuing Wendy
Rescuing Mary
Rescuing Macie (novella)

Badge of Honor: Texas Heroes Series
Justice for Mackenzie
Justice for Mickie
Justice for Corrie
Justice for Laine (novella)
Shelter for Elizabeth
Justice for Boone

Shelter for Adeline
Shelter for Sophie
Justice for Erin
Justice for Milena
Shelter for Blythe
Justice for Hope
Shelter for Quinn
Shelter for Koren
Shelter for Penelope

Ace Security Series

Claiming Grace
Claiming Alexis
Claiming Bailey
Claiming Felicity
Claiming Sarah

Mountain Mercenaries Series

Defending Allye
Defending Chloe
Defending Morgan
Defending Harlow
Defending Everly
Defending Zara
Defending Raven

Silverstone Series

Trusting Skylar (Dec 2020)
Trusting Taylor (Mar 2021)
Trusting Molly (July 2021)
Trusting Cassidy (Dec 2021)

Stand Alone

The Guardian Mist

Nature's Rift
A Princess for Cale
A Moment in Time- A Collection of Short Stories
Lambert's Lady

Special Operations Fan Fiction

http://www.AcesPress.com

Beyond Reality Series

Outback Hearts
Flaming Hearts
Frozen Hearts

Writing as Annie George:

Stepbrother Virgin (erotic novella)

ABOUT THE AUTHOR

New York Times, *USA Today* and *Wall Street Journal* Bestselling Author Susan Stoker has a heart as big as the state of Tennessee where she lives, but this all American girl has also spent the last fourteen years living in Missouri, California, Colorado, Indiana, and Texas. She's married to a retired Army man who now gets to follow *her* around the country.

She debuted her first series in 2014 and quickly followed that up with the SEAL of Protection Series, which solidified her love of writing and creating stories readers can get lost in.

If you enjoyed this book, or any book, please consider leaving a review. It's appreciated by authors more than you'll know.

www.stokeraces.com
www.AcesPress.com
susan@stokeraces.com

facebook.com/authorsusanstoker
twitter.com/Susan_Stoker
instagram.com/authorsusanstoker
goodreads.com/SusanStoker
bookbub.com/authors/susan-stoker
amazon.com/author/susanstoker